BAKING & ANGELS

BAKING & ANGELS

MEGAN MACKIE

Baking and Angels
Copyright © 2025 Megan Mackie. All rights reserved.

Cover by Oxford
Typesetting by Autumn Skye
Edited by Laura Mita
Proofread by Aysha Rehm

This is a work of fiction. All characters, organizations, and events portrayed in this novel are either products of the author's imagination or are used fictitiously.

Paperback ISBN-13: 978-1-965097-41-0
Ebook ISBN-13: 978-1-965097-36-6

To my sister Amy, who
knew when to walk away
to find a better life

The butterfly is only beautiful because the
caterpillar was brave enough to accept the
painful change

- Unknown

Table of Contents

Chapter 1   My Renewed Beginning 1
Chapter 2   The Earthly Authorities Showed Up 9
Chapter 3   I am Completely Human 17
Chapter 4   My Flawless Accent 28
Chapter 5   At Least We Had Each Other 36
Chapter 6   Angelic Consequences, I Guess 43
Chapter 7   Fix Everything! 51
Chapter 8   More Than Anything. 59
Chapter 9   Dreams of the Future. 67
Chapter 10 Then I Threw Up 76
Chapter 11 The Next Morning Sucked. 84
Chapter 12 We Confessed Everything 96
Chapter 13 It's Technically Not Illegal? 105
Chapter 14 Then Helena Had a Brilliant Idea. 113
Chapter 15 My First Train in Ages. 121
Chapter 16 Memory Devoured 129
Chapter 17 Bless-ed French Toast 137
Chapter 18 Mother of Vengeance 149
Chapter 19 Food Battle the First 156
Chapter 20 Battle Commenced 165
Chapter 21 Helena Had a Plan 180
Chapter 22 Tendrils of Doubts. 190
Chapter 23 We Talked Honestly 199

Chapter 24   Not Safe for Work 209

Chapter 25   Food Battle the Second................217

Chapter 26   A True Competition 226

Chapter 27   Divine Intervention....................236

Chapter 28   Home Again 244

Chapter 29   Like a Damsel in Shining Armor 252

Chapter 30   Tasted of Honey......................260

Chapter 31   Deal with a Demoness 268

Chapter 32   The Temptation 277

Chapter 33   Dressing Down.......................288

Chapter 34   Lavender Lemon Sugar Cookies.......297

Chapter 35   Breaking Limbo 307

Chapter 36   Explanations 318

Chapter 37   Ghosts of the Past.....................325

Chapter 38   Coming to an Understanding.........334

Chapter 39   Renegotiations 341

Chapter 40   Rising Stakes 352

Chapter 41   A Simple Entry......................361

Chapter 42   Enough was Enough 369

Chapter 43   I Acted Without Thinking............380

Chapter 44   Saving an Angel......................389

Chapter 45   Acceptance of Myself.................397

Epilogue   To Forget is Human..................404

Book Club Questions 413

Author Bio 415

Chapter 1

MY RENEWED BEGINNING

His entire life, the whole thirty minutes of it, Rafferty had not known what he looked like. He had dreaded getting up off that kitchen floor where he had been born, a new and complete adult human; he didn't want to see. He would have continued to lie there if the woman he trusted with his entire being hadn't pulled him to his feet.

"Rafferty, come on," she urged, backing up until her shapely backside bumped the counter behind her. She had gotten dressed, having run into her bedroom to put on the clothes she now wore, while he had remained naked trying to wrap his head around the new facts of his existence.

Up until thirty minutes ago, he had been a demon, bound to hell, in a body made of unholy energies.

Now he was alive.

As he let her leverage him up, he immediately unbalanced. The wings that had once weighed on his back whenever he had existed in the real world were gone. His renewed body had no idea how to handle that. The world around him swam and turned upside down. Nausea flushed through, and there was nothing he could do about any of it.

"Woah!" Helena called out as she tried and failed to catch him. His larger being flopped against her. She staggered back against the counter, her arms coming around to catch him. His hands slapped hard as they instinctively caught his momentum on the edge of her counter, the cold stone easing into his sweating palms. As uncoordinated as it currently was, *this* body was strong. He still had a long, lanky frame, but it was also muscled and healthy. Nothing like the depleted nearly skeletal thing he had been before, even underneath the illusions he had woven. This was real.

"Rafferty, try to breathe slower," Helena urged, her arms still around him as she stabilized his shaky legs. Her hand came around, pressing against the muscles of his back, his skin sweaty and slick.

"What's wrong with ..." His mouth felt dry, and his tongue wouldn't work properly. So much had happened so fast. He cascaded up and down various emotions like a plastic bag caught in a violent wind, upending from elation to dread to anger to giddiness to tears and everything in between. Feelings he was hopeless to completely define or understand, all happening at once. What reaction was he supposed to have?

Helena, beautiful Helena, tried to give him answers. "I ... I don't think anything is wrong with you. Just... everything has changed. I'm sure this is a normal reaction to being ... alive ... suddenly."

He shook his head. "This isn't possible ... it's ...."

A miracle.

He wanted to say a miracle, but to express it out loud filled him with terror. Miracles didn't happen. Nothing was ever given for free. *What terrible price was paid in exchange for this?* he thought but dared not ask. What more had he lost? What more did he stand to lose? What was left to take that hell hadn't already stripped from him?

"I feel so heavy," he said instead, and he did. He felt so solid and dense. The dulled edge of the counter pressed hard into his palms, and he lifted one of them to look at it. The indented line was so strange, so real, even as it faded.

He ran the hand through his hair and was shocked not to hit any of the horn that should have been cresting out of his skull.

"What's wrong, Rafferty? Talk to me!" Helena insisted. "You were alright a minute ago, what happened?"

"My wings ... my horns ..." he said. "They're gone."

She wrinkled her nose, clearly confused. "But Rafferty, they've been gone before."

He shook his head, understanding what she was referring to. "That was just an illusion. So I wouldn't scare you. They were always there. At least, to me."

"But ..." she huffed, struggling with this concept. "You wore normal clothes, and your wings didn't inhibit that."

He shrugged. "I could always feel them," he said. It was the best explanation he had. She was right, when he had looked like a normal man, a hat set on his head would sit properly, and yet when he moved his head, he would also feel the horns shift weight.

Now they were gone.

And he missed them ...

He closed his eyes, pained. "Why would I miss them?" he asked aloud, the thoughts too loud inside to remain there.

"Changes are complicated. It's nothing to be ashamed of," she assured him. He wasn't sure he believed her, but ...

She felt more real, too, as his hand landed hard on her shoulder, squeezing it. He could feel her, truly feel her. Bones covered by muscle and skin and the cloth of her shirt, all so very, very *real*.

"Rafferty ... are you ... do you think you're going into shock?"

He finally met her eyes. "I wouldn't know. What's shock?" Then he collapsed backward, flopping onto the kitchen floor, right back into the middle of the circle that had burned itself into Helena's kitchen tiles. Though there were no traces of demonic energy, maybe just lying there was safer anyway.

"Oh, no. Your head!" She was there by his side, gingerly touching around his head. He was only vaguely aware that he had thumped it onto the ground, but it didn't hurt. Nothing hurt.

"I'm ... I'm fine ..." he tried to say, giggles chasing his words.

Helena was still panicking, but not about him possibly having hurt himself. "No, Rafferty. We can't do this. We have to get out of here. With everything that happened to Scarlet and the demon ... dammit, there's a demon that's been set loose in reality! We need to go to the cops. Or we need to run from the cops? Oh God, I don't know what to do. I need to take you to the hospital. But *how* when you don't exist ... I mean in the system ... But you could be dying ..."

Her hands were cool on his face, and he held them there a moment and focused on his breath. Breathing! He was actually breathing ... because he needed to breathe ... this body *needed* to breathe, not just to speak. The idea of that felt joyful too.

"I don't think I'm going to die. Again. I just ..." But then words failed him once more.

Maybe it would just be better to lie and wait for his fate to be decided by someone else. Apparently, that person was going to be Helena, and he was okay with that.

"Just stay there. I'm going to go get you a blanket," she said, and she was gone again. Laying his arm down, Rafferty's hand landed on a book also lying spine up next to him. He grasped it to bring it up to look at it.

It was the cookbook, the one that had summoned him in the first place.

He opened the pages, letting them flutter above his nose, wafting that old book smell into his face. It smelled of familiarity, the closest sense he had had to taste in the before times. He brought his other hand up and opened the book wide. Assembled in tight little paragraphs, the typeface inside was an older style he didn't know the name of. Yet, it was the margins he focused on, filled with the swooping cursive letters. Written by a woman he knew once but would never see again.

"Nana," he whispered, saying her name. She was someone he had done wrong.

As fast as the elation washed over him, darker emotions took their familiar places, swamping him with his recent memories.

This is all my fault, his mind rang out to him. He had summoned his fellow demons, a whole kitchen of them.

He had been too distracted with Helena, too reckless in his actions and emotions, too angry at her to realize what Vassago was doing, that he hadn't gone back to hell with the others where he belonged.

If only Rafferty had talked to Helena before Vassago had made his move. But Rafferty had been so sure that he was right, that she *hadn't* cared for him, that she had just used him like so many of those that had come before ...

Why had it been so important to prove I was right? he asked himself.

The weight of a comforter dropped down over him, covering his cold, naked, vulnerable new body. Warmth seemed to have been clinging to it, washing back over him. His warmth. He was generating *warmth*. It wasn't the stinging burn of hell that was neither hot nor cold. The smell of that place was still in his sense memory, but he wasn't there. He was in reality.

The place he belonged. Right?

"Just stay right here. I'm going to try to pack some things and figure out what we're going to do next, okay?" Though she was asking, her gaze was already far away. "I need to call someone about Scarlet and Yosef."

"Scarlet ... Yosef ..." he repeated, even though she didn't hear as she rushed back out of the room. They were names Helena had spoken of: her boss and coworker. Names that didn't really mean anything to him until he met ... well, Yosef that night. Scarlet, he had only seen briefly at a distance, until Vassago had made his deal with Yosef ...

The image of the poor man's head being crunched between Vassago's teeth shot a fresh spike of pain and regret through Rafferty. And recognition. He knew that desperation that Yosef felt, to do *whatever* it took, to make *any* deal to save the thing most important to him, and he, Rafferty, had put a vile thing like Vassago in his path. The reborn man knew better, knew the price that such an action would take, and now ... Yosef was paying for it. Rafferty could have ... should have ... tried to keep him safe.

He *had* known better. And he hadn't cared when it mattered because all he was concerned with was Helena.

"I'm so sorry," he said, the words falling out of him unbidden but true.

"Rafferty, Raffie, what are you sorry for?" Helena asked.

She had returned, but he hadn't noticed. A small pile of clothes sat on the floor next to where she knelt at his head. Gently, she ran her fingers, her blessed fingers, through his hair over and over. He reached up to touch them, to make sure that she was still, in fact, real. Would he ever be able to trust it?

"I'm sorry, I ... I can't seem to get up off this floor," he said, still realizing her urgency, even if he couldn't feel it himself. He gave her a smile. "I don't know what's wrong with me." Maybe it was a lie or rather a truth that covered up a different truth.

"It's okay," she assured, petting his hair again. Damn, he loved that. "Just take your time."

"No, it's not," he said. "I know we got ... we're in trouble, aren't we? Or you're in trouble. Scarlet ..."

Her beautiful eyebrows pursed together, concerned. "I don't know. I don't know what we need to do, but ..." She leaned forward and kissed his cheek. "I'm sorry. I don't know *what* to do. Should we run or do we just call the authorities and turn ourselves in?" She ran her anxious fingers through her own hair.

"Don't be scared," he pleaded softly, brushing her wisps of hair back from her face. She was so beautiful. "You've just been through hell and back. Of course, you are scared." He needed to get up. He needed to help her save them.

"Maybe I can call Cindy. I shouldn't after everything she's going through but ... she'd also kill me if I needed her, and I didn't call."

His brain had to chug a moment, but then he remembered Helena's friend. Cindy was the emergency room doctor who had almost ended her own life under the stress of her existence and a little accidental push from his demonic energy. He truly hadn't intended to do that, but he hadn't really cared that it could have happened. Another surprise slice of guilt knifed through him, echoing the same cut as Yosef. He had always told himself that whatever the humans chose to do was not his fault or problem. And he had believed it.

Now, he had his doubts.

But I also helped save her life, he reminded himself.

Yet, it didn't count, did it? He did that for Helena's sake.

Cindy owed him nothing.

"I'm going to call her," Helena decided while he was thinking all this, standing with urgent, sharp movements. "Where's my phone?" That brought her up short. "Oh, crap. I left it at the table at the venue. I don't have a landline."

"Helena," he croaked out. He reached his hand out for her again. "Don't be afraid."

She took it and kissed the back of his knuckles, then set them against her cheek. "I'm going to take care of you, Raffie. No matter what happens," she vowed.

Then Fate tested that pledge.

The doorbell rang.

Chapter 2

THE EARTHLY AUTHORITIES SHOWED UP

Helena's shoulders stiffened as she walked toward the door. Skittering energy seemed to spike up and down her limbs. Rafferty's own mouth felt like sandpaper as he forced himself up, his legs more stable now, following her to the swinging door that separated her kitchen from the rest of her house. He had it held open, only a crack since he was still naked, but it was enough to see all the way to the front.

His beloved lifted up onto her toes to look out the window at the top, but she didn't seem reassured by what she saw.

"Oh, no," she breathed, then shot a glance at him. Whoever it was, it was bad, which meant he needed to put pants on to face it. She seemed to mutter something, but he couldn't hear it anymore. When he had been a demon, he could have heard her whisper halfway across the world.

9

The reminder of his lack of powers ratcheted up his anxiety even more.

Turning away, he let the door fall softly shut so he could grab up the clothes she had left him. He heard the front door open.

"Can I help you?" she asked, her voice as neutral as possible if distant, muffled through the kitchen door.

Changing his mind by an overwhelming urgency to see, he went back to the door with an unzipped fly to silently press it open again.

Two women entered. Both wore professional peacoats over suits. His heartbeat kicked up a notch as one of the women held up a badge on a chain around her neck. The other woman opened a wallet to flash her credentials.

What if it was Vassago in disguise, come to get another snack?

"Hello, my name is Agent Archon. I work for the BDI, and we are investigating an incident of demon summoning that you might be connected to. Do you have a few minutes for some questions?"

Rafferty's brain went completely blank. The BDI? He had no idea what that acronym stood for. What he did know was they were clearly the Earthly authorities, they had found his beloved Helena, and whatever they were going to do to her was all his fault.

Helena didn't answer Agent Archon's question, her gaze shifting from the badge to each woman's face.

The agents, of course, noted it. "First off, Ms. Rhodes, are you aware of the events that took place last night at Wrightwood Ballroom between the time of midnight and 1:30 a.m.?"

While the first agent asked the question, the other agent lifted up a device in her hands, studying its readings.

Helena stood there, her mouth opening and closing. She clearly had no idea what to say. Agent Archon read her nonanswer with calculating eyes. "Ms. Rhodes, may I ask where you were last night during that time?"

"I was ... at Wrightwood Ballroom," Helena said in a small voice.

"So you were present last night?" Agent Archon confirmed. "And did you see and/or speak to Ms. Scarlet Kovacs during that time?"

Helena closed her eyes and pressed her fingers against them as if that would help her not see it, not relive those final moments before they had fallen through hell.

"Ms. Rhodes," Agent Archon said gently, coaxing, "you saw something, didn't you? Something happened to Mr. Yosef Cantor, didn't it?"

"Yes," Helena squeaked out.

The other agent's voice was softer, gentler. Enough to lull her into a false sense of security. "It's alright. You're safe now. We can protect you. You just have to tell us what happened. Tell us what you saw."

"What happened to your coworker? Did it involve your boss?" Agent Archon's tone of voice matched her partner's. Coaxing and soothing.

"It wasn't Scarlet's fault," Helena said, "Yosef, he ..." Helena's voice thickened, and she stopped speaking again. She clearly didn't know what to do.

Rafferty didn't know what to do either. He had always been instructed by his masters to stay away and keep himself from view whenever anyone other than his summoner appeared. He realized too late he was doing that exact thing without being compelled. He had to get out there and protect her! He knew what *they* were doing. Demons used these same sorts of tricks all the time.

"Did *he* summon the demon?" the agent asked as Rafferty threw the door open.

All three women turned to look directly at him.

"I don't want to get anyone in trouble ..." Helena shouted, moving to place herself between the agents and him.

Agent Archon furrowed her brows as her attention went back to Helena, her mouth continuing to talk while her brain struggled with his shirtless appearance. "Ms. Rhodes. I don't think I have to tell you that demon summoning is not only highly illegal but also highly dangerous. We need to know if the demon that killed Mr. Cantor, if it escaped after he summoned it, or did it manage to get sent back."

"Hi, who are you?" the partner asked, having not looked away from Rafferty as he quickly crossed toward the authorities, stopping when Helena intercepted him.

"Rafferty, don't—"

"Sir, my partner asked you a question. Who are you?" Agent Archon repeated, her brain finally switching tracks.

Helena spun around. "I think ... we need to speak to a lawyer," her voice stronger but respectful as he placed his hands on her shoulders protectively.

Agent Archon's whole stance shifted.

Her partner *hmm*'d, but nodded. "That's fine. That's your right, but I'm going to have to ask you to come into our offices and give a statement then. If that's okay?"

But Agent Archon wasn't having it. "Ms. Rhodes, every moment we spend taking you downtown, waiting for your lawyer, and compromising with you to get you to testify is another moment when someone else could be eaten alive by this creature. Or worse. That will be blood on *your* hands if you *are* involved," she growled. "I want to pretend we have all the time in the world to follow procedures, but if you are somehow involved, every one of those victims will be another charge against you if you don't tell us what you know right now!"

Her partner looked at her alarmed. "Arc, this isn't how due process—"

Agent Archon took an aggressive step toward Helena, clearly due process be damned. "Where is the demon?!"

"Here!" Rafferty said. Gripping Helena's shoulders, he stepped around her, this time to shield her behind him. He wasn't going to let anything happen to her. "I'm right here."

He knew what they saw. An ordinary human man, dressed in ordinary jeans and not much else. Agent Archon's eyes raked up and down, her eyebrows pinching together hard when her gaze rested on his bare feet as though they offended her for not being hooves.

Not that Rafferty had ever had hooves.

Then Agent Archon glanced at her partner before they both examined the device in the partner's hand.

Her partner shook her head, clearly confused. "Nothing."

Agent Archon swung her attention back to Rafferty. "Sir ..." The words died on her lips as she took in the grave seriousness of his face. It disconcerted her and she had to start again. "Sir, what makes you claim that you are a demon?"

Now it was Rafferty's turn to be confused. "Because I am one," he said.

In times past, that declaration should have been enough to have him hauled off. The Earthly authorities didn't mess around with demonic anything, and a confession was usually enough to get one burned or beheaded then burned. Or disemboweled. Or drowned. Whatever the prescribed remedy of the time for disposing of demons was.

It had happened more than a few times.

Helena seized his arm protectively. "No, you're not!" Then she turned to the agents. "Not anymore. He's not a demon anymore. He's a man—"

"I am yours," he shouted, attempting to drown her words. He pulled his wrist free from her grasp and put his hands before himself toward the agents as he dropped to his knees in submission. "Do with me what you will, but please spare Helena. She has done nothing wrong. She is innocent."

"Rafferty!" Helena pleaded. "You have to stop talking. I'm going ... I'm gonna get a lawyer, okay? We need a lawyer. A lawyer."

Agent Archon patted the air with her hands as if to say *calm down*. "Possession?" she asked her partner.

"It's not unprecedented. I did this case study in school where the victim believed they were—"

"Later," Agent Archon hissed, then turned once more to Rafferty, gently lowering his proffered hands with a light touch. "Sir, I don't know what you've been through ... what *both* of you have been through, but ..."

This was infuriating. "I *am* the demon you seek! Do with me what you will!" Rafferty repeated. He thrust his hands toward the agent again. "I am responsible for the man Yosef's death. I am the one who attempted to corrupt this good woman, Helena, in order to acquire her soul. I am the monster you need to destroy to save yourselves. Cut my head off, burn me at the stake, I don't care, but you *must* take me into your custody."

Agent Archon's partner squatted down onto one knee in front of Rafferty, smiling kindly. "Sir, you don't have a trace of demonic energy about you," she insisted, showing him the screen of her device as if he would have any idea what the wavy line in its viewer would mean. "I know this is confusing, but we're going to help you. I promise."

Huffing, Agent Archon pulled a cellphone out of her pocket. "I'm going to call for an intervention team all the same." Then she looked to Helena. "If you want to call a lawyer, now would be the time."

"So, we're not under arrest?" Helena asked, with tentative hope.

"I would speak to your lawyer first," the agent replied, moving across the porch to speak into her phone.

"Right. Right." Helena nodded as she moved away to find her own mobile phone, only to pull up short remembering she had left it at the venue.

Rafferty's mind spun. What was happening here?

"Sir, I am going to ask you to get up off the floor," the second agent coaxed, gesturing for Rafferty to rise with her.

"You need to destroy me! Before it's too late! I am the one who summoned the demon Vassago!"

"Rafferty! Stop! Please," Helena begged, putting her own hand over his mouth to emphasize stopping him.

"It's alright, he doesn't know what he is saying. You're not under arrest, we're going to get you help," the agent assured. "Sir ... I know you think you're a demon, but if that were the case, we would be reading demonic energy from you, and there is nothing."

"Wait, Sophia," Agent Archon interjected, pressing her phone to her shoulder. "If he were possessed, there *would* be a trace of some demonic energy. Right? And you said you are reading *nothing*?"

"Well, I ..." Agent Sophia—at last she had a name—hesitated, not knowing how to respond.

"Go to the kitchen!" the former demon barked, pointing the way. "If it is evidence you require, it is there you shall find it."

"Rafferty, shut up!" Helena begged, clearly terrified. "Officers ... or agents ... I mean ... please. We can explain all of this."

But Agent Archon seemed to be at the end of her tether. She bolted past the kneeling man, heading for the swinging door that led to the kitchen.

The agent swung open the door and stared down at the kitchen floor. "Agent Sophia! We have a summoning circle."

Chapter 3

I AM COMPLETELY HUMAN

"Yes, he's completely human," the doctor said, flipping his stethoscope over his head to lie across the back of his neck before slipping his gloved hands into his pockets.

"You're sure?" Agent Archon stressed.

"Look, I have run every test known. I even got his bloodwork back already since demonic anything is the only way to get high priority around here," he grumbled with the air of an old complaint. "He is a healthy, fairly average human male, approximately in his mid-twenties. When did you say you were born again?"

"In the time of King Louis the XIV," Rafferty answered obediently, feeling uncomfortable under the paper sheet and the strange paper shirt that opened to the front they had asked him to wear. He had every intention of complying with *anything* that was asked of him, but he had not imagined this. "Why aren't you simply running me through with holy weapons and being done with it? Or attempting to burn me at the stake?" he muttered.

Agent Archon and the doctor both looked at him with neutral faces and pity in their eyes.

The doctor sighed. "Whatever is wrong with him, it is definitely mental. Considering there is no trace of demonic power, it could be something as simple as PTSD due to stress. You saw a man's head bitten off, correct?" the doctor asked.

"Yes," Rafferty conceded. While it had not been the worst thing he had ever witnessed, it was the most recent.

"Yeah, there you go. But I would want a shrink to make the final determination," the doctor said. "But it's not that big of a surprise. If this guy was a witness to your other guy getting eaten in half, I'd probably lose all my marbles, too, and be better off for it."

"Thanks for the medical opinion," Agent Archon said dryly.

With that, she left the room.

"You're welcome," the doctor said just as dryly as he turned to write some more things on a chart, glancing over at Rafferty. "You can put your clothes back on."

The man didn't leave, so Rafferty simply did as he was bid, standing up and letting the paper sheet fall to the ground. Retrieving from a nearby chair the precious clothes Helena had given him, he dressed himself.

"What … is going to happen now?" the former demon dared to ask as he sat in a chair to slip the shoes on.

The doctor didn't even look up as he went to leave. "Don't know, my friend. All I do know is my part with you is over."

"Where is Helena?" Rafferty asked.

"Who?" the doctor asked, pausing with the door already partially open, clearly impatient to leave.

"The woman I came with. Where is she?" Rafferty asked, fearful of the answer.

Outside in the hall Agent Archon's partner Sophia leaned inside, glancing between the doctor and him with a questioning expression.

"No idea, you'll have to ask her." The doctor gestured at her with his clipboard before handing it over to Agent Sophia. "He's all yours."

She took it, but before she could mutter any thanks, the doctor left as abruptly as he had come.

"Um, alright, why don't you come with me? We'll get you something to drink, and we'll just talk, okay?" Agent Sophia gestured down the hallway. "Don't forget your coat."

Rafferty had already risen to follow her, only to double back into the room to grab it with alacrity. They had brought him to their stronghold, but it was the strangest dungeon he had ever been in. Mostly it was cubicles and offices, but there were a few rooms with specialized functions like the one he had just left. Not a single rack or whip in sight.

"Don't worry, Mr. Lares. Everything is going to be okay," she assured, catching him looking around and probably interpreting it as anxiety. She flashed her sympathetic smile as she gestured for him to turn left out of the room.

"Are you serious?" He was disgusted by this whole ... farce!

"Look, I understand. We all understand. Something really terrible has happened to you. It's alright. It's not unusual for people who have been victims of a demonic attack to be confused. You might even have supplanted memories that are preventing you from—"

"What are you talking about? I am who I say I am!" Rafferty stopped in the hall, blocking traffic both ways, utterly aghast at what he was hearing. "I am a demon!"

Agent Sophia hushed him, holding her hands up to calm him down his shouting. Other agents were glancing at them with equal parts concern, pity, and professional indifference from their cubicles, but no one intervened. This was worse than flaming hot pokers.

Maybe he really was going mad.

"Why don't we come in here?" Agent Sophia asked, gesturing toward a nearby room.

Helplessly, Rafferty complied with her request. Inside the new room was a couch with a coffee table and a regular small kitchen table. Both seemed completely out of place in an office. Along the right wall were a couple of cabinets and a bin full of toys. The table had paper and a small bucket of crayons waiting. It also had a padded rocking chair in the corner.

"Where is this? A nursery?" He sneered at his new torture chamber.

"This is where the counselor meets with kids, but it's also the only room with a couch in it. In case you want to lie down," Agent Sophia said, moving to the cabinet to pull out a pillow.

"Fine! Fine," Rafferty snapped, dropping to sit on the couch, his elbows braced on his knees as he covered his face with his hands.

"It's going to be alright. You're not in trouble. There is plenty room for mercy here, *whatever* you might have done. We're not the bad guys. We want to help you," Agent

Sophia said gently and carefully. Her words brought him to tears. "I'll ... I'll get you some water."

Rafferty had never been so frustrated in his entire existence. This was worse than dragging Helena into hell. As he sat there, it came back to him. All he could see in his mind's eye was Helena suffering in torturous blackness and him unable to get to her, to shield her, to save her.

Despite the horror of those memories, he felt a sense of calm, or at least a sense of *calmness*, settle over him.

No. *That* had still been worse. There was nothing worse than hell.

This was ... a different kind of *bad*, but still nothing compared to *that*.

Yet, why wouldn't they believe him?

The door opened and closed, but he didn't lift his head. He expected a small cup of water to appear in the tunnel of his vision, but instead, someone pulled the rocking chair forward to the other side of the small coffee table. A person sat down and crossed their legs.

Rafferty waited for what he assumed was the agent to start babbling more inane words at him, but the silence continued. Gooseflesh skittered across his arms as a feeling of familiar wrongness prickled his skin, then worked toward seeping into his bones. Inhaling a sharp breath, Rafferty's head snapped up.

Vassago grinned too many teeth at him. "Salutations, mon vieil ami," he said, his French lilting and musical.

Fear, the sort that Rafferty hadn't felt in centuries, gripped his heart. His very mortal, pounding heart. Suddenly, it hit him how much he had gained back and how much he had to lose again.

"Retourne dans les ténèbres, immonde démon," Rafferty intoned, his mother's old words coming back to him. Return to the darkness, foul demon.

Vassago's grin remained sharp. "You are not my caller anymore. You know that. And our obligation to each other is paid." He had switched back to English, but for whose benefit, Rafferty wasn't sure.

The demon cocked his head to the side as his eyes roved over Rafferty's body as if he could see through the clothes he wore and relished the skin with lustful intensity.

"What the ever-hating hell did you do to get such a fine body? Is it yours? Did you manage to trade for it?" Vassago leaned forward, dropping his crossed leg and mirroring Rafferty's posture, his uncanny black eyes, two whirling pools of ink, staring unblinkingly. "How *did* you do it? *How* did you do it?"

Rafferty curled up his lip as his answer.

Holding their standoff a second too long, Vassago sat back again, recrossing his leg, his giggle uncannily disconnected from the move. "Well, you didn't sacrifice your 'old soul' I see. Checked in on her."

That snapped Rafferty's control, and he jumped to his feet and over the coffee table in one fluid motion. The demon laughed as Rafferty grabbed the front of the kitchen garb he still wore. The momentum shoved the rockers of the chair, sliding it backward into one of the cabinets. Rafferty pulled back a fist, righteous fury filling him.

"So, you are human!" Vassago crowed as if he had just proved something. "My hells, this is some sort of reverse miracle."

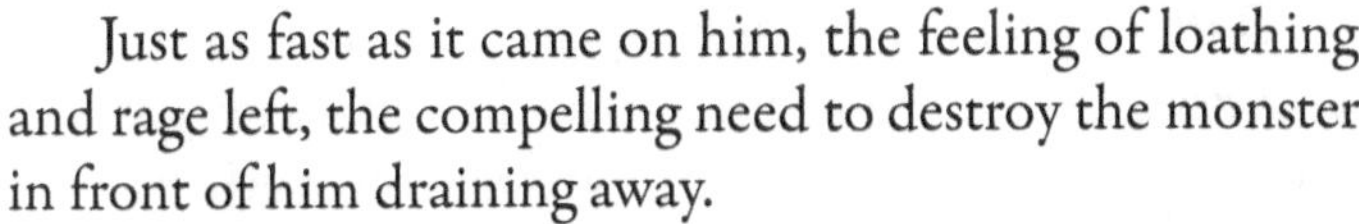

Just as fast as it came on him, the feeling of loathing and rage left, the compelling need to destroy the monster in front of him draining away.

Vassago's demonic aura.

It had an effect on humans, often making them violent and hateful, pushing them to do acts their higher minds would resist.

The fact that it had affected him like that was as much of a shock as any of the others he had experienced in the few short hours of his rebirth. Then Vassago pulled back on the aura, shielding it behind his fake human facade, and Rafferty found he could breathe and think clearly again.

"Hmm, better put that away. Don't want to alert the other fishies," Vassago cooed, pleased with his discovery, not at all bothered that Rafferty still gripped his shirt. "They got all sorts of nasty devices in this place and too many things of protection or whatever. I only got in through the tiniest crack in their armor and even just sitting here my skin's all itchy. They already want to destroy me, just like you. Best not to throw gas on an existing fire." He grinned again, too-sharp teeth and all. "If only I had your skills, shift that anger into lust. Ha, and you weren't even a proper incubus."

Another tendril wafted through Rafferty, this one pinging his groin into a spiderweb of sensation throughout his body.

Rafferty let Vassago's shirt go and stumbled back, breathing heavily. "No," he said.

"See, I'm too ham-fisted to play on lusts," Vassago crowed, clearly still pleased with himself. "Boy, if you ever needed proof that you were alive, you got it."

Rafferty ran his hands through his hair. "But what ... what does this mean?" He hated that he was asking Vassago this, but so far, the old demon was the only other being in existence who had some understanding of the context Rafferty was dealing with.

"Look at you, Lares. A demon, not only risen from hell but also ... *redeemed*," Vassago continued, purring. "I have no idea what it means, but I'm excited to find out." Vassago licked his lips, his own desire for what Rafferty had unmistakable.

Then the old demon shuddered, wincing in sharp pain.

Cocking his head to one side, Rafferty suddenly understood something. "You have no anchor here, do you? You ate him. And the circle has been closed and sealed." They both knew what that meant. A demon couldn't exist in reality without either a human anchor or the active circle they had been called through. The manic tension in every twitch and flinch betrayed Vassago's nonchalant posture.

"How much energy are you spending to just remain here in reality?" Rafferty asked, already knowing the answer.

Shrugging, Vassago turned away. "I'll figure that out. And don't flatter yourself. I'm not offering a deal of that sort to you ... since you and I have already done that tango?" An eyebrow arched with the implied question, testing if his statement was, in fact, true.

"Never," Rafferty affirmed, a smile slipping over his face. He had no intention of endangering himself or Helena further by making a deal with this same demon who had tricked and condemned him the first time. But deals were something familiar. Something he felt confident in now. Despite all the changes, deals were nothing new.

"So, I'm glad I didn't ask." Vassago sniffed with the indignity a cat would admire. "Besides, I think your little old soul has everything well in hand."

Rafferty flinched. "And you can't touch her. You know she would never accept a deal from you," he warned.

"Well, of course. She's not an idiot," Vassago chuckled, his implication clear.

Rafferty didn't rise to the baiting. He only waited and smiled. Even though he said he wouldn't make a deal with Vassago, they both knew that was a lie. It just needed to be the *right* deal.

They stared at each other, smiling, until finally, Vassago shifted away, yielding to Rafferty first to study the scarred arm of the rocking chair. It was a kind of tactic to make the mark feel superior to the demon. A false sense.

"What I want is really simple. Peace," Vassago finally said.

Rafferty furrowed his brows.

"No, I mean it. I leave you alone. You leave me alone. You don't tell anyone what you know about me. We go our separate ways, and that's the end of it."

Letting those words flow over him, Rafferty parsed them in his mind to try to find the flaw. "Define leave alone."

"I will do no physical harm, exert no influence, and make no bargains with you and your little old soul, other than this bargain I'm making with you right now. I can take no action that would do either of you any mental harm either. No driving either of you insane. You'll have to do that on your own. You will both be completely safe from me. You can just get on living your lives."

"Not just us," Rafferty added. "Her friends, too."

Vassago's eyes narrowed, then he let out an exasperated sigh. "I'm going to need specific names," he conceded.

The demon was serious.

It also meant that Vassago feared what Rafferty's knowledge could do to his chances of staying in creation.

But Rafferty conceded. He didn't have the stomach for this. The humans didn't seem to be interested in sending him back, or even believing his story, but if they were going to let him, he would prefer to just be done with all of it. To live a life with Helena.

"Helena's friends. Cindy, Charlie, Chris," he said, reciting the names he knew for them, hoping it would be enough for Vassago. "And Scarlet."

Vassago's lips thinned at the mention of that name; his latest victim and the one most likely to want to make a deal with him to undo the damage caused.

"Fine. Agreed. I will extend my amnesty to those individuals as well. Satisfied?" Then Vassago cocked his head to one side. "And we speak of this agreement to no one."

Rafferty was surprised that Vassago didn't even try to haggle about Scarlet. He felt emboldened to push it. "And one additional condition. I can tell Helena about this deal," Rafferty countered. "I won't keep anything from her like that."

The demon huffed through his nose. "Agreed. But just your old soul. Anyone else *you* tell voids the agreement."

Only one step left. "These terms remain in effect as long as we both uphold them in letter and in spirit?"

Vassago returned a thin smile. This was all part of doing business as demons. It was impossible to craft a perfectly worded contract that couldn't be loopholed and exploited eventually, so smart humans, or other demons, would bind contracts to the "spirit" of the meanings as well as the literal.

"I swear by my mind, body, and soul," Vassago intoned.

"I swear by my mind, body, and soul," Rafferty repeated.

And just like that, it was done.

Which was strange. There was no uncomfortable feeling of power creeping over Rafferty's skin, but Vassago shivered. He could feel the power of the contract.

Then his shoulders dropped a half in a semblance of relief. "Thank you, my boy. I'm glad we could come to an accord. And in the spirit of our old friendship, I'll give you this. No other strings attached." He pulled a spiral-bound book out of his pocket. It was uncanny to watch as the book was clearly bigger than the pocket and yet popped out of it all the same. Vassago dropped it onto the table with a definite thump.

Rafferty stared at the cover.

It was Helena's grandmother's cookbook.

Before he could lift his head to ask, Vassago moved to the door. "We've got our agreement. If we both keep it, you'll never see me again. Have a good life, mon ami."

And he left, leaving Rafferty alone in the quiet.

Chapter 4

MY FLAWLESS ACCENT

The door opened once more.

The two agents who held his fate in their hands filed in, followed by beautiful Helena.

To his relief, she came straight to him, offering her hands, which he took in both of his, his heart leaping at her touch. She squeezed, smiling reassuringly as she sat down on the couch with him. Her eyes alighted on the cookbook in his lap, that he had moved there because it felt safer. She reached to touch its cover, giving him a questioning eyebrow, but there was no time or safety of space to say anything about it. He slid it off his lap and tucked it under his coat on the couch as the two agents took seats across from them.

Agent Archon sat in the other normal chair which left Agent Sophia with the rocking chair, but she seemed plenty cheerful with the option. He knew this was it, and he would do whatever it took to protect Helena.

"We have come to a preliminary conclusion that you, Ms. Rhodes and Mr. Lares, were victims of a demonic possession," Agent Archon stated.

Rafferty couldn't believe what he was hearing. "What?"

Helena seemed surprised too. "But the summoning circle in my kitchen—"

"Is completely benign," Agent Sophia said, clearly trying to be reassuring.

Agent Archon shook her head. "Just carving a summoning circle into a floor doesn't make it a real summoning circle, and the symbols around it are just utter gibberish. It is most likely that the real demon summoner planted that to convince you, Ms. Rhodes, that you had done the deed and that your boyfriend was that same demon."

"The agency has seen this before," Agent Sophia added. "One time it was a husband who the demon summoner had convinced that his wife was a succubus that he had summoned. She survived but he did not."

Agent Archon folded her arms protectively across her chest. "This sort of deception," Agent Archon said, shaking her head in disgust. "It never works, but some of them try. All it accomplishes is just more people getting hurt."

"Then ... what do you think *did* happen?" Helena asked, utterly perplexed.

"We aren't going to comment further on an open investigation, only on the details that concern you." She sighed. "I know this is going to be very hard for you to accept. But with time and counseling, you will be able to get on with your lives."

"For the time being, we would like you to stay under our protection," Agent Sophia said. "The demon that caused all this is still out there, and it may focus on one of you to become its new anchor."

"Without the anchor, it will be ejected from creation naturally, but it will cause a lot of destruction before that happens. We would rather find it before anyone else gets hurt." Agent Archon flipped open another folder and showed her a brochure. "If you will allow us, we can put you up in a hotel. It's already prepared with a protection circle and other charms, so you wouldn't have to worry about the demon coming to get you while you sleep."

"I ... I just want to get back to my life," Helena said.

Agent Sophia nodded. "Of course you do, this is just until we can get your house inlaid with its own protections."

Helena nodded, wrapping her arms around herself protectively. Rafferty slid his own arm around her shoulders as well. He knew they were safe now, that he could rely on the deal he made with Vassago, but mentioning it now would only tip off these agents and void the deal.

Pulling out another set of forms from the folder, Agent Archon handed them to Helena. "If you sign this, we can have the protection circle set and everything over the next couple of days. It's all covered by the state's Demonic Barrier Act, so there is no cost to you. You won't even notice that it's there, but if the demon should get desperate enough to return, we'll also be alerted."

"And then you can go home," Agent Sophia finished.

"But ..." Helena bit her lower lip, "What if ... what if what I said was true, even if you are having trouble finding evidence for it. I summoned a demon; shouldn't I still be punished?"

It was Agent Archon's turn to sigh but remain otherwise professional. "If you had, in fact, summoned a demon, as you say, and it was an accident ... the worst that would happen to you is you would incur a fine and require classes on the dangers of demon summoning."

Rafferty blinked. "That seems ... incredibly lenient."

"There is a degree of mercy in the laws as written," Agent Archon explained, reusing the phrase Agent Sophia had said earlier like it was a creed.

"Nor is it really justice to lock away people who simply made a mistake and to ruin their entire lives," Agent Sophia added. "Especially if it's teenagers. They are often rebelling by doing something stupid with Ouija boards, that sort of thing. If no one gets hurt and they learned their lesson, it's not something to destroy their lives over."

"The demon is worse than any punishment we can dole out," Agent Archon agreed. "We are only interested in the unrepentant who will continue to be a danger to society. Nothing you've told me today, if true, rises to meet that standard."

"Well ... I'm not going to lie, that does make me feel a little bit better," Helena said.

Rafferty, frankly, could not believe what he was hearing. Mercy? They were going to show them mercy? He wanted to laugh out loud and would have if it hadn't been for the centuries of discipline to control giving away too much.

"You have a good life, Ms. Rhodes, Mr. Lares," Agent Archon assured.

"And you clearly love each other dearly," Agent Sophia piped in.

Agent Archon only hiccuped a moment at her partner's interruption, her one eye twitching before continuing. "Take our advice, stay at the hotel at least for tonight but for as long as you need. Let the professionals take care of the rest."

"Oh, also, Mr. Lares, do you have any identification?" Agent Sophia asked. "We can't find you in the system."

"Um, well, he's French," Helena said. It was true.

"Oh! I see," Agent Sophia said, her gaze shifting from surprise to confusion. "But he doesn't have much of an accent?"

"He hides it because ... well, I think, I don't know if this is true ... but I think you ... grew up here, but his citizenship is ... I mean, I don't really know. I'm sorry I don't know." She was clearly trying so hard not to lie, but it was a struggle to find an answer that they would accept.

They all looked at him.

He sighed, then said, "I don't know what to tell you since you haven't accepted any of my answers yet."

"Are you French?" Agent Archon asked directly.

"Yes. I was," he admitted. Was he really going to get away with this by just telling the truth?

Agent Sophia nodded. "We understand, Mr. Lares. Don't worry, we'll reach out to the Embassy on your behalf. Try to see if you can find your identifications, but if you can't we'll help you start the process to get them reissued. It's also not uncommon for identity theft to occur in these cases."

"But we just need an answer about the protection," Agent Archon interjected. "Do you want it or not?"

"We'll take it for tonight, for sure. Thank you," Helena relented.

Relieved at getting an answer she wanted, Agent Archon wrote on another form, had Helena sign it, then stamped it, before sticking it back into her folder. "If that's the case, then you are both free to go to the hotel now. Agents will go to your house to collect anything you need. Just give Agent Sophia a list."

Then Helena sat more upright. "Oh! My cat, Pooka. She's still in the house."

"Yes, our agents have already secured her and taken her to a holding facility," Agent Archon said, reopening the folder to retrieve another piece of paper.

"Holding facility?" Helena asked.

"Yes, you'll be happy to hear that nothing demonic has happened to your cat either. She has not been made a familiar and has a clean bill of health. Are her vaccinations up to date?"

"Uh, yes, yes, I think so. But I don't understand what you mean by 'holding facility,'" she pressed.

"Think of it as a pet daycare but federally funded," Agent Sophia piped in. "Pets are often targets, so she is also a protected person just like you now are. I can help sign you up for our check-in app so you can get updates on how she is doing."

"Thank you," was all Helena could say.

Everything was working out in their favor, and Rafferty felt numb. He couldn't trust this yet. It was almost as if a demon were working some impossible magic.

And maybe he was.

But whatever dastardly plan or mischief Vassago was concocting with this, Rafferty simply could not discern it.

"If we both keep it, you'll never see me again," he had said.

Have I already done something to jeopardize that? Rafferty wondered to himself.

Agent Archon stood, her face a stoic, analyzing mask. "Vous êtes libre de partir, M. Lares," she said in French.

"Merci, m'dame," he responded automatically, bowing his head respectfully, his French flawless compared to her rough, American-accented French.

Her eyebrows popped the tiniest bit, the crack in her poker face.

"Ton accent Américain est impeccable, je dois dire," she continued.

Rafferty's face ticked at the realization of what was happening. He hadn't even realized what he had done. But yes, he could speak his native tongue clearly, and it sounded indeed *like* his native tongue.

He licked his teeth, unsure. "J'ai passé beaucoup de temps en Amérique. J'ai tendance à adopter l'accent dans lequel j'existe," he answered. Again, it was the truth, and the truth had carried them this far.

Satisfied, Agent Archon switched back to English. "Thank you for your cooperation," she said, and finally left.

Agent Sophia stepped up. "If you come with me, we'll get you out of here."

Helena grasped Rafferty's hand to pull him after her, and they exited into a stairwell.

"Put your coat on," Helena urged just before they went out a pair of glass doors to leave the building. She already wore hers, though it was unzipped in the front. "It started snowing again."

Rafferty did as he was bid, a smile starting to crack his face. *Really? That is it? We are free to go? No need to prove our innocence?* he thought.

He looked down at Helena's angelic face. As long as she was safe, he was fine with that.

But it could still be a trap or trick. He couldn't let his guard down yet.

An unmarked, black car waited for them outside with a large, intimidating-looking driver in a formal, long black coat with a smart hat on his head. He opened the door of the car as Helena and Rafferty approached.

Agent Sophia went straight to the passenger side up front. "Next stop, the safest hotel in the city," she chimed.

Chapter 5

AT LEAST WE HAD EACH OTHER

Rafferty slipped his long, warm fingers between Helena's and squeezed.

During the car ride, he felt like he lived in a bubble of tension just waiting to pop. Agent Sophia checked them in once they got to the hotel, a nice one with valets and everything. The agents produced their bags from the trunk, the ones Helena had packed when she had thought about running. The valets took them without another word. Agent Caruso, the driver, escorted them on the elevator and then off of it at the fifteenth floor. It wasn't the top floor, but it was pretty high up. Their escort then deposited them into a suite with a couch, dining table, and a king-sized bed.

A few seconds later, Agent Sophia came in behind them and immediately jumped into explaining the amenities of the room as she flipped on the lights in a beautiful bathroom with two sinks and a decent-sized shower with two showerheads. Helena listened politely, but she moved to look at their view of the city, which was mostly dark buildings studded with lights and glowing streets where cars continued to move as if it were midday.

"Call me if there is anything else you need. I'm going to get out of your hair now so you both can get some sleep. Your dinner should be delivered shortly, and don't worry, everything is taken care of, including the tip. Just get some rest, and I will come see you tomorrow morning. Don't leave the room for any reason, please." Agent Sophia moved toward the door. And as she opened it, a covered cart appeared with their dinners.

"I'll take that," Helena insisted, grabbing the two covered trays before Agent Sophia could. "Have a good night."

It was a bit rude, but Agent Sophia only smiled and left.

At last, they were alone.

Helena deposited the trays on the dining table. It seemed too quiet, after all of the hectic franticness of the day.

And the day before, for that matter.

Just like that, Rafferty didn't know what to say to the beautiful woman regarding him expectantly.

"Are you okay?" she asked first.

"I feel ..." As if bidden, emotions flooded through him, zipping down his limbs and bubbling out his throat.

He laughed.

He had seen humans go mad before. This felt like how that looked as more laughter kept bubbling out of him. His eyes filled with tears as he looked up at Helena. Her surprised expression made it worse. It was just so damned funny!

"Why are you laughing?" she asked.

"I have no idea!" he crowed, throwing his arms wide. "But it feels really damn good!"

Now the laughter was working its magic, washing over her face, enhancing her beauty, making her eyes shine.

He rushed across the space, throwing his arms around her, like he had when they had dropped through hell. Instead of dissipating into nothingness like she had before, this Helena felt solid and real. She tucked her head into the space where his neck met his shoulder, burying her face there. The smell of her hair hit him, and his body responded. She was real and whole, and he didn't deserve this miracle.

"We're alive," he muttered. "I'm alive! I won! I won!!"

He hadn't noticed right away that while he was riding high on his elation, Helena's laughter had died away too fast. Not until she lifted her head to look up at him, tears bubbling in her eyes.

"This is going to destroy Scarlet Promotions," she mewed as if she were embarrassed. It sobered him immediately. "And after everything I did ... *we* did to try to save it. Even if they are not holding us responsible for ..." She shook her head. "Damn it. It seems so stupid to be worried about it. I mean, Yosef died! A man lost his life, and I'm worried about ... But Scarlet Promotions was his whole life too. Literally Scarlet's whole life and now ... she's ruined and he's dead and I can't do anything to fix any of it!"

He cupped her face. "I am sorry for everything," he repeated. He couldn't tell her that he didn't care about all that. Those people and places didn't mean very much to him at all, but they meant something to her, and she was in pain over it. He wanted to do anything to take it away.

She took one of his hands, pulling it away from her face so she could plant a precious kiss in his palm. "How could you have known? When all you've ever known before were people who used you? What do you have to compare it to?"

Dammit, her mercy and compassion for him seemed to have no end. "I should have …"

"Shhh," she hushed, breathing on his lips, blowing away his half-formed arguments.

Then she rested her forehead against his and savored the feel of him. It was intoxicating and he succumbed to it. "I saw hell. I know what you've been through and where you come from. And I love you."

There were so many other arguments to make. So many things left unresolved. Things he wanted to say, but … he couldn't get the words out or his thoughts to order.

There was only Helena.

And she loved him.

And he had won.

Then those lips were pressing against his. He opened his mouth to their demands and let her tongue in. She caressed along his own and she tasted wonderful. Heady and rich. His fingers slipped through her hair, holding her, while her hands slid down his chest, leaving a different sort of fire trail that felt like it burned him through the cloth of his shirt.

God, he craved more.

And she offered it without being asked, pulling up the edges of the shirt to slide her hands over his skin … his real, warm skin … and up his back.

The groan that shuddered out of him broke their kiss as he arched back. She wasn't bothered by the interruption at all. Instead, she moved in closer to press her lips to his exposed neck, then just behind his ear, and across his vulnerable throat, where her teeth could cut him open and spill his blood, ending him forever. The irrational danger of it sent more shocks of pleasure bolting through him. She could do it, but she never would, and that was hot.

He had had all sorts of sex before. Other than making food, making sex had been the most requested task of him.

This was different. He felt *everything*. Every touch that had come through the body formed from demonic magic had been nothing compared to this and making love to Helena had been intense in that form. She had elicited such sensations that had burned through the layers and layers of numbness, yet even then the sex and subsequent orgasms had been more in his own mind than in his body. Now her touch consumed him.

"Rafferty?" Helena's voice cut through the chaos of thoughts inside him.

Opening his eyes, he panted, wondering why she had stopped. She looked at him with concern.

"It's just so ... much ..." he gasped out. At some point, she had gotten his shirt off, her fingers still resting on his heaving chest.

"I'm going too fast." She started to pull away.

"No!" He wrapped her up against him again, to keep her in place. "It just ... I just feel so ... much."

"It's okay, come on." She tugged him away from the window, toward the bed, pushing him down gently but firmly. He laid himself out before her, like a dish being served. She stripped him out of his pants, and he felt vulnerable and exhilarated at the same time before her appraising eyes. He hoped she liked what she saw. She must have because she smiled warmly, shedding away the rest of her own clothes. This body had something to offer her. This body wouldn't drink her essence when she touched him and gave herself to him. He couldn't harm her by simply loving her.

Holy hell, I'm alive!

He welcomed her as she came to straddle him. He longed to be inside her, even as he relished her exploring fingers.

"Tell me if you need me to stop or slow down," she whispered.

"Just kiss me, please," he begged, and her mouth was on him again, devouring him like a ravenous beast. He lost all sense of her fingers until they gripped around his fully erect member, to direct it into herself. Crying out with unabashed sensation, he broke the kiss, once more bowing against her, his hands slapping her hips as he gripped them. It only encouraged her, and she lifted up to repeat the motion, slowly gaining momentum with each of her thrusts. She was in control; he was the reborn virgin.

"Raff," she breathed, and he loved it. He loved the sound of his name from her lips; the name *she* gave him. He was alive. This wasn't a dream, confirmed as she took him faster and faster.

She rose up, glorious. Her breasts bounced as she rode him, her mouth open with her moans, her eyes closed. Alive and vibrant.

He felt the pressure build up inside. Urgent and real.

"Rafferty," she sang out.

"Helena," he offered back, her name guttering out of this throat roughly. He was barely able to speak.

Now he pulled down, his grip on her hips, forcing himself even deeper into her, thrusting as hard as he could as fast as he could.

"Ahhhh!" she cried out, her arms spreading wide as she came around him, her body shuddering, her mouth open and her eyes closed with intensity, her back exploding as a pair of wings burst and stretched to either side of her body.

Chapter 6

ANGELIC CONSEQUENCES, I GUESS

Her cries of ecstasy stuttered into cries of shock, just as he came inside her, unable to stop what had already begun. Under his fingers, her skin felt uncomfortably strange. In reaction, his hands flinched away, but the feeling persisted around his waist and genitals, tingling sensations that had nothing to do with the acts that had just taken place.

Further startled by his reaction, Helena tried to get off him, but he bucked at the same time, throwing her off onto the bed. Thankfully, she got one of her new wings out of the way before she crushed it. She continued to scramble like she thought she could still escape the alien things now attached to her.

Rafferty leapt to the other side, his toes grinding into the carpet as he stared wide-eyed at the being that had replaced his Helena.

She looked very much *like* Helena, but now her skin had a golden-white sheen to it like gold-dusted porcelain. Ethereal was the only word that came to mind. On top of her head were a pair of horns. They were golden in color. Not metallic gold, but the creamy gold that some rams would have. And they curved together in a circle over her head, the tips imperceptibly touching. Like ... like a *halo*. She looked at him straight on where she stood, holding her hands before her. Her nails were golden as his had once been black, her eyes wide. All of it seemed to make her rose-gold hair shine even brighter.

He knew what he was seeing, but he shook his head as if that would be enough to deny it.

"Rafferty ..." she asked in the smallest voice possible. "What's happening to me?"

To him, she looked like a demon, but the most beautiful demon he had ever seen.

"I ..." He stared at her, his mind completely blank as to what to say.

It was the wrong reaction to have because Helena only panicked harder. Clambering over the bed, she bolted past him to go into the bathroom, her feathers scraping against the door as she forced her way through. The light flipped on automatically as she stood in front of the wall of mirrors behind the pair of sinks, staring at herself.

"Oh my God," she breathed, her eyes wide as saucers. "Is this real? Is this real!?"

She tried to run her hands over her head and immediately encountered the horns. Gripping them, she pulled. All she accomplished was to wrench her head back and forth as her panic rose.

"Don't!" Rafferty cried, snapping into action, finally. Seizing her hands, he pulled them away from her new appendages. "Don't hurt yourself."

Then Helena's legs went out from under her. She stumbled back into the shower space, landing to sit on a small bench in the middle attached to the wall.

"Ow!" she cried as her winged back hit the wall.

"Helena!" Rafferty bolted forward again.

Yet she kept thrashing, her mind struggling to understand the wings shifting and slapping against the walls of the showers.

"Stop. Stop. Stay still," he urged, holding his hands out to her placatingly.

She looked up at him with wide, truly frightened eyes. "Am I demon?" she asked. "Rafferty! Please tell me!"

He shook his head violently. "No, absolutely not. Never," he lied.

Gently he took her hands, and the same strange feeling skittered up his arms. He felt a pressing urge to let go but willed himself to hold on. "Something is going on, yes. But ... but ..." He raked his eyes over her, trying to find something he could latch onto. And then he did. "Feathers. Look. You have feathers."

"Feathers?" she repeated, then looked, her eyes wide and innocent as a child.

"You're ... you're an angel." He cursed himself. He had known other demons with feathered wings, though none as beautiful as hers.

"An angel?" she stammered. She struggled to stand up again, which caused her to whap her wings against the wall as she battled for equilibrium. "Angels don't look like ..."

But this time, she stopped and stayed completely still, really looking at her reflection in the mirror across from the shower. "I've never seen pictures of angels that look ... like ..."

She tugged on her wavy, rose-gold hair, streaming around the horns. Her wings drooped a little, then she lifted them again, fluffing them out, as if she could finally see the white-gray feathers instead of the bat-like membranes Rafferty once had. He found himself as enthralled as he had been shocked. Gently, he ran his hands over them, feeling the soft pinions.

Helena continued examining herself in the mirror, the worry line deep between her brows. "How do I undo it? I mean, how do I return to normal?"

He almost said, "This is your normal now," but caught himself in time when he met her reflected scared eyes. He couldn't.

"Whenever I wanted to ... shift ..." He blinked, trying to recall the memory, except ... he couldn't. He remembered it happened as a fact, but not the experience of it. "I don't know ... I just ... understood that I could and then did. It was more like ... I would focus to dampen my demonic aura and not only appear as human but feel human to you."

"Focus on what?"

"I don't know," he repeated, embarrassed.

"Okay, great," she said dryly. "That was very helpful." Her wings flexed, twitching off his probing hands. "And stop it!"

"Sorry," he said.

She looked at herself again. "So ... so that means ... demons and angels ... they're not very different, then."

"I ..." But Rafferty had no idea what to say. As far as he knew angels didn't exist. At least, he had never met one. They had always been demons pretending or misnamed by the mortals they were serving. "I don't know."

"I think I know why this has happened," she said, calming down.

As she calmed, Helena returned to herself. Rafferty didn't know how else to explain it. One second, she was this beautiful, ethereal creature, and the next, she was the very human woman he had known and fallen in love with. The wings and horns gone, her skin and eyes were back to their normal shades.

"You're right," she said with detachment, "I just knew how to do it." Then she gave a serene little giggle.

Her serenity disturbed him the most. He felt so disjointed. Even though she looked normal, to him she still felt a little uncanny and untouchable now.

Maybe it had been his eternity of paranoia, but he couldn't help feeling there was something more she wasn't tell him. Some agenda he didn't understand but could see the negative space of.

Demons played tricks on each other all the time. Even as he thought that he forced those thoughts away.

This was Helena.

She wasn't a demon.

She couldn't be!

And he was human.

Have we switched places? he thought, the question breaking over him on a wave of new fear.

"I would say this situation is both our doing, so it makes sense we're going to have to fix it together," she had said only yesterday.

Helena kept her arms wrapped around herself, and the urge to do something, anything, to make her feel better compelled him back into the main room. Immediately, he spied the tray of food still waiting to be consumed. Tearing the cover off like it was his only salvation, he scoffed at the meal before them. It was a burger with steak fries that someone had tried to dress up with some sort of pink aioli and sliced vegetables, the whole thing skewered through to hold it together. What sort of comfort would this give her, especially now that it was tepid at best? He tore off the other tray to find what was essentially a grilled chicken that someone had termed "blackened" with a pile of vegetables and cooling whipped parsnips. It too seemed inadequate to serve to comfort Helena with.

He stretched his hand toward it to use some demonic energy to reheat it, only to be reminded too late that such a thing was impossible now.

"Dammit, dammit, dammit," he muttered, panicked at what to do. Should he call back downstairs and order something else? March into the kitchen himself and cook her something that would actually bring her solace in her time of pain?

"Oh, you're hungry," she said, coming from the bathroom herself to see where he had gone.

He covered the food as if ashamed, though he hadn't been the one to prepare it. "It's not ... We can order something else ..."

Still naked and beautiful, Helena came the rest of the way to their suite's table and took the lid from him to look down at her burger. "No, this is fine. It's what I ordered," she said, setting the lid aside, sitting down too calmly before the plate as if her entire fundamental being hadn't just irreparably changed.

Her ability to radically accept all of this was remarkable.

He snapped his hand to hover over her plate, even as she moved to pick up the burger and bite it. "No, but it's not ..." But he didn't know what to say. He felt stupid and useless. "It's cold."

"Yeah, but it would be awful to let it go to waste," she countered. "And I'm honestly too hungry to wait. It doesn't matter what it tastes like."

He had never heard a more horrifying statement in his life.

That horror must have reflected on his face because Helena looked up at him, then her own eyes went wide as she covered her mouth, realizing what she had said. "Oh, dear, I'm sorry. I didn't mean it like that. I just don't want you to worry about me."

Her apologizing for something as absurd as dismissing his sentimentalities at a time like this deflated his indignation.

"Helena, I'm sorry," he said, kneeling down before her and grasping her hands. "This is all my fault. I did this to you."

Gently, she cupped his cheek. "No, you didn't," she said softly. "I was more than willing to pay this price to save you. I gave ... whatever that was ... I paid the price for our souls ..." She shook her head again. "I don't really understand what happened. I keep feeling like I can *almost* remember it, but the part of my mind capable of understanding it ... isn't ... able to right now."

That did not set him at ease. He had always felt there was some sort of higher, or maybe lower was a better word, consciousness that held them in their suffering in hell. *Had she spoken to them directly?* he wondered.

She then turned once more to her meal and took a bite. After a few moments of chewing she slowed, furrowing her brows as she looked down at it.

"What's wrong?" he asked fearful that he knew the answer.

"Nothing. It's just … it occurs to me … what you said about simply understanding how to …" She held her hand out to the plate of food, her eyebrows pursing together as she concentrated on the plate. Then before their eyes, steam rose out from the food. A fresh smell of cooked deliciousness wafted from the plate, as if the food there had just come out of the skillet or pot. She did the same to his plate, and within seconds, more steam wafted up.

Helena's face burst into a genuine smile. "I did it! I did it!" She grabbed Rafferty's hands squeezing them with excitement. "I just performed a miracle!"

Chapter 7

FIX EVERYTHING!

"**I** can fix everything!" Helena cried, unable to contain her relief. Her face was flushed with excitement as she wriggled in her chair. "We don't need Vassago's help after all."

Rafferty's heart lurched in his chest. "Vassago?! You saw him?"

"Yes, but now that I'm an angel, and I can perform miracles, I can fix everything!"

Rafferty couldn't take that point in. "He *saw* you? Or you *spoke* to him?"

"Yes, I tried to tell the agents about it, but they didn't see him, and they didn't believe me. He wanted to make a deal with me to undo everything that happened, but I told him no." She nodded with conviction, and he didn't think he could love her more at that moment. "Then he said he would see what you thought. Did you ..."

"I spoke to him, too," Rafferty admitted, affirming that she hadn't been delusional.

Helena's eyes went even wider. "Do you think ... this is all his doing?"

"Getting us out of trouble with the Earthly authorities, yes. This ..." He gestured up and down at her. "I don't know."

"But why would he do that? Why would he help us like that? *Neither* of us made a deal with him, right?"

"Demons will do that occasionally. Expend a bit of free power to show what they offer when they are trying to tempt someone."

"But we're safe here?" Helena asked, looking about the room. "I can ... I can feel it, all around us. The protection circle. It feels wonderful."

Rafferty shifted, clearly uncomfortable at the observation. He didn't feel a thing. Instead, he reached for the thing that always grounded him. He stuck his pinkie finger into the whipped parsnips on his plate and scooped some into his mouth, chewing anxiously. Then he stopped, a groan slipping out of him, his eyes rolling back and going closed while he shuddered.

"Are you okay?" Helena asked, alarmed by the reaction.

He gestured at his mouth; his eyes still closed in savor. "The taste ... I ..."

She smiled, not needing him to finish. With everything that had happened, he had forgotten that he had gone through great changes as well. The restoration of his taste was the most important to him. His punishment was over.

Hers was just beginning.

At that thought, he froze and opened his eyes, "Do you taste anything?" he asked urgently.

"What? Yes, I ..." She regarded the burger, then took another bite. "Yeah, it tastes fine to me," she said around the mouthful.

He took another bite of the parsnips.

"I don't ... I don't taste anything ..." He contracted his eyebrows.

Helena wrinkled her nose. "But you looked like you were—"

"I mean power," he corrected. "When I was a demon, I couldn't taste the flavors of the food, but I *could* taste the power I used to create it or influence it."

"But now you can't taste the power, just the flavors?"

"I taste ..." He sighed again, unable to resist scooping up some more food into his mouth. "Everything," he growled lustily, going for a third scoop. On his fourth scoop, she leaned in and licked it instead, trapping his finger in her mouth.

His eyes went wide as she suctioned her lips to him, slowly sliding off his digit in a playfully suggestive way. Now that she was back in a human form, he felt nothing but the usual reactions this body had to such an act, and since it was naked for her to see, see she did. His reaction made her giggle so hard she almost choked.

But as she moved the food around in her mouth, her expression became sober.

"What is it?" Rafferty asked, catching the shift.

"I think I taste it. The demonic ... or *celestial* energies, I guess. There is an after-tang. It is almost a sickly sweet sort of taste, and this is usually a decidedly savory food. It's sort of what I would imagine ... turquoise would taste like, if that makes any sense?"

He nodded slowly, then glanced at the table, spying a dessert tray, something her power hadn't touched. Prying off the plastic lid, he pinched off a bite of the chocolate cake within and held it out. "Taste this," he said urgently.

She licked that off his fingers too, albeit with less sensuality than she had with the parsnips.

"How is it?" he asked, the worry rife in his voice.

She took her time, letting her taste buds inform her. "It ... is very rich, and chocolatey. Yeah, I don't think I taste any celestial energies."

Growing thoughtful, Helena brushed her fingers down the side of his cheek. "I don't know much, but I do know ... at least I'm pretty sure ... This angel thing isn't happening to me because of some divine punishment ... and I don't know why, but I'm *sure* ... I *am* sure that it isn't anything Vassago did either."

He pressed her hand against his cheek. He really wanted to believe that. "We don't know that for sure."

She gave that a thought. "Okay, let's test it out. Ask me for something."

He blinked and recoiled. "What?"

"Ask me for a miracle. I have celestial power now. Ask me to do something for you. Something that would require otherworldly abilities."

He stood up, backing away from her and her offer, shaking his head. "No. No, we shouldn't do that."

"Hey, it's okay," she tried to assure him, lifting her hands to take his, but he pulled away even sharper.

"No, it's not!" he shouted, losing control. "This is not how the rules work. You cannot get something for nothing, there is *always* a cost. Always. Throughout the entire universe, this one rule is absolutely true."

"But this is divine—"

"It's coming from you!" he shouted, only for someone to bang on the wall. He swallowed down a breath and forced himself to soften his voice. "The energy it takes to make something like this happen, it can only be coming from you, your essence. You can't just spend it like it's renewable."

"But you said I am an angel," she said, her voice coming out small.

Another invisible stomach punch. "I don't *know* ... okay? I don't know ..." He could feel his lie exposing him. "So many things in history that have been attributed to angels were just demons whose gifts worked out well for everyone. There have to be some wins or humans would not even try us."

Helena's expression was unsure. She didn't understand, but before long, she would realize she needed to make a deal to have enough energy to stay. Just like with Vassago, she wouldn't be able to remain in creation, at least not without an anchor point and a supply of energy to resist creation trying to expel her.

Since she was not privy to any of these thoughts, she tried to reach out to him again, but he recoiled even more, taking several steps back to put space between them. He surprised himself with his reaction.

Rafferty had never felt rawer and more vulnerable in his life. A cold chill rolled up his spine, sending shivers and forcing him to hug his arms against himself. He had never felt more naked.

I won. So why doesn't it feel like it anymore, he thought.

"Rafferty," she whispered, his name a plea.

"I'm sorry, but … I can't … I just … I need …" He shook his head as he turned around, plucking up his discarded shirt from the ground to dress himself with. Somehow that small action felt just as much a rejection of her as everything else had. But he didn't know what else to do. He needed space from her, time to think.

Helena turned away, too, but went to the unopened suitcases. She tore through the first one, which luckily was the one she wanted, and yanked on a set of pajamas. By the time she was dressed, so was Rafferty, who headed to the door to their suite.

"Agent Sophia said to stay here," she said, alarmed as he reached for the door.

"I just can't," he repeated, but he hesitated, unable or unwilling to look at her. "I'm sorry."

And then he was out the door.

Rafferty never felt so shattered in his entire existence. Not like this.

"I'm a coward. I'm a coward. I'm a fucking coward," Rafferty repeated to the echoing sound of his feet hitting the concrete steps as he went down the stairwell. He knew he could have taken the elevator, but the point wasn't to get away. The point was to move and try to think, not to feel so much only inside. Fifteen floors gave him a lot to think about.

He hurt her.

He *knew* he hurt her by rejecting her like that. Whatever had happened to her, it wasn't her fault. There was nothing she had done that was evil, but he also couldn't stay. The squirming terror inside at what she had become drove him.

Too soon, he reached the bottom, out of breath. Pushing his way through the door jarred him as he emerged into the opulent hotel lobby, an extreme contrast to the plain, beige walls and echoing emptiness of the stairwell.

A couple standing near the door to the stairs shot him startled, offended glances at his sudden appearance. Breathing noisily, he ignored them and scanned across the carpeted space with its warm lighting and elegant clusters of furniture to find a semicircle dais that proclaimed itself a bar.

The carpet gave way to a marble floor then back to carpet as Rafferty cut across the space before the check-in counters. The staff there gave him a passing glance, but only enough to see if he was approaching them to ask for anything.

There was nothing that he needed they could offer him at that moment.

A part of him was aware he still felt elated at his new existence. He moved about the world with freedom; everything he saw was for the first time with his new eyes. Though he had been taken to bars and had appeared in restaurants—they were the most common places desperate chefs would summon him—this was different.

He was free.

Dropping into one of the high chairs at the bar, his elbows hit the top, and he grasped his head as if that would help him keep it from exploding at the war raging inside him. His joy at being human again and his horror at Helena becoming … something else. He had no idea what he was about to do, but he had arrived at his destination. It was all he could focus on in that moment.

"What can I get you?" a voice asked, mildly cautious.

With a sharp lift, Rafferty dropped his hands onto the bar, aware of the scene he was making.

"Huh, I ... I don't know."

"Okay, no problem," the bartender said, smiling a thin smile as he slid over a menu. Rafferty didn't look at the menu, though, but instead studied the worker's clothing. It was a simple ensemble of black slacks with a white shirt held back with a black vest and a bowtie. What undid the formal appearance, however, was that the man had rolled his sleeves up to the elbows, and one of them looked on the brink of coming undone.

The chef in Rafferty reacted. "How are you getting away with that?" he asked, gesturing to the sleeves.

Predictably, the bartender looked down, raising an eyebrow. "Get away with what?"

"Your sleeves," Rafferty said, his words tensing up.

"Oh, you know. They don't really care too much as long as the shirt is clean, and I don't cause any trouble. I'm really vigorous when I shuffle up the ice, and I hate getting my sleeves wet," the bartender said, just as someone waved at him down the bar. "I'll be right back. Take your time."

Rafferty let it go.

"You truly are a chef, aren't you?" a familiar accented voice asked.

Chapter 8

MORE THAN ANYTHING

Rafferty's eyebrows popped up, surprised to see one of the waiters from the Winter Rose Ball standing next to him, holding a short glass half filled with an amber drink. He grinned at him, then gestured at the chair beside him.

"You mind if I join you?" he asked.

"Uh, no, not at all," Rafferty said automatically, feeling strangely more at ease as the other man took his seat and set his drink on the bar.

"I can tell you are trying to remember where you've seen me before," his new companion said, flashing his white teeth as he adjusted his suit jacket over the casual button-up shirt he had on.

"No, I know who you are. You were the head waiter at the event the other night. The Winter Rose Ball."

The former waiter held out his hand. "Éliott," he said, in that rich, familiar rhythm of speech that Rafferty had once shared in his original life.

"Uh, Rafferty," the former demon responded, taking the hand and shaking it. It felt strange to introduce himself. The only real people he had ever interacted with were those who summoned him, and they already knew who he was when they did.

"<I imagine you are here for the same reason as I am,>" Éliott said, speaking in easy French.

"<And what reason is that?>" Rafferty answered, then flinched as he realized that not only had the language easily rolled out of him, but it had been fluent like Agent Archon had said. As a demon, he had adopted whatever manner of speech his masters had, some quirk of the summoning. He hadn't spoken French in ages before talking to Agent Archon.

No, wait, that is not true, he thought, realizing. *I spoke at the restaurant Helena took me to on our first ... date.* He blinked again, also realizing *I spoke to this man. So he already knows I speak French.*

"<You are here because the agency brought you here,>" Éliott replied, then gestured to the building at large. "<We are all here. All the wait staff. Anyone connected to what happened. The tragedy.>" He shook his head soberly.

"Yes, it was," Rafferty said, returning to English, that voice still speaking with Helena's accent instead.

"Did you know her?" Éliott asked, also making the adjustment, though he kept his lyrical voice notes.

"Ms. Scarlet? Not really. Only through my ... girlfriend." He wondered if he should be saying these things, but it was true after all. Harmless information. Though he wondered, *Is any information truly harmless?* Demons would often probe marks for every drop they could use to manipulate.

Somehow that thought relaxed him more. He was a demon. He could handle a conversation with a waiter, even if that's not what he proved to be.

"Ah yes, you are the beau of the pretty lady. The one actually in charge?" Éliott said, setting down his glass to pull the menu Rafferty hadn't even glanced at toward himself.

"Helena," Rafferty said, wondering if they were together after how he had left upstairs. He wouldn't blame her if she cast him aside.

"Is she alright?" Éliott asked, sounding genuinely concerned.

"I …" Rafferty had thought to lie for a moment, but there simply was no point. "No. She's not alright."

"Hmm, I suppose that is to be expected," Éliott intoned, then waved his hand at the bartender, who was already on his way to returning.

"Do you know what you would like?" the bartender asked.

"Another bourbon for me and one for him. We both need it tonight. Then your charcuterie board, s'il vous plaît," Éliott ordered. "Please charge it to the room." He glanced at Rafferty, smirking cheekily. "I love saying that."

Rafferty nodded but couldn't offer anything else, not even a thank you for ordering for him.

Éliott didn't seem to take offense. He clapped an overly friendly hand on Rafferty's shoulder. "Do not worry," he said. "This is not your fault."

"You don't know that," Rafferty growled, the truth coming out harsher than he had intended. Yet, he had already thrown himself on the mercy of those in power for these crimes and had been more or less ignored. He had been deemed crazy and pitiable, and then dismissed.

"Oh, I understand how you feel. The woman you love was in danger, and you did not know what you could do to help her. I, too, feel the same. My cousin, he is in a lot of trouble, mostly of his own making. He cannot find his way out when he is like this. There is nothing I can do to help him except sit by his side and wait for him to find his own way."

"Your ... cousin?" Rafferty repeated, trying to parse what Éliott had just said.

"Yes, the chef who was supposed to work the Winter Rose Ball before you came in like a superhero and saved the day." Éliott shook his head and sighed. "This is not the first time he has ruined an opportunity for himself and run away, leaving me to pick up the pieces. I just did not expect it would lead to demons."

Rafferty's bourbon appeared on the bar before them, and he flinched, wary of what the bartender had just overheard. The bartender passed a glance between the two of them, but he said nothing, only turning away to continue with his own business.

"You shouldn't talk about such dangerous topics here," Rafferty chided.

Éliott nodded, noting the faux pas with his eyes as the bartender walked away. "You are right. I apologize. I am just as shaken up as all of us about the whole situation. The need to talk is strong."

The charcuterie board appeared, and Éliott didn't hesitate to tuck into it.

Rafferty only watched him eat.

"Please, join me," Éliott invited, as he spread some jam over a piece of cheese on a cracker. "This has something fiery with the sweet."

Rafferty wanted to say no, but his fingers moved before he realized it, taking the offered morsel of food and popping it into his mouth. Sweet apricots hit his tongue as fiery steeds trampled right behind it. Taking in a sharp breath through his nose, Rafferty chewed, mixing the creamy cheese and dry, crunchy cracker with the battling storm of the jam's tastes.

"Exciting, no?" Éliott asked, elbowing Rafferty lightly in the side as he assembled another bite.

While Rafferty could admit that the tastes were exciting, and so potent on his taste-starved tongue, there was something missing.

Helena wasn't here to share it with him.

In fact, this was just like their first meal together, when she had offered him the gift of existence, asking for nothing else in return.

Tears filled up Rafferty's eyes. Folding over, he hid his face in his hands, surprised by how intense this felt, too.

"How about this one, I think it is blueberry, but it might be something—" Éliott's voice died off, clearly having noticed Rafferty's show of emotion.

Rafferty didn't know what to expect, but it wasn't the hand that rubbed at the center of his back. "Yeah, yeah," Éliott's voice soothed along with it. "I know, man. I know."

Sniffing hard, Rafferty lowered his shield, regarding the charcuterie board and trying to refocus on the moment.

"What would you like to eat instead?" Éliott asked. "If you could pick anything in the world, right this minute. What would it be?"

He sniffed again, letting his mind wander. "Gruau," Rafferty said truthfully, which made him chuckle despite his thick throat and wet eyes.

"Oh?" Éliott asked, sounding intrigued.

"<It sounds like the most comforting thing right now,>" Rafferty replied, letting his old tongue slip from him.

"<A taste of home?>"

"Oui." Then Rafferty shook his head, switching back to English. "But they would not be able to make it right here, even if they would do such an off-menu thing."

Éliott nodded, then stood up, shooting back what remained of his bourbon like it was water. Then he slapped Rafferty's shoulder twice. "Come with me. Bring your drink," he added, swiping up the charcuterie board himself.

Rafferty didn't question it. Honestly, he hadn't questioned anything that had happened during this conversation. His defenses were down, and while a whisper of warning slipped through him that he was being too trusting, too open with this stranger, he needed it at that moment like the desert needed rain.

That is how the devils get you, isn't it? he thought as he followed Éliott through the small clusters of tables toward where the other waiters of the bar/restaurant were entering and exiting through a set of swinging doors.

They didn't stop them as they approached. In fact, one of the busboys paused to hold the door open for Éliott as he passed through, slapping hands, then snapping as they passed in some sort of salute to each other.

Walking into that kitchen felt like walking into a long-lost home.

The bevy of smells, the clanks and clatters, the rushing sounds of water and frying oils. A sense of urgency danced in the air. It was the one room that Rafferty had always felt safe no matter what century it was—except for Helena's bedroom, lying in her arms. There had been a different sort of safety there.

Rafferty stopped a few steps from the door and breathed it all in deep into his lungs. While he soaked in the atmosphere, Éliott continued forward, stopping next to a woman wearing a white jacket and apron with three buttons next to her shoulder. Her hair was tied back in a short ponytail under a white pillbox toque. She didn't look happy to see the intruders, but she leaned in to listen to Éliott speaking in her ear. As soon as he was done, he planted a kiss on her cheek, and she finally, reluctantly, grinned at him, then gestured toward a corner while speaking softly. He then snapped a second surprise kiss on her other cheek before he turned to gesture for Rafferty to follow him to the counter.

"She said as long as you stay out of the kitchen's way and clean up your mess, you may cook whatever they have in the kitchen," Éliott informed him, tapping at the empty counter, then pulling up a stool to sit at its corner with his charcuterie board.

Stunned, Rafferty asked, "Truly?"

Éliott met his gaze, already chewing another morsel, and nodded. "Oui." Then he gestured to the room. "I know the sous, and she owes me a favor for when I bailed her out of a different tight jam."

"And you don't mind using your favor for me?" Rafferty questioned.

Éliott spread his hands, including the one holding the board, with enthusiasm. "What else are favors for if not to help a friend?"

A friend.

Again, that feeling of ease washed over Rafferty, urging him into motion. It inspired a grin to crack across his face as he eagerly grabbed up one of the aprons hanging from the end of the counter.

"Do you want me to help?" Éliott asked, slipping into *his* familiar support role as easily as he slipped the apron over his head.

"You're sure?" Rafferty asked, obeying his natural wariness.

"Of course, more than anything. I want to taste your cooking."

Rafferty nodded, accepting that answer. It was one he understood. When he finished tying his apron strings, he pulled a large bowl toward himself. Oh, to cook again, and this time, he would taste the food he made with his own hands. "I need steel-cut oats, butter, salt, sugar, nutmeg, and brandy."

"Ahh, you are going to do it the way my grandmother would," Éliott noted with a grin.

"Yes, the correct way," Rafferty said as he moved to a small sink to wash his hands.

Éliott grinned wider and set off to find the requested ingredients.

Chapter 9

DREAMS OF THE FUTURE

Rafferty could not stop laughing. It was a deep belly laugh shared with this fellow countryman many generations removed. They had been laughing for so long that Rafferty had forgotten what they had been laughing about. It just felt good. His hands had continued, however, adding the final touches to his meal, passing his new friend's bowl to him, steam wafting from the top.

"This tastes excellent," Éliott moaned as he took another bite. "I think it's been ages since I've had something like ... Words fail me. No, wait! The brandy flavor sings! It is warm and savory-sweet, and ..."

Rafferty agreed, but he couldn't provide better words for it. He laughed then went still as he tasted his food. A memory, something he had thought he had lost long ago stirred up in his mind, drawn out by the taste. His mother making this for him, showing him how it was done over a real fire in their hearth. He couldn't recall her name, but her smile was as beautiful as antique lace.

"What is that?" A woman's voice, which was not his mother's, interrupted his thoughts.

Another white-coated woman stood there, this time with a short bob under her white cap. From the looks of her, she had just murdered something made of chocolate, as she was spackled in blips and bits of the substance.

"Oh, hello, Eleanor," Éliott said. She shot him an annoyed look, then directed her gaze back to inside Rafferty's pot.

"What is this?" she asked, lifting up the ladle to pour some of the substance back in, examining its texture.

"Gruau," Éliott said, unperturbed and, in fact, seeming rather delighted by her irritation.

"Gruel," Rafferty amended, giving the English word for it.

"Gruel?" she exclaimed, wrinkling her nose at it. "Like what Oliver Twist ate?"

Rafferty looked inquisitively. "I'm sorry. I do not know who that is."

Eleanor narrowed her eyes as if trying to decide if Rafferty was making fun of her or being an idiot.

"Oliver Twist, you know. Dickens. Great novel, several okay movies, and one musical," Éliott offered, nudging him with his elbow like it was a private joke.

"Sorry, I ... I don't really read much. Except cookbooks," he said, and it was true. His ability to read English or read at all came along with the ability to speak it and then all he had ever been able to find when summoned had been cookbooks.

"He's a chef," Éliott piped in, the words escaping him before another mouthful cut them off.

"Oh, I see. A purist then." Eleanor practically sneered, crossing her arms.

Rafferty had no idea what this woman's problem could be, though he wasn't really that bothered by it. Just wary. It wasn't uncommon for humans to have blatant hostility toward him, especially if he had invaded their kitchens.

She didn't let up, though, as she planted her fists onto her hips. "So, you think, just because you're a 'real purist' chef, you can just waltz into any kitchen you want and just start cooking whatever you want."

"I'm sorry," Rafferty said evenly, the safest answer he had ever been able to give any of his masters. The only one they really wanted to hear, and only sometimes it worked.

This time it did, and she backed off, her guarded eyes trying to figure him out. Then she slipped a spoon out of her pocket, presumably a clean one, and dipped it into the pot. Blowing on it once, she stuck her sample of his gruau into her mouth. Rolling it around. He could tell she was truly tasting it, and he waited with bated breath for her thoughts. Then her eyes closed as her mouth stilled, no longer actively tasting it. A shiver ran through her body, and she swallowed, bringing her fingers up to her lips as if she could touch the taste.

Then her eyes opened, and the guard came back up.

"*That's* gruel?"

"It gets a bad reputation," Rafferty said, grabbing up his bourbon to down a swallow, reigniting the brandy flavor lingering in his mouth.

"Is this your thing?" she asked, nodding toward it, her arms crossed still, but less actively aggressive. "You specialize in gross-sounding foods and make them taste delicious?"

"I don't specialize in anything. I just make what I'm told," he said, taking another bite, affecting like he wasn't both pleased by her reaction to his food and delighted with it himself. Maybe it hadn't just been the demon magic he had put in it all these centuries to make it turn out.

"Hell, I hear that," Eleanor said, recrossing her arms the other direction.

"Eleanor is the pâtissier at this hotel," Éliott said, then gestured over at her station, where a gorgeous statue of a unicorn with a flowing rainbow mane and tail sat on a long, silver slab.

"What is that?" Rafferty asked, getting up from his little corner to go look at it. It was only as he got closer that he realized the unicorn was in fact ... "A cake?" he asked.

"Yeah. There's some rich hedge fund manager's daughter's birthday party. The inside is entirely chocolate cake, though I was tempted to make it red velvet." She chuckled at her joke, but when Rafferty didn't join her, she let it go. "I have a bit of a dark humor."

"It's beautiful," Rafferty said instead, leaning in to examine it. "But how?"

"It's all edible. I used either cake or chocolate to build it up. The skin is fondant. Just takes time. I make cakes like these all the time. And chocolate sculptures. I make videos of them and post them online. You should check them out." Eleanor leaned against her counter, her arms still crossed, but her face seemed more relaxed now.

"She needs to run her own studio," Éliott said, sticking his finger in one of her frosting bowls to steal a bit. It

earned him a slap from her, but he only grinned undeterred as he stuck it into his mouth.

"A studio? Not a shop?" Rafferty asked.

"It would be a studio and a shop," she conceded. "The idea being I would make my creations, make video content of them, then put the creations up for sale, that sort of thing. I've almost got it together. It would just go faster if I had an investor. I want to buy a space, but not many banks are so keen on my business plan." She looked Rafferty over again. "Have you ever heard of *Baking Underground*?"

Rafferty could only blink at her.

"It's sort of like those cooking show competition things like on the Food Network channels, but this one is more homegrown and lower tech," Éliott explained.

"It was a fun thing a group of us did. Started out as just a way to learn tricks from each other, but then we started recording them and putting them on the internet. It's real rough, but now it's sort of taken on a life of its own. We have live audiences now and everything. And it's still a good networking opportunity."

"I think it could be a big thing," Éliott said.

Rafferty wrinkled his nose, trying to understand what they were telling him. "How does it work?"

Éliott spread his hands out before him, mischief in his smirk. "Twelve enter, only one survives!"

"No, Éliott ..." Eleanor shook her head in disgust then huffed a sigh as she brushed her hands off on her apron. "There are three rounds. You get about an hour each, everyone makes a dessert or a dish, though we've done other baking rounds, too, like casseroles and stuff. Everything is blind taste-tested and the winner goes onto the next round until there are three of us."

"Then it's an all-out battle," Éliott crowed, taking the narrative back.

Another huff from Eleanor. "In the third round, it's about making the most stunning piece possible. What makes the 'better dish' becomes subjective. Some people have won by visual surprise and artistry, others by extreme tastes. Or being innovative."

"It becomes very strategic, which is what keeps it interesting," Éliott added.

Rafferty nodded, understanding. "And the ideal encapsulates all."

"You've got it," Eleanor agreed. She took a small step closer, and there was a bit of a change in her energy. No longer hostile. Rafferty would almost guess … inviting? Like he had passed some kind of test. Or maybe cooking just turned her on.

"And where do you call home?" she asked, shifting so she perched on the edge of the preparation table they were eating at.

Another basic question that he had no answer for. Rafferty shifted on the kitchen stool he sat upon, wondering if he could say he lived with Helena. Did he live with Helena? Their future was so uncertain.

"You mean where he works?" Éliott asked, before glancing at Rafferty. "I only know I met you at … that job." Clearly, they weren't supposed to talk about the Winter Rose Ball—which suited Rafferty just fine.

Rafferty nodded his understanding. "I don't have a home. Not like that. I just do … one-off gigs, whenever someone needs me," he said.

Eleanor smirked. "What are you, a trust fund baby?"

"I … I have a girlfriend," he said.

"Oh, my dear Lord, you are kidding me," Eleanor decried, clearly disliking that answer. "So, you're a deadbeat?"

"No ..." Rafferty said, desperately trying to parse her meaning. "Deadbeat" must be a new idiom; he just hadn't heard Helena say it yet.

"He is from France, you see," Éliott again interjected. "He hasn't been here very long, yes?"

"You're French?" Eleanor asked, getting more and more skeptical of their story.

"Oui," Rafferty said. "I ... I don't have an accent because ..."

"Because he does not want to be judged by it like some of us are." Éliott raised a poignant eyebrow at Eleanor, who ignored him.

"<Oh, so you're a real French chef then?>" Eleanor asked, in American-accented French.

"<Why does everyone try to make me speak in my mother tongue?>" Rafferty asked, getting annoyed with the practice.

This time Eleanor blinked multiple times at Rafferty's perfect French. "You know you would have an easier time getting jobs if you didn't try to suppress your natural accent. People love that sort of thing."

Rafferty shrugged. "I'm sorry to disappoint." He turned away to go back to the small bit of counter by the stove he had used. He snagged the brandy bottle he used for the gruau. His glass received a healthy refill.

Damn, this brandy tastes good, he thought after an equally healthy swallow. Alcohol had no effect on him before, as ashy tasting as anything else he put in his mouth.

Eleanor's gaze followed him, the wheels clearly turning in her head, but he didn't care anymore. His head swam with the drinks he had already consumed. He wasn't tipsy drunk; he didn't think he had the emotions needed for such a thing. Even in his first life, he had been a sullen drunk, and that much hadn't changed now in his second life apparently.

"You know, people are really into antique recipes too. You could fill a real niche for someone. Also, I could refer you to a couple of places if you're looking for steady paying work," Eleanor suddenly offered, eyeing his gruau.

"In exchange for what?" he asked.

She frowned. "Nothing," she said.

That made him pause. "Why would you do that for me?" Rafferty immediately questioned.

"Because I'm not as much of a bitch as you think I am," Eleanor responded, finally giving him a grin. It changed her whole face, and for a brief moment, Rafferty's swimming senses got caught up in it. She didn't look away from his naked appraisal, then she reached into one of her apron pockets and pulled out a business card. It was a bit of cardstock that had seen better days, the corners roughed up and creased, but everything needed on it was legible.

"Feel free to call me. I remember how hard it was to get started, so if you are interested, I have enough favors I need to pay forward that I can at least make a few introductions."

Rafferty took the card, knowing he would never call it. "Thank you," he said politely.

She nodded and went back to her cake.

"What is it you *would* like to do?" Éliott asked, refilling his own glass with fresh inebriant as soon as Eleanor left them. "I mean, if you could do anything, nothing in your way."

Rafferty stared over his glass into the far middle distance, where the past and the future collided. "I always wanted my own place, like a shop or a café, where I could explore and push the boundaries of cooking. To follow my curiosity and do whatever catches my attention. There are so many recipes I have never gotten to try, so many ..." It was definitely the drink talking, pulling those words out of his heart like shards of glass long lodged inside. He didn't even entirely know what he meant by them. It was certainly nebulous as far as dreams go.

The sick part of his heart reminded him that once he had wanted to be the head chef for the king, and he had done anything, including selling his own soul, to try to achieve such a thing.

"You don't want to have your own full-blown restaurant or something?" Éliott asked, clearly a bit flummoxed by his answer.

He shook his head. "No. I've already been there. Done that. Worked my way up the ranks, cutting every throat I could, making choices and compromises no one should ever make." He downed the rest of the brandy. "I never want to do that again. But I still love the work."

"Wow. You are like a tragic noble in a romance story. A fallen man seeking redemption," Éliott whispered sincerely, propping his cheek on his fist.

"There's nothing noble about me, I assure you," Rafferty said, not stopping Éliott as he refilled his glass yet again. Why not? "I've just been given a second chance that I don't deserve, and I have no freaking idea what to do with it."

Chapter 10

THEN I THREW UP

The world rolled and swirled around Rafferty. And he hated it.

"What the hell is wrong with me?" he asked.

"You drank like a fish, and I get the distinct impression that you've been on land a long while," Éliott said, his voice coming from Rafferty's left. Apparently, his arm was around the other man's shoulders, and without his help, he was pretty sure the ground would be rolling more.

"This is all your fault," Rafferty declared as they walked off the elevator. Or at least he thought he declared it. It was startling to realize they hadn't already been in motion, so who knows how the words actually sounded.

"Yes, it was me that made your Adam's apple bob up and down," Éliott said dryly, or at least his version of dryly. He always sounded like he was about to burst out laughing.

Which made Rafferty giggle.

Just then there was a tentative knock at a door. Éliott's hand lowered, so he must have done it.

"Hang on a second, someone is here," came Helena's voice.

"Don't open the door!" another, smaller voice ordered.

"I'm not, I'm just looking out the peephole," she responded softly.

Éliott straightened, lifting Rafferty so his wobbling head looked more or less straight at the peephole. "Oh, dammit, it's Rafferty."

"Good to know how soundproof these doors are not," Éliott noted. "That cuts down on my amorous plans considerably."

The sounds of the locks undoing cut off any follow-up questions, which spilled out of Rafferty's head as fast as he could even form them.

He really wanted to throw up.

The flap at the bottom of the door scraped across the carpet as Helena opened it. He had hoped she would be asleep when he got back. How late was it? Or maybe how early?

"Good evening," Éliott said cheerfully, as if hauling back another man whose arm was draped over his shoulder was the most normal thing in the world. "I believe this belongs to you."

Helena had a mobile phone in one hand on speaker, though when she got it back, he had no idea, but she hit a button and pressed it to her ear. "Charlie, I have to call you back. Rafferty just came back," Helena said as she stepped back, pulling the door with her.

"Uh, I am sorry, but I cannot go any further," Éliott said, hesitating at the threshold.

"Oh, it's okay. Please come in," Helena said, gesturing welcome, but Éliott shook his head.

"I had about as much as he did, and I am afraid I will disgrace myself if I stay here any longer. I am just down the hall, and so I will pass him to you and then take my leave to visit my own porcelain god." Éliott laughed and wavered on his feet.

Had Éliott only gotten them this far on sheer will alone?

Before Rafferty could remember enough words to even form the question, he found himself more or less tossed into Helena's arms.

Despite having said good-bye already, she was still speaking to her friend on the phone, the gadget pinned to her ear with her shoulder, while she also tried to juggle his disorderly limbs. "No, Charlie. Don't come," Helena insisted as Éliott slapped Rafferty's back, then saluted sloppily and jetted down the hallway, pulling his card key from his pocket.

Not wanting to be a burden to Helena, Rafferty pushed himself away, stumbling his way toward the bed.

Letting him go, Helena went to shut the door, still talking to Charlie, a friend who was having trouble with his husband. That was all Rafferty remembered about him. The husband had harassed Helena a few times, though, and that Rafferty *did* care about, and he had a brief thought of leaving right that moment to go take care of that problem. If only he could remember where the door was.

Or how to stand up.

He did attempt to turn around to go, but Helena still had her hands on him and his flailing nearly knocked her over.

Throughout all of the jostling, Helena's voice kept speaking to her friend. "Not until I know what's going to happen next. Ideally, not until I'm back in my house. No, you don't have to stay with us. We're safe. At this point, you'd have to stay here at the hotel with me anyway, and I'm not paying for this room, so ..."

She paused in her speaking while Rafferty flopped face forward and just lay there, grateful for something steady to focus on. The sheets smelled like detergent, which he found oddly comforting. But only for a few seconds, because he found that position difficult to breathe in, so he turned his head to look at Helena.

Still on the phone. "Get some sleep. I'll keep you updated. I promise," Helena swore, glancing at the clock by the bed. Rafferty followed her gaze, which turned out to be more difficult than it should have been. He also wasn't entirely sure, but he thought it said it was 2:00 a.m.

A beep signaled that Helena had finished her call. She dropped the phone onto the table and moved to help Rafferty.

"Raffie?" Helena asked softly, brushing back his dark hair from his face so she could see him. "Honey, do you need to throw up?"

"No," Rafferty said with a stubborn whine.

"Okay, then can you slip off your shoes?" she asked, kneeling to help with that. He toed them off himself, but she cleared them to the side. "Are you sure you don't need to throw up?"

He didn't deny it this time. Instead, his shoulders jumped as he gagged at the idea.

"Yup, you're going to erupt," Helena said, seizing him under one shoulder, leveraging him up bodily to stumble-walk him into the bathroom quickly before it was too late.

Helena tried to help with stabilizing, but he bowled her out of the way once he got going. She had to let go before she got sideswiped off at the bathroom threshold. A second later, Rafferty's entire back seized, and the contents of his stomach went into the toilet.

Mostly.

It felt so good.

Or rather, it felt like such a relief.

He did it a second time, and that hurt, his whole stomach aching as it used too much muscle to accomplish the job.

The next oasis of relief came when he rested his cheek against the cool surface of the toilet seat.

"Is that it?" Helena rubbed gentle circles against his back.

Why isn't she disgusted with me? he thought.

"Are you done?" she asked.

Rafferty didn't reply, just stuck out his fist and gave a sloppy thumbs up.

"No more coming up?" she continued, needing reassurance even as she hit the handle and flushed his disgrace away.

Rafferty still wavered in his squat but shook his head back and forth. Helena brought him a cup of something.

"No! No more bourbon," Rafferty croaked, lifting his head toward the wet sound, his stupid brain not understanding liquid noise and assuming it was more firewater.

"Bourbon?" Helena asked, truly confused. "You were drinking bourbon?"

Rafferty shook his head. "No, not bourbon ... Or yes, bourbon. We drank bourbon, but also brandy. It was for the gruau ... eh, gruel I think you would say?" he said, lingering too hard on the *l* sound to try to make the word come out in English.

"Gruel?" Helena repeated, wrinkling her nose. "Where did you find a place that serves gruel?"

"We made it. I have a friend in this hotel's kitchen," he explained, as he looked into the cup and realized she had brought him water. He attempted to fumble at the cup of water, only for her to bat his hand away and hold it to his lips herself. He felt like how a wilted house plant looked.

"Yeah, but gruel?" Helena pressed.

Rafferty shrugged. "Oatmeal. It's like really fancy oatmeal." He glared up at her, taking her aback. "What you think? People ate shit food before the modern times ... all through the ... the ... history ... times ... whatever ..." He pushed himself up, actually steadier on his feet now. At least, steady enough to use the door and wall to guide himself back out of the bathroom.

"I am sorry. I should not be speaking to you like that," he said, the words he usually kept inside his head coming out his mouth with the ease of chickens flying free from a coop.

"It's alright," Helena lied, wrapping her arms around herself.

Has she always lied to me?

Rafferty managed to sink onto the bed, his thoughts discombobulated, and jumped to a similar thread to what they were just talking about. "Brandy with the nutmeg adds a warmth ... Pairs well with the nutmeg. Makes it more together than apart. I should make it for you when we go home," he muttered. "Add blueberries ... golden raisins ..."

"Okay, my love, let us get you to bed," his savior insisted, tugging at his shirt. From the smell, he guessed he had gotten some puke on that, too.

Once the shirt left him, Rafferty flopped and curled, tucking the pillow hard under his head. Sliding up, Helena sat down beside him in the space left by the crook of his body. Gently, she brushed his hair back from his face, but he didn't so much as twitch. It felt so good.

"I'm sorry I dragged you to hell," he murmured. Yet, hell didn't seem so bad right now. And how could this be hell if she was here? The only ones who touched you in hell gave pain, but her touch soothed and eased. He uncurled, exposing his neck then his belly to her. She could consume him whole if she wished; he would cease to exist happily for her. Instead, she lay down beside him and tucked her head into the crook of his shoulder, her fingers resting lightly on his chest, making small circles in the chest hair there. Her hips tucked up against the side of his own, her crooked leg settling a delightful weight across his thighs.

"Thank you for coming back," she said.

He smiled and nodded. *Of course, I came back. I'm sorry I ran,* he thought but didn't say. Talking had suddenly become hard.

Instead, he moaned and covered his face with his hands. He could already tell his head would be pounding soon. It was pre-pounding now.

"Do you want me to make it better?" Helena whispered, her fingers finding trails through his hair, sending soothing shivers through his sick head.

He could barely feel her shifting next to him until her wings spread out over him like a blanket. In his blurry vision, he saw the strange creature with its circle of horns lean over him with eerie gold eyes.

What color were Helena's real eyes?

Stretching her gold-tipped fingers toward his temple, he could feel power gathering at those fingertips. She would heal him from the damage he had done to himself. A shiver ran through him.

She was about to perform another miracle.

"This is going to make you feel a lot better, Raffie."

Then his hand seized her wrist.

Helena jumped at his sudden move.

"No, don't," he said, but it was too late. The power gathered in her fingers snapped like static into him. Light glowed down his arm, leaving it with a pearlescent sheen so much like Helena's own. Then it dimmed as it disappeared under his clothes, glowing brightly through the weave of his shirt. Then she leaned forward and kissed his forehead gently. The energy popped like a soap bubble, and Rafferty's forehead burned warm, not painful, but intense.

"There. You'll be alright," she whispered, then gently touched his lips with hers.

He whimpered. He owed her now. "What do you want from me?" he asked, fighting to stay awake. "In return?"

"Nothing. I just want you to be happy," she promised, but her eyes ... they glowed hungry gold in the dark of the room. It was the last thing he saw before he slipped into oblivion.

Chapter II

THE NEXT MORNING SUCKED

Rafferty didn't feel as bad as he thought he should have when he woke up. Instead of a pounding headache, he just felt dry. Like he really needed to soak up a whole bunch of water in a shower or tub. Opening his eyes, he found Helena lying beside him, curled up under the blanket, which he had clearly passed out on top of.

Light streamed through the curtains, cutting a slice of it over her cheek, giving her red-gold hair an outline of fire. He couldn't drink the view in enough. She was so precious and sweet, sleeping like that, he could convince himself that nothing had changed about her. Even as he studied her, he couldn't resist lifting a finger to caress down her cheek, only to hesitate an inch above her skin.

His forgotten shame filled him again, the alcohol having done nothing to wipe it truly away. He had abandoned her when she had been at her most vulnerable. And yet, she had just forgiven him.

Disgusted with himself, he withdrew his hand and slowly sat up so as not to disturb her.

After everything she had done for him, all the times she had shown him mercy and compassion, and all he could think about was his revulsion at the idea of touching her. The uncanny feeling she had given off whispered underneath his skin, and he rubbed at his fingers to try to dispel it. *How can I do this to her?*

This beautiful creature had become a demon for him, traded her life for his, and he couldn't even bear to touch her. He had called her an angel, but he knew what he had seen, what he had felt. She had become what he had been, something that needed to go back into hell. His whole being told him the truth in the presence of her unnaturalness. And last night, she had used power on him to wipe away his hangover. *It is only a matter of time before she will need to take energy back in. Who might she harm when that happens?*

Not that he really cared about those theoretical victims. He had never cared before what other demons did or to whom, but to think of Helena that way ...

Hating himself for thinking such thoughts, he slipped from the bed and tiptoed into the bathroom, shutting the door as silently as possible.

The hotel had provided an automatic sensor for the lights and the one over the shower stall clicked on in response. With a sigh of relief, he turned the handle within the stall, immensely enjoying the patter of the water as it fell against the floor. He had seen showers before, he had even eyed the one in Helena's house, but had never dared to ask her if he could ... take one.

Now, it felt almost sacred as he undressed, removing the jeans he wore and feeling his own hands slide down his very real skin. He felt pleasure at touching himself, where he had always had the equal and opposite sensation before. The same abhorrence at touching himself as he had at the thought of touching Helena now.

"I will master this," he ordered himself. He couldn't abandon her; he owed her too much. Even the thought that he *could* leave her, that maybe he wanted to, after everything she did for him, horrified him.

Jerking his own hands away from himself, he opened the glass door of the shower and entered it. Immediately, he leapt back out with a small cry as his still-warm skin was hit by shards of icy wet. Guessing he hadn't cranked the handle far enough, he reached around the stream to yank it all the way the other direction. Within moments, the water shifted from glacial to pleasantly warm. Sighing, Rafferty stepped into that, letting the gobs and gobs of water flow over his whole being, washing away his thoughts with it.

Maybe it was the absence of active thoughts that allowed something else to take their place. A memory. Standing in a kitchen before the cooking fire with a large bowl filled with heated water and a rough bar of soap, washing himself with a cloth. Everyone he knew did it this way. Only the wealthy nobles would get to surround themselves with water, bathing in tubs that they could sit in, and that was only once or twice a week at most unless they were the king or queen. Ordering up bathwater was time-consuming. If he wanted to bathe more than that, he would have had to go to a stream, and those were often a brisk experience, only pleasant on the hottest of days. He had wondered then what it would feel like to simply let himself soak in so much warm water.

Rafferty didn't get much of a chance to dwell on the memory as, almost too late, he realized his artificial waterfall had turned into a lava-fall.

Another sharp cry escaped him as the shower scalded him out of it.

"Dammit!" he cursed.

"Rafferty? Are you okay?" Helena's voice came from the other side of the bathroom door.

He panicked. "Yeah, I ..." He reached for the handle and tried to turn it back just as Helena opened the door. "No! Don't come in!"

Predictably, he slipped. Falling out of the shower, he hissed as his knees banged on the ground, those sensations just as intense as all the others he had been experiencing. In fact, it felt like his knee had exploded, the nerve there shooting electric pain up his leg, overwhelming every other thought and stealing his breath away.

"Oh crap! Are you alright?" she said as she entered the steamed-up room. All he could see from where he had landed on the ground were her ankles as she stepped past him to the shower itself, reaching in to turn it off.

Desperate for some shred of dignity despite everything, he swiped for a towel hanging on a rack bolted to the wall, but he only managed to drape it over himself. *Why did I do that?* he thought. She had seen him naked before. Not only that, but he never cared about *being* naked.

When he didn't really have a body.

"I'm an idiot!" he declared as he rolled on his back, not daring to straighten the throbbing knee.

"Are you hurt?" Helena asked, squatting down next to him.

"Only my pride," he muttered, then winced. "And my knee."

"Yeah, I can see that," Helena said gravely.

He stiffened. "Is it badly damaged?" he asked, unable to keep the fear from his voice.

Helena glanced down at him, then she averted her eyes away. Dread flooded through him.

"Does it feel like icy electricity shooting up your leg and snatching your breath away? But now it's fading into a dull throb?"

"Yeah," he asked, the anxiety thick in his voice.

"Yes, I think you have done the worst thing in the world," she continued gravely. "You banged your funny bone."

She said it so deadpan Rafferty didn't realize it was a joke until she broke out into an enormous grin and started giggling. "You're going to be fine, don't worry," she assured him, and leaned in to give him a kiss on the cheek. "You never banged your knee when you were alive the first time?"

"Not that I remember." For a split second, he almost flinched away but instead forced himself to hold still and receive her kiss.

"I am sorry about last night," he said instead, letting her help him sit up on the bathroom floor.

"How are you feeling?" she asked, brushing her fingers through his hair tenderly.

"Embarrassed. Stupid," he muttered.

"It's alright, we've both gone through some ... big changes the last couple of days." She stood up and then offered him a hand, but he didn't take it. "Did you at least have fun with Éliott?"

"Yes, yes, I did," he said truthfully, a grin threatening his lips at the fresh memory, whisps of the sound of the other man's laughter ringing through his head.

To have a friend again ...

"Does your knee still hurt?" she asked.

"No, it is better now," he confirmed. "I just need a moment." He gestured to the door, asking her to leave.

She gave him a sad smile that pained him to look at.

"I just need a minute," he said, and it sounded weak even to him.

But she left as he requested.

Then he lay back down on the cooler bathroom tile and sighed angrily.

"Ungrateful," he murmured. "You are ungrateful."

Finally, he had to screw up his courage to come out of the bathroom. Their eyes touched briefly, but then he looked away, moving toward his borrowed suitcase to pull out clothes himself. He laid them out on the bed, then turned his back to her. Without hesitation, he let the towel fall so that he could get dressed. From his periphery, he saw her only take in his nakedness a second before shyly looking away.

He thought she would say something, hoped she would.

Instead, she grabbed up her toiletries bag and went to the bathroom herself.

They continued in that tense silence, each plagued by their own thoughts, until she broke first. "Who is Eleanor?"

He jumped at the question. "Who?"

Helena didn't answer but went to the side table by the bed and picked up a dog-eared business card. Only then did he remember. "Oh, right. She is a pâtissier, a dessert chef, here at the hotel. I met her last night in the kitchen. She makes cakes."

"Oh, I see," Helena said, looking down at the card as if it could verify his words for her. "Why did she give you her card?"

"She said she could help me find work. I suppose I will need to find a job now." He stared at the card and this new reality it symbolized.

A fresh panged look crossed her face. "God, I don't even know if I *have* a job now," Helena said, handing him the card. "Is this what you would like to do?"

He didn't answer that, so she continued.

"Because I've been thinking, you know, while you were gone last night ..." She went and fetched her mobile phone. "I was doing searches last night, and I found some things. And I mean, I was searching everything, you know, just jumping from rabbit hole to rabbit hole, but I ended up on this realtor's site where it lists restaurants, cafés, and kitchens that are up for sale or rent in the city, and I thought we could go and look at some of them today. Not make any decisions or anything, but just go check them out. Get some ideas?"

She held out the screen to him, showing him exactly what she described, small thumbnail pictures of beauti-fully decorated cafés with location and catchy words in the titles. There were a few restaurants ranging from classy to working-class, each with a price tag that suited them. As he scrolled down, looking at what Helena called possibilities, he paused on one that was familiar.

"Isn't this that kitchen, that catering place we went to that had the awful food?" he asked, tapping the image to direct her attention, but the action opened up the entry even further.

Helena hovered over his shoulder, wrinkling her nose at the picture. "Yeah, I think so. That address looks familiar. That bastard went under, huh? Can't say I'm sorry. Couldn't have happened to a nicer guy," she said dryly, still clearly bitter from the experience.

"I don't know," Rafferty said, a grin sneaking onto his face. "It gave me the opportunity to be your knight in shining armor."

That reminder allowed his grin to infect her, and she even blushed a bit before slipping her arms around his neck.

"I love you," she whispered into his neck. "You know that right? I meant what I said at the Winter Rose Ball."

He didn't say it back. He couldn't. Instead, he made himself wrap his arms around her smaller body and pull her against him, shielding her with his whole being from the world, and himself. "I believe you." Somehow, that meant more to him than the other words at that moment. "I believe *in* you."

They squeezed each other harder, and while they did, everything felt right.

"I know everything is weird and complicated right now, but we will figure this out. Right?" Helena asked.

"Yeah," he agreed. Because he had to agree. He had to have faith.

Breaking the hug at last, he looked down at his ... girl-friend, delighted to call her such, even if just in his own mind. "Do you think the agents will allow us to just leave?" he asked.

"Well, we're not prisoners. I think. They encouraged us to stay put, but I don't think they can make us. And besides,

I'm less worried about Vassago now than I was before." She stepped back from their shared embrace, grinning mischievously. "I betcha I can take him now."

When he didn't smile back, she sobered a little, cupping his cheek with her hand.

"I need to tell you something," he breathed. "It's about Vassago."

Worry quirked her eyebrows. "What about him?"

He rubbed his fingers at the lines her worry made. "We don't have to fear him anymore. I wanted to tell you sooner, but ... I guess I'm telling you now. I made a deal with him."

Helena shifted away so she could look him full in the face, her eyes alarmingly wide. "What do you mean you made a deal with him?"

"He came to see me at the agent's office."

"Yes, you told me that. I saw him, too."

Rafferty continued. "Well, we made a deal. He won't harm us or anyone." He hoped his words would reassure her, but those lines between her eyebrows only deepened, her eyes reflecting more alarm.

He thought she would ask a million questions, demand answers, but she didn't. Instead, she wrapped her arms around him tighter, hugging him hard, and buried her face into his shoulder. "You are such a good man."

"It wasn't that kind of deal," he whispered into her hair, answering the question she didn't ask. "I promised him I would not reveal any information about him to the authorities, and he promised he would leave us alone. You, me, your friends, even Scarlet. It's demonbound; he's obligated to keep it as long as I don't speak of the deal with anyone but you."

She remained silent for a thinking moment.

"And if I tell anyone, then it voids your deal as well?"

He swallowed. "Yes. The language of the deal covers that, but I couldn't not tell you, so I made it a stipulation. I don't want to keep secrets like that from you."

She pulled away again. "So instead of demanding your mind, body, or soul, he bargained for your silence," she said, working it out on her own. "But what about anyone else he might hurt in the meantime?"

Of course, her mind would go toward that. After all, she was a good person.

"That sort of thing would have too high a cost. I protected what I could. We're all safe." He thought about it a moment longer, seeing the situation through her eyes. "I ... I didn't want to risk my soul or my life again. That may be terrib—"

She grabbed his head and pulled it down to kiss him firmly. "Thank you," she said when she broke it, gratitude flooding her eyes.

"For what?" he asked, startled by her gesture. She clearly didn't understand what a piece of shit he was to bind her to a promise like that without asking her.

"For saving my friends. Trusting me to keep your promise and protect you," she said, then she kissed him again, a soft, chaste kiss filled with blessed tenderness. This he didn't pull away from; ease washed through him. "Okay, so we're safe, but specifically which friends, besides Scarlet? What about Cindy? And Charlie?"

"Yes, and Chris."

Helena rolled her eyes, "Well, I don't know about protecting Chris right now ..."

"A person like Chris would be a perfect target for a demon like Vassago," he said. "Chris is important to Charlie and could be used to get to the rest of us indirectly."

Her brows furrowed as she understood that. "And to save anyone else would make the price too high. I understand."

Rafferty nodded. "If I'm honest, as a demon, he paid way too much for my silence, really." A grin spread across his face. "It's a really good deal."

She nodded, even though she clearly didn't like it. "And that's what Agent Archon was trying to tell us. It's not our job to stop him or catch him. We're just supposed to keep ourselves safe and just try to move on?"

"Yes. I suppose so," he agreed.

"I see." She nodded, thinking about it. "Then we are ... okay?"

"We're okay," he agreed. "I care for you," he said quickly, catching her other hand in both of his. "Deeply."

"I know, Rafferty. You went through Hell for me," she assured. "I suppose you could look at it like ... when you were my demon, I was your whole world. Now you can have the actual whole world. And ... if your feelings for me change, I'll understand."

"That won't happen," he insisted, hoping it wasn't a lie.

"I'm not worried," she also insisted, another possible lie. Then she turned to grab her coat and pulled a purse from her suitcase. "Come on. If we are safe now, then let's escape this place."

A knock came at the door.

Alarmed, their eyes met, reflecting back the same questions.

Helena moved first toward to door to answer it. "It must be the agents."

Yet, when she swung it open, there stood an unfamiliar woman, wearing a long, expensive winter coat, a scarf wrapped over her hair, and wide dark glasses perched on her nose. In one hand, she clutched a purse, in the other kid leather gloves. With shaking hands, she slipped off the glasses and pinched her eyebrows with worry.

Rafferty did not recognize her at all.

"Can I help you?" Helena asked, politely, clearly not knowing the woman either.

Then, the worry line between the stranger's eyebrows deepened, wrinkling it even more in the young face. Even though she wore no makeup, she clearly was beautiful and sophisticated.

Maybe there was something in the tilt of her head, but then Helena squeaked, her fingers flying to her lips. "Scarlet?"

Chapter 12

WE CONFESSED EVERYTHING

Tears bubbled up at the bottom of Scarlet's young eyes. "Oh God, Helena," she whispered. "I am so sorry."

Before anyone could say anything more, Helena's arms flew around Scarlet, pulling her into a tight, desperate embrace. Scarlet's arms returned the hug, and the two women held each other in a shared grief. For the first time since waking up in her kitchen, Rafferty felt like he was finally seeing Helena's true pain shared with someone who actually understood exactly how she felt.

"I'm sorry. I'm so, so sorry," Scarlet kept trying to repeat as a sob wracked her.

"No, no, it's not ..." Helena tried to admonish her, but it didn't do any good.

Finally, becoming conscious of the impropriety of this show of raw emotion in the hotel hallway, Helena pulled her boss into the room and shut the door.

The change of location seemed to give Scarlet a degree of control for her emotions, and she straightened, the poise Rafferty expected from an aristocratic lady like herself reasserting control.

"You must be the chef." Scarlet's damp gaze landed on him, then she stretched out her hand to shake.

"How did you find us?" he asked, the only question he needed answered. *Vassago couldn't have told her,* he thought, but he didn't have another answer for it and that scared him.

Scarlet didn't seem flummoxed or disconcerted by the question. "I have a private detective on retainer. He's very good and very fast." She licked her lips, squaring up with him. "I am so sorry for what I have put you through."

The formal words sounded wrong, but Rafferty took her offered hand, tipping her knuckles up so that he could bow over them. It may have been deeply old-fashioned and old country, but he didn't care. It reflected how deep his own guilt went. Scarlet took it in stride, not at all surprised by the gesture.

"This is not your fault, lady," he said when he straightened.

She shook her head, firmly, the tears threatening her eyes again. "No, sir," she stated. "I won't accept that this was only Yosef's choice and only he is to blame."

"Rafferty," Helena said, meeting his eyes, using them to give him a warning about saying too much.

Scarlet looked between the two of them, the once-older woman seeing more then they wanted to reveal. "So, you two *are* a couple, then?" She turned again, speaking to Helena even as she continued to hold Rafferty's hand.

"I wondered how you found him for the Winter Rose Ball so fast."

Squeezing his fingers once, Scarlet let them go. "I just wish that all your effort hadn't gone to absolute waste." She moved to the table, setting down her purse so she could remove her gloves.

"What happened? The other night after ..." Helena's question died on her lips as her voice thickened. He could see the memory of the terrible events playing in her eyes, the ease and joy they had struggled so hard to gain back that morning washed away.

Scarlet continued. "The other night ..." She cleared her throat. "This is partly why I came, even against the advice of my lawyer. I wasn't even sure you would see me. As you can imagine, Scarlet Promotions is utterly destroyed. Despite everything we did over the last year, there is no point in trying to save what remains. Half of the staff have already jumped ship, and I told the other half that they could continue to draw salaries while they looked for another job. I am even calling in every favor I have left to try to get them placed in new situations so the fallout from my disgrace doesn't taint their résumés."

"Your disgrace?" Helena repeated, taken aback. "But this wasn't your fault. You didn't do anything wrong."

"Whatever the facts are at this point are irrelevant— at least in terms of business. The news outlets and social media are feeding conspiracy theories back and forth, claiming that I ..." More tears beaded her eyes. "That I sacrificed my own assistant in order to gain youth and beauty. You have to admit it's a very compelling, classical narrative."

The weight of everything forced Scarlet to pull out one of the chairs from the table and sit down with an unladylike heaviness, as she lost herself to tears again.

Urgently, Helena retrieved the box of tissues from the side table near the bed and offered them to her mentor, her movements jerky as if she itched to do something, anything.

"Scarlet?" she asked softly.

The other woman blinked as if coming back awake, then grabbed Helena's hand instead of the tissues to give it a little squeeze. "And you most of all, my darling girl. I had thought to leave you with a legacy, and now I've brought you down with me!"

"It's my fault," Rafferty interrupted, his back ramrod straight, his arms at his side, like a soldier at attention. "I summoned demons to the kitchen that night. I am the reason your lover is dead."

Stunned silence.

Rafferty knew the risk he was taking. He had not used Vassago's name. He had in fact summoned many demons to the kitchen that night to help him. The spirit of the bargain would remain preserved. Probably. He understood the dangers of making deals with demons; this sort of thing was very hard not to do, but it was too late to regret it now.

"What?" Scarlet asked, swiveling her head toward Helena. "What are you saying …?"

"No, it's not that simple. It's my fault," Helena insisted.

Rafferty's heart skipped a beat. What if he couldn't trust her after all? In her hurry to defend him, would she condemn him by revealing …

"I brought Rafferty in and asked an impossible task of him …"

The surprise and relief he would have felt evaporated instantly. He shook his head, growling, "You asked for help from your boyfriend. I'm the one who took it too far—"

"It's not your fault! I shouldn't have put you in that position to ... Or I should have explained—"

"I should have believed in you—"

"I should have—"

"Stop it!" Scarlet barked, silencing the fight before it could grow. The now-young woman fidgeted violently with her gloves like they were a squirming animal, as she struggled with what Rafferty could only imagine were turbulent emotions.

She then indicated Helena. "You. Go. Speak."

Helena took a deep breath in. "A few months ago, I ... accidentally summoned a demon. It was the night of my dinner party in fact, the night you came—"

Scarlet nodded and waved. "Yes, yes, I remember." She gestured for her to get on with it.

"It was a complete accident. I still am not entirely sure how I did it, but once I had summoned Rafferty"—she gestured to him where he still stood straight as an arrow—"he ... he did me a favor, and I was able to send him back safely, but then I felt ..." She struggled for a moment, her eyes flashing him apologies. "*Sorry* for him. I summoned him back again, not to get anything from him. I just wanted to give him a break from Hell, you know. I know this sounds insane, but we ... we became friends and then ..."

"I seduced her," he interjected. "I wanted to stay here, and it was a means—"

"Rafferty!" Helena barked. "You don't need to do that. You don't need to lie to protect me." She turned back to Scarlet, her hands out, urgently pleading with their chosen judge. "He went back on his own to save me from paying the price of him staying."

Scarlet didn't look at her. Her gaze remained fixed on Rafferty, an intense haunted depth in her eyes.

Desperate, Helena continued. "We ... we fell in love. Truly. He's not a monster. He's not like what other demons are. He would never hurt anyone if not forced to—"

Rafferty closed his eyes, wincing at her words. To her, they weren't lies, she truly believed everything she said, but to him ... he knew better. "Helena—"

"You're not!" she insisted. "You're a good person who made some terrible mistakes. Why can't you see that?"

"Helena, leave him be," Scarlet commanded, fully in control of herself once more. She gestured at Helena. "Continue."

Helena's whole body shook, but she obeyed. "And ... and then the night of the Winter Rose Ball came, and when the chef didn't show up ... I didn't know what else to do so I ... I summoned him for help."

Falling silent, Helena hugged her arms around herself, having reached the end of her confession.

Instead, Rafferty took over. "I summoned many demons to that kitchen to make a feast fit for kings."

"And you let them free once they had?" Scarlet asked. Her gaze returned to him, and Rafferty felt as he had all those centuries ago when he had been face-to-face with the King of France. Though, to him it felt like only a couple of years ago.

He *would* tell her the truth, though he also was sure she wouldn't believe him.

"I ordered them back and they all went. I had bound them to my word."

Helena's eyebrows creased.

"So Yosef summoned him back," Scarlet finished for him. "He called the demon from the circle himself."

"But how do you know that?" Helena asked.

"I was there when he did it," Scarlet said, her long gaze haunted and heavy.

Rafferty licked his lips and continued. "What most likely happened is he spoke with a demon while it was under my thrall. That would be enough. The demon would have told him how to summon him back and offered him something he wanted more than anything." All things any demon could and would have done. "I was too preoccupied to have noticed, but that is not an excuse. I took a huge risk, and he paid the price." He shook his head.

"Therefore, we would have gotten away with a demon summoning that night if he had not done what he did," Scarlet said as if she were perfectly okay with that. Like it was something she would have done herself in those circumstances. Maybe she had. He didn't know much about Scarlet, but her lack of appalled reaction made him think this had not been her first encounter with the demonic before. "And he bargained ... for this."

Scarlet held up her hands, the wrinkled skin now tight over her bones, the flesh restored to supple strength. Gently, those hands probed at her angelic face. "He traded his youth ... his life ... to restore mine."

"If I were to guess, yes, as the ... deal was completed, all the essence that was Yosef transferred to you. You are now the same age in body as he had been," Rafferty confirmed.

A coughing laugh escaped Scarlet. "God. To be twenty-six again." She closed her eyes once more, sorrowfully. "I wanted it more than anything, but never at this price."

Abruptly, she stood up, zeroing in on Rafferty. He didn't move away as she approached, but he did flinch as she raised her hands to his cheeks. He waited, expecting her to slap him, to punish him for what he had done to her lover.

But when it didn't fall, he opened his eyes. Her face was fixed into an expression he hadn't expected to see.

Compassion.

Her hands gently cupped his face, holding him and his gaze locked with hers. "You are a demon?" she asked softly. He wanted to recoil from the question but didn't have the will to pull away from her grip.

"I ... I'm not sure anymore," he breathed.

"I saw you both drop through the summoning circle," Scarlet continued, as if she were afraid to voice her fears aloud. "I thought you both had to be dead. But if you were a demon, then you chose to protect her instead of dragging her there? You guided her through hell and out again?"

"Sh-*she* saved me," he said, Scarlet's eyes compelling him. Her eyebrows pinched, and then she set a hand against his chest. Those same eyebrows popped up with realization.

"You are alive," she whispered. Her gaze drifted down to her hand, and he knew what she felt. His thumping, beating heart, pounding fast against his ribs.

"He's human again, yes," Helena confirmed.

"Demons do not have a heartbeat. They don't have real bodies," Scarlet continued, as if she hadn't heard. Then she broke her own spell, taking a step back. "I will help you."

She retrieved her purse and opened it to pull out a silver cellphone.

"Scarlet, what are you doing?" Helena asked.

"I know someone who can help us. We can get him a new identity and a back history. Birth certificate, credit history, the whole works. Though we can't do it here. We will have to go to the office. You are free to leave, correct?"

Helena hesitated. "Uh, it's been strongly implied that we should stay here, but I don't think we're being forced to."

Scarlet nodded as she brought the mobile phone to her ear. "Lord, it's been ages since I've had to do this for someone. I hope he will still answer this number."

"But I don't understand," Helena said, completely flummoxed by her boss's actions.

"Why are you doing this?" Rafferty asked.

Scarlet turned to look him full in the face, a confidence returning to her expression. A strength only inspired by purpose. "Redemption is a rare thing. It must be protected at all costs."

Chapter 13

IT'S TECHNICALLY NOT ILLEGAL?

"Okay, I got what I need from you, just give me a couple of hours, and I will have this all sorted," the friendly man, whose name they were not supposed to know, said as he lowered the digital camera he used to take Rafferty's picture.

Shifting his feet, Rafferty rubbed his eyes against the afterburn of the flash.

"You alright?" Helena asked him, stepping beside him.

"I've ... never had my picture taken before," he said.

She smiled at him. "There are probably going to be a lot of firsts now," she said. She glanced over at the nameless man who was helping them create a new identity for Rafferty, nibbling nervously at her lower lip.

"What is it?" Rafferty prompted.

"It's just, I know this is technically not legal, but ..."

"Oh, it's legal," the nameless man affirmed. "These documents will be perfectly legit once I process them. Don't worry. My clients never have any troubles with these, I guarantee it. <You said you are French, correct?>" He switched to speaking Rafferty's mother tongue to ask the question.

"<Why does everyone keep asking me that?>" Rafferty asked in disgust.

The nameless man nodded. "You have a really good American accent. Props," he said, and then he returned to the plastic cabinet he had rolled in when he had arrived in Scarlet's office, opening the different drawers and pulling out the needed documents. "Okay, so work visa and US residence permit. Unless you want to be a naturalized citizen? Oh! Or I can make you a dual French and American citizen. I haven't done one of those yet."

He eagerly pulled out more documents, then paused. "Do I need a marriage certificate as well?"

He looked between Helena and Rafferty for that answer.

"Oh, uh. No, not ..." Helena glanced at him, but Rafferty didn't have a better answer than that. "Not just yet."

"Yeah, okay. No problem. You can always get one later. Or you can just, you know, get married, after I have these documents sorted and legitimized," the nameless man said and returned his focus to the next steps. He went back to his prep, only to realize a second later that Helena and Rafferty were still standing there staring at him. "You need to go away now while I do this. Go get some lunch. I'll call you when it's ready."

Helena nodded, taking Rafferty's hand to lead him out. That was their entire existence right now. Something happening, and she leading him through it. His personal guardian.

He couldn't believe his luck. If this many good things had happened to him in his first life, he never would have taken Vassago's original deal. Everything he needed was just happening for him.

Out in the main room of the office, Rafferty could see what an amazing place this once had been. He had seen a handful of offices before, but those had been taupe limbos all their own, with little squares to keep the workers in place and isolated. This room was beautiful, with the open workstations separated by vibrant plants instead of fabric-covered walls. A tall glass wall with water cascading down it protected the workers from the view of visitors in the foyer.

But for all the signs of vibrancy in the room, it was half empty of the people that made it an office. So many of the desks were stripped of anything that made them personal and unique. To emphasize the emptiness, about every fourth desk did still have someone sitting at it. Amongst the remaining workers was a tense hush as they poured over job sites on their computers, looking for new employment, or played videos games while waiting for callbacks. They just didn't seem to realize how lucky *they* all were. They were alive, safe, and still being supported to do nothing. Like royals or nobility.

Helena nibbled at her lower lip as she regarded them all. Her own desk lived in Scarlet's office, now forbidden to her while the nameless man worked. The head of the organization had gone to a meeting with her lawyers and the Bureau of Demonic Investigation.

"Come on," Helena said, tugging him again toward a side room. The lights came on automatically as they entered a kitchenette. Like the rest of the office, this room housed hanging plants in the corners and had a large window letting in sunshine from outside. A long, granite counter lined the wall to the right with cabinets above. Two refrigerators sat side by side to the left of the bay window, now unnecessary for so few people.

"There should be some leftover food in the fridges. We were bringing in catering every day leading up to the ball," Helena said as she went to the first refrigerator.

While she did that, Rafferty went to the counter. A few machines lined the back edge of it including a microwave, a panini press, a toaster oven, an electric griddle, and a standing mixer. Opening one of the upper cabinets he found several bags of bread products, including bagels, and crackers.

"Here, sandwich meat." Helena set a plastic tray partially covered with folds of sliced meat. From a glance, Rafferty guessed it was the standard turkey, ham, and beef. Still, he slipped the clear plastic cover off and selected one of each, taking a tiny bite per slice.

"They are still good," he affirmed.

"Well, yeah, it's only been a couple of days." Helena returned with another smaller tray, which included several kinds of cheese. At a glance, he recognized Swiss, cheddar jack, and straight cheddar. The other two white cheeses he confirmed as Havarti and provolone after he tasted them.

"Is there butter?" he asked, a plan forming in his mind. It appeared beside him. He mulled over his options, not satisfied with the simple sandwich he would make out of what was available. Still, his stomach growled with even this much before him.

He was hungry. Actually hungry!

The excitement of satisfying that hunger took him over. He went to the refrigerator to look inside.

"There is also some lettuce, but the other toppings are a bit picked over and not looking so good anyway," Helena added from the other fridge, pulling out a very sad-looking plastic plate with a few scraps of wilted lettuce on it.

"Are there eggs?" Rafferty asked, instead of commenting on the pathetic greenery.

"Eggs?" Helena glanced back into her fridge. "No. Why would there be eggs in an office?"

"I suppose no milk either?"

"Oh, that we have." She pulled out a carton, exchanging the greenery plate for it. She popped it open to smell it. On the side, he saw a name written in Sharpie along with the words, "Don't drink!!!"

Helena passed it to Rafferty who took his own whiff. "Henry doesn't work here anymore. He left with the first wave."

"Was he the sort to drink directly from his carton?" Rafferty asked, taking the okay-smelling find to the counter.

"No, definitely not," she assured, following him to all his finds. "So what masterpiece are you planning?"

He sighed. "With what is here, something very functional and boring. I'm only just now realizing the limitations of my new existence."

"What do you mean?" Helena slid over one of the chairs so she could sit in it sideways to watch.

"As a demon, any missing ingredients I needed for what I wanted to make, I could simply create from my store of power. Without it, I'm stuck with what I have."

"And you want eggs?" she asked.

"I was thinking of making those savory French Toast sandwiches that you liked so much," he said, opening another cupboard and finding a hodgepodge of spices and salts. He pulled down a salt shaker and pepper inside a plastic grinder. "I have everything else."

"Okay, then here you go. One miracle," Helena said, slapping her hands together.

Energy flowed between them before Rafferty could object, and then there she was, holding a carton of eggs.

"Oh!" she breathed. "I think I get it. It's like you use your energy to rewrite one ... piece, I guess, of reality." She held it out to him proudly.

"No! You shouldn't have done that!" Rafferty cried, seizing the eggs from her as if they could hurt her now.

"What? It's no different than what you used to do," Helena said, surprised by his reaction.

"That is the point! Everything has a cost! You're the only one paying it."

"But look, I'm fine. I'm alright." She held out her hands in proof. "I didn't even break a sweat. It's just a small thing. It's just eggs." Then she thought for a second. "Or are you worried about my intentions? Right? When you make something this way, you imbue it with intentional magic."

"Don't call it magic."

"I just wanted to make you happy. How can that be bad?" She looked up at him with her beautiful, sincerely sweet eyes. She was the same person she had always been, her human appearance and the touch of her hand on his forearm felt so very real and normal that he could forget that she had changed at all. She was just his Helena.

His resolve melted like butter on the electric griddle. "Okay. I guess, this won't really hurt anything. And it's just us eating this ..."

"Well, actually." Helena looked at all the ingredients laid out. "Really, we could serve this up to those that remain of my coworkers. It's a lot of food that's going to go to waste otherwise."

His lips thinned at that suggestion.

Then she batted her eyes at him, pleadingly.

"Fine."

Her smile bloomed on her face. "I'll go ask everyone."

She left the little kitchenette as Rafferty dipped four bread slices into the batter and slapped the batch onto the griddle to a hissing sizzle. Within minutes, more people filed into the room, all sullen and dour. They received their plates of the fresh sandwiches with barely a word of thanks, but Rafferty didn't mind, he just focused on making up the next batch, enjoying every second. This was what made him feel alive.

While he worked, drinks were retrieved from the other refrigerator. Condiments were applied as needed.

Soon, the atmosphere of the room shifted. The remaining employees started to talk to each other. Then there were brighter faces accompanied by laughter. The room felt more like a party.

People slapped Rafferty on the back, complimenting his work. A couple of them even asked for his recipe. It fed his soul even more than food ever could, but it was a close contest. Helena beamed at him proudly. And all the while, he kept making sandwiches until every egg and slice of bread and meat was gone. The conversations continued. It felt good to just be a part of a group like this, a temporary community. He even got to eat some of his work, and it was as delicious as everyone around him said.

He set his anxieties about her eggs aside. There was no way her intention didn't get into the food with them, but it seemed to be as she said, she just wanted to make everyone happy. She couldn't affect their minds, anyone who chose not to be happy would resist the pull of her energies, but they would still feel her call to that emotion.

Sometimes a demon can do miracles, he thought as he took another delicious bite, full of flavors.

Just as the plates were piling into the sink and Helena started the water before he could think to, the door to the kitchenette opened and the chatter in the room went silent as if a switch had been flipped. It was so jarring as Scarlet entered the room she jerked to a stop as the wall of eyes focused on her.

"Oh. Hello."

Chapter 14

THEN HELENA HAD A BRILLIANT IDEA

"Hi, Scarlet," Helena said a delayed moment later, turning off the water and rubbing her wet hands on her jeans. "Would you like something to eat?"

That seemed to break the spell on the room. "Thanks" was murmured by all, and everyone filed out with excuses that they needed to return to this, that, or the other thing. Scarlet didn't even try to heed them. She simply walked past and took the offered plate with the last sandwich on it from Helena. Then she went to the table and set it down as she assumed a seat, placing herself as elegantly in the chair as if she were in a five-star restaurant.

Then she paused, a sad smile on her face. "That is so easy now. It used to be such a production to simply sit at a table."

Then both women looked up at Rafferty, who had been in the middle of grabbing one of the chairs that had been pushed back so that he could pull it up to the table to join them.

He froze as he realized they were both staring at him, his stomach clenching.

"Come on, sit down," Helena encouraged, tapping the bare space next to her. Then she turned to Scarlet and gestured at her plate. "What do you think?"

Scarlet refocused on the sandwich, hesitating as if looking for a fork or knife to eat it with, then slummed down her manners a bit and picked it up. She took a tentative bite, and when it didn't burn her like acid, she took a bigger one.

After a few seconds of chewing, her eyes fluttered. "Oh my," she said with food still in her mouth, with her fingers leaping to cover her societal faux pas. "This is delicious."

"I know, right?" Helena squealed, popping the last of her sandwich into her mouth.

"So you really are a chef?" Scarlet asked, taking a sip of the sparkling water. "You weren't just a demon?"

"Rafferty was a chef, yes, when he was last alive," Helena said, as if that were a natural occurrence, for a man to be alive centuries later than anyone else he had been born with. His girlfriend nudged him with her elbow to speak.

"I ..."

"One thing is terribly clear that needs no further explanation," Scarlet said, already halfway through her sandwich. "You are a most talented cook. This, the dinner party, and what was served at the Winter Rose Ball. Now that you have your second chance, are you going to do something with this gift? Would you like to see what my connections can find you? I know several high-end restaurants that would appreciate you."

"I ..." Rafferty trailed off again, staring down at his plate. He had only one idea that excited him. "There is this underground ... thing."

"Underground?" Scarlet asked, wrinkling her nose.

"Does that have something to do with that business card I found?" Helena added.

"Eleanor," Rafferty said, picturing the chef in her kitchen scrubs and her warrior's smile. A different kind of hunger slid through him. "She is a chef who is trying to create a sort of..." He struggled for a moment, then related the idea to the only analogy he knew of. "Cooking show, but one she shows online. She does these *fantastic* cakes," he added, his voice reflecting the awe he felt at the memory of her masterpiece. "She told me about this ... competition. I don't know much, but it sounds ... fun."

He felt damn near predatory thinking about it. A battle of cooks. Not for the attention of a king, but then everyone in these times thought themselves kings and queens.

"And this is a thing?" Scarlet asked, looking to Helena for confirmation.

She shrugged. "I don't know, but maybe we could check it out. Here. Let me go get my computer. I'll be right back." Standing up eagerly, she left without another word.

Rafferty and Scarlet sat there awkwardly now that Helena had left the room.

"Have you got your new identifications yet?" Scarlet asked politely.

"He said he'd let us know."

He thought they would lapse back into silence, but instead, she scooted her seat a little closer, leaning in to pitch her voice down. "You must excuse me, Mr. Lares." She hesitated, her mouth opening and closing as if she couldn't believe she was doing this. "Your existence as a demon. Tell me about it."

He pulled back as much as she leaned forward. "You want me to tell you about what it is like in Hell?"

"I want to know how much my poor Yosef is suffering right now," she said softly and fragilely.

And here it is, he thought to himself, realizing what she was really asking. None of her help was out of any goodness in her heart. "You want to know how to bring Yosef back," he said in a low voice, his eyes half-lidded.

"I ... want to know if it is possible, yes," she admitted, with equally fragile hope in her eyes.

"Up until recently I would have said no, not at all possible," he said dryly. "But I know you would say I am lying."

"Because here you sit," she said.

"Because here I sit. And I have no idea how or why."

Scarlet's eyes narrowed, her shoulders squaring. "But you do have some theories." It was a statement, not a question. She could see that he did. He could tell she was a formidable dealmaker.

He sighed and looked away. He supposed he was in her debt. While not bound by any outside forces, what this woman giveth, she could taketh away. And Helena would pay that price. But he also knew this woman wasn't going to like what he had to say, so it was risky either way.

Fuck it.

"If he were on the brink of dying, something could be done. You could trade your life for his. It would take that much to pay the price of the imbalance to stop a death."

"But he's already dead," she said, her voice cracking.

"Yes."

"And the price would be ..."

"It's been attempted, as far as I know, but never succeeded. Not in the way you wish."

She shook her head. "That makes no sense. Here you sit." Her hand gestured frantically at him.

"Yes, here I sit. I …" Tension built at the back of his neck. He was so loathed to admit this. "I just don't know why."

"Is he a demon now? Because of what he did?"

Rafferty straightened in his chair. "If you wish me to tell you, I will tell you. But you will not like any of it."

Scarlet's jaw stiffened as she lifted her head imperiously. "What you have to say cannot be worse than what I am imagining in my head," she declared.

He wasn't going to argue about the validity of that statement.

"Yosef … is in pain now. Feeling all the emotions that a body insulates you from. There is no buffer now. And he is alone. Completely alone. No one is going to care for him or be safe for him. If he tries to reach out to the others, they will only take what little of him remains for themselves."

She pursed her eyebrows together hard. "But what are they taking?" she asked, fear in the undercurrent of her voice.

"First, they will take his memories. The good ones will be the most prized. They will have the most energy. If he can't fight them off, they can consume him entirely until there is nothing left; nothing will remain of him. But if he figures out how to fight back, he'll realize he needs to do the same to the others around him or everything he ever was will be gone forever."

"And there is no way we can help him?" Scarlet asked, her voice cracking with her urgency to act. "Couldn't we summon him, at least? Get him out of there and hold him here in creation."

Rafferty gripped the edge of the table hard, keeping control of his own emotions. Bile kept threatening at the back of his throat. "His presence would slowly consume everything around him, corrupting the world as the price continues to eat at creation. He would also need to be bound to a living being here as an anchor, or creation will try to force him back."

"What if we closed the circle? Minimize the damage?" she asked, her eyes darting back and forth as she thought hard about solving the problem.

"That would only last as long as you, his summoner and anchor, hold out. It wouldn't buy you time, it would lessen it. The circle cuts down the cost. He could eventually drag you back with him sooner."

"Then I would go," she said firmly, tears breaking ranks from her eyes. "Then he wouldn't be alone."

Rafferty shook his head. "It wouldn't work like that. You would eventually try to consume each other, just to resist the pain. Whatever love you had for each other would be destroyed."

A strangled cry of pain escaped her. "My poor Yosef," she cried, and pressed a fist against her mouth, thinking about the hopelessness of the situation.

They sat there quietly like that for several long minutes, each plagued by their thoughts. Rafferty had the passing thought that he wondered what was taking Helena so long, but then Scarlet lifted her head again, calmer now, her grief tucked back into its box.

"I knew another demon once. An incubus," Scarlet suddenly said.

Rafferty smirked. So here it was, the answer he had been wondering. "Did you summon him?"

She shook her head as she took her napkin and dabbed at her wet face with it in a vain attempt to preserve her makeup. "No. My sister did. I watched as that thing ate her up from the inside out. When she died, my parents covered it all up and used their money and influence to bury the whole mess."

"Then you know what I say is true," he said.

Scarlet nodded, her jaw stiffening again. "I also saw the things *she* did to *him*. My sister had always been a selfish, hateful bitch. And while I know it is thought to be wrong, I don't know if I can fault him for what he did to her, considering what she took in return."

Rafferty didn't need to hear more. He knew. Again, they sat in the heavy silence. While they did, he studied the grief hanging over Scarlet's being as she stared off into memories.

"I never saw this part," he said aloud, the words slipping from him like thieves stealing his thoughts.

"What part?"

It was too late to deflect his misspoken words. And he didn't really wish to. Something was happening to him, something he hadn't expected from anyone who wasn't Helena. He gestured between them. "This. The hurt, the suffering. The grief. This is all demons do. Even if you were to call him back, he wouldn't be your Yosef anymore, he may not even remember you, but he'll tell you anything you want to hear, simply so he can consume you to alleviate his own suffering. And it won't work. Nothing will ever alleviate it."

Scarlet studied him a moment. "Is that what you did to Helena?"

He didn't get to answer that question, and he was glad for it.

Just then Helena returned carrying her computer.

"I found it, I'm mostly sure," she said excitedly. "Here, look. This is a schedule of all the places where there is a food battle and, look, this is the next one." She pointed to the screen, holding it out so that both of them could look. "It's tomorrow, and see here, it's near Cindy's house in the far reaches of the suburbs. We can go, and I can check on her, too. It's perfect!"

She looked between the two of them.

"Are you both alright?" she asked, finally reading the mood in the room.

"Yes, yes, my dear," Scarlet said, fetching up her purse and standing. She then nodded to Rafferty. "Thank you for lunch."

He wasn't sure what to make of that. By all rights she should have pressed him to repay his debt to her, but she didn't even give him a knowing look as she left.

"Sorry that took so long. Was that really awkward? Did you guys talk about anything?" Helena asked, watching her boss leave, clearly sensing the mood, finally.

"No," Rafferty said. "No, it's fine. We're fine."

Chapter 15

MY FIRST TRAIN IN AGES

Helena would not stop grinning at him as she held his arm walking down the platform. They were both carrying overnight bags slung over their shoulders, looking like the dozens of other travelers boarding the train. He followed Helena's lead as she led him into one of the cars. Having consulted her ticket, she let go of his arm so she could navigate down a narrow hallway until she stopped by the middlemost compartment.

"Here we go; this is us," she pronounced, and slid the door to one side to enter. "What do you think?"

"It is not how I last remembered," he said, following her in, sliding the door shut behind himself.

Plopping down on the gray two-seater to the left, she dropped her carry-on bag on a single seat opposite. "What were you expecting?"

Rafferty ran his hand over the top of the seat, all efficient gray vinyl.

"Jewel-colored velvet. Ruby red or sapphire blue, wrought iron filigree."

"Hmm," Helena cooed. "That does sound more romantic."

He grinned as he settled down next to her, dropping his bag onto the floor, and she immediately cuddled into him, slipping herself under his arm, fitting against him as if made to be there.

"This is nice too," she said, relaxing in a way she hadn't in the last few days.

He knew that they were headed to a possibly stressful situation, but there was something golden about this moment. That ecstatic feeling echoed inside him from the first time it hit him that he was alive. Running his hand along Helena's back, breathing her scent in, as long as he forgot the new truth of her existence, he could just be happy.

"So you didn't just get summoned into kitchens, if you've ridden in a train before," she said, picking up the conversation after a moment of blissful peace. They both gazed out the window, though there wasn't much to look at yet except the side of another train waiting in the depot.

"Yes, I've ridden in a train before," he agreed. "A long time ago by your perspective."

"It wasn't for anything cooking related then?"

He shook his head. "No, that particular mistress wanted something very different from me. I'm not even sure how she got my name to summon me."

"What did she want?" Helena rested a hand on his chest, brushing slow circles through the fabric of his shirt, slipping under the edge of his coat and out again. It felt so soothing. "If you want to talk about it. You don't have to."

He pressed a kiss to her temple. "I will tell you anything you ask," he assured, then took another moment to collect his answer. "Being a demon is more about being willing to say yes to anything than it is anything magical or mystical. The power of yes seems to be just as rare, if not rarer than anything I could conjure."

She snuggled into him as she listened.

Rafferty cleared his throat and continued. "I don't remember when it was, what year. People wore hats in public. I was dressed in a vest and jacket. It was hot, so probably summer. She ..." He swallowed. "She was escaping her parents and their designs for her future. She wanted me to protect her as she journeyed out to the west and adventure."

"Hmm, I wish I could see that, you in old-timey clothes," Helena said, as the whole car jerked, shuddering into motion. "Did she fall in love with you?"

He twitched. "She ... lust maybe ... or at least ... I wouldn't have called it love."

Helena spun around, her expression delighted and teasing. "Oh, really?" she asked, setting her cheek on her fist, her elbow propped against his chest. "And?"

He felt like a bug pinned under a particularly delighted cat.

"You said you wanted to be honest with me," she continued to tease, her eyes dancing merrily like candle flames, reflecting gold flashes over her natural stone blue.

"When did I say that?" he countered, just as playfully.

"Oh, I don't know. I feel like it was recently." She pouted, which made her even more achingly cute.

Words were failing him. He had never needed to speak of such things and normally he wouldn't feel so shy about it. Shame about sex was not something he could ever afford, and he had done too much too many times to really be affected by a trivial emotion. But what he felt and did with Helena was different. It was more than simply desire and heat, it touched his soul and cut through the shield of disinterest he had used to protect himself. It was terrifying and yet healed him at the same time.

Or at least it had before when she had been human and he the unnatural monster.

Closing his eyes, he brought his forehead forward, cupping the back of her head to draw hers to meet him.

"What are we doing?" she asked after a second, her words barely forming out of the whisper.

"You may eat the memory," he said. He felt her go completely still under his hand.

"But ... won't that destroy it for you?" she asked.

"I don't care. It's not one I treasure," he said. "You may have it."

She pulled away a moment, her golden eyes studying his, glinting hungrily.

"I offered myself to you, mind, body, and soul," he affirmed, so there would be no doubt. "You need to feed your power to stay here. And I want you here."

"But won't I be doing to you what the others in ... that place did to you?"

He cupped her face and pulled her in for a kiss.

It happened then. Her resistance gave way, and he could feel her slip into his mind. It was slower than the first time he had eaten her memory of the taste of chocolate cake. Then he had simply wanted to do her as little harm as possible. In quick and out again, capturing the delectable memory of the taste of cake. At the time, it was a shadow of what a real taste would be, but more than he had known in ages.

But he recognized this was Helena's first time. She was cautious, reaching out on instinct to go where she didn't belong. Ice knifed through his brain.

"I'm sorry, I'm sorry," she breathed, pulling away, but he locked his hand behind her head to keep her in place.

"It's alright," he breathed. "I'll live. Just take it into yourself."

"I don't know what I'm doing," she whispered. Her hand snaked around to cup his own head from behind.

"That's it," he confirmed as he felt her move into him again. And then the memory ignited, playing out ...

She sat across from him in the car. She had been smiling shyly at him all morning. He could smell it from where he sat. The musk of her desire, the rapid beating of her heart as loud as a drum, at least to his ears.

He knew what was coming before she said it. He simply waited, with his ankle crossing his knee, his hands resting on both as the train rocked them hard from side to side. After five days of traveling, he was getting used to the sensation.

The motion was also making his mistress's desires worse.

"If I order you to, you have to do anything I ask, correct?" Her handfan fluttered as she asked the question, which did little to move the summer air in the car.

"As you command, my lady," he said.

She snapped the fan together. "Then, kiss me," she ordered, sitting up a little straighter in her seat, the training she had received in being a lady who could command a room manifesting itself.

He dropped his crossed foot and leaned forward, letting his grin slide onto his face. This had been easy. Barely a week and this innocent ingenue was ready to partake of his pleasures. But it wasn't the prospect of sex that excited him; it was the thrill of taking the energy of her body. She was a rich vein that would increase his wealth significantly.

"Lift your skirt," he said to her, his voice low and rumbling.

It was bold. She could buck.

Maybe that was why he did it. Some small part of him wanted to give her a chance to escape what was about to happen. She would never be the same afterward. There was a good chance that if she only did this with him once, she wouldn't even notice that she had even lost anything until she was quite old and it was too late. If she only congressed with a demon once, the damage would be minimal to her long-term health.

Her eyes went wide, her breath caught.

Then slowly, she lifted her skirt, bringing it up past her knees, the cloth trembling with the excitement and terror that always came with defying the forbidden. She hesitated when the cloth reached her mid-thigh. The garters she wore were now clearly visible, but as he suspected, she didn't wear any drawers due to the heat of the year. It was more than enough.

He slid his hand along that exposed skin, and she gasped in a sharp breath. Fearfully, her eyes flitted to the door of their little private compartment. It hadn't occurred to her to save money by taking a lesser class. The shade over the window was drawn down, and the door would not open without a warning knock.

Just so, he expended a little bit of power to encourage all those who would interfere to continue past as quickly as possible, automatically skipping the door.

No one would disturb them, but he wasn't going to tell her that. The thrill of being caught added to the aphrodisiac.

He pulled at his cravat and undid the top button, showing her a scandalous amount of his neck. Pure as the driven snow, she gasped again, her own fingers lifting to touch the beckoning skin. That alone made her moan, and it was at that moment when his fingers darted in past her defenses.

She gasped and squeaked. As she did so, he moved in and slipped his tongue into her opening mouth, swallowing her cries, as his digit slicked along her wetness. He didn't enter her. Not yet. Only traced along her folds and back, feeling for the erection of her clitoris, already sparking.

Her hands grasped feebly at his shoulders, yet she did not push him away. Only hesitated as she tried to comprehend what was happening. His fingers moved again, exploring her, mapping out her responses to the touch, all while he continued to ravish her lips.

There was a temptation to slip one of his fingers inside her, test out that virginity she had been so proud of a few days before.

"Oh Rafferty," she moaned.

That was wrong. That ... that wasn't his memory.

Breaking the kiss, he looked down at the young woman before him, but she had changed, been replaced by an angel with golden-red hair.

Helena smiled up at him, wrapping her hands around his neck to pull him back into another robust kiss.

There was nothing he could do. He couldn't change what had happened. This was a memory.

But guilt was introduced, a feeling he knew he hadn't felt as he deflowered ... he couldn't remember her name. That was gone, consumed by the demoness invading this memory. The woman beneath him as he opened his trousers to set his cock free was a different woman. And she was consuming him instead of him consuming her ...

MEMORY DEVOURED

"Oh wow," Helena breathed as she arched back. At some point in their exchange, she had come to straddle him. "I feel amazing!"

She settled back on his legs, rolling her shoulders as she savored the delicious feeling of power feeding her being.

Blinking, Rafferty realized his eyes were already open, even though he had been enveloped by that memory. A memory he realized he still retained. He could see it all in his mind's eye. The train, the woman. The taste of her in his mouth, the feel of her body around his fingers.

Except, the memory was now changed. It was Helena he remembered there. Even though it wasn't possible.

Helena's eyes opened, and she smiled with so much affection it hummed through him. It was an expression of kindness, warmth, and a little bit of mischievous delight. Slowly, she kissed him affectionately, then nuzzled his neck, settling contentedly against him. "Are you alright?" she asked.

"Yes, but I don't understand. You didn't eat my memory?"

She sat up and cocked her head to one side. "I didn't?"

He shook his head. "I still remember it."

"Who was that woman anyway?"

"I ... I can't remember that part. It's different now." He pressed his fingers into the ghost of the ice pick still inside his brain.

"I'm sorry, I wasn't trying to hurt you."

"No, that's not it. I'm fine. But it's weird. When I think of that memory now, I don't see her. I see you." He met her gaze but didn't find any answers in her confused eyes. "Now I'm a bit worried."

Then there was a knock at the door. "Dessert and snack cart. Do you want anything?" a voice called through the door.

Helena's eyes went wide with delight. "Oooh, dessert cart," she said, bouncing off his lap to open the door. "Oh, dear Lord! Rafferty, you have to come see this."

Joining her at the door, he stared at the white, multi-layered cart. It had a little awning above with a cheerful blue-and-white striped pattern. Hanging from around the top were pretzels dipped in various kinds of chocolate and pressed into sprinkles, candy, or nuts. The two shelves below had three different kinds of cakes and a mini–ice cream station with so many possible toppings in jars all around. There were also brownies and cookies in drawers along with several prepackaged candy and nut mixes.

"Oh my word, Rafferty, look! They really do have everything!" Helena pointed at a medium-sized bowl in the middle.

"Are there eggs in that raw cookie dough?" Rafferty asked, gesturing to the bowl.

"No, sir. It has everything else, but not the eggs. So it is safe to consume," the attendant said. "Would you like a scoop of that along with a scoop of ice cream?"

"Yes! Please!" Helena squealed.

"We also have some RumChata in a chocolate shot glass," she said, indicating an unmarked bottle in the back of the cart.

"I'm dying. I've died. This is amazing, yes, please!" Helena cried, overly giddy.

"And what would you like, sir?" the attendant asked as she finished preparing Helena's order.

"I ..." He looked over the cart. "May I have some of that flourless chocolate cake?" He gestured at the plate in the middle near the back.

"It has a hint of orange if that is alright?" she added as she reached for a small paper plate to dish the pre-cut slice on.

"How can it not be?" he said, and he accepted the dessert.

"Anything to drink?"

"Milk!" Helena called from inside their compartment, having already retreated back to the seat. "Definitely need some milk."

The attendant retrieved two cold bottles from the end of her cart. "Would you like me to charge it to the car?" she asked.

"Yes, please!" Helena called back, and Rafferty accepted that the issue of payment was taken care of.

"Oh my gosh, I am so glad that lady at the ticket counter offered us the free upgrade. This is the best!" Helena declared once the cart moved on. She had already devoured half of the small train-shaped bowl the scoop of cookie dough and ice cream had come in.

Rafferty settled into the single seat across from her since she had decided to sit cross-legged and take up the entire double-seater. He didn't mind. He enjoyed watching her enjoyment.

"This is so nice," she said, smiling at him. "Getting to travel with my boyfriend. It's like a slice of normal, you know?"

"Is this normal?" he asked. "I have no frame of reference."

"Hmm." She nodded around a full mouth, sliding the spoon out with a sensual slowness. "When Cindy and I were coming home from college, we convinced our boyfriends at the time to come with us."

"At the time?" Rafferty asked.

"Yes, I've had quite a few before I met you," she said, then cocked her head. "Is that a problem?"

He shook his head. "No, of course, forgive me. I know you had a life, and lovers, before my existence."

"We did just share a memory of one of your own," she pointed out.

His jaw stiffened. "She wasn't my lover," he said, the words making the chocolate cake taste bitter. "I wouldn't call her that. Nothing I did with her I would call love. Love requires a choice, and I had very limited choices."

He stuffed a larger bite of his dessert into his mouth, simply to have something more to do than talk.

"I suppose I know that," she said, her words soft and tender as a feather brushing the air. "I know we never really talked about this before, but if someone would summon you, what happens to you if they ask something of you that you don't want to do?"

He swallowed, the cake sliding down his throat like a rock, threatening for a moment to choke. His gaze went long as he remembered the calculation. "There is a price that has to be paid when we are summoned. If we don't do as our masters' command, if we break our word ... There is something in all of this, that binds us to our agreements. There is also something that prevents us from taking what we need without one. We aren't sure what it is. Our summoners can send us back without paying the price if we don't make a deal. Then it falls on us. If we break the agreement, the price is higher than if they simply sent us back. If we fulfill our end, then we can take what we were promised by any means and there is nothing our masters can do to stop us."

Watching her take this in, he could see her reliving the consequences of such an imprudent deal like the one Yosef had made. Helena's gaze had gone long as she listened, tapping her spoon in her bowl. "So when I accidentally summoned you the first time ..."

"I kept the price low. My trip there and back and the tiniest bit of power to make the ingredients I needed. It only cost you a memory. A vibrant memory. I didn't gain anything from it but didn't lose anything either. We can't risk saying no to anyone. Though, we don't want those who summon us to know that if they don't already. Then we can get away with all kinds of things." It didn't exactly feel good to say that aloud, but there was some strange relief in it as well. These were things he would have never said to anyone, but revealing them to Helena felt right. He was safe with her.

But she pursed her eyebrows as a thought occurred to her. "Is that why you pledged yourself to me, mind, body, and soul? You weren't just being romantic?"

He realized what she was getting at. "Just in case, you know?"

"Does that mean I have to do anything you say?" she asked, releasing one of those worried eyebrows so it could arch up inquisitively. Mischievousness returned as well.

Yet, he couldn't find the humor in it. "I would never do that to you," he assured. "I may have been a monster for centuries, but I would *never* do that to you."

Setting down her bowl next to her on the seat, she crossed the breath of space between them and wrapped her arms around him. Then he felt her wrap her wings around as well, filling in the remaining space until they were contained in a small cocoon of feathers. He sucked in a sharp breath.

Wanting to pull away, he forced himself to stay, to let her hold him. Even as the eerie feeling washed over his skin, his long discipline of doing things he didn't really want held him firm.

"I'm so sorry, Rafferty," she whispered, his hard work keeping her oblivious to his true feelings.

She is just trying to comfort me. She loves me, he thought, and it helped.

The sensation eased as she reverted back to herself, apparently completely oblivious that her wings, horns, and even tail had been visible. Instead, she smiled and brushed her fingers down his cheek. "Good thing I'm not really a demon, right?"

"We don't actually know what has happened to you," he said carefully.

She nodded. "I know. I'm aware that I might not be … an angel. But I don't feel particularly compelled by anything, if that helps?" She blew out a sigh and retreated back to the double-seater to reclaim her abandoned treat bowl. "It's probably why I want to go see Cindy so much. You know? Just focus on what I can do, what I can control, until I figure out some answers."

She blew out another breath. "Do you think … we should tell the BDI … about me?"

"Absolutely not," he answered, forcefully shaking his head. "They may not have believed us about me not being a demon, but if we show them you …"

"They'll send me back," she agreed, finishing for him. He was grateful. The words he would have said would have been far worse. "I know. We just hadn't said it out loud yet."

"It is agreed then," he said, nodding as he took up the last of his own cake, even though he didn't really want it anymore. There was no bringing himself to ever throw away food given to him.

"Are you okay, by the way, with all my … changes?" she asked. The vulnerability in her eyes at asking the question sliced through him like a knife.

"Of course. I would be a hypocrite if I weren't," he lied. "You let me touch you when I was a demon."

"Well, if I'm honest, it wasn't always easy. That aura you put out gave me the heebie jeebies."

"On some level, you recognized that I didn't belong here," he explained.

"But you don't feel like that now," she encouraged. "So that means you *do* belong. That's good."

"Yeah," he said, but he wasn't sure that was true either.

"What happened to that woman, the one that you helped." Then Helena wrinkled her nose. "If you don't mind me asking. You don't have to answer if …"

"She died," he said. "Not right then. Not when she had me, but eventually, years after she sent me back. I don't really know. I don't know if I care. That's what it means to be a demon."

He wished he hadn't said it. Helena's face sobered, all the joy she had been feeling about their trip sucked out. He just couldn't stand her perkiness right then, and now that he had destroyed it, he regretted it.

And if he was still a demon, he could have devoured the foul-tasting memory, and she could have gone back to being perky.

"Rafferty, *do* you think angels exist?" she asked.

He had uttered so many lies up to that point, he couldn't give her another one. "Not every demonic deal turns out badly. The people that get good results, like the woman in that memory, they herald us as angels. Our gifts are 'miracles.' There are no angels. Only us."

He dreaded what she would say to that, and if she would apply those rules to herself. He would have given anything at that moment to know what she was thinking, but a voice came over a speaker somewhere, mumbling some words that he hadn't been focusing enough to understand.

Helena appeared to, though, and she perked up. "We're almost here!" she said, her excitement returning after their sobering conversation.

Chapter 17

BLESS-ED FRENCH TOAST

"I'm so glad you came," Cindy's mother, Ms. Hawthorn, said as she led them up the stairs of her house. It was a nice place. Had the touches of money to it without being ostentatious. Rafferty had cooked in several places such as this, all for various reasons, very few of them good. But Cindy's mother didn't seem like a woman who would summon a demon for any reason, even as she unknowingly welcomed a former one in.

"Thank you for picking us up at the station," Helena said, pitching her voice low to match the tenor of Ms. Hawthorn's soft words.

The matriarch waved it off. "She's been in bed for ages. At first, we just let her rest, you know, after everything. Recover. But then she stopped getting up at all. She's barely eating unless I sit there and make her. I've never known her to be like this. She's always been such a go-getter. So driven. I am starting to get concerned." And that was evident from the fretting she did with her hands. Rafferty was pretty sure she hadn't drawn breath since they crossed the threshold.

"It's okay, Ms. Hawthorn. I know some tricks to get her going again," Helena said self-assuredly. Anyone else may have looked down their noses at such a bold statement, but Ms. Hawthorn seemed to take comfort from it.

They reached a landing, treading softly over beige carpet, wearing only socks. It struck Rafferty as odd to be required to remove shoes at the door, especially since they hadn't walked through mud or anything. Yet, he didn't question it; he only followed Helena's lead. She didn't seem to think it odd.

Past a banister that lined the hall, there were several doors, all closed. He guessed they were most likely the bedrooms of the family. Cindy's mother stopped at the one at the end, knocking twice before cracking the door open.

"Cindy, honey. You have visitors," she said with a soft, sweet voice.

She opened the door wider, and Helena moved past. Rafferty only followed when Ms. Hawthorn looked at him with expectation in her eyes. All of this felt awkward. He hated it. He didn't know Cindy. She wasn't his friend.

The inside of Cindy's room was dark and sleepy. He could make out a bed against the farthest wall and some other furniture only by the light coming from the open door, or rather coming from the slit since Cindy's mother shut it most of the way and retreated, giving them some privacy.

Helena didn't seem to have any trouble with the dimness, though it bothered him that his eyes weren't adjusting as fast as they used to. She went straight to Cindy's bed and sat down on the edge of it next to the lying form.

"Hey," she said with kindly warmth, and brushed at Cindy's hair.

"What are you doing here?" Cindy asked, her voice coming out small and heavy with sleep.

"We came to see you."

"My mom called you, didn't she?" she said bitterly.

"No, I came myself. I was always going to come see you," Helena said, continuing to brush Cindy's hair. It was how she would brush his own hair. He found watching her do that to someone else, even her longtime friend, maddening.

"What about your Winter Rose Ball event?" The other woman lifted her head a bit. "Has it already happened?"

"Yeah, it went well," Helena lied, or semi-lied, neatly stepping around the things that had not gone well immediately after the things that had. "I'm sorry I couldn't come sooner."

"What were you going to do, watch me wallow?" Cindy grumbled, laying her head back down. "I've fucked everything up. My career, my life. Did it all to myself."

Helena glanced up at Rafferty. The eerie feeling of her aura strengthened, and he shivered with it. He knew what she was tempted to do. He shook his head at her.

"Hey, Cin, would you like to get up? You hungry?" Helena asked, her aura pulling back. "We just had dessert on the train, but it's almost time for a late lunch."

"We?" Cindy lifted her head and looked straight at Rafferty. "Oh. I remember you."

He nodded his head to her in acknowledgment, only to realize she might not be able to see it in the dimness. "Hello."

"What are you hungry for?" Helena asked.

The form on the bed shrugged.

Rafferty felt something shift in the atmosphere in the room, as Helena kept stroking Cindy's hair. "How about Bless-ed French Toast in a cup?" she said, emphasizing the *ed* of the word. "All you have to do is say yes and it's yours."

She lay there, considering it a moment. "K," she finally said, her voice becoming stronger, livelier. "But I should probably get dressed or something."

"That's fine, we can go down and get started, and you can join us when you're ready," Helena said, getting up. "Besides, I got a world-class chef here. Maybe we can find a way to take it all up a notch."

Cindy looked to Rafferty, and he gave a small wave.

The former doctor finally sat up and grasped at her bed-mussed hair, running her fingers through it in a vain attempt to look presentable. "God, you should have said. I'm sorry you have to see me in such a mess."

"*My* apologies," Rafferty insisted as he backed out to the hall. Honestly, this sense of embarrassment was new for him.

Helena said something, but he didn't quite hear it before Cindy added, "Breakfast for lunch," with a chuckle.

"Meal of champions," Helena agreed, just as she appeared to fill the crack in the door.

"Thank you for coming," Cindy added.

Helena turned around and gave her friend a gentle smile, her fingers resting on the doorknob. "It's going to be okay, Cin. I promise. I'm here to fix everything."

"Hel," Cindy grumbled. "You can't just fix this. No one can just fix this."

Standing there, Helena clearly didn't know what to say to that, so Rafferty interceded, speaking over her shoulder so as not to invade the woman's privacy again. "We'll see you downstairs."

"Thank you," Cindy called.

Rafferty could see that it was hard for Helena to leave her friend, even for that short amount of time. With a small bit of encouragement from him, they shut the door firmly behind them and retreated down the hall to the stairs. They didn't say much as they went down to the kitchen, Rafferty again following Helena because she seemed to know her way around this place.

Cindy's mother greeted them in the kitchen, where she was nursing a cup of coffee and staring off before they walked in.

"She's going to come down, and we're going to make French Toast if that's alright," Helena said.

The woman popped up from the stool that was pulled up to the kitchen island. "Oh, yes of course. Let me pull the griddle out for you."

"Oh no, that won't be necessary," Helena said, extending her hand to stop Ms. Hawthorn. "We're actually going to do it in coffee mugs."

"Coffee mugs?" Cindy's mother repeated, blinking at the suggestion.

"Yeah, it was our favorite dorm meal," Helena explained as she knelt in front of her bag, unzipping it. "I thought something like that would help ground her, you know, reconnect?"

"Oh, that's really clever," Ms. Hawthorne said, pressing her fingers to cheek as she shook her head at herself. "I forgot you two met in college. It seems like you've been friends forever."

"Cindy was my roommate all four years of undergrad, not after," Helena said, directing the explanation to Rafferty.

He knew the words, but felt like he was missing the context, or rather the modern context, of them.

Ms. Hawthorn nodded, "I know that's right, but it doesn't make sense to me. How can I be a mother of a grown woman." She chuckled and redirected to pull down a set of over large mugs. "Would these work?"

"Oh wow, yes!" Helena said, surprised at the size of the mugs, which to Rafferty seemed like they were more akin to soup bowls.

"Do you need anything else?" the anxious mother asked. "We have bread and cinnamon. Syrup is in the fridge, and eggs. If you need anything I can run to the store."

"No, no, all that's great, it's all we need. We'll take care of the rest," Helena said, then she set a hand on the poor woman's shoulder. "Is there anything you want to go do? We'll take care of her."

There it was again. The *eerie* feeling.

Only this time Rafferty knew what it was. Her demonic aura was bleeding through her human disguise, but Helena didn't seem to be aware of it. She was instinctively trying to influence the human before her. The little flashes of hungry gold popped in her blue eyes.

Cindy's mother creased her eyebrows. Clearly, it was affecting her too, or maybe she had seen Helena's eyes flashing.

Ms. Hawthorn backed away to press her fingers against the spot on her forehead some humans would call her third eye. To Rafferty, it was a sure sign she thought something else was affecting her sight. "I do need a break," the older woman conceded. Her faux cheerful worry she had been using to mask her weariness dropped away.

"Yes, go ahead and take one. Everything is going to be better after this," Helena pressed, a little too hard.

A shiver ran through Ms. Hawthorn; she flinched and backed away a few unsure steps. Her desire to escape the uncanny feeling warred with her understanding that this was her daughter's friend, a person who should be safe. Someone she had known for years. She had no obvious, sensible reason to be unsettled by her or to mistrust her.

Helena's eyebrows pinched a little at the mother's odd shift. Still intent on her mission, Helena smiled encouragingly. "Go ahead and run some errands or whatever you need. We'll take care of Cindy now."

"No. No, that's alright. I'm just going to finish my coffee," Ms. Hawthorn said, reassuming her seat, before clearing her throat and dragging her eyes from Helena to the open paper on the counter before her.

It was Helena's turn to shift uncomfortably, glancing at Rafferty, but not knowing what else to say or do. He thought about leaning in and telling her to pull back on her aura, that it was causing the strange behavior in their hostess, but it lessened on its own anyway. With Ms. Hawthorn doing such a poor job pretending not to watch them, he thought it best not to draw more attention or act any more suspiciously.

"What do you need me to do?" he asked.

"Um, can you ... get out some bread?" Helena asked, her worried gaze stuck on the brewing problem at the end of the counter.

He turned to what looked like, and turned out to in fact be, a bread box. Pulling out the plastic-wrapped loaf inside, he brought it to the island where Helena met him with a cutting board and a serrated bread knife.

"Um." Helena shook her head, refocusing. "Chop up some of those slices into cubes and fill each of these cups." She turned and went to the refrigerator. With a bit of clatter, she gathered up the aforementioned eggs, butter, and a small jug of milk from the door. "Okay, put like a tablespoon of butter at the bottom of the cup then put the bread cubes in."

Rafferty paused mid-slice, having filled the first two cups with the bread cubes already.

"Shoot, sorry," Helena said, realizing. "I should have told you that part first. That's on me." She shot a nervous glance toward Ms. Hawthorn, who still hadn't moved or even turned the page of her newspaper. Every muscle in the woman's body exuded tension and anxiety.

"It's not a problem," Rafferty replied with the same detached voice he would use working under any chef, the kind that said everything was fine and under control. He simply pulled down a sheet of paper towel from a standing roll nearby and dumped the bread cubes onto it. He then eyeballed the butter to cut a tablespoon off, only to realize that on the paper, the producers of this butter had already measured out and marked how much was a tablespoon along the whole length of the paper. If that had been there before, he hadn't noticed it. The tiny innovation made him smirk.

"Okay, then when you got that, here's another bowl," Helena continued, setting a small mixing bowl next to him. "Mix together the eggs, milk, and cinnamon, then pour over the cubed bread, I mean once you put them back in the cups. Pop each cup into the microwave at a time and cook it for about two to three minutes each. Maybe three since they're bigger, and then we got it. You got it?"

"How many eggs to milk?" Rafferty asked as he replaced the bread into the now buttered cups.

"Oh! Uh," Helena paused as she was pulling a book out of her backpack. "One egg per cup, three tablespoons of milk per egg. Cinnamon to taste. Then we add syrup to it after or more butter if you're Cindy. I did whipped cream once, but, I mean, we had so much sugar on the train, I'm good."

She set the book down on the counter and let it fall open. Only then did Rafferty recognize it. It explained the same rambling nervousness Helena seemed to be displaying. She was going to mix up one of her grandmother's hedgewitch potions, written in the margins.

Ms. Hawthorn's eyes locked onto it with round alarm. "What is that?"

"Oh." Helena put her hand over the pages protectively. "Just my grandmother's old church cookbook." Belatedly, she lifted up the opened book in both hands to show the printed cover with its pencil drawing of a church and the year below it behind roughed-up, once-clear-now-yellowish plastic sheets. The title *Trinity Church* graced the very top.

Ms. Hawthorn's eyes narrowed as she studied the worn page, but there simply wasn't anything obviously wrong with it. Still, Rafferty waited, poised to step between the two women if one decided to irrationally attack the other.

To his relief, Ms. Hawthorn sat back down. She rubbed a hand to her temples. "I apologize," she said, closing her eyes. "I haven't been getting very good sleep lately. Every time I lay down, I keep thinking about what she almost did."

Dammit, Rafferty thought. He recognized what was happening here. Another effect of the demonic aura. The longer someone was exposed to it, and the weaker willed they were, the more they spilled their secrets. Whether the demon wanted to know them or not.

Ms. Hawthorn was no exception. "I blame myself. I wanted her to succeed so much. She had such a bright future ahead of her, and now it's all just ... gone!" She threw her hands into the air as if it were Cindy's career turning to confetti.

"Don't worry," Helena assured her, setting the book down to leaf through. "She'll bounce back, and everything will be fine. I promise."

Ms. Hawthorn's lips tightened. "Don't do that. Don't make promises we both know are impossible to keep without some sort of miracle."

Helena's aura strengthened again, invisible but stronger. "Well, I intend to do everything I can." She found whatever she was looking for in the book. Then she went back to her backpack, which put her just out of Ms. Hawthorn's sight.

"What are you doing with that?" he whispered quietly as she sank next to him to reach it.

She looked up, a little guilty. "What?" she mouthed. Then her lip pouted a little as she drew her mouth in tight.

"Helena—" he tried to warn, only to be cut off as he violently shivered. His mouth tasted of pennies and irrational rage flooded through him. Her aura grew even stronger, enhancing his fears. The urge to fight flooded his mind with visions of grabbing the knife and stabbing flesh over and over. Gripping the edge of the counter, his eyes widened as Helena removed three metal canisters from her pack that he knew for a fact had not existed moments before.

Helena remained oblivious to everything as she popped one open with a satisfied grin.

"What the hell are you doing!?" Cindy's mother screeched at the top of her lungs, startling Helena. Bits of dried leaves leapt out of the canister at her flinch. She also dropped the third canister, which rolled across the floor toward the door.

With fierce enraged eyes, Ms. Hawthorn stood at the end of the counter, her hands gripping it with white-knuckle intensity like he was. If it hadn't been made of granite, Rafferty could imagine her cracking it with that amount of force. She was also wobbling forward and back on her feet, wrestling between her fight and flight responses.

"It's tea!" Helena said, truly confused, holding out the open end of the canister to show. "It's just tea. I ... I got the mix from my grandmother's recipe book, to help with Cindy's depression. It's just tea, I swear!"

"It's just tea," Rafferty repeated, his voice steady and strong with reasonable assuredness that he had often used on his summoners who went into an utter panic at his presence. While he did not have the same demonic juice in it to influence his mark, it steadied Ms. Hawthorn all the same. Maybe it was because he understood what was happening that allowed him to maintain control.

"It's just tea?" she also repeated, clearly not believing it, looking to Rafferty, the only other human in the room, even if she didn't realize it, for confirmation.

He nodded, his centuries of practice in the art of lying helping him not to oversell it.

"Is the Bless-ed French Toast ready?" Cindy called from the hall just as she entered the kitchen, actually dressed, tying her unwashed hair up into a ponytail. She stopped and picked up the canister that rolled away. Then she looked up at the scene in the kitchen. "What the heck is going on?"

Chapter 18

MOTHER OF VENGEANCE

"Uh, nothing," Helena tried to cover. She came over to Cindy holding the open canister to show her friend. "I just brought you some tea. I got the recipe from my grandmother's old church cookbook. I thought it would be fun to try."

"She can't drink something like this," Ms. Hawthorn shouted. She crossed the space to place herself between them.

"Mom?" Cindy protested as she was jostled backward.

"There might be a bad interaction with the medicine you're now on!" she said, while staring Helena down, who also retreated before the other woman's fierceness.

The doctor rolled her eyes. "I'm not taking what Dr. Mellon prescribed." Then to Helena over her mother's shoulder, she added, "It's fine."

"Why not?!" her mother demanded, whirling on her daughter, whose jaw stiffened in response. Helena took the opportunity to scurry back to her bag, stowing away the offending tea canister.

"Because the side effects are going to make me lethargic and foggy-brained," Cindy countered. "I *actually* read the study on it."

"Dammit, Cindy!" Her mother slapped her hand hard on the cabinet by the door. "What are you doing with your life? Are you giving up? You need to *fight* this!"

"There's nothing to fight, *Mother*," Cindy shot back.

"This is your fault!" Ms. Hawthorn said, whirling back to point at Helena with the accusatory muster of an Inquisitor.

"Don't you dare bring Helena into this!" Cindy shot back.

Rafferty could feel it. The energy Helena was pumping out now was reaching a boiling point. Now, it was a defensive response as Helena panicked. She didn't even seem to realize she was doing it, but the more she desired to fix things, the worse it was getting.

It egged on Ms. Hawthorn's tirade. "You listened to her about taking the job in that city hospital instead of joining your father's and aunt's practice. You would have been successful there! They needed your help. We could have been here to support you and take care of you—"

"I'm not a fucking child!" Cindy screamed back.

"You're acting like a fucking child, refusing to take your medicine, having a tantrum in your room, getting waited on hand and foot—"

Cindy interrupted her mom, throwing her hands up in the air and spinning around. "You know what? I don't have to take this, do I? I keep forgetting that I am a grown-ass adult, and I can just LEAVE!"

The shouting continued into the hall, and her mother started to go after her, but at the last moment, she spun on Helena. "Get the hell out of my house, you monster!"

"Ms. Hawthorn, I—"

"And take this sinful stuff with you!" Ms. Hawthorn continued, picking up the second canister from the counter island to throw it at her.

Rafferty stepped between them as she did, blocking the too-light-to-do-any-harm object from hitting Helena in the face. Instead, it hit his shoulder, and the lid burst off, cascading the dried tea leaves everywhere.

"GET OUT OF MY HOUSE!"

More objects came flying, whatever Ms. Hawthorn could get her hands on, including her half-empty coffee cup. The innate desire to fight the thing that terrified her had possessed her; she was all animal brain and no higher thinking.

"Go, go!" Rafferty bodily pushed Helena toward the hallway, the way Cindy had gone. He knew the only thing they could do was run.

"My backpack!" Helena tried to go back for it, but he shoved her forward.

"I'll get it! Let's just get out of here."

"Get out of here!" Ms. Hawthorn continued, a panting, red-faced mess. He ducked under a crock of flour, the white stuff going everywhere and covering half his back and shoulder as he scooped up the backpack by the handles.

Helena hadn't retreated far, waiting for him as he exited the kitchen, her hand outstretched to him. "Are you hurt?"

"No," he laughed, as more things crashed behind them. Maybe he was going mad since he was starting to find this funny.

"What's wrong with her?" she asked as she patted at his flour-covered shoulders, trying to brush it off, even as he was still determined to get her to go out the front door to safety.

"I'll explain later. We need to get out of here. Now," he urged.

"Wait, what about Cindy?" Helena countered, moving toward the stairs, but Cindy was already coming down carrying a duffle bag and talking into a mobile phone.

"Dad, you need to come home," Cindy said into it. She pulled on a coat from the rack at the bottom of the stairs and then sat on the lowest step to pull on shoes. "Because she's lost her damn mind! And I'm leaving."

In the kitchen, Ms. Hawthorn had stopped throwing things. From what little he could see, she had collapsed into screaming wails onto the floor, as if her heart had shattered into a million pieces.

Cindy stood up and gestured for Helena and Rafferty to follow her. "I didn't do a damn thing."

She listened for another moment and then hung up her phone.

"I'm done listening to him, too," she snapped, then seized her purse. "Come on, let's get out of here."

"Cindy, I'm so sorry. I don't understand what I did wrong," Helena said as she grabbed her suitcase handle while Rafferty seized his own.

"Nothing. You're ten years too late to have done anything wrong, just get me out of here," Cindy growled, and they all went out the door into the cold, sharp air.

Cindy took a deep breath of it as the door shut hard behind them. "You've rescued me not a minute too soon."

Then the door opened again. "You ungrateful child, where are you going?!" Cindy's mother shouted. Her arms were wrapped around herself, and her face was the shattered ruin of the simple, well-off housewife she had been only an hour or so before. "Where the hell are you going?!"

"Out of this house!" Cindy yelled back, spinning on her heels to march down the street.

"How dare you speak to me like—"

Then Cindy spun back. "I'll be right there. Can you take this for me?" she asked, passing the duffle bag to Helena before charging back. She pushed her parent back inside and shut them both in.

Standing on the cold sidewalk, they could hear the shouting continue albeit more muffled. Helena looked to Rafferty, her face drenched in guilt and worried.

"What did I do?" she asked hopelessly.

He worked his lips. "This happens when mortals are confronted by too much of something otherworldly. It triggers their instincts. They will fight or they will flee. Some freeze."

"But I was just making tea?" Helena defended weakly. She understood what she had done but was struggling to accept it. "She went from zero to a hundred and sixty so fast?"

"You didn't just make tea, and you know it." He could feel his own hostility rising toward her. Helena took a half step back, cowering away from the sharpness in his voice.

"I was just ... I was just trying to help," she said, and a tear dripped down her cheek.

"Dammit," he muttered under his breath. Then took a deep one in before blowing it out. Again, he had the urge to eat her bad memory of this incident. It was also occurring to him that maybe he did that a little too often in his previous existence, and he wasn't as socially suave as he thought he was. Pushing that personal analysis away, all he *could* do was wrap his arms around her, all while being careful to keep his own instincts under control.

"Just take a deep breath and let go of the need to help right now," he said.

Helena's aura flared a moment, even stronger, but then she nodded against his chest and took a breath in. When she exhaled the aura retreated, giving him some relief at last.

"Do you feel what you did?" he asked.

"Yeah," she said thoughtfully. "Yeah, I do. Dammit. I did make it worse, didn't I?"

"You've just got to be aware," he agreed.

She's just Helena, he repeated to himself, trying to quiet all the other doubts plaguing him.

"I'm so sorry. I was trying to help," she said into his shoulder.

"I know. But you can't force things," he whispered into her hair. He had a stray thought that they should just leave, get away from the situation entirely, without Cindy. Cindy's problems were not Helena's. She had enough to deal with, and he, if he was honest, didn't like sharing Helena's attention. This was ... unnecessary and superfluous to Helena's goals.

She doesn't need her needy friend anymore, he thought. *She has me!*

But before he could figure out why that didn't sound quite right, the front door opened and closed so hard it echoed down the street.

Cindy stood there, her face red, her eyes on fire for the first time since they arrived. "Alright, let's go," she declared. "Anywhere is better than here. We can get a taxi or something down the street. Otherwise, she might come out and keep this up."

"And there are too many eyes," Rafferty added. He couldn't see them, but he could feel them coming from the neighboring houses.

"Too much of everything," Cindy said, "I should never have come home."

"Well, do you want to go to a cooking contest?" Helena asked.

Cindy raised an eyebrow, then simply said, "Sure."

Chapter 19

FOOD BATTLE THE FIRST

"Okay, this is a little bit more than 'underground,'" Cindy said as they entered the high school gymnasium, dragging their suitcases and backpacks with them. "I was picturing an impromptu rave-like thing in a basement, or something."

Helena nodded. "I think that's where they started, but things like this, they have a way of growing quickly."

The doors had been standing open, welcoming any and all into the vast room. The bleachers in the gym were fairly full of people all chattering away which made the gym space thrum with sound. Tables were everywhere, covered in white tablecloths with cooking equipment, including toaster ovens and hot pads, still in the process of being set up. On the furthest table were several bins and plates of unprepared ingredients as well as three mobile refrigerators lining the wall and even an ice cream maker. Amongst all this were several people in different colors of culinary wear, ranging from perfectly correct to incredibly ironic, all with numbers pinned to their backs. They were talking, laughing, sharpening knives, or reviewing notes.

"Wow." Helena breathed as she took it all in. "Okay, this is a thing that has legs." She laughed as she swept her gaze over the organized chaos.

To Rafferty, a sense of coming home washed through him. This was familiar, no matter what era he was in. It was the feeling he most looked forward to whenever he had been summoned. It was why he was almost unsurprised when his eyes locked with Eleanor's.

They both held that stare for too long before Eleanor sighed and made her way from the middle of the room to the gaping trio near the door.

"So you came to check it out?" she asked, offering her hand to him to shake.

"A long way to go for a cooking competition," Helena noted, and Eleanor's smiling eyes tightened again.

"We're near one of the bigger culinary schools in the area, so you know, it makes sense," she countered. "And who are you?"

"Oh, hi!" Helena said, offering her own hand with her smile. "I'm Helena."

Eleanor didn't take the hand, only looked at it like it offended her. "Yeah, I know," she said instead.

"This is my girlfriend," Rafferty said, covering the awkwardness.

The other chef arched an eyebrow. "Girlfriend?"

"Yes," he said. It felt good to actually claim that, and his ears burned a little at the admission.

You'd think I was a youth again, he thought.

The other chef sniffed again, not finding his answer as amusing as he did. "Fine, whatever," she muttered under her breath, then crossed her arms. "So you jumping in?" She addressed the question to him.

"Jumping ... in?" he repeated, trying to parse what she meant.

"The registration table is over there," Eleanor said, gesturing to a folding table with a green tablecloth tucked into a corner of the gym. Two people sat at it, talking to each other with a bunch of clipboards and numbers sitting on the surface before them waiting to be used. "I hear there are still a couple of slots left."

"Can he just do that?" Helena asked, glancing over her shoulder at the table.

Eleanor sneered. "Yeah, why not? You just have to throw in for the prize money: $100 participation fee."

"I have ... I have no equipment," Rafferty said, directing his gaze poignantly toward the other competitors.

"That's fine. Everything you need is provided. People just like to bring their own equipment if they can. Because of the gym, the challenge is all based on things that can be made in a toaster oven."

"We were just here to check it out, but if you want to, go ahead, Rafferty," Helena encouraged, setting a hand on his arm. He could tell she wanted him to do it.

"I'll find us good seats," Cindy said, offering her hand to take his rolling suitcase for him.

He relented, and Eleanor nodded with satisfaction before turning around and heading back to her prep area. "Good luck."

He followed Helena over to the registration table where she picked up a clipboard. "Hi, he's participating," she said to the two figures waiting there.

They broke off their conversation with an air of annoyance, but one of them pointed to the surface of the clipboards. "Fill this out. The fee is $100."

"Got it," Helena said, already reaching around for her backpack.

Rafferty stopped her with a hand. "What are you doing?" he asked softly, trying to cheat away from the two contest officials, who were now more interested in the potential drama before them.

"I got you covered. Don't worry," Helena said, then she winked. "You can make it up to me later."

His mind went to exactly what she was implying, which made him blush, and then he chuckled when he realized he was blushing. She grinned, very pleased with herself as she paid the fee. They needed to laugh after the events at Cindy's house, especially since Cindy had made it very clear she didn't want to think let alone talk about it. Full stop.

Even when Helena offered to abort this plan, Cindy insisted that they go anyway. And so here he was, signing up for this very competition. Not the strangest turn of events in his life, but he wondered if he had had days like this in his first life or this was just how things were in this time.

With the fee paid, it only left the clipboard, which he did mostly himself, only pausing when he got to the line asking for his culinary school.

"I don't ..." he said to Helena, indicating the line with a finger to finish the sentence.

"Hey, is it necessary for him to be from a school?" she asked the officials.

"No, you can leave it blank. The bare minimum of what we need is his name, email address, and the fee. The challenge is baking something involving a toaster oven. You can do anything else you want, but something in the dish has to come out of a toaster oven," one of the officials said. "Oh, also since you're the odd number, you get a pass on the first round. We're cutting off applicants now, so you can just sit in the stands and watch. Congrats."

They went to join Cindy, who had indeed found a spot on the less crowded side of the gym, mostly near the front, but with enough space to tuck their suitcases between two bleachers. Suitcases they didn't need now that they weren't staying.

"Well, I guess that's lucky," Helena said as she settled down next to her friend.

"I do not think so," Rafferty murmured as they sat down.

"What happened?" Cindy asked, tucking her mobile phone away when they approached.

"He's in, but he's the odd man out, so he gets a pass on the first round," Helena reported to them. "Though I think he's disappointed; he wanted to cook." She cast teasing eyes at him.

"How is this a contest if I get a pass?" he responded, following her lead and playing up his disappointment to comical levels. "I tell you it is a fraud!"

The two women giggled.

Satisfied with his joke, he cast his gaze over the contestants. After several moments of observation, he realized he could beat most of them with skill alone. And yet, in his mind, each of these cooks were far worthier to be called such than he was.

I've got to stop thinking like that. I won. This is my reward. I get another chance, he told himself.

Still, it was fascinating to watch the process. The drama before them played out as some dishes succeeded, while others were utter disasters and everything in between. Once the plating was finished, they were taken to another official who numbered the plate the same as the contestant before setting it on a table to wait for tasting. Eventually a timer went off, and all the remaining contestants, no matter where they were in the process or whether they started over again or not, had to either turn in their dishes or forfeit. Two chose the second option, yielding their rounds.

"Looks like Eleanor is moving on," Cindy said, nodding over at the whiteboard they had rolled in to keep track of the brackets.

Sure enough, Eleanor's name moved to the next rung.

"A lot of desserts," Helena noted.

"Well, yeah, it's hard to make much else in a toaster oven," Cindy said.

"No, it isn't," Rafferty countered, as he studied the dishes listed on the board.

"He's right. Eleanor made a lasagna," Helena pointed out.

"That's not that spectacular," Cindy sniffed. "At least according to my mother." She folded her arms as she said the last. Rafferty got the impression she was stewing about the fight she had just had.

Helena eyed her friend, then gestured over to the table. "She even plated it like she's in a restaurant."

"Looks are as important as taste," Rafferty added.

"Sure, but we're not even getting *that*. I can barely see it from here and they're definitely not letting us try it," Helena noted. "There should be an emcee or something. Or let the judges talk about each dish."

"For twelve dishes, that would take forever," Cindy commented.

"Well, okay, but highlights then? The unusual or the interesting, with like a film camera or something. Have it up on a big screen," Helena said, gesturing with her hands as if that would make the screen in her mind appear along the wall. With enough power it would, but Rafferty was relieved that she seemed to finally take the incident at Cindy's parents' house to heart. On reflection, he realized that there had been a strong degree of unspoken negative feeling already there, like methane gas building up in a cellar. Helena's spark set it off.

"I don't think they have the money for that," Cindy retorted, her sharper than necessary words pulling his attention away from his thoughts to the present. This would get tiresome if she kept being angry at everything that had nothing to do with her mother.

"ALL THOSE PROGRESSING TO THE NEXT ROUND, YOU ARE NOW FREE TO SET UP YOUR PREP," an announcer declared over the gym speakers.

Helena pointed at the ancient-looking thing in the corner. "See, they have that, they could be doing a lot more with all this."

Rafferty only grunted as he stood and shed his coat, handing it to Helena, who smiled as she took it. "Go kick their butts," she said, wrinkling her nose in that cute way.

Their fingers touched briefly. Before he could think better about it, his other arm went behind his back, his feet came together, and he bowed over her hand with all of the gallantness he would have been expected to show to a high lady who had come down to compliment one of his dishes. Maybe too gallant as he would not have been allowed to touch her hand like this, but historical accuracy be damned.

Now, *her* cheeks burned pink, and her eyes flashed gold, marring the picture. He let go of her a little too quickly. Their fingers snapped. He corrected with another apologetic smile, which she returned, probably assuming the action had come from nerves, and then he turned to walk straight to choose a table.

Before he could decide, Eleanor appeared at his side. "You ready?" she asked before he could swivel his head very far.

"I ..." he hesitated, still trying to look around.

"There's no point in trying to pick the best station. There isn't one," she said, crossing her arms, which wasn't smooth as she held a long piece of cloth in one of her hands. She aborted the habit and thrust it toward him instead. "Here, I have a spare apron."

"Oh. Thank you—" he said so belatedly that she didn't even let him finish.

"Good luck." Then she turned her back to him to go back to her station.

Rafferty's cheeks burned as he watched her walk to a table right next to where he stood, resolutely not looking at him. The apron was of heavy-duty material with leather straps that went over his neck and tied in the back. Sturdier than he would think necessary for an apron, but it felt like armor as he donned it. Then he fastened the number they had given him with his copy of his registration, fixing it to the large pocket in front with the provided tiny safety pin.

"You claiming this one?" An official gestured to the table set up nearest him.

"Uh, yes," Rafferty said.

"Okay, once you claim a station, you can't switch until the round is over," the official said even as they walked away, then added as he addressed everyone nearby. "We're breaking down the empties and removing them, so make sure you're satisfied with what you have."

That forced Rafferty to do what he had always done when he entered a kitchen, put aside everything else that was happening in his life and just focus on the cooking.

A wicked grin split his face as a shiver of delight coursed through him.

"Time to cook."

Chapter 20

BATTLE COMMENCED

"How are you doing?" Helena asked, thirty minutes later. Her presence wasn't forbidden by the officials apparently, but Rafferty wished she would go sit down and let him concentrate.

"Fine," he answered.

"So it's a pot pie?" she asked, not getting any of the hints, leaning on the other side of the table and watching as he laid the crust he had made over the top of one of the provided ramekins. It was large enough to make one serving per person.

"It was something I could make with the time available and the ingredients that remained." He glanced back at the ingredients table at the far end. "There is even more of a strategy to this thing. You have to make food out of what is provided, and while they have provided quite a lot, there is still something you are going to want that isn't here. It forces you to think."

Helena noted what he referred to. "Why didn't you use the pre-made crusts? I see someone else doing that," she asked.

"Pre-made ... crust?" he asked, his lip curling in contempt at the concept. "How ... how is it *pre*-made?"

Helena laughed merrily. "I know you've been to hell and back, but you have been cooking up here over the last few decades right?" She then boldly leaned over to the other competitor next to them, laying a hand on a thin, red, opened box. "Are you done with this? Can I borrow it?" she asked.

"Uh, sure," she said, then went back to working on her own creation.

Leaning back, Helena held out the box to him as he set the last cutout of a leaf in dough on his decorated savory pie and wiped his hands before taking it.

What little surface of the box there was showed an image of a pie and declared exactly what she said, two pre-made pie doughs. "Huh" was all he could say to it.

"You've seriously never used anything pre-made? It's always been from scratch?" she asked, and again, he struggled to understand the question.

"Everything I've ever made has been with my own two hands," he said, turning the box over.

"And a little personal magic?" Helena quipped, giving him a cheeky wink when he looked at her, alarmed.

"Very little," he said dryly. "Only what I absolutely needed. Or what my master—"

"Client," she corrected.

He blinked, realizing her word coding was safer in this time period. "Client required." He regarded the red box again, before dropping it into the shared trash bin between him and the table behind him. "While I can recognize the convenience of such ... pre-made fare, I don't see how one could use something like this and not be considered cheating? It is the work of someone else, not themselves?"

"Time constraints," Eleanor said, coming up beside him, wiping her hands on a towel. "Don't get me wrong, I'm not disagreeing with you, but this challenge is using toaster ovens and so many people have done really clever things with pre-made stuff that it was decided not to handicap them."

"I could see how this would have a public appeal, too, showing that good food can be made out of anything," Helena added.

Eleanor nodded at her, then nodded at Rafferty's potpie. "You better get that in, you only got thirty minutes left. That's cutting it really close, don't you think?"

Rafferty slid in his own pie into the heated oven and shut the door firmly. "I didn't realize that I could have used pre-made," he said.

"Don't worry. Yours will still taste better," Helena assured him, giving him an encouraging smile.

"Rafferty Lares, you are going on to the next round," one of the officials stated, matter-of-factly. The cook he had been competing with swiped the beanie off her head with a curse. She spun once in a circle, then thrust her hand out to him to shake. It was clearly a formality. He could tell her anger was directed at herself, not him. There was a time he had done that dance himself. As soon as they performed the two-second ritual, she was already off.

"You have fifteen minutes to go to the bathroom and prepare anything you need to for the final challenge. I would go claim your table, too, and let the official know so they don't break it down on you," the official advised, and Rafferty took it to heart.

More than half the room was already in a state of "breakdown" as they kept calling it. Much of the audience had left, too, as their favored participant failed to advance, leaving half the bleachers empty. He moved back to reclaim his station, only to stop in his tracks as he spied a familiar pair of humans talking to an official near the end of the bleachers.

"Agents Sophia and Archon are here," Helena said softly, coming up beside him with worry painting her face.

"Yeah," he acknowledged as he kept his gaze on them.

"Who?" Cindy asked, joining them, following his directed gaze.

"The agents there," Helena answered. "They are looking for the demon that ... ate Yosef."

Cindy mouthed the word "oh," apparently already knowing most of that story, then followed their gaze. "Does that mean ... *it*'s here?"

"Not necessarily," Rafferty said. "They could be keeping an eye on ..."

More people walked by so Helena slid her hand down from Cindy's shoulder to take her friend's hand. "I'll tell you later. Just trust me. We're safe. From it at least."

To Rafferty's surprise, Cindy accepted that with a curt nod.

It was only then that he realized his delay had allowed the officials to start breaking down his chosen station.

"Wait, wait. I'm still working here," he said, bursting his way past the two women to slap his hand on the table. It didn't stop the official who had already disconnected the toaster oven and coiled the cord beside it, fastening a twisty tie to keep it together.

"Go claim one of the other tables, I'm not setting this back up," he growled, and continued with his breakdown.

Rafferty thought about fighting it, but the ire wafting off this official held his tongue. He was right, there were other stations that no one had touched yet and what difference did it really make? With the agents here, the last thing he wanted was to cause a commotion and attract attention.

"What happened?" Helena asked as he shifted to his new table.

"They broke down my setup already," he explained, wiping his hands down his slightly floured apron to disperse his own irritation.

Helena's eyebrows shot up. "What? That's bullshit. What kind of way is that to run an event like this? I mean, this whole thing is a mess."

"It's fine. They are all supposed to be the same. I need to decide what to do next and not worry about it," he said, fixing his sleeve, which had unrolled itself, while letting his gaze wash over the ingredients table. An itch at the corner of his eye made him look toward Helena, who was smirking at him.

"What?" he asked.

"You look so damn sexy right now, you know that?" she said, her smirk evolving into a grin. She brushed a bit at his upper lip, removing some of the flour that had gotten stuck to his bristles. He was actually growing facial hair. "I'm going to need to show you how to shave."

"You don't know how to shave? How old are you?" Cindy asked, while he brushed his own face, realizing she was right, he was growing a beard.

"I know how to shave," he countered, getting annoyed. This was a distraction, and he needed to focus.

"Cake," he said, confidently. "There isn't really much left that can be made with the remaining ingredients." Only to stop as he saw the other contestant who wasn't Eleanor claim the last six eggs from the tray.

"Oh, come on," Helena said, catching it at the same time he did. "That's hardly fair!"

"It's a competition," Cindy argued. "It's part of the challenge."

"Thank you, little Ms. Devil's Advocate," his girlfriend and defender groused.

"It's fine," he said. "I can make it without eggs." And went over to claim his other ingredients.

He wasn't surprised that when he returned, he found Agent Archon and Agent Sophia waiting for him at his table.

"Mr. Lares," Agent Archon said, her eyebrows conveying a healthy amount of suspicion. "Imagine meeting you here."

"Hi, Mr. Lares," Agent Sophia said with that gently sympathetic smile. "Are you doing any better?"

"Uh, yes, madame," he said without thinking, then realized what he had said, then wondered if it would make him more suspicious or less. He had never called someone madame ... at least not in this century. Or on this continent.

Agent Archon's eyes narrowed at him, but he held his nerve, and his chin steady, his eyes looking at her without actually meeting her gaze. "Do you still believe you're a demon?" she asked.

Now he couldn't help but meet that piercing gaze.

It seemed to be enough of an answer for her.

"Do you mind if I ask what you are doing here instead of staying in the hotel where we told you to stay?" Agent Archon asked next.

"Competing in a cooking contest," he answered. It was the truth after all.

"Have you seen the demon Vassago around here?" Agent Sophia asked softly, taking a small step forward even though there was no one around near enough to overhear. "Has he been stalking you or haunting you or anything?"

"He's not a ghost, for Heaven's sake," Agent Archon muttered at her partner, before turning back to him, bracing her fist on his table. "I hope you haven't done something unadvisable, like make a deal with Vassago or something? This is a strange way to get started in the culinary industry. A cooking competition."

"Looks fun though," Agent Sophia piped in, grinning at the board. "I love cooking shows. I would watch the heck out of something like this."

"Vassago has nothing to do with me being here," Rafferty said, meeting Agent Archon's eye. "If anyone does, it's Helena, my girlfriend." He nodded over at where she sat with Cindy, looking worried as they watched him talk to the agents.

Agent Archon narrowed her eyes a little more, studying for cracks in his steely mask.

Then she straightened. "We'll leave you to your business, Mr. Lares," she said, stabbing her hands into the pockets of her coat as she nudged Agent Sophia in the shoulder to head toward the doors.

Agent Sophia gave an apologetic smile and nod as she followed. "Good luck with the final round."

He warily watched them go. "If they would just kill me, this would all be so much easier," he muttered.

"Forty-five minutes left in the round," the official declared over the speaker, and Rafferty focused on his work.

His hands flew as he opened the condensed milk and measured out what he needed, adding it to his dry ingredients, chasing it with his wets, including adding the apple cider vinegar at the end. Mixing it well, he felt confident in his creation, eyeing the available fruits to garnish with, or maybe even turn into a glaze.

And then he opened his toaster oven.

Cold.

"Crap," he muttered, and dropped to his knees to check that the cord was plugged in. It was and when he quickly traced his fingers over the power strip they were all plugged into, he confirmed the strip was on and the other cooks all had power. "This would never happen with fire."

He unplugged, gathering the cord up with the broken machine and spun to one of the tables that were still waiting to be broken down.

"What do you think you're doing?" a gruff, familiar voice intoned over his shoulder as he went to grab the hopefully working machine.

Rafferty nearly jumped out of his skin as he turned to meet the swirling whirlpool of black ink eyes of Vassago. The demon in human form grinned wide, his teeth looking normal at first glance, but too sharp the longer you looked.

He also was wearing one of those green shirts the other officials were wearing.

"My toaster oven is broken," Rafferty stated, the words falling out of him in a small voice, like a boy knowing he'd been caught and was in trouble, not because he had done something wrong, but because the bully had caught him. He could feel Vassago's aura washing over him, emphasizing the fear and self-doubt that always lived in the background. When he had been a demon, he learned how to fight back against it, but he had never felt more fragile or mortal than he did at that moment.

"No," Vassago said, seizing the machine from his hands. "No substitutions. You have to use what you have."

"It's broken," Rafferty repeated, knowing it would do little good.

"What's going on?" Helena demanded, suddenly appearing at his side, her fists planted on her hips, ready for a fight. The feeling abated some. Was Vassago using his aura to influence him? That wasn't quite a violation of their agreement. A negative aura spread out from the one producing it, and the longer a demon was in creation the harder it was to suppress.

Realizing that, Rafferty steeled himself against it. "My toaster oven is broken. I'm trying to swap it out," Rafferty said to Helena, willing her to be careful. Oldest trick in the book, get the target to fear that the demon had violated the agreement, so they violated it themselves.

Helena flinched as the demon's aura washed over her, but she furrowed her eyebrows and wrinkled her nose. "Are you one of the judges?"

She didn't seem to recognize Vassago, but he was unsettling her. The pinch in her brow conveyed that she didn't know why. Since she had only met the demon a couple of brief times and under a great deal of duress, Rafferty didn't blame her.

Vassago gave Helena a small leer as he said, "The rules state that he has to use the equipment he was assigned when he starts the round. Switching out equipment in the middle is an automatic disqualification. It's in the official rules. I didn't write them."

"That isn't fair!" Helena argued, now crossing her arms.

"No, it isn't fair," Eleanor agreed, stepping up to the other side of Rafferty, crossing her own arms. "His equipment isn't working."

Vassago narrowed his own eyes at Eleanor, which made his leer seem hungrier. Rafferty's heartbeat sped up. His deal didn't extend protection to her, he hadn't known her until a couple of days ago, and Eleanor would clearly be the perfect target for a demon like Vassago.

"You're not allowed to mess with me," Rafferty said, his ears ringing in his panic. Why were they ringing?

"I didn't," Vassago said. "It's not my fault either if the equipment gets broken. I didn't do it, nor did I make the rules. Like I said, I'm just enforcing them. The rules are the rules. Finish your dish or be disqualified." It was clear that he was mocking him, but mocking wasn't a violation of their deal.

With that, the demon turned on his heels and walked back to the official's table, having done whatever he needed to at the crucial moment he needed to do it. He may not have broken the toaster oven, since he couldn't have even made sure that Rafferty ended up with it. That would have been a violation, but enforcing existing rules made by others at the exact moment it hurt Rafferty insulated the demon from the "spirit" of the agreement.

It was very clever.

And the only reason the demon would do that was because ... "He's made a deal with someone," Rafferty said softly, putting it together out loud.

Helena looked confused by what he said, but Eleanor spat on the scuffed gym floor with contempt. "Yeah, but good luck doing anything about it. Even if you could prove he took a bribe, in the grand scheme of things, these stakes are way too small to get anyone to make a difference."

She stared down Vassago, but the demon-in-human-clothing noticed her and simply shrugged as if to say, *"Not up to me. Take it up with a higher authority. Oh, wait, there isn't one."*

Eleanor sneered after him, then she looked at Rafferty with regret. "I'm sorry I can't do anything to help you. I'd let you use my oven, but there won't be time to finish up my dish and get yours in. I'm using up every bit of space in there."

Rafferty looked to the ingredients table and the refrigerators beyond, his ears still ringing. What was he going to do?

"Rafferty, I could ..." Helena was saying, but he didn't register it. What he did feel was her hand touching his arm, her skin pressing his, her strength flooding into him. It was like golden light turned into a warm liquid, and he felt the freezing in his muscles let go. His mind cleared of Vassago's fog, and he could think again.

"I can fix it," he said, as his eyes zeroed in on the one thing that no one had touched. The ice cream maker.

As if he had been brought back to life from stone, he quickly snatched Helena's hand, kissing the back of her knuckles as his eyes locked with hers. He could see she didn't realize what she had done, but he could explain it, and chide her for it, later. For now, he just needed her to know how grateful he was.

Then he was off, his long legs eating up the meters between him and the ice cream machine. Grabbing up a half-pint-sized measuring cup, he slid it under the spout to test. To his surprise, the machine was already preloaded with ice cream base, so all he needed to do was dispense it. Filing that under how-is-that-not-cheating, he accepted it as his advantage and left the ice cream unpulled to return to his station. Snapping out the industrial cooking sheet that came with it, he grabbed his batter and proceeded to dump the whole thing onto the sheet, spreading it out with a spatula.

He glanced up at Helena, who had returned to her seat next to Cindy. Their mouths were moving, clearly talking, but he couldn't hear it. Her worried eyes met his, but he smiled back with a wink. This was when he thrived the most, when things had gone terribly wrong in the kitchen, but he *knew* he could fix it. And make it better than it had been before.

Having prepared his batter into the thinnest layer possible, he charged again, this time toward the refrigerators. Opening the frozen compartment, he had no compunction against throwing out whatever was in his way inside onto the ingredient table next to him and shoving his cooking sheet inside. The two officials who were supposed to be assisting with the ingredients just stood there flabbergasted at his boldness as he charged past them to the ice cream machine.

Leaving nothing to chance, he test-pulled the machine again and a smooth, cold swirl of ice cream emerged. This time he tasted it. It was vanilla. Perfect.

But it would take at least ten minutes, fifteen would be better, to chill his dough in the freezer.

Vassago *could* do a whole lot in that time.

Despite the agreement, he was leaving nothing to chance.

So, Rafferty needed to make it expensive for him.

"Helena," Rafferty said, not raising his voice very much, but knowing she could hear him all the same. "I need your help."

Sure enough, across the space, his beloved perked up, her eyes fluttering in surprise. She said something to Cindy and then got up and came directly over to him.

"What do you need?" she said, her fingers rubbing together.

He grabbed her shoulders and planted a quick kiss on her forehead. "Just stand here and don't let anyone near the machine," he said. "You can't help me, I'll be disqualified, but you are allowed to watch. Watch the machine."

He could tell she wanted to do more, but she only nodded. "You got it."

Leaving the only person in the world he could trust to stand guard, Rafferty went back to the ingredients table and grabbed up more sugar, butter, cream, and salt. This was going to take all his remaining time, but he knew he could do it. Everything in his world zeroed in on the caramel sauce as he set the sugar to melt in a pan on the hot pad provided. That was working at least.

As soon as his caramel was ready, he poured it into a bowl to cool, and he rushed back to the freezer. Pulling out his cake batter, a finger test told him it was firm, but not frozen. Which was fine, he could work with that. Returning to his table he glanced at the clock.

Seven minutes.

He didn't even have time to curse as he laid his sheet down to carve up the batter. Then he went back to the ice cream machine. Helena's influence worked, as it served up four dishes of ice cream in short order. Using his longer fingers, he gathered the glass dishes by their short stems and returned to his prep area. Rolling up the cake dough into spirals, he stabbed them into the piled ice cream, then reached for his caramel. It flowed from the end of the spoon over the creations.

"Five …" Vassago called over the speaker, "four … three … two … one! Utensils down!"

Rafferty slammed down his spoon onto his table with a mighty clatter.

All four dishes were ready to present.

He was out of breath as he took up another tray and set the dishes on it to take up to the judging table. Glancing again at Helena, she was jumping up and down and cheering with Cindy. Only then did he hear the roar of applause from the gym all around them. Apparently, they hadn't been the only ones invested in his success.

But as he approached the judging table, he saw Vassago whispering something in the ear of the judging official. He retreated as soon as he reached her, offering his tray.

"I'm sorry, sir, but apparently you've been disqualified," she said, only to shrink back as the room erupted into screams and boos. "The challenge in the event was to use … was to use a toaster oven and this dish …" she tried to explain, but the room wouldn't let her.

"His toaster oven was broken!" Eleanor shouted, coming up beside him, again to his defense. "What the fuck was he supposed to do?"

"But the rules state ..." the judge said, clearly unprepared for this level of pushback.

"What's the point of the rules if they aren't fair!" someone else shouted.

"This is rigged!"

"What was the whole point ...!"

And more shouts echoed in the gym's space, drowning out any individual words.

At last, the judge took Rafferty's tray in shaking hands, cowering from him as if he had been the one who had been shouting. "Look, we'll take it, but we're going to have to discuss this ..." And then she retreated away after setting down the tray with the rest of the entries, to the huddling group of green shirts nearby.

With nothing else to do, Rafferty turned to Eleanor. "Thank you, but you didn't have to defend me."

She huffed as she recrossed her arms. "I want to win, but not like this," she scowled. "And besides, I'm the one that encouraged you to participate, and then they go pull this shit? What the ever-loving ..."

"Are you alright?" Helena asked, cutting off Eleanor's color to hug him.

"Yes, I'm alright."

"What is going on?" Cindy asked, joining them as well.

"They are deciding my fate," he said, and somehow, he didn't feel sour about it. Instead, he wrapped his arms around Helena's waist and squeezed. "Thank you. For being here for me."

Chapter 21

HELENA HAD A PLAN

"So what is this?" Cindy asked as she brought the cup to her nose to smell the brew.

"Uh, nothing," Helena tried to cover. She leaned over to Cindy holding an open thermos to show her friend. An open thermos she hadn't had a few minutes ago.

Dammit, Helena, he thought, as he realized she had used her power to create it and her poignantly avoiding his gaze was the confirmation of it.

"I just brought you some tea. I got the recipe from my grandmother's old church cookbook, like I said. It's supposed to be good for anxiety and stuff. I thought it would be fun to try and that maybe some old witch medicine might help you."

"I mean it smells good, even cold," Cindy conceded, then brought the cup that made up the top of the thermos to her lips and took a sip. "Though I really just feel better having gotten out of my parent's house."

"Yeah, I'm glad I brought this thermos of it, but I was going to make it for you fresh at the house," Helena lied.

She glanced over at Rafferty, who sat on the other side of her on the bench, feeling calm in the cool air of the train station platform. There were very few people around on the open-air platform. Most other passengers waited inside the small train station fieldhouse where there was heat and a bathroom.

Helena nudged his arm to offer him some of her tea as well, but he refused it.

"I'm good," he said, his arms lying limp on his lap. He felt tired, but it was a good kind of tired. A triumphant tired. He knew he should be upset with her spending her power to make them some of that don't-be-depressed tea from before, but he just couldn't. His emotions were all wrung out after the competition.

Cindy glanced at him, shaking her head. "I still think we should have fought harder," she said over her cup rim.

"With your mom?" Helena asked.

"No! At the competition."

Helena sighed, leaning back on the bench. "I mean, there are worse ways they could have resolved it. It wasn't technically a disqualification."

"They should have done more than just give you your entry fee back," Cindy insisted.

"Like what?" Rafferty asked.

Cindy huffed out a breath. "I don't know," she admitted. "But they could have at least made a real attempt at apologizing."

"I didn't fulfill the challenge," Rafferty said, closing his eyes. "What more is there to say? An apology would have meant nothing."

"Why aren't you more upset about this?" Cindy asked.

He shrugged. "There are more things in life that are far more unfair. It was fun, and it was free. I win either way."

Helena shook her head. "I mean, let's be honest, the whole setup was a mess. There are a ton of things I would do differently," she countered, her gaze far off as she was imagining it while she ticked off her fingers. "If I was in charge of something like that ... well for one thing there would be a whole lot more promotion. Guest commentators. Appropriate judging criteria. I would make sure all the equipment *worked* and have a recourse if it wasn't. I mean there are just so many little details that could be taken care of that would make the whole experience so much better."

Cindy looked at Rafferty again. "Are you okay with that Eleanor chick winning, though?" Cindy retorted.

"It was not her fault either. It just happened," Helena said.

"It didn't just happen," Rafferty said as he glanced at Cindy. "You-know-who was there."

"You-know-who?" Helena asked, looking quizzically. "You mean the agents?"

He met her gaze meaningfully. She gave him a little shake of her head. Sighing, he leaned forward and set his forehead to hers, quietly inviting her to take the memory. He would rather that than risk breaking his deal with the demon in question.

Helena understood that at least and touched her forehead to his.

"Okay, I'm going to the bathroom, you love birds," Cindy said with wry humor. "Don't let the train leave without me."

They waited a few seconds for Cindy to disappear into the little field house, then Helena leaned back, his memory uneaten.

"It was Vassago, wasn't it?"

Rafferty nodded.

"Damn it," Helena cursed, "I thought I felt like something was wrong, but I couldn't put my finger on it. It was that guy, the one who wouldn't let you switch out your toaster oven. *He* was Vassago? What ... what a jerk!"

Rafferty chuckled. "That is probably the mildest thing anyone has ever said about him."

She shook her head. "And there is *nothing* we can do about it?"

"He kept his end of the deal. He did us no harm," he pointed out.

"He sabotaged you! I would say that's doing harm," she argued.

Shrugging, Rafferty folded his arms. "Not really. He could have been the one that got you the entry fee back, resolving the issue. I wasn't entitled to win, and there were no real consequences for me *not* winning. It came out as neutral as possible."

"Cindy is right. You seem really chill about this," Helena pressed, her ire cooling.

"If anything, I find it reassuring. If we hadn't kept our end of the deal up to this point, he would not have been compelled to bend over backward to do the same. And besides, I still had fun." He smiled so hard it made his face hurt. "I still feel like I won."

Helena laid her head on his shoulder. "I'm glad. Now I just need to finish figuring out how to win, too."

"What would winning look like for you?" he asked.

"I want to do it," she said, her voice soft and intense. "I want to run one of these events, but I want to do it *right*." She straightened and dug out her phone. "I was looking at the organization's website. Anyone can host one of these, they just have to register it, and Scarlet Promotions could do this if I can convince Scarlet not to give up."

He nodded. "I see what you're trying to do."

"I *can* fix everything. I can help everyone," she insisted, smiling. "I can fix Scarlet Promotions and save her legacy. I can get you a life you would love, a real restart, and show people what a good chef you are. And it's like with the ice cream machine, if I'm there, then Vassago can't act." She paused, then asked, "You think he's targeting Eleanor?"

Rafferty blew out a breath, considering his answer. "She's who I would target. Talented and hungry. She's so full of energy and drive. He could feed off that for a while if he can convince her to make a deal with him."

"Do you think they're already in a deal?"

He licked his lips. "If they are, that is not your fault or your problem. She's a grown woman making her own choices."

"Yeah, but she can't understand what it means." Helena licked her lips. "Not that I knew either, but demons ... they aren't really like you, right?"

"Like me?" Rafferty raised an eyebrow.

"You know. You were so ... merciful, I guess." Helena wrinkled her nose in that adorable way.

Rafferty chuckled dryly. "No, demons are not like me. Not *even* me."

"What do you mean?" She wrinkled her nose again.

He looked at her, drinking her face in. "I have no idea why I spared you. Honestly. You were the perfect mark.

I had you over a barrel, but I don't know. Maybe it was because of ..." His throat started to close up as he thought about the last person, the one before Helena, who had summoned him. "Because I was so tired of it. All of it."

Helena seemed on the brink of saying something when her eyes drifted over his shoulder toward the train station field house. She suddenly had a look of concern, and her lower lip slipped between her teeth to anxiously bite. Cindy was returning, but something seemed to be bothering Helena.

Then Helena spoke again. "I've been thinking about telling Cindy the truth about me."

His whole body flinched, and she refocused on his reaction. "It won't violate the agreement, right? What happened to me is my secret and really has nothing to do with Vassago."

"Uh ... no, no it doesn't," he said, his mind spinning up into a jumble. "But why would you do that with everything you have going on?"

No, he thought, *that is the wrong tactic with her.*

"She's my best friend. I have to," Helena answered as if that rule was obvious.

"It's not lying to her ..." He scoffed at the notion. He leaned forward, fighting to keep his voice down with the urgency of what he needed to say. "How shocked were you when you realized for certain that demons were very real and not just a story you hear about on the news that happens to other people?"

Helena's eyes went wide with the memory.

He continued. "You almost lost your mind with that big of a paradigm shift, and you hadn't tried to harm yourself a few short weeks prior."

"But ... but I don't want to lie to her," she repeated in a small, childlike voice.

"There is a big difference between lying and *privacy*," he answered.

Helena bit her lower lip and pursed her eyebrows together hard. He could tell she understood what he was saying. In a few more seconds, she would agree with it. A familiar smug feeling bubbled up inside him, and he hated it.

I'm not telling her this because I care, he realized, *or rather, not only. I'm ... I'm jealous!* He could see what he was doing. But he wasn't sure if he cared.

"Helena, I ..."

Just then Helena set her fingers to his mouth to stop him, as Cindy returned to sit down next to him, but she wasn't listening to them; she had her phone pressed to her ear. Whatever lightness in her expression they had achieved over the last few hours had been completely obliterated.

It annoyed him. Why was she doing this to Helena? Burdening her with her own problem? If they had been in the other place, Cindy would be another dark soul, reaching out to suck the energy out of whomever she could grab. The urge to protect Helena from that burned inside him.

"Dad, I ..." Cindy said, but the voice coming from her phone only shouted at her. Words like "ungrateful" and "disgraceful" came to him clearly, but that was it.

Helena's lips drew into a straight line as she heard every word. She opened her mouth to say something, probably "hang up," but urgently Rafferty moved to put his face in her sight line to block her view.

You have your own problems, he thought.

What he said, though, was "Do you think Scarlet will go for your idea?"

She pinched her eyebrows deeper, and Rafferty wished he could use just a little bit of his demonic aura to make it harder for her attention to drift from him, to be more of a draw on her attention than her friend's pain.

"Do you?" he pushed.

Helena looked back and forth between him and her friend, unable to choose. "Yes, I think so. This is a project Scarlet Promotions can totally handle," Helena assured him as her gaze shifted back to Cindy.

"Dad, please listen—" Cindy's face became more and more despondent.

Helena leaned over Rafferty to gently set her hand over the phone. The two friends made eye contact, tears welling at the bottom of Cindy's. Quietly, she yielded the phone, and Helena pressed down on the hang-up button on the screen to do just that, cutting off the still-ranting voice. Helena then pocketed the phone so that it couldn't hurt Cindy anymore.

The burning raged in Rafferty's chest.

Above them, the overhead speaker binged three descending tones. "Attention all passengers. The train going north will be arriving in three minutes. Please stand back from the blue line for your safety. Have all baggage with you and tickets ready to board."

"Let's get on the train," Helena managed to communicate over the announcement.

Rafferty and Helena gathered up their bags, but Cindy simply sat there, staring, as if she were numb and detached from all of it. Finally, Helena picked up her duffle bag to pass to Rafferty before taking her friend's hand and tugging her up to her feet as the train rumbled into the station. Cindy let herself be led up into their waiting coach.

Helena handled passing their tickets to the conductor, waiting at the doors to punch. None of them said anything to each other outside of functional directions to their first-class private room, the fortuitous upgrade coming in handy again: Helena and Rafferty side by side on the two-seater and Cindy dropped in the single seat across, her gaze returning to staring out the window.

Helena's fingers laced in between Rafferty's, gripping hard enough to turn her knuckles white, while she watched her friend sink back into her own personal hell, the last few hours only a small rise above the surface. He laid his own hand over hers, squeezing, trying to communicate without words that there was nothing she could do. He had seen this sort of darkness before.

"Cindy? It's going to be okay," Helena said softly.

"Don't say that," Cindy responded, but she didn't look away from the window as the train jerked into motion. "Just don't."

"I'm just ..."

"I'm going to stay with Chris and Charlie when we get back to the city," Cindy said, crossing her arms.

The hairs on the back of Rafferty's arms stood up. He could feel the eerie energy coming off of Helena and knew intuitively what she intended.

Digging in his pocket, he slipped out his phone. There were only two other numbers in it, one Helena's, and hit he autodial on the other one.

A weak voice answered on the other end. "Hello?"

"Scarlet? It's Rafferty," he said loudly, capturing all the attention in the train car.

"Oh, yes, Rafferty. How can I help you?" she said, clearly speaking the words automatically, despite the fatigued undertones. "Oh, wait, you were just at that cooking competition event. How did it go?"

"I enjoyed myself. It has some real potential, but I will let Helena tell you about it." He then passed the phone to her.

Her eyes glanced at her friend but put on the spot like that with her boss, she couldn't not take the phone.

"Hi, Scarlet," she said into it, turning her guilty eyes toward the window.

As they launched into talking, Rafferty glanced at Cindy. She didn't look at him, only settled back, her face clean of emotion. He recognized it, but he couldn't let her drag Helena down with her.

Chapter 22

TENDRILS OF DOUBTS

Helena talked to Scarlet the whole way back to the city, going over her idea. They got into details and minutiae Rafferty barely understood. Cindy, for her part, stayed quiet and didn't do anything to distract. Once they reached the station, Cindy parted ways with them, heading to Chris's house to stay. While she continued to talk to Scarlet on the phone, Helena hugged Cindy, and that was just as well.

Over the next three days, Rafferty barely saw Helena. They were still staying at the hotel, but she would get up in the morning and leave for her work, eager to get out of the door while he remained in bed.

He spent much of his time sleeping. Sleeping was such an interesting experience. He remembered doing it in his first life, but not what it was like. Sleeping was not something a demon did. You simply existed. He felt like the

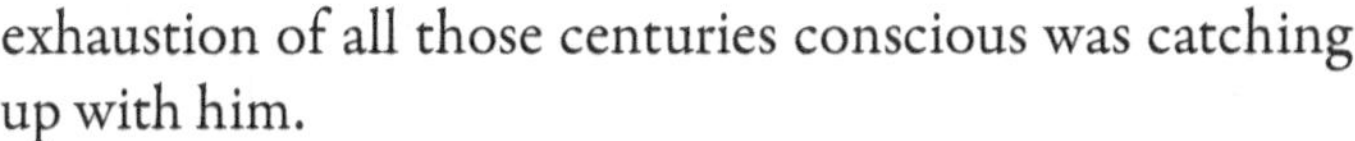

exhaustion of all those centuries conscious was catching up with him.

It made Helena's peppy energy ... annoying.

But the second she was gone, loneliness would overtake him, and he would long for her to return.

So, it was a surprise when he woke up on the third day and Helena was still there. She looked freshly showered and dressed for her day, but this time she wore jeans and a sweater instead of her work slacks.

"Good morning!" she said brightly as she ran her brush through her beautiful red-gold hair, currently darker from being washed. Waves appeared after each stroke, and he found it mesmerizing. "I have a surprise to show you. Something I've been working on for Scarlet Promotions." She grinned, her eyes bright with excitement. "I want you to come look at it with me. Give me your expert opinion. Please?"

Rafferty sat up, the comforter dropping from his bare chest as he ran a hand through his longer hair. He wondered if he shouldn't cut it to be more in line with the fashion of the times he now lived in.

"Come on, you've been cooped up here for days now. Have you done anything but eat and sleep?" Helena asked, pulling clothes for him from their suitcases. They needed to wash them if they didn't go back to her house soon.

"Watched TV," he said, kicking his legs out from the covers as well so he could stand up.

"Watching what?"

"Cooking channels," he said truthfully. He had spent a lot of time on the cooking channels, of which there were many, all full of marathons.

"Oh my!" Helena said, as he stood, her cheeks shifting to red. "I didn't realize you were sleeping naked."

Rafferty looked down at himself. "How else do people sleep?"

"In ... pajamas?" she offered. Then she laughed. "What did you wear when you were alive the first time? Nightgowns? Or maybe you called them nightshirts?"

He frowned as he searched his memory, surprisingly, finding a scrap. "Oui, we wore something like that. But I never did. I would either wear my clothes because I was too busy to change, or I would sleep in nothing at all."

She giggled again as she crossed the space, sidling her hands along his sides, giving his hips a gentle squeeze as she nestled her nose into the crook at his neck. "Too bad there isn't any time to make more of it," she whispered, the promise of those words waking his body the rest of the way. His breathing sped up and blood rushed through him. Her lips brushed against his with a million little kisses in quick rapid succession that left them tingling even as her touch made his skin crawl. She felt like too much, too intense, and he wondered if it was always going to feel like this. He still wasn't used to it.

Then she squeezed him around the waist in a quick hug before releasing him to hunt for her shoes. "Come on, get dressed. We need breakfast—"

Helena's phone rang out.

Huffing a sigh, she went to pick up the errant thing. "Yes, hello?" she said into it. She gave him an apologetic smile, which he returned, then moved to the bathroom.

"Scarlet?" she asked.

Rafferty halted in place as Helena's expression fell.

"What ... what's wrong?" The alarm in her gaze as it hit his made his heart skip a beat. "We'll be right there."

The doorman didn't argue or even question Helena and Rafferty's need to enter the towering building with its beautiful maroon canopy and decorative statuary on either side of the door. He just jotted down their names from their state-issued IDs (Rafferty had dismissed the idea of a driver's license when offered until he had actually learned to operate one of the machines) and pressed a button next to an elevator to let them in, then another on the inside to send them up.

The door to the elevator opened immediately into a foyer, instead of a hallway like most buildings did. Scarlet clearly lived on the whole floor of the building. Lined up to one side of the foyer were a series of wheelchairs: folded up, clean, and waiting to be used. There was another stand beside them with various arm crutches and pushing walkers for when she had fought to move regularly under her own power. Seeing them lined up, no longer needed by the old-woman-turned-young, they seemed almost sinister. Memento mori.

Beside him, Helena tensed, alerting him to look for danger, but he didn't see nor hear anything.

She set a hand on his arm. "Can you just ... wait here a moment?" she asked softly.

"What is it?" he asked, his voice matching hers.

"I hear her ..."

A crash drew their attention to the main door at the end of the foyer.

Helena rushed through and no request of hers was going to stop him from following.

The door led them both into the main room of the apartment, a cavernous space where the tile gave way to warm wood. The furniture was the light-colored creams of the modern era that spoke of wealth in the way brocades and jewel colors once had in the century he had been born in. Like her office, Scarlet's apartment was also a study in the elegant ways that water and greenery could be incorporated into a space, to make it have a garden-like feel, but this one also used the floor-to-ceiling windows to make it seem almost like a terrace amongst the clouds. A haven of the gods.

Helena didn't savor the view at all as she turned to the left and passed through a large alcove where a long dining set sat, looking more like it was waiting for pictures instead of dinner guests. This continued again into another room, set up with lounge chairs and a fully stocked bar, picture-perfect and untouched. Nothing about this place spoke of a real home to Rafferty.

And then they turned past the bar into another hallway.

Here were the signs of life.

Clothing and shoes of all sorts were thrown and scattered over a softly carpeted surface. Wine stains cut red slashes over the lighter fibers as well as the shards of the glass that used to hold that wine. More alarmingly, Rafferty picked out the sight of different colored pills amongst the refuse.

Helena ignored it all as she tripped her way through like a deer in a thick jungle. He had to resist the urge to sweep her up in his arms and carry her over it all or to start cleaning it up.

Another crash of glass spurred Helena faster, and she turned about halfway down the hall, through a doorway. "Scarlet? It's Helena. Are you alright?" she asked as she passed through, Rafferty right on her heels.

It was a man's bedroom; he could tell that by the clean masculine smell that greeted him. Like the hallway, clothes were thrown over the floor and the bed, though now there was a place of origin as their throw patterns suggested that they all came from the small walk-in closet off to one side. Scarlet was kneeling in the middle of it all, beside the messed-up bed, in a bathrobe and a slip of a nightgown, picking at the glass from a broken frame on the floor. Tears streamed down her face, even though she didn't make a sound.

"Oh!" Helena said as she rushed to drop to Scarlet's side. "I'll get that." She tried to take over, but Scarlet only batted her hands away before looking up in surprise at their sudden entrance.

"Helena? No, no, child. I've got it," she said, but she abandoned the glass she had been gathering to pull the picture from the frame, dropping back in an unladylike, heedless way to stare at it. "It's my fault. I shouldn't have done that to him."

Over her shoulder, Rafferty could see the image. It was of Yosef standing behind her, his hands on her wheelchair, laughing and smiling. Her older self laughed, too, and they were dressed in colorful shirts with balloons and streamers all around. There were also strings of flowers around their necks, though Rafferty was pretty sure they weren't real flowers at all.

Tenderly, Scarlet's fingers brushed over the image of Yosef. "I was so disgusted with my own ugly face, I forgot that he was in the picture, too." The tears streamed afresh, but still she didn't sob. Her voice didn't even thicken as she spoke. "I was sixty years too old for him. He didn't care. He was a baby, but ... he said he didn't care. That age was just a number and that he loved every inch of me." Her head dropped into her hands, though she was careful not to crush the picture, unwilling to let it go from her fingers. "I was preparing him to live without me. It wasn't supposed to be the other way around."

"Here, let's get you up," Helena said, moving to take her arm to do just that, but Scarlet slapped her away.

"Leave me alone," she barked.

While Scarlet couldn't see their faces, Helena gestured with her hands, then she mouthed the words *Help me* silently.

He had only one idea. "What would you like to eat?"

It was strange to ask that question with no other agenda but to help Helena, and he needed to help her. Judging from the smell of alcohol, he would bet that she hadn't eaten anything to counter it properly. Food did many things: bring comfort, sanity, and a sense of connection back to the consumer. Scarlet clearly needed all three.

The socialite blinked, lifting her head to look up at him standing over her. It took a moment more to process that there was someone else there, and he was male. A heartbeat later, she clutched at the top of her robe. "What ... what are you doing here?" she asked, the thread of imperial authority returning to her despairing voice.

"I'm here to help," he said, and he reached down to hook his hands under her shoulders to lift her back up to her feet.

She meeped as her equilibrium changed, forcing her to put more effort toward clutching at her robe than fighting his assistance.

Helena stood up as well, bringing the picture frame and all its glass shards piled in the middle with her. "Let's go to the kitchen. I can get you something cold to drink," she offered.

Scarlet opened her mouth as if to argue, then she looked away and cast her gaze over the rumpled, abandoned bed. "You must both think I am a disgusting old woman. That I planned all *this* or something." She gestured at Yosef's room. "He moved in on his own. To better take care of me. Other than the cleaning service, he did everything for me. Cooked. Bathed me. Administered my medications. Made me laugh. Made me feel beautiful and worth loving again. He gave me everything. Everything."

"What did he make you?" Rafferty asked gently. "What was your favorite thing that he would cook for you to eat?"

She laughed dryly. He could see it just behind her eyes. She had an answer.

"I wish to take a shower," she said instead of giving him an answer. She turned away from them and walked with forced dignity out of the room to another across the way, shutting the door firmly behind her.

Helena then made a hesitant motion to follow Scarlet but came up short when she got to the closed door. Instead, she leaned her ear to listen. Closing her eyes, she focused. "It's so strange," she whispered. "I can hear her in there so clearly." Another moment later, she opened her eyes. "The shower is running. I ... I don't think she'll do anything."

"I don't either," he said, hoping it assured Helena. "Why?"

"Her life is Yosef's gift to her. She loves him too much to throw it away. At least, just yet."

Helena went still a moment, thinking that over. "Yosef is keeping her alive in more ways than one." She backed up from the door and crossed her arms, hugging herself. "Do you think he did the right thing? I mean, obviously it was the very wrong thing and very wrong for him, but ... for her sake?"

He shook his head. "Right or wrong is pretty much irrelevant."

"Irrelevant seems like the wrong word, too," she said, nibbling at her lower lip as she thought.

He sighed, understanding what she meant. "It is possible for something to be both," he said. "Right and wrong don't cancel each other out. They are independent of each other, and neither are irrelevant. They're both important."

She smiled at that. "You know, I think you are wiser than you think you are."

That was a hard statement for him to swallow, so he cleared his throat and looked away. "Does she have a kitchen?"

It was an asinine question. Of course she did, but it was the first one his brain spat out.

Chapter 23

WE TALKED HONESTLY

Rafferty didn't have many moments in his existence where he thought something was truly unfair. He had seen the pain and suffering of the people he had been forced to serve from every level and walk of life, from the ultra-poor to the ultrarich and all the layers in between. All of them believed that they weren't getting their fair share no matter what they actually had.

The former demon believed he would continue to think that ... that is, until he walked into Scarlet's kitchen.

"Oh my ..." He didn't know who to direct those words to, but it didn't matter because he could barely process anything at that moment.

It was the ultimate, state-of-the-art kitchen. It was more than a restaurant-style space. While it had a multi-range stove lining one wall, it had also been designed with modular units for every type of cooking his heart could desire, including an induction surface, an inset steamer, and something called an air fryer. Throughout the rest of the room, there were dedicated task stations and a work-horse sink with a faucet that extended on a metal hose, one that could be pulled all the way across the room and that would snap back home when released.

"Oh wow," Helena said, impressed herself, and a warmth slipped in through his chest. He couldn't have loved her more than in that moment.

Two different fridges, set at different temperatures, had touch screens reporting data on their surfaces. When he tapped the screen to see what was inside, a list appeared beside a picture of the items along with tags like "date bought" and "date expected to expire." The screens even went further to show a meal plan, laid out three months in advance, typed and organized with ingredients listed and buying requirements. There was also a list of forbidden foods and another with foods that could be consumed once in a great while.

"She was on quite the restrictive diet," Helena commented as she slid her finger over the surface, scrolling the list.

Rafferty nodded as his eyes scanned it, still trying to take everything in. "So much"—he turned to look at it all—"thought and design went into this room. And it was *used*."

"Looks like by Yosef," she said, tapping at the list. "He used to make notes like that. His own little abbreviation system that I had to learn just to understand his emails. He *lived* here. They really were a couple."

Rafferty had no doubt about it. He just let his eyes linger over the list of Do Not Eat. "If we are going to make her something, it should be from this list. She is well now. There is nothing forbidden to her now."

"I suppose so," Helena said, but waited as his eyes scanned the list again. "Food of the Gods?" she asked, basically at the same time he saw it himself.

He tapped the heading, and, sure enough, it opened up to a typed-up recipe and a link to a paused video; a paused video of Eleanor.

"As you can see there are many versions of this recipe that call themselves the Food of the Gods, but this one is my all-time favorite," his rival's recorded self said, doing her thing of preparing herself to make what looked to Rafferty to be a dessert of some sort.

"This is it," he said, pausing the video and refocusing on the ingredient list.

"Are you sure?" Helena asked.

"Yes," he said, turning to go to the cupboards to see what supplies they had.

Helena didn't simply accept that. "*How* can you be sure?"

He couldn't help smirking a little. "I have always had a knack for knowing what people truly want or need to eat."

"Oh." Helena wrinkled her nose. "That's not ... I guess, I thought ... that was all a part of your whole demon thing?"

He shook his head. "No, that belongs to me alone. My mentor used to call it the 'Sense.'"

"Oh," Helena said, but she sounded distracted, cocking her head to one side as if listening. In fact, he was sure she was. When she noticed his scrutiny, she looked up. "Sorry. I was just making sure she was okay. It's so weird. If I just focus long enough, I seem to be able to hear her no matter how far away she is."

That gave Rafferty pause, the only thing that really could distract him from his marveling at the stockedness of the cupboards.

"Oooo, whipped cream!" Helena declared, grabbing up a can from the shelf. She popped off the top, brought it to her mouth, and did the most horrifying thing he had ever seen: blasted white foam into it.

She smiled as her lips tried to wrap around her mouthful, taking in his shocked expression. "What? You've never done this before?" she chided, shaking the can. Then she offered it to him to blast some in his mouth for him.

"No, thank you," he said, pulling his head away. She only pouted for a second before redirecting the nozzle back for another hit, filling it up again with white cream.

His pants grew tighter at the visual.

Swallowing, he looked back into the cupboard.

He reached up into it and pulled down a jar of rich, golden honey. Palming the jar, he looked at her and lifted his eyebrows in a suggestive way. She giggled around her whipped cream, catching the implications. Painting her with that honey, then licking it off her was a something he needed to add to his list of things he wanted to try.

He reached for a package of dried apricots and a box of graham crackers required by Yosef's recipe. But he couldn't focus; Helena was being so distracting.

While he rooted around amongst the ingredients, she opened the honey jar, pulling the lid away revealing a small honey dipper attached to the underside. It trailed a thin glob of honey, which she lifted over her head and spooled into her mouth. Strands of honey clung to her cheek and dripped down onto her blouse.

"Oh, shoot, that was dumb," she said, realizing it.

As she tried to look down at the mess, he thumbed up the honey escaping to drip just below her collarbone. She went still at his touch and watched as he brought his thumb into his mouth. The honey tasted of sunshine and warm days. Some part of him wanted to believe it also tasted of her.

Helena watched him, her eyes running calculations. "Do you miss sharing tastes with me?"

That wasn't what he thought she was about to say, and his sharp flinch conveyed it.

She flinched in response, screwing the cap of the honey back on. "I mean, I'm sure you don't miss not being able to taste anything and being at my mercy for some scrap of it, but it's like … there's some connection that we used to have that we don't really anymore. At least, that's how I've been feeling. I don't know. So much has changed so fast."

Lifting her fingers to her mouth, she went to suck off the sticky, but he caught her wrist. Leaning forward, he did it himself, locking his gaze with hers as he did. Her finger made a loud smack as his lips slid along the digit, then released at the tip. "I still feel very connected to you," he assured her in a husky voice. "But yes, I do sometimes miss sharing tastes with you."

"I suppose there are all kinds of advantages when demons make deals," she said, reclaiming her hand sadly, and suddenly, something that hadn't occurred to him yet … did.

"Did you … make a deal with her?" he demanded, alarmed, his heart revving up.

"What?" Helena asked, her eyebrows knitting, confused.

Rafferty let the cupboard doors he had been holding drop and they banged closed, reflecting his anger. "Did you make a deal with her? With Scarlet? Is that why you're trying to use your power on her behalf?"

"You mean like a *demon* would?" Helena asked, her eyebrows shifting to anger as she realized what he meant.

"Did you?" He knew this trick, answering a question with a question. He wouldn't let her deter him.

"No!" she exclaimed. "I'm just trying to help her."

"Like you tried to help Cindy?"

She huffed. "Yes, okay, I get what you're saying, but it didn't work. I don't even think I helped Cindy. I'm going to need to call her and make sure she's okay over at Charlie's as it is. Why are you getting so angry at me?"

"Because I can't understand how someone as wise and smart as you keeps insisting on doing things that will cause them harm. Spending what little power you have doing favors for every broken person in your life will only drag you back there."

She looked questioningly. "Back where?"

"To hell!" he shouted, which forced her to press her hands to his mouth to shush him, glancing anxiously at the closed kitchen door.

"Keep your voice down! I don't want Scarlet to hear," she hissed.

She huffed a breath. "It's not like I'm doing anything wrong trying to *help* people. I haven't done anything I wouldn't have done before. Maybe how I'm doing it, but it's only been a sliver of power, if at all. And for that matter, how is it any different when you used *your* demonic powers to *help* me?"

"I was trying to get your soul!" he growled, but she waved her hand at that.

"No, you weren't, not even a little bit, and we both know it," she replied defiantly. "So why are you thinking I would do the same thing?"

"Because it's the game," he said.

Her eyebrows furrowed deeper, her expression asking the question her lips didn't. *What game?*

"It is what we demons call all this. The bargains, the acquiring of souls, and the energy they generate—it's the great game. The only game worth playing for us. In order to pay the price to stay in creation, we risk and bet what little we have in the hopes of getting the jackpot. To do what Vassago is doing and be so flushed with power that we can stay a time in creation away from the suffering."

Helena took that in a moment, then asked, "Is that a game you can actually win?"

Now, it was his turn to blow out a sigh. "I would have said no a week ago. But"—he dryly laughed and gestured at himself with both hands—"here I stand. I won. And you ..." He almost couldn't say it, the words threatening to choke in his throat. "You lost. And I don't know how to save you from that fate."

Helena nodded, her lips drawn into a thin line. "I'm not going to lie. I've been thinking about that these last few days. I'm really a *demon*, aren't I?"

He shook his head again, reaching to grasp her hands. "No, you aren't. Not to me," he lied. He set his forehead to hers. There it was again. That uncanny tingle. "But please, stop risking it. Why won't you listen to me about this?"

She forced a shuddering breath. "Because I can't just stand by and do nothing. I can't ... I can't just bring Yosef back. But I need to help *her* somehow." She shook her head.

"How did you do it? I saw you, I felt it. You were able to keep me calm when everything was happening with Cindy."

"That wasn't me." He shook his head, wishing she would get it. "That was a strength inherent to yourself."

"Then what is it that demons do?"

He laughed dryly. "So much of what we would actually do would be normal things that anyone can do, but so few have the incentive to. You have to understand, Helena, a demon's goal is to extract as much power as possible while expending little. If we simply do what a mortal asks and it takes no power, we will do it and take all the credit we can for our 'miracle.'"

It felt good to actually explain this out loud, like it was something he needed to hear as well, to process the actions he had performed for years without giving them much thought.

Helena listened but still shook her head. "But there must be something more I *can* do with just a snap of my fingers. I can make anything I want: a pile of gold, a feast for thousands. And you keep telling me I can't. Then what is the damned point? Why can't I just snap my fingers and make this Food for the Gods? I could even put the intention of helping her feel better."

"Demonic magic can only hold grief back for a time, but we can't alter it any more than we can other human emotions. We don't control that; we just try to momentarily influence them. You can't make people feel anything they don't want to, and you're going to waste all of your power trying to force it, and fail, and then have nothing to show for it. People want to use and be used, so you might as well use them."

"Is that what you did to people?" she asked in a small voice.

A strange shudder washed through him. He knew that she was seeing him in a different light than ever before. He hadn't been lying to her about who he was or what he had done, but now she seemed to be accepting it. He hated it and craved it at the same time. It had felt all along that he had been tricking her, that she loved something so vile, but she truly didn't understand how loathsome he had once been. How loathsome she was becoming.

Helena cupped his face with her hand, then slowly skimmed her fingers over his ear and through his hair. The petting washed through him, feeding his touch-starved soul. There was nothing more to it; he could tell. She wasn't using any demon energy to invoke this response in him. The fact that it was so innocent and pure was why he craved it so much. He craved it as much as he could revile it.

It was confusing.

She ran her fingers through a second time, and his mouth fell open while his eyes fluttered closed, confusing his feelings further. He wanted more.

Then she paused.

Opening his eyes, he gazed into Helena's real gray ones, the human eyes he lost himself to. "I know you're not sure about me now that I've changed. I know you are afraid of what all this means. I know. I *know*," she said with all the strength and earnestness that he loved about her. "But it's not who I choose to be. Even if I *am* actually a demon." A tear pricked at her eyes, but her voice remained strong. "It's not who I *choose* to be. And honestly, I think it's the only thing that matters in all this." Her strong eyebrows quirked a little. "Do you understand?"

Rafferty swallowed back the thickness in his throat, imprisoning any other words he could say. He nodded. Then reached for her, wanting to hold her close, ignoring the uncomfortable tingling her aura washed over his skin. The need to feel the weight of the body housing her unchanging spirit in his arms far outweighed any discomfort.

"I love you," he whispered. And oh, did he mean it.

"I love you too. I know I always will," she replied, digging her face into his chest and shoulder, snuggling and squeezing as hard as she could as if he were her buoy in the storm of changes she was living through. "We'll figure this out, right?"

"Yes," he said. "Whatever it takes. However long."

For a moment, he could see it. See how he could be perfectly happy with her, how wonderful this long life he now had could be. And he dared to say the thing he had been holding back.

"I do love you, Helena."

Chapter 24

NOT SAFE FOR WORK

"I love you, Rafferty," she answered, and snuggled her nose even more. They savored each other for long moments he wished would last forever, but moments never did.

At last, she pulled away and looked up at him. "I know what you said, but I am still going to do something to help her feel a little better." She broke from the hug and turned to lean against the island counter beside him, her gaze falling onto the smart surface of the refrigerator. "How about this as a compromise: it can be like with the eggs the other day, right? I'll make an ingredient *you* will cook with and give it a positive intention. That was a very low cost, and it had a big impact, right? We made a whole office of people feel better."

Rafferty sighed, finally understanding that he was the one that hadn't gotten it. This was Helena. She would do whatever it took to help whomever she could. She was a woman who risked her own soul to give a demon like him respite from hell.

Rafferty moved closer until his body was just on the edge of her aura, and it sparked a memory. Something he used to know, and just then realized he had forgotten.

She inhaled sharply at his approach, lifting her face to him as she sensed the shift as she woke up from her deeper thoughts.

Without a word, he raised his hand, brushing it over the edge of that otherworldly aura, hovering just outside the uncanny feeling. The action sent a shiver through both of them.

"What was …" she started to say, but closed her eyes as he did it again, savoring the sensation.

"Do you remember, the second time you summoned me to your kitchen … do you remember throwing the frying pan through the glass?"

She snorted, the memory apparently a funny one for her now, and she opened her eyes, the sensual feelings disturbed.

He reset his hand again, hovering it just over her head, the pulsing of energy feeling so real to him. It should have been subdued because she hid it behind a physical body in creation, but she had no control or, apparently, awareness of it. That needed to change now.

Brushing down his fingers again, this time, he shifted just a little more into the aura and her giggles disappeared. A quirk of worry appeared between her eyebrows, before she caught his hand, stopping him.

"What … is that?" she breathed. "What are you doing?"

"You know," he said. "It was the same thing that you felt around me."

She shifted on her feet, confirming the truth. "Touching you was like caressing a battery. I'm doing that too, aren't I?" She closed her eyes tightly. "I wasn't sure based on how you were acting, but I have that weird aura thing going on, don't I?"

He nodded.

"Does it hurt you?" she asked, her eyebrows showing full concern.

Shaking his head quickly, he attempted a reassuring smile. "No, it doesn't hurt. But it is intense. It can be very intense when you are not hiding yourself fully behind the human form."

She nodded. "I know what you're talking about. It was the hardest part about ..." He wasn't sure what she was going to say, but she shook it away. "But you're touching it right now?"

"I know." He moved his hand, caressing the aura just inches from her neck. Another shiver washed through her and her lips parted in a pleasurable "Oh."

"You don't have to do that," she breathed, even though she clearly liked it.

"There is something about it that I want to help you explore," he said, stepping from her side to in front of her, bracing his hands on the counter to either of her sides. Trapping her there but not touching her. Yet.

Again, she inhaled at the sensation as he moved his presence into her aura, her eyes going wider, her lips parting as if ready to be kissed.

"There, you felt it again, didn't you?" he asked.

"Yes," she said, letting her gaze go soft, concentrating on what she was feeling. This time she raised her hand toward him. "I sense you, too. Your space. Your aura."

This time she caressed down his human aura, and he arched toward it, the sensation skimming down his skin, straight to his groin, which was rushing to fill with blood.

The surprise on her face was comical.

"Oh! Oh," she said as she put together what was happening. Her fingers moved, wafting around his head, and his body obeyed the motion, tipping himself toward her, like a flower bending its face toward the sun. He longed now for her fingers to sink into his hair once more. Every fiber of his being ached for her to grip him and take him, force him to submit to her will and scream in pleasure.

"This is how succubi do it!" she whispered, shocked.

"Hell, yes," he agreed, the rumble deep in his throat. "Our auras influence each other and are a potent tool against humans. It can inspire them to great acts of violence and terror, but if you pull it back enough, manipulate it just so, it does ... this ..." At last, she sank her fingers into his hair, the eerie feeling continuing its shift to something intoxicating, overwhelming his senses. He lost control and pressed his body against hers, grinding his aching groin against her leg.

"Rafferty," she breathed, her own fever pitched up as both her hands came around his head, pulling him into a kiss. And she devoured him.

She wore a long skirt, and it was up past her hips instantly. The winter stockings gripped her thighs, leaving a strip of bare skin between them and her panties. He lost all control at that sight.

His hands tore at her underwear, ripping it aside while her own fingers dug at the zipper of his jeans.

He groaned again as her fingers found his member, giving it the smallest sip of relief as she squeezed his hardness. Her eyes glowed gold. It was too late. He hadn't expected this to happen, but he wasn't surprised. He was human now.

She scooted up against him, inviting the tip of him toward her entrance. "What are we doing?" she asked, nearly begged, even as he entered, slipping into her wet body, right there on Scarlet's kitchen counter. Cuddling around him, she rested her head on his shoulder, and they clung together as they joined. "We shouldn't be doing this," she gasped, but it did nothing to stop her as she rocked her hips, grinding her bud against him.

He couldn't say anything. Gripping her from behind, pulling her as close as he could, he started pounding into her. Her gasps came out small and sharp with each thrust. It was going too fast. Yet there was no stopping, no slowing. He could feel her draining on his energy as they coupled ... as he *fucked* her. He didn't care. She could have it all. He just needed to thrust.

Legs wrapped around him, pulling him tighter. She pressed her lips against his shoulder: a vain attempt to quiet her screams. Liquid gushed down his thighs as he thrust deeper and deeper. He could feel her trembling around him, spasming in pre-orgasm. Grasping her by the throat, he pressed her back onto the cooking surface, violating it with their musk, which only made what they were doing hotter. With his other hand, he tugged her hip hard against him. More leverage to thrust even harder, deeper.

"Rafferty!" she strangled out, and she came. All her muscles clenched around his cock. Her body arched back and her breasts strained the buttons of her shirt, showing him peeks of the lace underneath.

It sent him over.

He thrust hard one final time.

For one dangerous moment, it all went, all of his essence and energy flowed into her, feeding her with his mind, body, and soul. She took it all, glowing brightly like a nova star being born. She would transcend and leave him behind, having completely consumed him, his deep satisfaction filling the void. To give her everything of him so she may be more ... death would be sweet, oblivion a righteous reward.

And then it came back.

He didn't understand it, but the life force flowed back into him just as his heart had slowed to dangerous stillness. The pleasure he had felt when he came reignited, and he came a second time. He didn't know such a thing was possible. Helena sat up, his angel burning bright, and wrapped her arms and legs around him again.

"I love you," she breathed, and those words burned away the dark oblivion, the void of hell, waking him to a warmth and light he had never known before but that he had craved his whole existence. He held on in return in the torrent storm of celestial energy, a mere mortal man grasping at a higher being.

And then it was over.

They were in the kitchen, having just fucked on the counter.

The light was the same, artificial trying to mimic real.

Already, the cold void of hell and transcendent warmth faded from his memory, leaving only the heavy reality and sparking tingles of bitter pleasure.

"Wow!" Helena breathed, sitting up to smile into his face. "That was insane!" Then she laughed; joyful, merry peals that skipped lightly over his heart like stones over water. "Oh my God, I can't believe we did that!"

Exhaustion weighed on his limbs then, and he slumped onto Helena, letting her hold him up as he tried to remember how to breathe.

She seemed to have boundless energy. "You okay?"

"Yes," he managed to say, though he wasn't entirely sure it was true. "Sex with one of us always comes with this sort of price." Though he was confusing himself now. He was the human, she was the demon, so he should have said you. But he couldn't say that.

Her laughter faded completely, giving way to her concern. "Did I hurt you?" she asked, threading her fingers once more through his hair.

He shook his head.

They held each other for a long silence, recovering while thoughts slipped in.

"Why wasn't it like that when we first slept together?" she asked finally.

"I ..." He shook his head. "I can't remember. I ... I wasn't trying to steal your energy from you ... I didn't want to hurt you."

"But it didn't feel like this," she said, her mind working now as she puzzled on it.

Rafferty just wanted to lie down on the floor and go to sleep. "I don't know. You're just better at sex than I am," he answered.

"Oh, that's not true," she chided, nuzzling his neck again.

He mirrored the action, placing a kiss on her soft skin. "I lost control with you," he said. "I always lose control."

"Hmm" was all she said, then she straightened, slapping his shoulder with comradery. "We better clean up before Scarlet comes in and we get caught." She slid past him to jump down onto the floor, fixing her skirt and what remained of her panties as she did so. Numbly, Rafferty bent over to draw his own pants up, feeling vulnerable as he did so.

"I can't believe we got away with that!" Helena said, her giddiness bordering on annoying.

Rafferty paused halfway up, looking toward the swinging kitchen door as a small, smugly smiling Scarlet shut it when their eyes made contact.

He didn't have the heart to tell Helena that they hadn't gotten away with it.

Chapter 25

FOOD BATTLE THE SECOND

"Very well. I'll consent to witness one of these food battles," Scarlet finally conceded. They had been sitting around her kitchen island.

"Really?" Helena asked, clapping her hands together in delight.

"Have you ever known me, child, not to be a woman of my word?" her boss said dryly. She sat with them now, wearing a long sweater the same color as her name over black slacks with a glittering black shawl draped over her shoulders. She may have had a shower, but her hair was perfectly dry and styled simply, its waves cascading around her lovely face. There was not a scrap of makeup on her, and yet she was one of those women who looked as if she had been done up in a salon all the same.

She slipped another bite of the Food of the Gods from the plate to her mouth, the morsel delicately balanced on the flat of her fork. Satisfaction burned in Rafferty's chest as the dessert disappeared and her lips allowed a small smile as she chewed. He had gotten the recipe right.

"I must say, Mr. Lares, I should hire you as my personal chef and forgo all this competition nonsense," she said, holding her fingers up to block the view of her chewing as she spoke.

"But that is part of the attraction. Like ... someone sponsoring a race car driver. He'll be your chef and represent Scarlet Promotions. It's excellent publicity for both of you!" Helena declared, her eyes shining with the energy of the idea.

Scarlet exchanged a glance with Rafferty, a kinship he didn't realize they shared, an understanding about the drive and dedication of Helena.

The other woman plucked up her cloth napkin and dabbed at the corners of her mouth. "Like I said, I am willing to go see what all this is about, but it is just that. I'm going to see. I am not agreeing to anything else yet."

"That's plenty. Let me go find your coat, and we'll get going," Helena said, standing up to do just that.

"What, now?" Scarlet exclaimed, her eyes glancing at the overly large, ornate clock ticking away on the wall. It declared they were approaching five in the afternoon.

"Yes! There is an event tonight, not too far away. You can see for yourself the potential here. And if we hurry, we can still enroll Rafferty into the competition." With that, Helena was gone, off to get the aforementioned coat. His and Helena's were draped over one of the stools at the island counter, ready at hand.

"Is this truly what you want as well?" she asked, leveling her gaze at him.

"Yes," he replied, letting his hungry grin take over his face. She needed to see the truth right now. "Oh, yes indeed."

The same familiar shiver washed down his spine as Rafferty entered the newest arena. It was taking place in the same hotel they were staying in, in one of the ballroom/convention halls attached to the space. Not their most lavish spaces by any means. The industrial carpet they walked on spoke to that, but it had plenty of space. The venue made the token effort of covering the various tables with black tablecloths.

As in the gymnasium, each cooking station was set up with essentials, including a few more appliances, such as grill surfaces and stand-alone hot pads with four surfaces. A supply table of ingredients waited on the far side, cooks preparing to cook their dishes were walking through making selections. From the sheer volume, it seemed there was more than enough to make three dishes. A larger crowd of audience members moved through the cooking stations, which had been spread out in the space randomly. There truly seemed no pattern to it, and Rafferty wondered why.

"This is certainly interesting," Scarlet noted, as a handsome young man in a plum purple chef's uniform and a ponytail walked by.

"Something's wrong," Rafferty said, noting that many of the chefs and cooks were standing in clusters talking urgently. Many had their arms crossed.

He spied Eleanor amongst the closest group and decided she was the safest person to ask, being she was the only one he knew. Leaving Helena with Scarlet, he approached his rival.

Her frown deepened when she spotted him.

Unable to resist, he adopted a swagger, a bad habit from the kitchens of yore.

"What's happening?" he asked as if they were old friends.

She huffed, then relented in a low, growly voice. "They changed the whole format. I'd blame your sugar mama, but it was apparently just decided for the pleasure of Mr. Tirrell. I guess all the Richie Riches think they can buy us now."

"I think I'm out," one of the other cooks she had been talking to said, slapping off his own toque as he turned to go to his station to gather up his things.

The others continued to stand around, unsure of what they wanted to do.

"What are they demanding?" Rafferty looked back at Eleanor.

But it was a chef with a white coat with black piping who answered. "They went from three rounds to one."

"It's an endurance round now," a gray-coated cook with an orange handkerchief instead of a toque interjected. "The one to get the highest number of plates served in the allotted time wins."

"One dish and you have to make as many of them as you can," the white-coated chef complained.

"They have a whole event going on next door, and we need to feed them all, for free. I'm working for *free*," the gray-coated cook complained, gesturing as he spoke with his thick accent.

"Technically for the prize money," the first one said.

"Oh, okay, thank you. They want me to work my ass off, after I've been working all day in my real job, for the chance of winning some chunk of change. It ain't even enough to make a damn bit of difference. You know what? I'm following that guy. I'm out." And gray-coated cook stormed off.

"I mean, he has a point. I do this to relax and have fun," the white-coated cook said.

"You were complaining just last week that the challenges were getting rote," Eleanor pointed out, switching her crossed arms to planting her fists on her hips.

"Yeah, but ..." white-coat waffled just as Helena walked up.

"What's going on?" she asked, tugging at Rafferty's sleeve.

"They're changing the format," he whispered back. "One round, cook one dish and clear the most plates to win."

"Oh?" Helena wrinkled her nose. "That's interesting."

"Well, most people are rebelling against change," Rafferty noted.

"Are you coming, Eleanor?" the white-coated chef asked, eyeing Rafferty with the wariness one gave an outsider.

"No. I'm in. I paid my fee, and I'm going to take their challenge," she said, turning to march back to her station.

"That's so Eleanor," the white-coated chef said, shaking his head. "We went to school together. She would be chef of her own kitchen by now if she wasn't so ... whatever she is." He glanced at them. "Don't get me wrong, it's not that she ever does anything wrong. It's not what you're thinking. It's just ... she never quite does anything right, either, despite her talent."

As white-coat walked off, Rafferty could feel Helena's aura bristle, like it had become porcupine-like and the energy of it was sticking him on the side facing her. Leaning in despite the prickles, he whispered in her ear. "Be careful."

Immediately, the prickles retreated. Helena closed her eyes as she breathed in deeply, tucking her demonic thorns away. "Sorry, sorry. That sort of thing … it just pisses me off," she said vehemently at the chef's back.

She glared daggers at the white-coated chef's back. The man flinched and came to a stop. As he started to turn, Rafferty turned Helena away as well, their widening eyes a mirror of each other's.

"What did I do?" she asked in a squeaky whisper.

"No idea, but keep walking," Rafferty coaxed, nudging her arm to reinforce it.

Thankfully, they encountered Scarlet, who was talking with another man in a suit. As they approached, she paused and gestured for them.

"Ritchie, let me introduce you to my protégé Helena. And this is her boyfriend, Rafferty Lares. This is an old friend, Richard Tirrell."

The well-dressed older man cocked his head to one side as he looked Rafferty up and down. "This is the one who did your spread at the Winter Rose Ball?"

Scarlet stiffened at the mention of the cursed event but didn't let her smile crack. "Yes, he was, as a matter of fact."

"Excellent. Best meal I've had in ages," the man named Ritchie declared, offering his hand to Rafferty to shake.

Rafferty shook, but the hairs on the back of his arms rose when he did so, and a familiar revulsion rose in the back of his throat. *A nobleman who thought very highly of himself but has nothing of real character. Only his entitlement,* Rafferty thought. He disliked this sort immensely.

They were always asking for substitutions and special off-menu items, even if it was the king's menu.

"Too bad it got overshadowed by all that demon business. I don't give a damn one way or another. Don't give a damn if it's not politically correct. All these cowards running away from my Scarlet and her cute little business, it's ridiculous. Who hasn't had a light brushing with the demonic before, really? We've been friends for too many years, Scarlet. Weak in the spine they are."

An awkward silence washed over them, but Mr. Tirrell just plowed right through it. "I'm looking forward to whatever it is you plan to cook today," he continued, turning to survey the room. "Maybe we should just forgo this whole thing, and I hire you on the spot as my own personal chef. What do you say to that?" He turned back and grinned with the satisfaction of a man who believed he had made an offer that couldn't be refused.

Rafferty offered his own sharp grin, not knocked off-center in the slightest. "I must apologize to you, sir. I just took a position in Ms. Scarlet's household. I'm not the sort to drop a position once I've said I'd take it."

"Ms. Scarlet?" Ritchie asked, turning back to the younger woman, who smiled indulgently, showing no signs of correcting Rafferty's presumption.

"It is what I insist all my staff call me. Ms. Kovacs was my mother, as you remember," she said.

Ritchie blinked, his courtier smile sagging as if he was struggling to reconcile his old friend with the young woman standing before him now. "Right. Right," he agreed, reforming the smile to full brightness. "Gosh, yes, the original Old Battleaxe. You'll have to forgive me. Your change is really throwing me off."

Scarlet nodded magnanimously.

"To be honest, I like my staff a little more on the pliable side," he said from the side of his mouth at her, as if he were sharing a great secret. "That's how I lucked into this sweet situation. I'm hosting a company appreciation next door, and I got this lot to cook for them all for free. All I had to pay for was their ingredients. Saved me a bundle."

"That is a way to get it done," Scarlet conceded, her mask not slipping an inch. Helena was doing a poorer job hiding her true feelings about that but managed to slip her fingers around Rafferty's bicep and squeeze until she had control.

Scarlet's vagueness was all the praise Ritchie needed. "Maybe I'll go ahead and buy this whole Underground Cooking thing. I can see lots of uses. No need to run another corporate gig again. No offense, of course. Your events were always the classiest, but for things for the regulars like this ... And these fools will do it just for a chance at a carrot."

He continued to chuckle until Scarlet cut in. "Well, that would be unfortunate as I am already in the process of acquiring the competition."

Ritchie's fluffy white eyebrows shot up to his hairline. "Oh, are you now?" A look of calculation washed over his face. "Alright, how about this? I'll wager you for it," he said.

"I don't think this group is yours to be wagering," Scarlet countered, raising one of her delicately arched eyebrows back at him in return.

"I mean, sure, we could do the whole outbidding each other, calling in favors, greasing palms, the whole nine yards. God knows, they took my money straight into their own pockets readily enough to set this up." A gambler's face washed over his expression, both delighted and aroused by his idea. "But that would be awfully boring. We both know I would win anyway. But this ... this would be fun. You have your champion." He nodded at Rafferty, then scanned the room, stopping inevitably on Eleanor. "And I'll have mine."

"Does she work for you?" Helena asked.

"No, but she will be in a minute." With that, Ritchie sauntered off to go speak to Eleanor.

"That ass," Helena hissed under her breath.

"This may be a little unorthodox, but I wouldn't disparage it. You're about to get everything you want, Helena," Scarlet scolded just as softly, giving her a knowing look when her protégé met her eye.

"So you'll go for my idea?" the truly younger woman asked.

"We'll see. First, our champion needs to win."

Chapter 26

A True Competition

Rafferty glanced at the standing oven beside him, grinning at the beauty of it. It had been built like a cabinet, with multiple sections behind the glass doors, sporting metal racks in each. It was possible to set each of the six chambers to different temperatures, but he didn't need that this time. Already roasting were several trays of diced-up, garlicked squash, the smell dancing in his nose as he rolled out the crusts for his creations. There would be six trays in all, one for each slot and even though they were given time to prepare, he had to use every minute if he was going to pull this off.

A few feet away, Helena sat with Scarlet and the socialite's "friend" Ritchie. The latter sat back in his chair, supremely satisfied and talking nonstop, not that either of the women were listening. Nor did he seem to need them to. All eyes were watching the few chefs that remained once the new rules for this competition had been properly spelled out.

Helena gave him an encouraging thumbs up, and he returned it, feeling the most relaxed he had in a while.

"We don't exactly have time to waste," Eleanor cut in as she walked past carrying an armload of ingredients.

Rafferty glanced at the large-faced clock on the wall, calculating the hands. There was an hour and a half to go until serving time, since they still had the full three hours reserved for the competition to create their entries, and at quantity, he simply wasn't worried. He could spare a moment for his girlfriend who was making this all happen.

He was supremely happy and ... satisfied. The truth was, he was loving this competition. It fed his sense of rivalry, excited his blood, and made his brain tingle with ideas. He thrived in this environment. Even if there was no prize or reward, and he would love to do this for the rest of his new life. And no one could really get hurt by it. He already knew what winning at all costs was like; he didn't need that anymore.

Despite the generous amount of time, he couldn't waste a second of it. His hands flew as he prepared the different ingredients for his dish.

"What are you making?" one of the observers asked, a teenage girl from the looks of her. She leaned on his table to look inside one of his bowls. There were observers, their potential diners, all over the place, watching the various chefs and cooks as they worked. It added an extra pressure.

"Please don't lean over my ingredients," he said as he slipped his pie crusts into a chiller, another appliance built much like the multilayered oven, only cold.

The teen responded immediately by straightening, taking her long hair out of the corruption zone. "Yeah, but what are you making?"

"Rainbow pie," he said as he removed two kettles, now whistling with boiling water, to replace them with four saucepans on each of the burners on his stove top.

She made a look of disgust. "A dessert? With spinach?"

He chuckled as he distributed the aforementioned spinach amongst the four pans, then dumped the boiling water. "It's a savory pie. It's going to have many layers and be full of color. Hence rainbow."

"What are you doing to the spinach?" she asked next without missing a beat.

"I'm wilting it," he said. "That way I can mix it with my prepared cheeses there, where you were leaning."

"Oh" was all she said and then she flounced away.

Rafferty wasn't offended. A young couple walked up, their arms wrapped around each other as they watched him mix his wilted lettuce in with the ricotta and hard cheeses, adding lemon zest and pesto. When the white and green of the mixture was fairly even, he roasted some peppers quickly, then pulled the chilled pie crust shells from the cooler.

A meditative calm washed over him as he layered each pie with breadcrumbs, then squash, his spinach mixture, the peppers, building the colors, until he covered each one with another pie crust, then added bits of extra dough to make roses with vines and leaves coming from them.

By the time he slipped each pie into their waiting slots in the standing multi-oven, he had accumulated quite a crowd.

"What? No meat?" one of the onlookers asked, twiddling his mustache.

"You take one bite of my food, you won't miss it," Rafferty answered as he focused on cleaning up his station and setting up his plates, so he could fill them quickly.

"I can't wait to taste his food," an older woman commented, sniffing at the air. "It smells delicious."

"He's taking a really big risk," Eleanor called from her own station. "He's only limited to how many pies he can bake at one time. It limits how many plates he can fulfill. He can't simply make more."

"I have made enough," he said, confidently.

Eleanor smirked and returned to her own dish. She seemed to be preparing to make stir-fry, setting her ingredients up in various bowls so she could chop and toss in one of the three electric woks she had prepared on her table. Next to that, there were three rice makers, steaming away. It was the complete opposite of his strategy: very little comparable prep with lots of fast, desperate work when it would come time to serve.

All he had to do once his pies were done would be to plate them.

Until then he had some time to kill while he waited, and he had a need that he wasn't used to dealing with. He loathed leaving his pies unattended though, so he waved Helena over.

"Yes?" she asked, leaning into him to ask in a soft voice.

"Can you stand here and watch my pies a moment?"

"Sure, are you okay?" she whispered back, looking warily around for any threat or danger. Damn, it was so cute.

"I'm fine. I just need ... to use the privy."

"Oh!" she said, "The *privy*, huh?"

He had a feeling it was the wrong word, but her teasing was a small price to pay for her help. "I'll be right back," he said, giving her a tingling kiss on the cheek as payment.

Nearby a group of teenagers giggled and whistled when he did that, only to have adults hush them for him.

It didn't take him long to find a pair of doors with a male and a female figure printed on them. Entering, he found the space empty, which suited him just fine. Along the wall were urinals, and he chose to take care of his needs at one of those.

"It isn't as easy to go back as you thought it would be, eh?"

In so many ways, Rafferty was not at all surprised to see Vassago standing beside him. On some level, he had known the demon had been watching him while he prepared his pies but hadn't dared to come too close. Not with Helena around for certain.

Glancing at the demon, Vassago had chosen his disguise well. He looked like he had before, a simple, unassuming man in a green official's shirt. The whole ensemble was so average and forgettable as long as you didn't look at his eyes for long enough to realize that the blackness there had no sparkle of life. They would just become whirlpools that would suck a person in if you dared to stare into them too long.

And Rafferty dared.

"Looking for your future, little chef?" Vassago asked, unblinking as his smile widened, showing too many teeth.

"I thought I would see you a lot sooner and a lot more."

Vassago chuckled dryly. "There are plenty of fish in the sea, my little man," he said.

"Then why aren't you out there fishing? Or have you already caught someone?"

The smile didn't evaporate from Vassago's face. At least, not entirely, but it did lessen. It was the demonic equivalent of having bags under the eyes. And it spoke to how much stress and pressure to return to Hell Vassago was really under.

Rafferty's eyebrows popped up in genuine surprise. "You haven't?"

Vassago leaned an elbow against the wall, and it was only then Rafferty remembered he came there to pee, and he unclenched. "I am being hounded by those mortal authorities. They are persistent and clever. They keep scaring off my prey. It's quite annoying."

Rafferty focused on the tinkling sound against the porcelain backsplash. "A big concession from one such as you," he noted.

"Simply an acknowledgment of my situation. I am not an idiot to want to pretend that those nasty, wicked humans who chase me, using whatever means is necessary…" Vassago chuckled dryly. "That they aren't the-ends-justify-the-means types."

"You mean Agent Archon and Agent Sophia?" Rafferty asked.

Vassago didn't respond right away. Instead, he stared off into space, seeing horrors Rafferty could only guess at. It was an educated guess. "Seeing flames? Or do you think they'll try drowning you? That one always takes forever."

The other demon blinked hard, coming back to himself, turning his toothsome smile toward his current target. "And how are things with your little … demoness?" he asked.

Rafferty had been expecting him to ask, yet hearing the words coming from Vassago's mouth filled him with an urge to punch and keep punching until his fist was covered in pulpy mess. Instead, he shook his member and tucked it away, then whirled away to wash his hands, but his anger made slapping the water on harder than it should have been.

Vassago's eyebrows lifted with delight at Rafferty's violent struggle with the appliance. "Ah, I see, she's got her hooks into you, hasn't she? You thought your experience would protect you, but your demoness is clearly cleverer than that. I told you before, my boy, a demon can trump any human, even if the human knows better. Especially when they know better. It'll only be a matter of time before you join us again." Vassago laughed. "Unless you want some help with her, of course?"

Rafferty felt like Vassago had just stabbed him through. Vassago knew.

Somehow, he knew what Helena was. The smirk on the other demon's face was unmistakably clear.

Of course, he did. Vassago was very good at finding things out.

"Get away from me, Vassago."

"You know the old adage. 'The devil you know.' And before you get your drawers in a twist, listen to my proposal. You at least owe me that, after everything I did for you."

Rafferty's fist swung before he realized it had.

It slammed into Vassago's face with a glorious smack, knocking the demon into the wall. Vassago hit the tiles and groaned in pain, only to look up at Rafferty and burst out laughing, even as he doubled over. Rafferty was shocked the tile wasn't cracked.

"Hey, man! What's going on?!" a bystander cried, as he entered the bathroom. He hadn't seen the punch, but Rafferty was sure their body postures gave them away.

"No, no, it's alright," Vassago said, lifting a hand to the man to stand down. "I had that coming. Trust me, I had that longtime coming. Everything is alright. It's alright."

At first, the defending bystander didn't seem like he intended to just leave things at that. But then a brief eerie feeling washed over Rafferty's skin, filling him with the urge to laugh.

Vassago kept chuckling as he expanded his power. The bystander's mouth cracked a grin, then laughed himself, shaking his head. He then disappeared into a bathroom stall, still laughing.

Despite the pressure toward joviality in the room, Rafferty resisted laughing himself. He hurried to the door, needing to escape and get back to the safety of Helena's presence.

Vassago shifted his jaw back and forth in his one hand as he followed Rafferty out the door. "Yes, my boy, I think I can give you that one."

"I owe you *nothing*," Rafferty hissed, refusing to stand down from his war footing. "You ate me!"

"You gave yourself to me!" Vassago hissed back, nodding and smiling at a couple of people walking past. His voice sweetened as he continued, folding his hands behind his back as he caught up to walk beside Rafferty. "Come on, boy. You know the rules. We can't take it without it being given. There was no way I could take your life unless you gave it to me. I had every right to take every slip and sliver of you, but I didn't, did I? I actually had some affection for you, even though you were an arrogant idiot who was only focused on himself. It wasn't because of me your poor mother and sister died. You abandoned them long before I showed up."

"I know what my sins are," Rafferty growled, clenching his fist again. If only he could forget them.

The demon lifted his hands defensively. "I'm just asking for the same mercy you've been shown. Isn't that what your pretty little old soul is all about? She gave your unworthy ass a second chance, and that's all I'm asking for."

Rafferty couldn't bring himself to fight again, not with so many eyes still watching them, so his only recourse was to flee. Unfortunately, Vassago was nothing but persistent.

"I mean, look at you! You're alive! I've never seen a miracle like you before. One of us getting to come back and get a second chance to live. That's all I want. Hey!" Vassago seized Rafferty's sleeve to slow him up. "Listen, please. I'm begging you. I'll get right down on my knees right here if you want, but please, Rafferty, hear me out. I don't want to hurt anyone anymore. I want to be just like you, now. A man. Alive. *Alive!*"

"I can't help you," Rafferty tried to say, but he could hear the wavering in his own voice.

"It wasn't a fluke, was it?" Vassago slipped his arm over Rafferty's shoulders, in that camaraderie-way this demon would do, that made Rafferty feel both held and trapped at the same time. "I've been thinking about it. I know you have, too. Helena took your place, didn't she? She's bearing all of your sins now, but somehow that has meant that she can still be here without any price. I've seen those agents. They tested both of you, but neither of you registered on their little evil devices. I just want the same thing."

"You want to fall in love?" Rafferty said, and instantly regretted it.

Vassago raised his eyebrows. "Love?" Then he started to laugh. "Oh, is that it? You got the little old soul to love you so much that she was willing ... Ohhhhh." The sound rolled out of Vassago with a breathy awe. "Oh, that's tricksome, isn't it? Love. People don't summon demons in order to love us. It's not inherent in the deal. We can make them think they love us, but they're still taking from us, so it doesn't work. No one ever just summons us for our own sake, do they? This little old soul of yours, you believe she truly genuinely loved you."

Rafferty, hearing the past tense, went stiff under Vassago's arm.

"Well, because it's not like she loves you still. She can't, can she? She's a demon now."

"*I* love her," Rafferty said softly. "I loved her even when I was a demon."

Vassago scoffed and withdrew his arm. "If you think that, you are lying to yourself. Or your human brain is misremembering. Rationalizing. We aren't chained down like they are by those sorts of feelings. Just like she's not weighed down now. But I'm not judging you. You always were a bright boy, and the fact that you figured this out all on your own ... I mean, I applaud you. You won the game. I never actually believed that was possible. So thank you." Vassago laid a hand over his nonexistent heart. "Thank you."

And, with *that*, he left.

Rafferty turned, managing to slam his way back to the bathroom and through one of the stalls to throw up.

Chapter 27

DIVINE INTERVENTION

Rafferty had a problem.

No one was selecting his dish.

He had cut into one of the pies and dished out the slices onto the plates provided by the hotel. To his eye, they all came out perfect, with even colors, and it smelled delicious to him. But when he set out his plates with a small bit of greenery garnish, no one picked one up to give it a try.

"Raffie, what's wrong?" Helena asked, coming up beside him to speak softly.

"I don't understand it," he whispered back. "There were several people who expressed interest in my dish, now where have they all gone?"

His eyes skimmed the room.

"There seems to be as many people as before. In fact, I would say there are more," Helena noted, and she was right. The room was flooded with people, and they were gathering around the other contestants, selecting plates of their dishes before moving toward other tables to sit and eat. There was a lot of energy and excitement in the room, while the "nobles" nearby, Scarlet and Ritchie, observed and commented while splitting a bottle of wine.

Eleanor's station in particular was raging as people cheered and clapped while she put together stir fries to order and made a show of flaring the fire and making the ingredients dance. Already her plate stack had shrunk, and the officials were keeping count as they added more. It was clear that out of everyone in the room, she was doing the best.

"Boy, she's really putting on a show," Helena said thoughtfully, then looked down at his offerings. "And your show was earlier when you were putting the pie together. But where are the people who were watching you then? They looked so interested."

"They came back and got a couple of plates, but that's it. No new people," he reported, wondering where he went wrong. "I don't understand it. The presentation looks appealing, right?"

A look of pity flashed on Helena's face, and a thrum of panic jittered through him. "What's wrong with them?" he asked, his voice nearly the whine of a child, and he cleared his throat.

"Nothing!" Helena assured him. "I think it's delicious. I had one, it's wonderful!"

He waved her compliment away. "Taste means nothing if the other person doesn't think it looks appealing."

"But it does!" his girlfriend insisted. "It's colorful and fun. It looks really good."

"Then why do they not come?" he asked. He was being surly and petulant. He could hear it himself.

"Maybe, it's not you," Helena offered lamely. "Don't panic."

"I have never had this happen before," he insisted. He could feel the panic infecting him despite her instructions, leaving his chest to make his hands shake and his feet itchy. The need to do something was strong, but there was nothing left for him to do. "I don't understand. I put out the food and normally the people just come and eat it."

"You've never had to market to people before," Helena said as if her words made any sense.

He was about to shout at her when she plucked up two plates and walked them over to Scarlet and Ritchie.

Ritchie grinned smugly at her as she approached, clearly aware that he was winning. Helena spoke to both of them, though Rafferty couldn't make it out. The smug nobleman's eyes glanced at him, twinkling in victory, and Rafferty had visions of taking one of his knives and stabbing it into one of the man's eye sockets, just to see how far he could cut through.

"Sure, I'll help out," the rich man said, his voice carrying just enough over the din for Rafferty to hear it. Helena set both plates on the table, waiting as they both dug in.

"Oh my, this is delicious!" Ritchie exclaimed, much louder, after his first bite, already cutting another chunk off for his second. "Oh, fantastic! You really must give me his contract, Scarlet. I really have to insist."

Helena said something more, then returned to Rafferty's station. "There. That's two plates down," she said.

"I hope he chokes on it," Rafferty murmured, his voice as dark as coffee.

"Oh stop," Helena said, bopping his arm with her fingers. "Just watch."

At first, Rafferty couldn't see what good she had done, really, but a single person peeled off from the crowd. They came up to the table and looked at his dishes, then back at the boss's before pointing at the plate. "Is this what Mr. Tirrell is eating?"

"Yes, totally," Helena said, and swiped up another plate. "Here, try some."

"But what is it?"

"Savory Rainbow Pie, of course! A beautiful balance of flavors all in a single magical pie," she continued, speaking louder as a couple more people walked up to look at it. They too were also glancing back at their boss.

"No meat, though?" one of them asked as they took the place of the first man, who walked off with a bite already on its way to his mouth.

"It doesn't need it," Rafferty snapped.

The pair flinched back, clearly offended, but Helena was there again, soothing their hurt feelings. "This is strictly vegetarian, but so good you won't even notice. It's a complete meal all unto itself."

Just then Ritchie walked up. "Oh, that was surprising. Are you sure you don't want to just throw this silly competition and come work for me instead? If you cook like that, I will double what she's paying you," he crowed, plucking up another plate. He didn't wait for an answer as he cut another mouthful and stabbed it with the tines, barely getting it to his mouth in time as he returned to Scarlet.

"Alright, alright. We'll try it," the two people said, snatching up plates and retreating away.

Rafferty couldn't stand it. He grabbed at Helena's wrist. Her head snapped back toward him at the abrupt motion. "What are you doing?" he asked, barely above a whisper.

"I'm helping," she said, patting his gripping fingers to reassure him.

While he couldn't feel it, he couldn't imagine she wasn't enchanting people.

"You can't—"

"It's not going to get you disqualified, don't worry," she said, giving him a wink. "I'm just another participant, recommending a dish I have tasted, just like everyone else here." She gestured over to another table where a pair of kids were trying to pick desserts between two other tables while a third was already munching down on a sugar treat.

Before he could say anything more, another handful of people came up to the table. Helena backed around it to stand close enough to whisper to him. "Just be nice and answer any stupid questions they may ask. You can win this thing yet."

And then she left him, weaving her way amongst the gathering crowd.

Rafferty had never felt so angry in his life. It was like someone held his spine against coals.

Still, he did nothing. There was nothing more for him to do; his work in the process was done. Plate after plate disappeared from his table, all without him doing anything more. It was all Helena. He watched as she moved around the room, talking, laughing, socializing with people, and one by one, they came over to claim a plate. As the time ticked away, he stood back and counted the plates, refilling new ones from his other pies still warming in the ovens. They, too, disappeared until only half a pie was left.

"What is the issue?" Scarlet asked, coming to stand next to him, her arms folded while one hand held a flute of wine.

"She's taking it away from me," he growled.

"Eleanor? I wouldn't say that. It looks like you two will be neck and neck. I'm tempted to ask for a plate recount just to be absolutely sure," Scarlet noted.

"Not her."

Scarlet went quiet for a moment before saying, "And how is Helena taking this away from you, exactly? If anything, I would say she is doing all of this *for* you."

"It's not my victory if she helps me. Then what am I really doing all of this for?"

"Me," Scarlet said, pinning him with a sharp stare. "That's what you both told me. You were doing this for me. To help me. Because everyone wants to help me." There was a twinge of contempt at the end of her last statement.

"I made a mistake," he snapped, then closed his eyes, already regretting saying that out loud. "Apologies, lady. I don't know what I'm trying to say. I feel it, but there are no ... right words for it."

"Maybe you're thinking of moving on, now that you have your second chance at life," Scarlet said.

His heart sped up at that statement. "No," he said with a sharp shake of his head.

"Helena is not the woman you knew anymore, is she? And she's not what you want now. But you don't know how to say good-bye and let her go, and that terrifies you, because it's what you really want, isn't it? You want to let him go."

Rafferty blinked as he caught the pronoun shift.

Scarlet didn't seem to realize it. She wasn't even looking at him anymore. Her gaze was long and far away. A second later, she snapped back to herself, then she swallowed down what was left of her wine as if to wash the words out of her mouth.

The two of them were like a weighted island of silence in a sea of laughter and chattering.

Eleanor shone in this environment. People were still gathered around her, watching her work. She had been going at it full tilt and showed no sign of slowing. She was energized by all this, her cooking and her social nature merging seamlessly before her audience. She was exciting and vibrant to watch. A goddess of cooking.

"I did not consider my making the dish as part of the ... performance. To attract the people to my food, not just by making it look tasty, but involving them in the process of making it." He shook his head. "This is too different a world for me. I'm used to being a faceless, behind-the-scenes player. My cooking is my only communication with my audience."

And it was true. Over at his station, a small crowd was gathered, eating and commenting on his works. They seemed very pleased, but the space behind his table, where he should have been standing, was empty. And the void he should have been filling seemed to be occupied by Helena.

She led another small group over and handed them each a plate of his pie, the last plates on the table. Her face practically glowed as she talked and laughed with everyone hovering around her. Like a queen bee in the middle of her buzzing hive.

Vassago's words rang in his ears. *"Ah, I see, she's got her hooks into you, hasn't she?"*

His old self would admire her work. She was pulling off a subtle trick, gathering the people around her, sipping off of their essences. Sustaining herself with their energy, willingly, if unwittingly given. His stomach twisted again as he watched her, even as he felt jealous that such a skill came so easily to her. It had taken him ages of nearly starving, rationing his power, until he could get his payoff before he realized he could do this trick.

It felt like she was cheating the game.

"This world is not the one I know."

"And you think you're the only one that feels that way," Scarlet said dryly. He blinked, unsure if he understood what the woman beside him was saying, but her gaze was also on Helena. Strangely, Scarlet was wavering on her feet. Then the noble lady stumbled a little, spilling a little of her drink, before resetting herself, compensating her unsteadiness with unnatural stillness. She had had more to drink than he realized. "If there is one ... *damn* thing ... I have learned from Yosef, that took me a lifetime to understand, that he just knew so naturally ... there is nothing wrong with letting the people love you and help you."

It felt like a slap of cold water, settling his anger back from raging fire to seething coals.

With a very focused, slow walk, she went back to her table, leaving him with that unhelpful advice.

Chapter 28

HOME AGAIN

"Oh my Heavens, did you see Mr. Tirrell's face!" Helena crowed as they exited the elevator on their floor. "It was everything I could do not to chew on my nails; I was so nervous. But you did it! We won!" She hugged him again around the shoulders, inhibiting his ability to pull their room key out of his pocket. Giggling and wiggling, she did not let go until they were almost to their door. "Also, your dish was soooo good! I was nervous when you did the pie thing, but it came out so tasty, I about lost my mind. Oh, I should call Cindy and tell her that we won the contest! I was texting her the whole time and ..."

Helena came up short, just as he managed to tap the key to the door reader, another bit of modern magic he wasn't entirely sure hadn't come about via demonic influence.

As angry as he was at her, he had managed to tamp it down into hot burning coals in his stomach, until he figured out how to deal with it. So, his voice sounded mildly concerned when he asked her, "What is it?"

"I missed a call. It must have come through when we were in the elevator." She pressed her device to her ear and waited, listening. A second later her eyebrows popped up. "We can go back to my house now."

My house.

She continued. "That was the BDI. They are giving us the go-ahead to go home. Oh, huzzah!" She grinned; her excitement renewed. "This day just gets better and better."

He didn't say anything to that; he simply spun around and went to set their suitcases on the bed. Clearly the maid had come in at some point during the day while they had been gone, as the bed was made up fresh.

"It seems a shame not to stay one more night," Helena said as she followed him in, scooping dirty clothes piled to the side of the room. "The agency will have to pay for it either way, but I also just really want to shower in my own shower and sleep in my own bed, you know?"

She dumped the load into the nearly empty side of her suitcase, stuffing it down so she could zip it behind a panel. "It's lucky, too, really. We were going to need to do laundry again, and my work clothes are dry clean only."

"Whatever it takes to win the game," Rafferty muttered as he turned on his heel to fetch the toiletries bag they were sharing, stuffing the brushes of various sorts into it, along with the other necessities of this modern life.

"Rafferty? What's wrong?" she called after him. "You don't seem alright. Why aren't you happy?"

"Why should I be happy?" he shot back, the internal anger bleeding into his words.

That took Helena back a half step. "Well, for one, you just won your first cooking competition, and for some pretty amazingly high stakes," she said, following him into the bathroom and leaning into the shower to retrieve the soap they had been using.

He took the opportunity to leave the small room where she was too close to him. "No, I didn't."

"What the hell do you mean? Of course, you did!" she cried, chasing after. He worked at stuffing the toiletries bag into his suitcase, but it wasn't fitting correctly, which led him to jamming and jamming it some more until her hands stopped his. "Will you please look at me and talk to me!"

The second he did, however, the anger retreated back into its cozy cave in his stomach. He didn't want to have this fight now. He didn't even really understand what the fight was about, so how could he tell her?

She bit her lower lip, clearly worried about his behavior, and he didn't blame her.

Forcing a breath in, he blew it out. "You're right. I'm sorry." He looked into her beautiful gray eyes, begging him to give her answers she could understand. "I'm not mad at you," he lied.

"Was it Richard Tirrell? I was wondering if he wasn't triggering something in you," she offered, and he accepted.

"He reminded me so much of the nobles I used to serve," Rafferty agreed.

"Oh, I was thinking he would be like the masters who used to summon and use you," she said.

"That, too."

She nodded, calmer now, more reassured by his explanation. "Well, let's get out of here and go home. Get as far away from anything to do with that pompous jerk."

He nodded, and they continued with their hasty packing. Helena kept talking the whole time, going over the events of the competition in detail. He listened and nodded or agreed when needed, but he wasn't really listening. Instead, a feeling of dread settled over him. One that seemed like it would stretch on and on for the rest of his life. At least, the rest of his life with Helena.

"Oh, dear Lord," she said as they entered through her front door and snapped on the light. After a second, she added, "Well, I guess it could have been worse."

It was clear that people had been in her house. Everything was slightly moved out of place, for one thing. As Helena rolled her bag through the door, she paused by one of her pictures on the wall and adjusted it back to straight. Then she turned a vase that to Rafferty didn't look like it mattered which way it pointed, but to her, it looked better. Then she shoved on the front of her couch with her knees, pushing it back an inch until it was back against the wall.

"If I wasn't so busy, I wish I could just take tomorrow off and straighten everything up, make sure nothing is missing. Not that I think they really would take anything, but you know."

"I will do it," Rafferty declared, shutting the door behind them.

"Oh, you don't have to," Helena said, waving her hands as if that would wipe away the suggestion. "You're not a servant anymore."

"I don't see it like that," he answered.

"Oh! And I need to let the BDI's Pet Care know that we're home, and I can come get Pooka back!" She grabbed her phone to do just that.

A doorbell interrupted whatever she was going to say next, and he was grateful.

Annoyed, Helena looked up from her phone. "Oh, come on!" But the bell rang again, so she pocketed the phone and went to open it.

A muffled voice came through the door before it opened. Then there was chaos as Charlie, followed by Cindy, dragged suitcases into Helena's home.

"I've left him, that's what's happening!" Charlie declared, clearly answering something Cindy had asked.

Rafferty didn't care. Cindy was saying something in response, while Charlie was trying to wrangle a small yapping dog that was refusing to forget about the squirrel it saw.

"I'm sorry. Wait, I'm sorry," Helena repeated, though what she was apologizing for, Rafferty hadn't the faintest idea, "What has happened?"

"No, *we're* really sorry," Cindy interjected, shooting a harsh look at Charlie. "We should just go to a hotel."

"How did you know we were here?" Rafferty asked.

"We didn't! That was my point!" Cindy declared.

Charlie picked up his little dog. "I just ... didn't know where to go. I wasn't thinking."

Cindy scoffed and rolled her eyes, exasperated since she had literally just told him to go to a hotel. Rafferty guessed she had been "just telling him" for a while now.

"No, don't be ridiculous, come in," Helena invited, now stepping back to clear the door. Rafferty left her side and grabbed the handles of two suitcases crowding the entry. Apparently, Charlie brought a total of six.

"Sorry," Cindy said, this one directly to him. "He's been freaking out for the past hour, and since I was staying with him ..."

"It's okay," Rafferty said. "You are Helena's friends. I am not a stranger to people freaking out." He was being serious, but it elicited a smile from Cindy.

"You're a good guy, Rafferty," she said. Her words hit him in his heart sharper than they should have, but Cindy didn't seem to notice as her attention was pulled back to Charlie as he recounted his story.

Charlie had been talking the whole time to Helena. "I mean *she* was just standing right there, in our apartment, wearing *my* bathrobe. To be fair, she looked as surprised as I was, but why would he do that!?"

"You mean, this girlfriend of his, she was in your apartment?"

"Yes! I mean, has he lost his damn mind?"

"I think he wanted to be caught," Cindy said, crossing her arms. "Like a cry for help or something. He knew we would be coming back."

"I don't know what he's thinking, I just know ... I just can't!" Charlie's face twisted up and Helena threw her arms around him. He didn't start crying, just shuddered and let himself be held.

"Charlie!" a shout came from outside.

Because Rafferty stood nearest the door, he looked out to see Chris, Charlie's husband. He ran from where he had badly parked his car on the street, the lights still on, the driver's side door standing open.

"No! I don't want to talk to him," Charlie said. "I can't just yet. I can't."

"Don't worry, I'll take care of it." Helena's face was full of determination, a battle look settling on her features.

"No, I'll take care of it," Rafferty said, not at all prepared to let her go anywhere near this so-called friend who had already threatened Helena a few times already. He didn't wait for her to agree; he moved out onto the small bit of porch she had and met Chris at the bottom of the steps.

"Charlie, I'm sorry. I mean it. Can we just talk about this? Please!" Chris shouted, even as Rafferty stopped him bodily from proceeding up the steps.

"No," Rafferty said firmly, blocking the other man's way. "He doesn't want to talk to you. You should go." Again, Rafferty thought to reach for his demonic energy to work on the human's emotions and compel him to obey. Even if such a thing would have been expensive, Rafferty knew how to make it work. As a man, his words lacked that sort of compulsion.

"Get off me!" Chris struggled, at first simply trying to push past the human obstacle, but when Rafferty proved to be determined, Chris laid his own hands on him in a weird ineffectual slapping motion.

"I said, 'No!'" Rafferty shouted, ignoring the slaps, as he seized Chris's shoulders, determined to walk this jilted lover to his car.

"Chris, please, listen to him," Helena called from the top of the steps, not daring to get any closer yet, for which Rafferty was grateful. Chris seemed determined not to listen to either of them.

It didn't help things that Charlie came out onto the porch at that moment, his own face tear-streaked. "Chris, you have to go! I need time!"

"How dare you do this to me? Do you understand you are humiliating me?!" Chris shot back, his rage replacing his pleas. "I said 'Get off me!'" he shouted inches from Rafferty's face.

Chris broke away from his grasp just enough to whirl back a fist. It landed across Rafferty's face as a haymaker punch. His head whipped to one side, and a wave of nausea roiled his stomach as the world spun. Like all the other sensations he had experienced since coming to life, this one was intense as well. His eye felt like it had exploded. Cupping his hand to it, the ground came up to meet his butt, and he decided to stay there until everything else in the world settled.

For his part, Chris loomed over him, cupping his hand in his other one, swearing in pain, having taken as much damage as he had given out. From what little Rafferty could see through his other eye, Chris's knuckles were split and bleeding.

Then another person stood between them.

Chapter 29

LIKE A DAMSEL IN SHINING ARMOR

"**S**top it, Chris," Helena said.

Not yelled. Simply said.

She didn't seem afraid or intimidated by the other man, who still had height and weight on her. Not now. What did a demon—an otherworldly being—have to fear from a mere mortal?

Nothing about her had outwardly changed, but Chris yielded before her, taking an unsure step back. "I just ... I don't want ..." he said, then ignored her and turned toward Charlie.

His husband still stood at the top of the porch with Cindy one step down, being a second-level human wall. With her jaw jutted forward, it was evident she had no intention of letting Chris get past her.

"Charlie, can we just ... *talk*?" Chris pleaded. "If you let me explain ..."

"Why there was a woman wearing my bathrobe in *our* apartment?" Charlie shook his head, his arms hugging himself as his heart broke. "I can't. Not right now. And not like this. I don't even know who you are anymore."

"You always do that! The second we start to get real about anything, you shut down ..."

Helena set a hand on Chris's shoulder.

"Get off me!" he screamed, swinging his arm back to hit her. Rafferty could see in his mind how it was going to play out in that split second. Her head would snap to one side, she'd fall. Rafferty wanted to move but his mortal body couldn't go that fast anymore. Couldn't bend time and space to protect her from the pain coming for her.

And then Chris froze.

He stared at Helena, like he had forgotten how to throw a punch.

There were shouts coming from Charlie and Cindy, but they had no effect on what was happening right there, just above where Rafferty sat. He froze, too, feeling the demonic power bending around them both, burning like ice.

"I'm going to call the police!" Charlie shouted, storming into her house.

"Cindy, stop him," Helena commanded. Cindy jerked at the command, closing her eyes as she wobbled on her feet.

"I should stop him," Cindy repeated softly, her own desire to do just that juiced with Helena's power. She followed Charlie inside, leaving Helena and Rafferty with Chris.

"Stop it, Chris," Helena repeated, setting a hand on the top of his head. "You need to leave for now. Not forever. Just for now."

Her touch stilled him, and Rafferty knew what she was doing as he watched her fingers sink into Chris's skull. Demonic power could not overwrite another's free will. That was impossible. But it could enhance feelings and sensations a human already felt, bring the ones buried underneath to the surface.

After a few seconds of her touch, Chris's face twisted into an ugly mask of sorrow. He dropped to his knees in front of them all. A sob ripped from his throat, ugly and broken.

"I'm so sorry!" he screeched, adding to the disturbance that had, in fact, brought some of Helena's neighbors poking their noses out of doors. "This isn't who I am!"

"Shh. Quiet," Helena commanded, touching him once more. Immediately, the wailing sound cut off. But he hadn't stopped crying. Rafferty could see through Helena's parted legs that Chris continued to sob and wail, but no sound could be heard. She was stilling the sound waves he should have been making, augmenting reality.

Helena looked down on Chris. Her eyes glowed like twin suns: unearthly, inhuman eyes with no trace of emotion. "You need to leave," she insisted, not unkindly, just simple facts. Her will was final, and there was no room for negotiation.

Chris nodded.

Then Helena helped him up to his staggering feet, lifting the larger man easily, as if he were a small child. Rafferty tried to get up to help her, but she shook her head. "You stay down. I got this."

He yielded automatically to her order. It seemed like the absolutely right thing to do. He wasn't sure he if he wouldn't have simply fallen over again if he did try to stand.

His vision whirled once more, and he closed his eyes to wait for the swimming motion to end.

Helena walked Chris all the way to his car and sat him on the driver's side. She stayed, one hand on the door and one on the roof of the car, talking to Chris. Rafferty didn't look away, deluding himself that he would be ready to spring up if Helena should need him, until Cindy knelt beside him. She set a black bag on the ground next to her and unzipped it but didn't remove anything. Instead, she took his face and turned it up toward the porchlight.

"Relax your head," she encouraged. "Let me see."

He obeyed, submitting himself to her scrutiny. She probed his eye very gently, encouraging the lids to pull back. The lower one hurt to do that, but he resisted pulling away.

"You're definitely going to have a nice black eye. Eyeball looks fine, if a little red," she pronounced, then reached into the bag to pull out a small flashlight. She shone the beam into each of his eyes, one at a time, though he wasn't sure what she was looking for when she did that. Whatever it was, she seemed satisfied as she traded the flashlight for a plastic packet.

Giving the packet a quick twist, she shook it out, then held it out to him. "Hold this to that eye until it goes numb," she said.

He obeyed that order, too, surprised to find the packet turning cold. Wanting to ask if it was some kind of magic, he resisted. Every time he returned to this plane of existence, there was some new technological advancement that shocked him. He learned it was best not to ask questions about them unless necessary. This cold packet was something he could simply accept.

"I used to be able to take punches better than that," Rafferty complained.

Helena's doctor friend cracked a grin. "A lot of fist-fights in the culinary world? Need help standing up?"

"No, I'm fine," he insisted, but even as he got up under his own power, Cindy offered a steadying hand until he was clearly, solidly on his feet.

"I would sit on the porch," Cindy suggested, already turning to go to Helena and Chris, who were still talking at the car. She muttered to herself, "I can't believe I'm going to go patch up that asshole's hand."

"Then why are you?" Rafferty asked as he dropped onto the second step from the bottom, still holding the cold packet in place.

"I swore an oath about it," Cindy murmured.

Rafferty wondered what sort of oath that could be, but she had moved too far away to make asking easy without shouting the question. It could wait for later, if ever.

"I'm so sorry about this," Charlie said, and it took Rafferty a second to realize the apology was for him. Helena's other friend remained at the door, watching what was happening outside while still shielding himself within her house.

The former demon grunted. Helena's friends were a lot of trouble.

"Still, I can't believe he did that. Chris has never hurt anyone before in his life. I didn't even think he knew *how* to throw a punch." Charlie pressed his fingertips to his lips as if he were tempted to chew on them and he was trying to resist, all while shaking his head. "I don't know who he is anymore."

"Charlie?" Helena asked, suddenly much closer as she walked up to the porch, holding her phone out toward her friend. "Do you know Chris's brother's number? I don't think Chris is in a state to drive himself safely anywhere."

"Uh ... yeah," Charlie said, taking the phone to type the number in.

As he did that, a police car rolled up, its lights spinning though its siren was silent.

"Did you call them?" Helena asked, alarmed.

"No, no. Cindy talked me out of it," Chris confirmed.

"Oh great. Someone must have called 911," she muttered, crossing her arms.

"Helena, I'm so sorry. This is all going to bring the BDI back on you, isn't it?" Charlie interjected, even as his thumbs worked across the phone screen.

A second car pulled up and two familiar agents got out.

"You are *sure* that this ... incident ... has nothing to do with the demon?" Agent Archon asked for the dozenth time.

"Yes," Helena said with tired assurance.

Rafferty and she had been talking to the agents for about an hour, and a light wintery sprinkle of snowflakes washed over them all. Chris sat in the back of one of the police squad cars while his brother, who had arrived twenty minutes ago, talked to the officer standing guard over him.

Charlie stood just within the door, talking to Agent Sophia. Cindy sat on the porch with her medical bag, staring off into space.

Helena indicated toward her friends. "This has been an"—she blew out a sigh—"ongoing issue, long before we had ... any concerns about this demon."

Agent Archon sniffed. "And you don't want to press charges?" she asked, directing the question toward Rafferty, standing by Helena's side.

"No," he said shaking his head. "He is a sad fool. He's suffering in a hell of his own making. But if he comes for me again, I will."

"Fine, fine. Don't need a whole speech about it," the agent dismissed, tucking away the notebook she had used to take down the basics of what happened. "Call me or Agent Sophia if you should be contacted by the demon, or any demon for that matter, or if anything else unusual happens. Which you are sure you haven't seen?"

Rafferty felt the hairs on the back of his neck bristle, but it was Helena who answered. "You mean like the demon I told you I saw at the agency, but you didn't believe me?" she snapped, which was quite uncharacteristic of her.

Agent Archon's eyes widened a moment, then narrowed. She said nothing more but headed over to talk to the police, presumably to talk to Chris and his brother.

"I think that is it, let's go inside," Helena said softly, and he nodded. His eye still throbbed, and the ice pack Cindy had given him had long gone warm. When they passed the doctor on the stairs, she took in a sharp breath coming back from her long stare. Then silently collected her bag and followed.

When they filed back into the house, they found Charlie sitting at her dining room table, his head in his hands.

"Should we make some dinner?" Helena asked, looking from Charlie to Cindy who deposited her bag onto Helena's couch.

"We brought food from Charlie's kitchen," Cindy said, shifting back to the door where their suitcases and a couple boxes of food Rafferty hadn't noticed earlier sat.

"I can do it," Rafferty volunteered, and went to pluck up one of the boxes, with Cindy doing the same with the other.

Helena nodded and went to sit down next to Charlie, but he got up to follow into the kitchen, so she did as well.

"So they fixed the floor?" Cindy asked as she set her box on a counter. Tapping a foot onto the tile where the lines used to be.

"I guess," Helena said, letting the door fall shut behind her. "I guess in case we get tempted to open the circle again."

"But it was a real demonic circle, right?" Cindy asked, crouching down to touch the nonexistent lines.

"Not officially, I guess," Helena answered.

"What did you say to Chris?" Charlie cut in before Rafferty could think of a suitable lie about the floor.

"I made a deal with him," Helena said.

Chapter 30

TASTED OF HONEY

"A deal?" Charlie choked out.

Rafferty's heart pounded hard in his chest. "You did what?"

She straightened, looking her friend directly in the eye, holding his shoulders. "And it's one I think you should consider making as well. He has agreed to go to therapy."

Immediately, Charlie's head shook. "No, no. I can't. I can't forgive him and just carry on like nothing happened. I can't even look at him again."

"I'm not saying you have to," Helena said. And Cindy chorused, "She's not saying that."

Cindy came up on his side, joining her hand with Helena's. "I see it all the time. I have a colleague who's a family therapist. They said that often people will go to see them not just to save their relationships—though it's what she hopes for—but sometimes it's also so that they can do the work to part well."

"I know you, Charlie. You don't want things to end like this right?" Helena asked, her voice heavy and hypnotic. She was doing it again.

"Helena! Stop it!" Rafferty hissed, but she only glanced at him before Charlie spoke.

His voice came out slow and thick as molasses. "Yes, you're right. This isn't what I want. Even if we don't end up together ..."

Cindy pinched her eyebrows together in worry, but Helena only nodded. "Yes, exactly. You're going to rest here tonight; I've got my guest bedroom and everything. I can also make up the couch—"

"No, that's fine," Cindy said. "We've shared a bed before on more than enough road trips."

"It's a queen. We'll be fine," Charlie agreed. Then he looked up at Rafferty. For a second, Rafferty thought their eyes met, but then he realized he was looking at the area around his eye. Where his husband had hit him. "I'm so sorry he did that to you."

"You are not responsible for what he does," Rafferty countered. He just meant it factually, but Charlie looked like he was about to burst into more tears.

"You are too kind."

Charlie swallowed the lump in his throat, then bent to pick up his little dog, who had come over to set a paw against his leg. "I didn't even know he knew how to throw a punch," he repeated.

"Oh, honey," Cindy said, rubbing his back. "Everyone can throw a punch but you."

Making a choking sound, Charlie let out a broken laugh, much to Rafferty's surprise.

Then they all laughed. It was infectious so much so that even Rafferty, who found no real humor in the situation, couldn't fight back a grin with some small chuckles. It tickled all the way into his belly, and somehow everything was lighter and easier when it died down. *When is the last time I laughed like this?* Some distant part of him knew he must have, for he recognized it for what it was.

As it died away, Charlie's shoulders dropped as if the laughter had relieved his great burden. "You are right, Helena. You have a deal."

A shiver ran down Helena, and she closed her eyes as she felt it.

Rafferty's throat tightened. He had let his guard down, and she had done it. She had bound her friend to a deal. Just like ...

But why did he care? These weren't his friends, they were hers. He had chosen to accept her and guard her secrets, so ...

I'm not responsible for what she does, a rebellious thought echoed back at him.

"You okay?" Cindy asked her.

Immediately, Helena's eyes snapped open. "I am so sorry. This has been ... well it has been a day. So much has happened that I would love to tell you about, but we need to go to bed soon, and I—"

"Oh God, yes. Go ahead. Go to bed. I didn't even realize what time it was," Charlie said, flipping into a mode that seemed closer to his nature. "We can take care of ourselves, don't wait on us. We can make our own food and everything, just go to bed. Go." Cindy nodded agreement as he shooed them out of the kitchen.

Rafferty went willingly. This whole situation made him incredibly uncomfortable as he beat it all the way back to Helena's bedroom.

As soon as he passed though the entryway, he whirled back to her.

"How could you—" was all he got out as the door shut behind her, and she attacked him.

The force of her grab shoved him back several steps. He kept stumbling until his back slammed against the wall with a definitive thump.

"What—"

Then her lips were on his. They devoured him. Heat knifed through him and went straight to his groin. A moan rumbled from his throat. Gasping, the kiss broke, and she was at the buttons of his shirt. He was still wearing his coat, and the buttons gave way quickly enough so she could slide the whole thing off his shoulders.

Another protest was choked out as her lips went for his throat. Her tongue and teeth nipped and sucked, setting his nerves on fire to shoot down his spine. Her hands washed over his skin, feeling every inch of his ribs and the muscles of his chest down to his stomach. They then teased just above the waistband of his pants, and he ached for her to go further. She then abandoned his neck to stick her tongue fully into his ear. Another cry squeaked out that he barely strangled back. Her friends would hear, and he couldn't ... why couldn't he ...?

As delicious sensations erupted from her ministrations, his knees went water-weak, bringing him down and even more accessible to her power.

Then, all at once, she stepped back, her warmth leaving him cold. To prevent himself from falling over, he braced his hands against the wall, panting.

To his shock, she was naked. She hadn't stripped her clothes off, he would have noticed that at least, but she stood before him as she truly was. Her wings framed her on either side of her form, her skin glittering white gold with dusky golden edges. The peaks of her breasts captivated his gaze entirely, the cream and golden edging making him think them twice-baked meringues. His appetite to devour them ached to his core.

Helena laughed, the haloed horns on her head sweeping her rose-gold hair from her face. She set her fists on her bare hips, smirking and elegant where he and his disheveled clothing were a mess.

With twinkling eyes, she then pointed to the ground before her. "Kneel, mortal," she said, teasing music in her voice.

He was headed there anyway, so he let go of all resistance and dropped to the ground before her. It was then he realized her legs were slightly parted, and he was captivated by the rose-gold hair of her sex. A longing to bury his face there filled him. A small voice in his head told him she was doing this, playing his emotions like a fiddle, but nothing else within him cared. She was hungry; she had to be from all the power she expended that day, and he was her meal.

The same fingers that commanded him came closer to slip through his dark hair. A shiver of ecstasy at the touch washed through him, and his mouth opened in another uninhibited moan.

"It's alright. I won't let them hear us. Sing out for me," she whispered, taking another step closer as her other hand cupped the other side. His head swirled with sensation and he didn't care. Then she gripped the back of his skull—a sharp pain of pulled hair, sweet and primal, as she drew his mouth down toward her waiting sex. And he opened it eagerly, parting her lips with his tongue.

A moan escaped his throat as he tasted it. He expected the less than pleasant taste of woman, not his favorite, but he had performed before when ordered. But Helena had changed herself somehow. She tasted of honey. Not metaphorical honey, but actual sweetness between the folds of her flower. The bee metaphor someone had told him centuries ago danced through his mind as he licked and probed again, arching the tip of his tongue down the smooth avenue that led to her bud, tapping it before leaping free. Now, it was her turn to shudder as he washed her nerves with pleasure. He then lost himself to the rhythm of his work, kneading and working her. She cried out beautifully, unabashedly, from his worship, her hands gripping his shoulders as he grasped her round buttocks in each hand, cupping her body open and toward him.

The moans and shudders announced that she was close, and he wanted her to gush into his mouth, more of the sweet ethereal honey, but then she stopped. Ripping herself away, she seized him and threw him to the bed with unearthly strength.

She was on him then, like a wild animal, tearing at the buttons and zipper of his jeans, yanking them off with his underwear so that his erection sprang free. He had never been so engorged before, standing at ready, aching attention. She didn't make him wait long as she mounted on top.

He about died as the head of his cock slipped into her tight folds, but then she paused. He wanted to push himself all the way to the hilt, but she pulled him out and waited. Looking up at her glowing face in the dark, he wondered briefly what was wrong, but her wicked smile sharpened as she once more let his head pass her portal and no further.

She was teasing him.

Over and again, she slipped the head in, taking immense pleasure, her breath and moans saying so, but denying him the relief he longed for.

"Helena, dammit," he muttered as she did it again. He seized her hips, a wild thought tearing through his mind that he would force her the rest of the way down, but he stopped himself when she resisted.

"Ah, ah, ah," she chided, her eyes glowing mirthfully in the dark. Then she leaned a little closer, whispering, "Beg me."

"Please," he twisted out. Rafferty hated begging, but she had all the power. She feasted on him even now. He could feel it, and he was helpless to stop her. Helpless to say no.

"Please?" she continued, dangling her bait, her hot lips barely kissing.

"Please," he growled out now. "Please fuck me."

Her smile sharpened a split second, then she dropped hard on him, his erection finally doing what he longed so hard for, capturing him inside her.

The force of it lifted him off the bed, her interior muscles tightening around his shaft. She didn't pull him out to start a rhythm, instead, her vaginal walls began to pulse. Fully inserted, she squeezed him, watching with detached eyes as his breathing came in gasps with each pulse.

"Let me hear you!" she ordered, as her hips finally rocked.

He cried "Ah," with the next breath, then repeatedly in higher and higher in pitches as she at last shifted to riding him fully. Her pace was perfect; she grasped his hands in hers. Eventually, one of her hands slipped away to play in time with her clit, her peaking breasts arching out as she leaned further back.

He gave her everything he had as he neared higher and higher toward the peak. He would explode inside her if she didn't ... if she didn't ...

His balls tightened and he came, hard. He bellowed like an animal as he felt himself shoot into her. His life energy drained into her being, through their connection, and she glowed like sparkling starlight.

His succubus.

His angel.

Chapter 31

DEAL WITH A DEMONESS

Barely gasping for air, he watched as she came next in all her glory, her wings spasming with her own orgasm, wringing out the last of him into herself.

Again, he could feel his heartbeat fading, the cold oblivion beckoning. Then she curled forward, dropping once more onto his chest. With the full contact of her skin on his, the warmth flushed back into him. He took in a sharp full breath as life filled him, even more than what he had given her first.

The urge to tell her to stop, to not give back what she had rightly taken from him, died before it could reach his lips. He had no real strength to stop her. All he could do was wrap his arms around and hold the snuggling female close. They were still connected, but he felt himself deplete inside her. She would just have to shift a little bit for him to fall out.

Her being shifted, and the eerie, unearthly form disappeared until he held a mortal woman once again. She cuddled into his chest, her eyes closed, a contented smile on her face.

"I love you," she whispered sleepily. And then there were a few soft little snores.

Rafferty stayed that way, holding her, for ages as he stared up at the dark ceiling above them. He had no idea how he felt, but he knew that sleep was too far away. As time ticked by, his legs, which were still off the bed, complained and ached. Her weight made it harder to breathe, and he grew irritated.

Finally, he shifted, arresting her tiny snores with a louder snort.

"I can't ..." he attempted to explain, but she just sleepily lifted her head and took in the situation.

"Oh, sorry," she murmured, then disembarked from him, shifting to the side so he could sit up.

In that position, he kicked off the pants that were trapping his ankles while she crawled around to lie on her side of her bed, burrowing under her covers still naked. Feeling like it was required, he did the same, crawling under her quilt with her. As soon as he was in place, she slid up closer, already most of the way back to sleep, and settled into the nook of his shoulder.

"Thank you," she muttered.

"For what?" he asked, whispering the words into the dark.

"For giving me so much ..."

He could sense her slipping away, slipping into sleep. "I want something," he said, jerking his shoulder to keep her from leaving him for her dreams.

"Yes?" she asked.

Licking his lips, his eyes searched the ceiling above for answers in its shadows. "I want a contract with Scarlet. Scarlet Promotions, I mean. If I'm going to be your champion in this competition, I want it in writing. Everything spelled out."

"Oh, yeah. Okay," she agreed so easily it felt like a cheat.

"And money, too. A guarantee."

"Mm-hmm."

He nodded then. It was only right. He was giving her so much of himself; it was the way of things, and he needed to get something back in return. It just felt more comfortable to have an agreement. This was how these things worked with demons.

"I have every right to demand this," he said out loud, but Helena didn't answer. Her breathing had already slipped into an even rhythm. "I have every right," he repeated, hugging her closer.

Yet, even in a better position, he still stared up at the ceiling, unsure what to do or say, wondering if sleep planned on coming at all.

In the morning, Rafferty woke in the bed alone. His head ached, and it only got worse when he opened his eyes. The edges of Helena's blackout curtain glowed brightly, indicating a bright, sunny day outside, and he hated it already.

He thought about rolling over and trying to find some more sleep to sweep away his headache, but a weight settled on the bed beside him, settling in the space left by the crook of his body.

"Good morning, sweetie," Helena's voice sang out softly as she brushed her fingers over his forehead, clearing his hair from his eyes.

The involuntary groan did not deter her as he turned his head away from her touch, the headache spiking again.

"Is everything okay?" she asked again.

"I feel hungover," he muttered.

"Ohhhh," she cooed, leaning in to kiss him on his temple. Immediately, the headache eased away. "I'm sorry. That's my fault, I think." Then she bounced back up to her feet. "Get dressed. Charlie's started breakfast. We've got a big day."

"What?" he tried to ask, but she was already gone.

Dragging himself out of bed, he wondered at his own reluctance. A night of passion should have invigorated him, and the news of someone else cooking should have alarmed him, but instead, his heart felt heavy, like it had been replaced with a stone.

"Is that my phone ringing?" Charlie asked, leaning against the counter in the kitchen, a piece of toast hanging from his mouth.

"It's there on the counter," Cindy said, gesturing at it with her head while she poured herself a hot cup of coffee.

Rafferty checked the underside of the eggs he had just flipped over easily, having taken over the cooking duties so Charlie could finish getting dressed for the day. He then picked up the whole pan and brought it to the four plates waiting for him beside the stove. With quick work of his spatula, he had the whole pan of eight eggs distributed to the plates.

"Hello?" Charlie said into his phone as he placed it between his shoulder and his ear while he attempted to adjust his tie. Somehow, he had tied it so the thinner end was longer than the thicker. His fingers tried to fix it, but he was making such a mess of it, though, that Cindy set down her coffee and took over.

"Yes, I'll be there in a half an hour. No, I haven't left yet, it'll take me less time … because I'm not staying at home at the moment, so I'm closer to the office … I'm sorry, but who works for who here? That's none of your business, just focus on my business, and I'll be there in a half an hour!" he said sternly. Then in the same stern yet sincere voice, he continued. "Thank you. I really appreciate you. Your work is valuable to me. Bye." He hung up with a press of his screen and lowered the phone. "I have no intention of being there for very long. I'm just going to go in and set things up so I can take the next week off because, seriously, I just can't with everything going on and stuff. I swear I'm just losing my mind, but if I don't set things up the whole thing may burn down before I can get back and are you done yet with that tie, oh my God!"

Cindy bopped him on the nose. "Yes, if you would just hold still and take a breath every other sentence, I would be finished—" Another yank and she had the tie straight, the ends measured perfectly.

Charlie turned away abruptly, seizing control of his tie back. "Oh it's fine, I …" Then he stopped and forced a breath in. "Thank you. I appreciate you. I'm sorry, I'm sorry. I am not being my best right now."

"It's not required," Helena said, coming in as well. She then laid her hand on his shoulder. The tension in the other man immediately deflated.

Cindy didn't seem to notice what just happened, and the bliss washing over Charlie's face made Rafferty's spine shiver. He covered his discomfort by pulling bacon out of the oven.

Helena smiled, satisfied, as she patted Charlie's shoulder and then moved to grab a stool next to her other friend. "I just hope the guest room was okay for you both?"

"Well, I've never slept better. It's like that trip to Mardi Gras all over again," Cindy said, grinning as she reclaimed her coffee cup.

"And I'm so sorry about this drama just showing up on your doorstep again," Charlie repeated for the hundredth time as he accepted the plate of breakfast from Rafferty.

"No, please, me casa, su casa, yadda yadda yadda," Helena said as she took her own plate, giving Rafferty a kiss on the cheek. She then led them all into the dining room. "And I have to go into the office, too. Scarlet sent me an email asking me to come in."

"So you still work for her?" Cindy asked, holding the door for Rafferty as he followed with his own plate. It felt strange to belong with this group of tight-knit friends, but they were treating him as if he had always belonged.

But all of them would not speak to me if I were to leave tomorrow. They are not my friends, he thought bitterly to himself. Somehow that made him feel even more alone.

Guilt washed over him, too.

She was winning the game. And he resented her for it.

They talked around him as they all ate at the table while he took slow, methodical bites of his food.

"You know that Cooking Underground thing that I told you about?" Helena asked as she sat down at the head of the table.

"Vaguely, but to be fair I've been a little distracted. I'm just glad you still have a job right now. It sounded like you were losing it," Charlie said as he went behind her to sit on the bench side, letting Rafferty and Cindy have the two easier-to-access seats. Then his watch went off. "And I'm going to be late, so that's it for me, good-bye. Tell me all about it later!"

Rafferty was at least grateful that Charlie cleared the remaining contents of his plate into his mouth before he grabbed his suitcase and went out the door.

Cindy finished her breakfast and gathered up the extra plate to take to the kitchen. "I'm going to be heading out as well. I'm meeting up with my supervisor. I mean, my former supervisor. We're going to have lunch."

"That sounds like a great idea," Helena added, taking up Rafferty's finished plate as well, following her friend into the kitchen, ignoring him entirely.

Rafferty sat there with his hands in his lap. Then a peculiar itch slipped into them. Pulling out his phone before he realized he was going to, he stared at the black screen. Then got up to go to where his coat hung by the front door to retrieve Eleanor's business card.

Typing the number in, he hit the call button before he could stop himself and overthink it.

His hand shook as it rang. Maybe he should have waited. At least have Helena sit here with him, guide him through this. *When did I become so dependent on her? Is it even right for me to rely on her like this? Shouldn't I just be brave and—*

"Hello," Eleanor answered.

A thrill of excitement slipped through him at the sound of her voice. "Hello. This is Rafferty," he said, a hint of his old, charming self flowing into his words. It was the voice he used in seductions, but Eleanor bulldozed right over it completely unaffected.

"I'm not available to take your call right now but leave me a message and I'll get you back when I've got a minute. Thanks." Then there was a beep. It took another half second for him to realize this was the time for him to speak.

"Uh, hi. It's Rafferty," he answered, his words coming out now in sharp detached sentences. "I'm calling you." Another long pause, his brain working so fast and coming up with nothing more to say.

So he hung up.

"What am I doing?" he asked the phone, but it offered no comment.

Just then Helena returned, dressed in a slate-gray women's suit with a skirt that went to her knees. She was flipping her hair up into a quick, professional bun. It was hypnotic to watch. And she smiled as beautifully as the sun.

I love her, he thought as he drank it in. He knew it and felt it burn in his heart. *So, what am I doing calling Eleanor?*

"I'll call when I'm on my way home. I love you," she said so easily and casually, as if such a declaration was no big deal. Leaning in, she gave him a kiss good-bye. "Are you going to be okay here while I'm gone?"

"Yes, of course," he said. "I have plenty of Food Network to watch."

She smiled but she couldn't hide her worried look. "I'm doing this for you, too. You know that, right? I know I've been leaving you alone a lot lately, but soon, you'll be more involved as we finish getting things set up. I've got meetings with a production company today, and I think they're really keen on working with us."

"Doesn't that seem ... rather fast for this sort of thing?" Rafferty asked.

Helena cocked her head at him curiously. "Do you know much about broadcasting?"

He shrugged. "I cooked for a TV executive once. He liked to talk while he ate. I did not understand much of what he said, but I am a very good listener."

A wary look passed over Helena's face, though he had no idea what he could have said to inspire it. Then she asked, "What happened to him?"

It was like she had punched him in the chest.

"He died," Rafferty said simply.

A tension stretched between them, then Helena shook her head, banishing the expression from her face. "No, let's not do that. Let's not spoil a good morning. I'll see you later," she said, grabbing her coat.

He felt the urge to go to her, to hug and kiss her one more time, but he didn't, and she didn't look to him for one. His stomach felt sick, and the overwhelming urge to bake something tickled at his fingers.

I'm not the man she thought I was. And she realizes it now. It's only a matter of time, his darker voice said in his mind, the one that had been with him in Hell keeping him existing.

Before he could turn to the refuge that was the kitchen, however, or pick up the remote control to lose himself in other people's cooking, his own phone rang. Glancing at the screen, a fresh hitch in his chest caught him

"Hello, Eleanor."

Chapter 32

THE TEMPTATION

Eleanor was a sight as she worked in the auxiliary kitchen of the hotel. A cooking goddess in her element, her tied-back hair under a bloodred handkerchief was striking. Her snow-white chef's jacket was a stark contrast to it. Before her was an array of tiny beige blobs, but Rafferty couldn't see what they were from that distance.

She wasn't alone in the room: two other people armed with a camera and another with a microphone on a stick documented her every move. Or rather the cameraman did. The mic guy was leaning against one of the empty counters watching as his counterpart zeroed in his camera on the surface that Eleanor worked on.

There was also a fourth, familiar, person in the room. Éliott stood on the other side of the workspace, getting in the way of the mini-camera crew while he talked at her in a low voice. Whatever he was saying seemed urgent, and not for the millionth time, Rafferty hated that he couldn't sharpen his hearing to catch it.

What really caught his focus was all four sets of eyes shifting up to him. A feeling of unworthiness washed through him.

"Let's take a few minutes," Eleanor finally said to the two working men, wiping her hands on a damp towel, but her stiff demeanor was reserved for Éliott.

He took the silent rebuke, straightening himself, then turned, walking toward the door where Rafferty stood.

"If it's alright with you, I'll go ahead and get some still shots," the camera guy said, clearly uninterested in what was happening.

"Yeah, sounds great," she agreed.

"Hi," Éliott said to Rafferty, "what are you doing here?"

"Eleanor asked for my help," he said simply. "What about you?"

But Éliott clapped his shoulder instead of answering. "I'm glad. That's good. She needs all the help she can get, and you are a good person to give it."

Rafferty frowned at him. "The one thing I am definitely not is a good person."

But Éliott only gave a sad smile. "And if you need help, brother, know that I am here for you." Then he exited out the swinging doors of the auxiliary kitchen, which rebounded into Rafferty's backside, as if giving him a little push to enter further.

Taking the impetuous, he crossed the space to meet Eleanor, still wiping up with her towel, which she tucked under her arm as she crossed them. "Well, there he is," she said, the hostility from the first time they met having returned with full force.

Instead of cowing him, he felt the familiar posturing of the king's kitchen slip through him. Crossing his arms, he leaned one hip into the table beside him, letting a confident grin overtake his face.

A twinkle appeared in her eye in response, despite her determination to maintain her scowl.

He had missed this game.

She huffed, relenting first. "I only called you back because I'm in a bit of a bind, okay? I want to make things very clear right now that just because you've got a patron or whatever, I have absolutely no problem kicking you out of my kitchen, so I wouldn't go throwing your weight around like you're the boss. Because I'll do it. I'll walk."

"You mean, *I'll* walk," he corrected. "Don't worry. I'm very good at working *under* people." The innuendo was not lost on her.

Her expression didn't shift, but the crimsoning of her cheeks and ears told him his tease had been received and understood. "As long as things are clear. This is a one-time gig, and I only pay you after the work is completed."

"Understood," he said simply, then shrugged out of his coat.

Eleanor flinched at his easy capitulation like she had been about to voice an argument in a fight that hadn't come. It set her off-balance, and she undid her crossed arms to set them instead on her hips. She clearly didn't believe him, but anything else she had been prepared to say didn't fit anymore, leaving her nowhere to smoothly go next.

Instead, Rafferty turned his head toward her worktable and asked the question every chef, cook, and aspiring wanted to be asked. "What are you making?"

She turned with him. "Oh." Her arms dropped completely, and she went back over to the worktable. The cameraman had moved around the table, carefully recording footage of what looked like a flight of tiny birds made of dough. "It's not much. Just a little feature on a local online talk show. A fun thing people can do with crescent roll dough. You know, for kid's parties and stuff. Thanksgiving maybe. People like cutesy videos like this. We can usually get two, maybe three out of this footage. One how-to video, and then another just watching us make it with some sort of beautiful piano music underneath. That sort of thing."

Rafferty cocked his head to one side. "People just want to watch you make it?" he asked, fascinated by the idea. "They don't want you to explain it or anything?"

"Nope. Not necessary. Some of our most viewed videos. People put them on a playlist and have them going in the background while they work," she said, nodding at her flock. "We also sell the footage to companies that make reels for bakeries or whatever. It's a business. It will pay the bills eventually."

He bent down to examine the little creations further. "What are you using for the eyes? Poppy seeds?"

"Mini chocolate chips, actually," she said, lifting a small ramekin of the tiny dots of chocolate to show him. "They melt just right when I bake them in the oven."

"Hmm," Rafferty said, and she offered the top of the ramekin to him, wordlessly inviting him to help himself to a couple of the chips.

He thought about refusing; he didn't want to corrupt her chips with his unwashed hands, then rethought that she might take it as an insult. She seemed to be done making her flock since there was an absence of waiting dough.

"This is worthy of the king's table," he said, popping the chips into his mouth, letting the chocolate burst and spread over his tongue. It took every ounce of willpower to keep from moaning.

"The king's table?" Eleanor said, wrinkling her nose at the compliment.

He realized too late that again he had slipped up.

"I mean ..."

"Oh right. Éliott said you are from France, right?" she continued, nodding at him. "He said you worked in the kitchens at Versailles, doing those recreational meals for the fundraisers and such. You know, donate a few hundred thousand dollars, and come eat like King Louis the XIV. Right?" She looked back at him to confirm Éliott's lie.

But why would he lie at all, and with something so close to the truth?

"I ... yes," he answered. It *was* true.

Eleanor nodded. "Then I'll take it as the compliment that it is," she said.

"Truly," he agreed. "It was a compliment. Food presentation at the king's table was as much showmanship as it was taste. These sort of novelties ... would have been all the rage in his court."

"Yeah, beautiful," the cameraman added so rotely, clearly the word had lost its true meaning to him. Why he had injected himself into the conversation, Rafferty couldn't clearly discern, but it was a good reminder that they were not, in fact, alone.

The interruption seemed to annoy Eleanor. "Great, now if you'll excuse me. I got to get these little guys in the oven, and then I got to get another cake started. That is actually what I need your help with," she said with an unenthused grimace.

"Great, can Pedro and I go get lunch?" the cameraman asked, setting down his amazing device.

"Oh sorry, Rafferty, this is Peter, my cameraman, and his partner Pedro," she said, indicating the mic guy who gave a halfhearted salute. "And yeah, that's fine," Eleanor dismissed. The two men didn't waste much time with further niceties. Peter simply hauled his camera to a door on the opposite wall, holding it open for Pedro to follow with the long stick holding the mic, and then they were both gone without a backward glance.

Eleanor noticeably relaxed once they were gone. "Okay, now, have you ever made opera cake before? I need to make five hundred of them. I know it's not something one would find on the king's table."

A grin cut across his face.

"So did she do it?" Eleanor asked as she flipped her cake pan over onto the work surface, popping the thin sponge layer from the pan before pulling off the parchment paper with one smooth, dramatic motion.

Rafferty paused as he poured a measure of brandy into a cup destined for the saucepan before him, where he was preparing the coffee syrup for the layered cake. He caught himself from overfilling it at the last second.

Eleanor grinned as she noted it. "Scarlet Kovacs. You were there, weren't you? You were the chef who worked the Winter Rose Ball? That's why she's doing this whole ... sponsoring-you-thing. To get you to keep quiet."

Rafferty didn't answer that; he knew a loaded question when he heard one. He just wanted to enjoy the peace and ease that came with preparing a decadent, multistep dessert that took his mind and focus away from his … life.

"Hey, Rafferty!" Eleanor called.

He blinked and jerked. "Sorry, what?" he asked.

"Your syrup, man!"

He jumped as he realized that the coffee espresso in the pan had been boiling too long.

"Dammit, dammit, dammit," he repeated as he set aside the brandy so as not to waste it, too. He grabbed up the pan and went to the sink to dump the ruined liquid. It hissed and smoked in burnt-coffee anger as it drained away.

He could feel Eleanor staring at him as he rinsed the pan, then set it on the back burner to cool down. Before he could go get a different, clean pan, the other chef set one down on the stove top for him.

"You don't have to talk about it because it's none of my business, and, frankly, I don't really care, but …" She paused and leaned, seeking out his eyes. He found he couldn't deny her gaze. "Are you alright?"

It was too hard. It was too hard to lie. Maybe it was this newly fragile human nature he had been saddled with, but his eyes filled up to blurry against his will. Even as he tried too late to look away, the words came tumbling out anyway.

"I saw a man bitten in half and eaten by a monster. And I just stood there. I couldn't do anything about it. I spent my whole existence trying to never be powerless again … and I couldn't do anything … I couldn't even protect *her*. She saved me." *Dammit, I'm weeping like a child!* he thought.

Rafferty sniffed hard, trying to clear his throat and bottle the feelings back down, but they didn't seem to care about what he wanted.

Eleanor stayed beside him, a horrible look of ... pity! Her eyes were full of pity for him. "That's not your fault—"

"If it hadn't been for Helena, we would both be dead. I wasn't able to save her or Scarlet, or the idiot who summoned the damn creature in the first place!" He grabbed the cup of brandy he meant to cook with and downed it. The burn sliced through him, hot as a knife and fortifying as it pinned his feet to the ground to keep from running away. He gripped the opposite sides of the stove, just to have something to hold onto; his altar to the only higher power he had truly worshiped in his heart.

"So ... she didn't do it," Eleanor said instead of asked, her voice barely above a whisper and full of acceptance.

"*No*," he growled. "No, she didn't do it. She could barely get out of her wheelchair, never mind ..." He shook his head again as his throat threatened to close up. "None of us should be alive. She is just as innocent as the rest of us."

He had never voiced it before. *Do I feel ... is this sympathy?* he thought. *Sympathy for Scarlet? Have I been feeling it this whole time? Do I care for someone other than Helena?*

Churned up, he stepped back from the stove. Anger had replaced his guilt, and he wanted to destroy something. The only safe thing to him was the measuring cup he had poured the brandy into.

He hurled it with all his strength.

It smashed gloriously onto the unyielding, tiled floor.

They both stared silently at it, and instantly, Rafferty regretted it. That wasn't his to destroy.

"Hey! Eleanor, are you alright?" the camera guy asked, his head popping out of the lounge. Even though he spoke to her, his eyes flashed warning at Rafferty.

"Yeah, we're fine, thank you, Peter," Eleanor said, waving the cameraman away. She didn't seem mad.

Instead, she went to get a broom and dustpan to clean up the tempered glass. "Look, I'm sorry. Like I said, it's not my usual M.O. to pry into other people's personal lives. I got enough of my own baggage and all that. But you clearly need to talk to someone."

"I don't ... talk," he said lamely.

"Yes, I know, I know," she dismissed. "The idea of sharing all your private whatever is intimidating, and then you run your car through your boyfriend's restaurant and lose your job and then your apartment and before you know it, you're doing underground cooking contests for extra cash."

"Or you're dragged into hell," he agreed, out loud, too late to rethink if it was a good idea to do so or not.

She paused, then dumped the shards in the large garbage can. "Yeah, and I'm sorry about that, too. It's just I can't say I have felt entirely comfortable with the whole Scarlet Promotions thing, taking it all over, you know? As much as I gripe about it, Cooking Underground saved my sanity, you know. I'm protective of it. But also, it's not like any of my other opportunities were working out." She sighed.

Rafferty could feel it. The signs of a mark. She was vulnerable; her gaze had drifted downward, staring long at dreams that have died before they got to live.

"So this whole thing with views and making videos and stuff, this isn't what you really want to do?"

Eleanor shook her head. "No, not at all. It's just what I *can* do. Once I had my ... issues with my boyfriend, no one would touch me after that. The investors I was trying to line up all disappeared. It's just that instead of quitting or moving away like everyone and their dog wanted me to do, I picked myself up, went into rehab, and have been working to raise my profile ever since. At a certain point of celebrity, all that past stuff is just, you know, quirky."

"And what is it that you really want, then?" he asked before he could stop himself, his instincts to give her that littlest push too hard to resist.

"A tea house," she said softly, before blinking and shaking her head. "Sorry, that's stupid ..."

"No, no, no," he assured. "It's not stupid. It sounds lovely. It was one of my favorite things to make. Tea cakes, sandwiches, and such."

It was all the encouragement she needed. "What I'm actually thinking about is a hybrid place. There would be two rooms with soundproofing between them. One side would do the full formal high tea. We'd also serve lunch and brunches, but the other side would be like a tea express with desserts and snack boxes. People could come in and work like they do at coffee shops."

Her eyes twinkled as she talked, going into more details about how she would lay out the kitchen and what they would serve, things she wanted to try. He listened contentedly as he refocused on making the coffee syrup. "That seems like a lot of work," he said as he stirred in the brandy and sugars into a few fresh cups of espresso.

"Yeah, but it would be work for myself for once," she muttered, the bitterness of her last few years slipping into her voice.

"I know what that is like," he agreed as he took the cooked-up syrup off the heat and poured it into a bowl to start cooling. Then he picked it up to hand over to the chef.

Their hands met as she reached to take it from him, and they both stopped. "You do, don't you?" Eleanor asked, her voice as dreamy as her gaze. A new spike, sharp and electric, leapt from where his hand met her skin. It wasn't literal, but it felt real. His heartbeat sped up as a sensation flooded through him. It was a different one from when he touched ...

Eleanor shyly tucked a stray hair back behind her ear. "You know, Rafferty, I was thinking, once we get this done, we could go grab a little dinner and maybe have that talk we didn't get to have?"

"Talk?"

"About what kind of future you're looking for," she smiled shyly. "Maybe, it's one in a tea shop?"

"I ..." he tried to say, but he was too lost in her eyes to remember what it was. Her hard-as-nails exterior gave way to a sweeter one before him, much like Helena's had been once ...

He stepped back, breaking the tension between them. Then his phone rang.

Desperate for any sort of escape, he let the bowl go too fast, forcing Eleanor to finish grabbing it. The liquid inside bounced dangerously close to the lip inside the bowl.

"Apologies," he muttered as he dug out his phone from under the borrowed apron, his heart jumping again when he saw Helena's name and number.

With shaking fingers he answered it.

She didn't wait for him to greet her. "Hey, Raffie. What are you doing right now?"

Chapter 33

DRESSING DOWN

"Hi! Hi, Raffie!" Helena called out as she leaned from the entryway of the clothing establishment 105th.

Unzipping his coat, he obeyed her frantic gesturing and entered the men's clothing store, only to be greeted by another woman.

"Hello there again, honey cakes," the bright woman with her Southern twang greeted him, opening her arms to give Rafferty a committed hug. He didn't return it, and she didn't seem to mind. Then she stepped back, holding him at arm's length as she looked him up and down with approving eyes. It was almost motherly. No, worse. Auntly.

"Rafferty, you remember Honey?" Helena asked as way of introduction.

Honey didn't wait for an acknowledgment. She seemed to believe that of course he remembered her. Which, of course, he did. "Well, let's go on back and nick those clothes off. I wanna see what we're working with," she declared, followed by a suggestive tiger growl, before turning around to head to the back of the store.

"What is going on?" Rafferty asked, feeling like he was undressed already in the market square, which shouldn't have bothered him. But it did.

"She's going to do your fitting for your new uniform!" Helena chirped, clearly excited as she tugged on his sleeve.

He looked around the store at the fashionable mannequins in their fashionable clothes. "This is the place you brought me before. Where you got me that suit?"

"Yes! For our first date," she said, giving his cheek an affectionate peck. She still wasn't seeing the problem.

"This does not seem like ... the right store?"

"Oh, I know, but that's alright, this store also has another service where they sell high-end clothing including tailored uniforms. What we want is in the back," she insisted as they passed through a pair of swinging doors.

The back area was starkly different than the front. For one thing, a small platform, covered in the same gray-blue carpet as the floor, stood in front of a semicircle of mirrors. A little stand stood next to the platform where Honey had placed an open notebook. The clerk had draped a roll of measuring tape over her shoulders and was jotting down something into that notebook. A second after they had entered, she looked up, beaming a smile as big as her hair.

"Come on in, don't be shy, sugar drops," Honey invited, gesturing toward the platform. "I was just joking before about getting naked. Though do shrug off that coat. I'm fairly good at eyeballing you, but for this special order, we need to get it right." She winked at Helena, who grinned like this was all some sort of joke.

Rafferty sighed. "Okay, let's get this over with," he stated, firmly stopping Helena's tugging toward the platform. "But I don't understand what's wrong with a standard chef's uniform."

Helena's cheerful face melted to concern. "This is for your new uniform, for the competition. It's like half kitchen scrubs, but also half costume, you know, for the show. You'll be a celebrity chef! You need to have a signature look!"

"I'm thinking of it like a Formula One racer's jumpsuit," Honey chimed in, spooling the measuring tape between her fingers.

"Oh, and before I forget!" Helena scurried over to a briefcase he hadn't seen before leaning against the wall with her purse and coat. She pulled a small stack of papers out of the briefcase. "I need you to sign these. This is your contract for the event, just like you wanted."

Rafferty's heart clenched at the word "contract." It made Honey pause as she measured around his chest. Their eyes met briefly, but before he could interpret that look, Helena came up beside him on the platform.

"And look!" She flipped the pages in her hands to one in the middle, then thrust it up to him, bending the papers so only the text she wanted to highlight was easily read. It wasn't a word; it was a number. "Fifty thousand dollars. That's your pay for doing this event."

"For cooking for one night? That's quite a deal!" Honey declared, shifting her tape down to measure first his waist, then his hips.

"Yeah!" Helena agreed. "And that's just what he gets paid for doing the show. If you win, the grand prize will be another $50,000!"

"Is that a lot of money?" he had to ask.

"It's a really good yearly salary. I made sure," Helena assured him.

"I don't make that much working here every day, that's for sure," Honey said pleasantly. "It looks like you're moving up in the world, my little crème brûlée."

The older woman then went around, giving his rear a little pinch in time with her crème brûlée endearment. He jumped out of his skin with a little yelp. Immediately, Honey put her hands up, closing her eyes in self-consternation. "I am so sorry. I've already been talked to about that. My fault, I'm aware. That is unacceptable. It won't happen again, I swear."

"It's fine," he assured, relaxing his shoulders back down. "Worse has happened to me in my time, believe me."

"Oh, but that just makes it more ... ohhhhh," Honey continued as she knelt down beside him to lay her tape along the outside of his leg, measuring from his waist to the floor. "I promise, Honey is going to be a good girl from now on."

Honey continued to chastise herself as she worked, but Rafferty stopped trying to put her at ease. Instead, he glanced at Helena, who smiled warmly, still offering him the contract. Except he wasn't taking it, and he couldn't return her smile. He just wanted her to get the damn thing away from him. Since he didn't have the will to do that, however, he remained frozen, unsure of what to say.

A moment later, her own smile began to falter, and worry lines appeared between her brows. "What's wrong? Is there something else you would want?" She turned the contract toward herself, flipping the pages again. "I can fix it. Just tell me what you want."

"No, it's not that," he said. "It's good. Thank you. That is very generous, but ..."

"But, what?" Helena urged with the eagerness of a puppy. Her beautiful gray eyes were stormy with the lightning strikes of gold flashing through them.

He cleared his throat. "Where is this money coming from?"

Why am I questioning this? he thought. *What do I care where the money came from?*

"Oh," she said, relief washing her face back to a grin. "I'm getting several advertising companies to agree to sponsor this event. I've also made a deal with another production company to do the TV production."

"All within a couple of weeks?" Rafferty exclaimed. He had very little knowledge of such things, but the TV executive who he had once cooked for in the '70s had waxed poetic on "What a real pain in the ass it is to get everyone to agree to any and every little decision." Which was why it would take years to even start production.

Helena blinked at his question, the pucker returning between her brows. "Has it only been a couple of weeks?" Her gaze went internal for a second. Then she started shaking her head. "No, no, it's got to be closer to a month."

"But still ..." Rafferty wanted to argue, but he wasn't sure it was truly worth it.

"This child's working like lightning," Honey chimed in as she shifted from the stand where she had been jotting down her measurements. "And now, chocolate muffin, I need to get in there for some more personal measurements. Do I have your permission?" She indicated his inner seam.

"Yes, yeah," he said, wishing she would just get this over with.

A song jingled through the air, stopping whatever additional thing Helena was going to say. Spinning to her briefcase and purse, she dug in the latter to pull out her mobile. "Sorry, sorry, I got to take this."

She didn't wait for his permission to answer, turning away to talk softly into the magic rectangle.

Rafferty huffed, letting his eyes drift up to the tiled ceiling above as Honey knelt down before him. Her action was too much like other views he had seen, ones he'd rather forget. Sweat trickled down his back, making his skin itch.

A few seconds later, Helena pocketed her phone and snatched up her coat. "I'm so sorry, but I've gotta run and put out another fire. Are you going to be okay here?" she asked him, her eyes pleading with him to be okay.

"I'm fine," he lied.

That was all she needed. She was gone.

"My that child is running around like her house is on fire," Honey laughed, as she stood to write down a few more measurements. "She's going to burn herself out at that pace."

"What would you know about it?" Rafferty responded in a surly voice, but he didn't mean to; this helpful woman had done nothing to warrant it except being just too damned cheerful.

She also didn't take offense, which was its own kind of annoying. Instead, she laughed some more. "Oh, I was young once. Thinking I could change the world if I just worked hard enough. Put enough energy in, and it would all simply get done. Then I would win because I was the hero of my own story. How could I not?"

"That isn't how the world works," he said, watching her in the reflections of the tri-mirrors before him. Again, he saw his face, one he didn't really recognize and so felt disconnected from. It was a feeling he hated, but in that moment, he also felt like he couldn't turn away. Honey moved behind him, pulling some things from a rack of clothing he hadn't noticed before. She put the first two back before humming, satisfied with the third, then changed her mind again and switched it out with a fourth.

She stepped up beside him, brandishing her prize, a suit of kitchen scrubs, only they were black with piping of bloodred. "The only thing I know for certain is no one knows how the world works. We all just try for what we think is best in any given moment, and we're lucky if we turn out to be right."

"Then what's the point of any of it?" Rafferty sneered. "If this is supposed to be winning, why doesn't it feel like it?"

The reflection of Honey cocked her head to one side. She studied him for another long moment, her gaze feeling like it was reading more of his soul than his expression. "If I were to venture a guess, it's because you haven't fully let go of who you used to be in order to make room for who you are trying to become."

"You make that sound easy."

Honey laughed. "Oh, I know it's not." Then she offered him the clothes. "But let's start with the outside of you. Please, go try these on and come back here. They won't fit perfectly, but I'd like to see the general layout."

There was another mirror in the changing room, and it took every fiber of Rafferty not to punch it. Instead, he quickly took off his clothes and donned the outfit Honey handed him.

While she had said it wouldn't fit, the feel of the black cloth as it slipped over his shoulders or pulled up over his hips, it was as if it had already been made for him. He paused as he looked at himself in the single mirror.

He liked it.

The red piping at his shoulders and down his sides at the seam made him look powerful, like a general, even though the cut was still one of a chef with the front panel buttoning at the shoulder. If he undid the button, a triangle of red appeared as it laid back. He felt strong and confident. Proud even.

"Why doesn't this feel like winning?" he asked himself. The reflection furrowed his eyebrows at him as the answer almost slipped from his lips, a traitorous answer that he had kept trapped inside of him, threatening to come out. He had to hold it back no matter what. Helena could never know.

"Are you dressed?" Honey called from the other side of the thin door.

Without a further glance, he opened the door forcefully and marched past Honey to go to the platform.

"Oh my, now that looks sharp!" Honey called, before giving an appreciative whistle. "Your lady is going to love you in this. What do you think?"

"It doesn't matter what I think. Whatever she wants," he said, stiffening his jaw like a soldier, his hands ramrod straight at his sides. His tri-reflection in the tri-mirrors repeated the gesture, but the three of him reflected back all seemed wrong.

"What do you mean it doesn't matter? You're the star of the show, cinnamon crisp."

Firmly, he shook his head. "My life is hers. I owe her everything."

A soft, gentle hand rested on his arm. "You don't owe her your life."

He ripped his arm away. "You don't understand. You can't understand."

Honey's eyes reflected back at him in the mirror, and he flinched. While they didn't change at all, they burned through him.

Then she sighed, shifting her stance. "Look, this isn't my decision. I am just here to facilitate your big transition. If there is something you need to tell her, then you better tell her. Otherwise, it will become the slow poison that destroys you both."

Chapter 34

LAVENDER LEMON SUGAR COOKIES

Rafferty didn't notice the ride home. It was like he had fallen asleep on the way back to Helena's house, but suddenly the driver spoke up. "Is this it, sir?" he asked. Blinking, Rafferty looked out the window and realized that they were indeed in front of it.

"How much do I owe you?" he asked as he slipped off the seatbelt.

"If you're paying cash, let's just call it $40 even," the driver said.

Rafferty had no idea if that was a fair price or not, but he counted out two $20 bills and passed it to the driver.

As he fit his new key into the lock and turned it, his nose was greeted by a very distinct and specific burning smell as soon as the door cracked open. It harmonized with a sharp, rapid beeping sound.

"Goddammit!" Helena's voice cried, followed by several metallic crashes followed by an unearthly animal scream. Spurred forward, Rafferty slammed the door and rushed through. The air in the house was filled with smoke, and more of it seemed to be streaming from the kitchen.

"Helena!" he called as he burst through into the kitchen, the swinging door whamming hard in its jamb at the force.

Then he came to a full stop in shock at what he was seeing.

Ingredients were everywhere: flour and sugar spilled on the counter next to a bowl filled with some sort of dough, a bit of it splattered on the walls. Smoke trailed out from an open oven. A baking sheet lay splattered on the floor with mounds of something burnt brown and black on its surface ... and across the floor. And Helena was chasing a black cat throughout the room whose tail was very much on fire.

"Pooka, stop!" Helena cried as she tried to catch her desperate animal, the creature's medium-long fur standing completely on end, trailing burning bits of ash from her cindering tail. Her eyes wild, she scrambled into the corner by the back door, desperate for escape and, apparently, determined to do it through the wall if she had to. Failing that, she then made a desperate attempt to escape through the rapidly swinging door behind Rafferty.

Thinking quickly, Rafferty only had enough time to grab a dishtowel from the counter closest to the door and drop it down as he pounced on the cat before she could pass through his legs. Using the towel to protect his hands from her scrabbling claws, he turned on his heel to head to Helena's bathroom. Kicking the handle of her shower with a foot, he stepped into the shower with the cat, just as the water hit them both. The stream hit the tail and put out the fire instantly, but now the cat had an even more distressing problem: she was completely wet. Bowing herself in an impressive show of flexibility, Pooka managed to twist around and sink her claws into Rafferty. Or rather Rafferty's coat.

It didn't hurt him but gave her the purchase to free herself from his grip; the feline fell splat onto the bathroom floor and took off to parts unknown.

"Rafferty, are you okay?" Helena called, appearing at the bathroom door in time for the cat to blaze, or actually not blaze technically, past her. She yipped as she jumped back while Rafferty cranked off the shower to stop it from making him more wet.

"Pooka!" Helena called, chasing after the cat, and he got his sopping self out of the shower.

"I guess the cat is home?" he called out.

"Yeah," Helena shouted back. "The BDI dropped her off for us. Not that I think she's happy now to be home."

Hauling off his wet coat, he let it slap onto the floor and left the bedroom to survey the damage in the kitchen. It looked as bad as he remembered. Braving the smoke, he went to the window and hauled it open, then turned to the fire alarm and tapped the button to shut it off. At last, there was quiet, and he could think.

Just then Helena came back.

"She seems to have hidden herself under the bed. I'm going to have to lure her out with tuna or something," Helena said, coming to a stop at the swinging door of the kitchen.

"What the hell did you do?" he asked, gesturing to the room.

"I ... have no idea."

Rafferty couldn't help it. He broke down laughing.

Helena didn't laugh with him, looking more mournful as she squatted down. "They were supposed to be cookies," she said as she picked up the dark-brown-to-charred pieces, putting them back on the cooled baking sheet.

Rafferty turned to her mixing bowl and brushed his fingers through his wet hair to slick it back. He picked up the bowl, stirring the contents inside and measuring with his eyes the texture and consistency of her future "cookies."

"I don't think these were ever going to be cookies. What did you do?"

"I told you; I don't know! I thought it would be so easy to *make* cookies of all things and that it might be nice for you to come home to the warm smell, you know? And I was *trying* to be good and not use any magic to make them since you don't like that." She threw some of the cookie pieces onto the sheet so hard that they bounced right off again.

He set the bowl aside and dropped down to help her. "Thank you," he said, trying to give her a smile to show his appreciation.

It did not seem to soothe.

She was too focused on her failure. "I just don't get it. Why does everything I cook turn into a disaster? I'm cursed!"

Rafferty sighed, "Your baking sheet is too dark," he said.

"What?" Helena asked, pausing to follow his gaze.

He picked up the sheet and traced a finger along the edge. "Too dark of a baking sheet absorbs more heat, cooking your dough faster, so it takes less time. And you're baking. You're not cooking."

She narrowed her eyes at that, then crawled over to her counter to pull down a familiar spiral cookbook. Sitting down with her back against the cabinets, she laid out Nana's cookbook against her thighs and scanned the pages. "So, ten to twelve minutes would be too long?"

"In your oven, yes. And"—he stretched his hand into the oven's body—"the other thing about your oven specifically, it doesn't heat evenly."

"What?"

"I noticed this before, it's always hotter in the back than in the front, so anything that is made in it has to be turned around partway through."

"You're kidding!"

"It's not a big deal," he said.

"My cat was on fire! How is that not a big deal?"

He scrunched his nose. "Yeah, how did that happen?" he asked.

"I seriously don't know! One minute I'm pulling the burnt mess out of my oven and the next thing I know, *fwoosh*! This oven isn't even that old. Dammit!"

"Also, I think your eggs were too cold. You took them straight out of the refrigerator, right? You didn't give them time to warm up or put them in warm water or something?"

"Why would that matter?"

He pulled down the batter again and gave it another stir. "Cold eggs prevent the dough from aerating properly, making it so they don't develop air pockets, so you won't get a good texture in your cookie. I'm guessing you didn't use room temperature butter either, you just popped it into the microwave and turned it to liquid ..."

"Okay, okay, I get it! I suck!" Helena shouted, burying her head in her arms. "I just wanted to do something nice for you!"

Setting the bowl to the side, Rafferty shifted until he sat next to Helena, but like so many times since he met her, he didn't know what to do. He wanted to put his arm around her, but she was so prickly at that moment, he was sure that would only make it worse.

But then she decided for him, lifting her head to drop it against his shoulder, her eyes closed. Automatically, his arm lifted, and she slid into them naturally. Cradling her to his chest, he buried his nose into her golden-red hair, breathing her in, erasing the burnt smell from his nose.

"Thank you for the cookies," he whispered, and he meant it.

They sat that way for a few peaceful moments, then she asked, "Did you like the uniform I picked for you?"

He stiffened. *Why is she asking this now?* The thought felt irrational, but it also had the gravity of fate. Inevitable. Like an execution.

"What is it, lover?" she urged, softly, cupping her hands around his face. "Rafferty? Talk to me?"

"Are you really my Helena?" he asked, his voice breaking under the strain.

He could feel her start to pull away, and he pressed his hand, trapping hers in place. "No, please. I'm sorry, forget it. Forget I said it. Please." But his entreaties did nothing. Her hand escaped, and she sat back a little more, her gaze piercing him, judging him. He deserved it.

"What do you mean, 'Am I really Helena?' Who else would I be?"

"Dammit, dammit, dammit," he muttered, and he covered his face. If he were still a demon, he could have blinked himself away. How do humans escape these situations?

"Rafferty. Do you *believe* I'm not who I say I am?"

"No!" Yet that wasn't true either. "I'm afraid ... I'm afraid ... I'm ..." He growled. "I don't know what to say!"

"I think you do. You're afraid of me," she stated factually.

He wouldn't lift his head, but the pressure of her next to him forced him to nod.

"Hey, hey, it's okay," Helena cooed softly, once more deigning to touch him, rubbing her hand over the back of his. When he didn't unfurl, she retreated again. "I get it. After everything you've been through, of course, you would doubt me. If I'm honest, I've been doubting me, too. But I am still me. I mean, I am still Helena, even if I'm different now. I'm not in hell. I'm here with you. That must mean something."

He still couldn't raise his head. He understood what she was saying, but he could feel this all falling apart. The carefully constructed lie he had been trying to build crumbled around him.

Still, she persisted. "Is there any way I can reassure you?"

"That's just it, I'm not sure," he said, his voice steadier. The worst of it was out, and if he was honest with himself, he felt a bit better for it. "If you aren't her, don't ever tell me. I don't think I could bear it."

"I'm still *me*, Rafferty. I swear. I *am* Helena."

No, you're not, he thought. He couldn't unsee it now. The Helena he knew was gone. The Rafferty he had been was gone, too. They had both become different people, and it had all happened so fast.

Still, the tension dragged out between them.

Finally, she stood up and went to get her broom, proceeding to sweep up her cookie mess. Somehow, her moving allowed him to do so as well, uncoiling from the tight ball he had managed to put himself in. Now, he let one of his legs drop to the side, opening himself up a little bit, while he watched her repair the damage she had done. The oven had cooled, and the smoke had escaped out the open window. While Helena dumped the mess that had been her cookies into the garbage, Rafferty noticed the cookbook lying face down on the floor. Picking it up gingerly, he turned over the pages filled with Nana's writing, interrupted with his own here and there. He stopped on the recipe Helena clearly had been using.

Lavender Lemon Sugar Cookies, the printed text read, followed by Nana's handwriting. *To soothe the soul!*

He could almost hear Nana's voice as she recited to him while she baked. "Lavender flowers represent purity, silence, devotion, serenity, grace, and calmness. Mix with lemon and sugar. Lemons symbolize light, love, heart, and soul. They also attract good fortune and help people embrace changes. Now the sugar ... well the sugar doesn't represent anything, but if you don't add it to cookies, then you got biscuits instead, and that's not what we're going for today." He chuckled then and he chuckled now at the memory.

Then he noticed at the bottom of the recipe, something more written in her hand next to a jotted-down recipe for making the lavender lemon sugar needed for the recipe. *When needed to emphasize the purity in the lavender, use the Shepard's prayer. When needed to emphasize the light, use the morning prayer. When both are needed, use Lares's prayer.*

Lares's prayer.

He remembered now. Back when she had summoned him. She had fed him these very cookies and he ... went to sleep.

No, I returned to hell without being compelled, he realized, his eyes going wide as he read the words of the spell with his name above it, hidden as a prayer there in the book. Maybe he should have felt betrayed by Nana's trick, but instead, he saw an answer. A terrible answer.

He could banish Helena back to Hell. And he would be free.

It *would* be a betrayal.

It *wouldn't* be his first.

He looked to Helena, whose back was turned toward him. She was looking in her bowl of cookie dough in disgust before picking up the whole thing, spatula in the other hand, and going to the garbage can to dispose of the remains. Before he could stop her, she had neatly swiped the whole mess into the pail. Taking them all back to her sink, she dropped the spatula and reached for the dish soap to squirt into the bowl. This he intercepted in time.

"Let's try again," he said.

"Try again?"

"Yes, you and I together. Let's do this together," he said, setting the bowl on the counter. He went to the small shelf on the counter where he had stacked the herbs and spices he had collected during the short stints when he had existed in Helena's world as her demon. He found the jar that he kept the lavender in already on the counter where she had made her first attempt at flavoring sugar. A lemon sat beside it, half flayed of its zest. He picked it up and passed the grater to her. "Go ahead and get some fresh off of that."

He grabbed the lavender and started sifting through it to find the best in the bottle. Moving about as she zested,

Rafferty set things to right, wiping up the spills between measuring out what he needed.

It gave him something to focus on instead of his rapidly beating heart.

Chapter 35

BREAKING LIMBO

"Oh Lord! These taste so much better," Helena cried, her mouth full and spilling crumbs as she took a too-big bite from one of the freshest lavender lemon sugar cookies.

Rafferty couldn't help grinning as he slipped the spatula between another of the cookies and the parchment paper he had laid over the baking sheet, touching the top carefully with his clean fingers before transferring it safely to a plate. He could keep this show of joviality up as long as he didn't think at all about what he intended to do. Just pretend this was all very normal. He found the calm inside his storm easy to slip back into, surprisingly easy.

Beside the cooling plate on the counter, Helena's electric kettle whistled.

Before he could react, she snatched it up and brought it over to a pair of cups waiting for them with teabags inside. She filled them up to the brim, then took the time to tend to both, bobbing the teabags until they were completely soaked through and steeping properly. While she did that, he cut out another set of cookies to place on a fresh sheet of parchment.

It was all very domestic and homey.

He pushed the combination of buttons on the oven that set the timer. "We have enough for a half batch after this," Rafferty said, rerolling up the dough to one smooth flat surface with a wood rolling pin, in preparation to punch out the last of it.

"Are you happy?" Helena asked, leaning against the counter with her back to it as she picked up her tea before it had finished steeping to blow over the surface of the hot water. "I mean with the cookies?" she added, taking a sip.

"They are alright," he said.

She cocked an eyebrow. "What's wrong with them?" Casting her gaze over their bounty, she took another sip.

"They're plain," he said, and they were. While he had found a nice flower cookie cutter from one of Helena's drawers to punch the dough with, there was no real style to them.

"But they taste wonderful," she said, plucking up a second one and bringing it to his lips. She waited, a twinkle in her eye, until he finally took a bite of the still-warm cookie. It burst over his tongue, shattering into thousands of little pieces by the pressure of his tongue with a fresh, light flavor. He couldn't help it; his closed his eyes, a moan rumbling from his throat at the taste.

"You're never going to get used to that, are you?" Helena asked, her amusement barely contained in her words.

"Never," he agreed around his chewing. Her fingers slipped into his and he paused, holding the tastes on his tongue. But he didn't dare swallow.

"I guess you don't need to hold my hand anymore to taste anything," she asked. Then he felt that same eerie shiver run up his arm from where she touched him.

"Yes, no more sucking the life from you," he whispered as his other hand drew the cookbook closer to him on the counter, the first line of the prayer resting on his tongue along with the taste of lemon sugar.

Lie down, lost one, lie down, he recited the words in his mind. He just had to bring himself to say them out loud. And this would all be over.

"You never sucked the life out of me," she whispered, her lips tickling his own.

"Don't ... don't patronize me," he whispered back, the intoxicating tendrils of her allure slipping into him.

"No, it's true," she insisted, setting a soft kiss at the corner of his mouth. "It wasn't like the first time when you swallowed the memory whole, and I felt this ... void then. It was like I knew something was supposed to be there, but it wasn't there anymore." She picked up his fingers she had captured to brush them over her lips, her warm breath making them tingle. "But after that, you gave it back to me. Whatever you took, came right back, more intense than before. More delicious." She met his gaze, her gold eyes burning through him. "It's how I knew you loved me ... when we could share the taste together."

Whatever traitorous words lingered in his mouth died as her words choked them. What was she telling him?

His memory raced back to before, when he had been a demon and she had so willingly given him her memories of taste, to pay his price and feed his soul.

"You mean"—he struggled—"I didn't hurt you?"

"Nope," she said, popping up on her toes to kiss the tip of his nose. "Anything I gave you, you gave me right back. You didn't realize it?"

"No, I didn't," he said, shaking his head. "So when you gave me the energy back … I mean as we are now …"

"Yes, we both get everything we need. Maybe if more demons realized that sooner, there would be less need for, you know, all the bullshit you all do."

His mind couldn't comprehend it. This wasn't true. It couldn't be true.

It's a trick. It has to be, his mind screamed. Demons don't return energy. There isn't enough for both. It was finite. She had to be lying.

"I feel like ordering in tonight, I think the kitchen has been brutalized enough," she declared, spinning to exit the room.

She has to be lying, he told himself.

"Helena," Rafferty said.

"Yeah?" She paused at the swinging kitchen door.

He didn't answer immediately, instead looking down at the flattened cookbook under his palm, the words of the prayer staring at him in surreal, faded ink. "Lie down …" he tried to say, but the pain in his heart forced his mouth around the first words of the prayer and his eyes closed.

"Raffie?" Helena asked.

He let the book go, stepping back from it. He couldn't do it. Maybe he could never have done it, but it didn't matter. He couldn't do this to her now.

"Yeah. Yeah, let's order takeout," he said instead, letting the cookbook go.

"Is everything alright?" she persisted, coming a step closer.

"Everything is ..." But the lie wouldn't come. The pressure of the truth made his jaw ache. "I can't do this," he admitted.

"Can't make dinner?" she asked, because, of course, she would. It was what they had been talking about. "I know, that's why ..."

He shook his head. "I can't be with you. I'm sorry." He hated himself for every word, and yet they felt so right coming out of the dark places of his mind.

Her whole body stiffened as he spoke. "What—"

"I'm a liar. And a cheat. I've deceived people my entire existence. Destroyed lives."

"Rafferty?"

"That isn't my name!" He whirled toward her, electricity shooting down his limbs even if none appeared in reality. "I *sold* my name. I'm nothing."

"You're the man I love!" Helena insisted, moving toward him to take his face, but he slapped those seeking hands away. She continued, unabated. "Just ... slow down. Slow down and we'll talk about ..."

"I can't!" He pushed past her to go to the door of the kitchen. To escape her.

"Raff—Whatever ... whatever it is, we can work through this. You're not a demon anymore."

"No, but you are!" He spun back, and she came up short just before him, her eyes wide as the truth hit her full in the face. "And I can't watch you become just like me. I can't. I just can't!"

His voice broke. *Fuck. Why does my voice have to break when I need strength?*

In place of strength, anger would do.

He growled as he turned away.

"You don't mean that. You're just afraid." She tried to touch him again, and again he slapped her hands away.

"Helena! You can't trust me. I will betray you!" He seized the cookbook, the damned cookbook, and showed her the spell. "I was going to use this to send you back."

"Send me back. Send me back where?" she asked, but as her gaze rapidly cascaded down the words, understanding broke over her, followed by horror.

"You were going to send me to Hell?" she asked, taking a step back from him.

He watched as her facade melted away.

Her other form emerged with the glistening skin and the horns that encircled her head. Her brilliant wings flashed white as if the colors of the rainbow washed down the filaments. Now she also had a long, thin tail, which whipped between her legs with its little tuft of hair at the end, shape implying the typical triangle. She was still so very beautiful and not of this world.

It brought him to his knees before her, overwhelming his senses as she amplified all the feelings she wanted him to feel, making them stronger than his negative ones: His love for her. A deep desire to fall before her in worship with his mind, body, and soul. He wanted to give his life for hers, and he would have no regrets doing it.

But he did.

He regretted.

Everything.

In that same moment, she realized what she was doing. She stared at her hands, each with golden-tipped nails, in shock. "I'm sorry. I'm sorry," she repeated, and she tried to dim her light. She writhed, desperate to get her true appearance back under control, and it broke his heart to watch her try to change herself for him. "I didn't mean to."

He got back up off his knees, and she didn't move to help him this time. She didn't dare. Instead, she wrapped her hands around herself, hugging tightly.

"Rafferty, I'm sorry. I'm sorry. I didn't mean to."

"I can't do this," he repeated softly, knowing this time she would accept it, now that she understood what she had done. "I'll keep your secret. I won't let BDI know, but I have to go. Please. Let me go."

Tears streamed down her face, and even though her head shook a little, he could see from the pain painting her form that she was relenting. "But where would you go?" she asked, her voice squeaking out of her.

He had only one thought. "I have a friend I can call. I do not ... I cannot tell you any more than that."

"Rafferty ..." She openly wept now. "I love you." Her last desperate argument; her last plea for him not to go.

He turned to leave the room, before it became too hard. "Good-bye, Helena."

"Hey, there he is," Éliott called as he pulled up to the curb. Rafferty sat upon a bench a few blocks down from Helena's house, his head resting in the palms of his hands. It had been all he could do not to grab his bag and turn back, to beg Helena for forgiveness and take back everything he had said. He knew that what he was doing was right, and he understood he wouldn't feel it. Not with a demon playing with his emotions.

Éliott reached across from the driver's seat to open the door. "Come on, get in. It is going to rain."

Rafferty obeyed, throwing his bag into the backseat before climbing into the front.

"Dog weather, all of it," Éliott muttered as he looked through the windshield up at the clouds.

"Un temps de chien," Rafferty agreed, letting the French fall from him, though he wasn't really speaking of the weather.

A few moments later, Éliott pulled away to the chorus of thunder and the flashing of lightning. "I picked you up just in time," Éliott commented, just as water pounded onto the car.

"Thank you," Rafferty managed to say, though he barely heard the other man as he wrestled with his own internal maelstrom.

"Do you wish to tell me what happened?"

Rafferty couldn't even say "no." Only silence stretched between them.

After a minute or so Éliott nodded. "I understand," he said softly. "Don't worry, my friend. It will all be alright in the end."

"I just broke the heart of the woman who saved my soul," he said. "I don't deserve ..."

Éliott's phone went off, interrupting. A strange feeling slipped down Rafferty's arms, making the hairs stand up straight. *What was that?*

"Sorry," the other man said, picking it up from inside one of the cup holders to glance at the screen. "Oh dear."

He set the phone down and hit a button on a little screen on his dashboard.

"Oui, hello, Eleanor?"

"Éliott," Eleanor's voice came over the speakers. "I need your help."

"Anything, belle. What do you need?"

Eleanor growled.

There was a crashing sound over the phone.

"Eleanor? Are you alright?"

"Just get over here before I destroy the whole kitchen!" Then she hung up.

Éliott swore beautifully in French, a phrase that made the corners of Rafferty's mouth lift. That phrase had apparently withstood the test of time. "Do you wish to be dropped off at my place first?"

"Yeah, it's fine," Rafferty said. He didn't really care one way or another anymore.

"Good, because we are here," he said, pulling up in front of another house. Rafferty had no idea where they were, and he blinked as he stared at the two-story building. It looked like someone's idea for a castle if it were a house. "I live in the second-floor apartment, but my landlady, she lives on the first."

Rafferty nodded, then got out and retrieved his bag. It wasn't until Éliott pulled away that he realized he hadn't been given a key or anything.

Slumping under the weight of everything, he dropped himself and the bag on the steps. The ice and the salt on the step ground into his butt through his pants, but he let it. He imagined himself freezing there. Then he would go back to where he deserved to be.

"This is all I've ever been," he whispered. A worthless being amongst countless other worthless, unimportant beings.

Then a door behind him opened.

"There he is. Welcome, angel food," a warm voice said as the yellow light washed over him.

A familiar woman stood at the door. She seemed to glow with the light behind her, her pale hair lit up around her face, making it harder to make out.

"Well, don't just sit there. Come in," Honey invited.

Rafferty felt his hackles raise. He wanted to ask about the strange coincidence of her being here, but more than anything, he wanted to be alone in the cold, where he deserved. "I'm here to stay with Éliott for a few days, but he took off without leaving me the key," he explained, hoping she would take the information and leave.

"Yeah, that sounds like him. Why don't you come in and wait for him inside? It's freezing out there," she urged, opening the door wider.

"No, that's fine. I'm fine out here," he said, even as another gust of cold wind cut him to the bone.

"And yet you are welcome," she said.

"Really, I am fine." He didn't dare look at her, keeping his focus on the frost- and salt-encrusted street.

"As you wish," she acknowledged, then shut the door once more.

Rafferty immediately regretted not taking her up on her offer as a fresh slice of ice-cold air cut through him despite his modern coat.

It had been Helena's last gift to him, using her power to dry it for him before he left. He hadn't even argued with her about it.

Shivering hard, he curled into himself, squeezing his eyes shut.

It felt like hell. Alone, in an endless dark, with only his pain and regrets for company. Well, that and the other condemned demonic souls feeding off of each other. He wondered if he just stayed like that on that frozen step, would he die and return to that place? At least there, he knew he belonged, and it was what he deserved. He understood it.

But he would be throwing away Helena's gift to him. Even more guilt compounded. While the touch of those in hell had always been something to fear, had always promised suffering, hers had been …

Burning hot tears pricked at his eyes and he pressed his shaking fists into them. Even that was gone, her loving and safe touch. She was becoming … had become one of the creatures of the dark, just as he had.

And that was all his fault, too. He had corrupted her. Corrupted her love.

He had failed her.

"Merde, Helena. I'm so sorry," he said, his voice squeaking out of him.

Only the cold whistled in response.

Then a weight dropped on his shoulders.

Chapter 36

EXPLANATIONS

"**D**ear Lord, it's colder than Hell out here," Honey said as she sat down on the step next to him; she was bundled in a quilt, just like the one she had dropped onto his shoulders. "Though I suppose that's not how the saying really goes, does it? Everyone says its hotter than, not colder. Oh, except in Dante's Inferno. One of those circles is supposed to be cold."

She continued to look him full in the face as if she were expecting him to comment on it.

He looked away under the pressure of it and cleared his throat.

"It's alright, I know," she said.

Flinching, her statement forced him to look back at her. She nodded with an air of confirmation, but he still wasn't sure what she was confirming.

"You can't know," he whispered.

"That you are a demon who has not only escaped Hell but found a new life here on this plane of existence known as creation or reality, for lack of better more comprehensive words. And that the woman who saved you is becoming something you struggle to define." Her smile faded down to one tinged with sadness. "I've been watching you for a long time, Lares. In fact, I am the one that gave you that name."

Rafferty's entire body went still, his muscles locking with a strange urge to run and an inability to do so as the skin covering them prickled.

This time she was the one who looked away, casting her sad smile out over the dark and cold. "It is the name of a Greek god of house and hearth. Protection god. It was aspirational." She glanced back at him, and he saw the metallic flash of power in her eyes.

"You ... you're one of ... you're a demon?" His voice cracked, his mouth dry.

"I wouldn't call myself that," she said, shaking her head. "I mean, I try my best."

Gripping hard on the quilt with his shaking hands, he pulled it tight, more terrified by his next question. "Or are you ... one of ... *them*?"

"You mean an angel?" Honey laughed a sparkling peal. "We do go by that. Others would call us such, but I thought you would know better. There are no such things as angels, right?" She gave him a conspiratorial smile.

"Ah." The sound burst from Rafferty's chest. It was neither a laugh nor a cry. More like a burst of relief and despair. "Are you here to send me back?"

She blinked at that. "Back? Back where?"

"To where I belong."

Her lips pursed a moment. "I'm not here to judge you, corn muffin. Nor punish you if that's what you're thinking. You've already punished yourself enough. And I bet it's not what you want. Not really. It's just what you think you deserve. Éliott and I have been debating this. He argues that you wouldn't have tried to work so hard to escape it to be here, but I think *you* think you deserve to be *there*. Or at least it is a more comfortable idea. That's why you're having trouble adjusting."

"It wasn't comfortable. It was torment." He growled at her daring to call it anything else.

"But you knew what to expect. You knew who you were. That is its own sort of comfort."

Rafferty blinked, following her strange sort of sense. "I *do* belong there," he agreed. His face dropped into his hands as he felt his being shattering at the admission.

They sat like that for a long moment. At first, he thought she was waiting for him to get it together, but that wasn't quite right. She wasn't ignoring him either; she still felt present with him, while not in a hurry for him to do or say anything more.

Finally, when he felt more in control of himself, he asked, "What happens now?"

"Well, one option would be to get off this freezing porch and come inside. The others are waiting to talk to you."

There were others. It didn't surprise him. "I'm ready," he agreed.

Nodding, Honey stood up, folding her blanket over her arm, and led him into her house.

Only it wasn't a house on the inside.

The last thing Rafferty saw as he stepped through was the light of the circle bursting from the floor. Then everything went white.

He is back.

He knows this place intimately ... and it knows him.

Despair cuts. He expects to be held in a small, enclosed space. The eternal crush. The darkness, the emptiness. A coldness that isn't coldness. Existing, but alone.

Yet, what he feels is ... space. A wide openness, filling and alive. Teeming with energy. There are no concrete shapes, no bodies or sense of physical form, and still so much ... existence. They welcome him, reach out to touch him. Though he does not hear it, he perceives laughter and a joy. And relief.

Grief fills him, tendrils of darkness that ignite his fear, that they, the others, will be disgusted by him and push him away. Yet, they don't. They do not recoil; they are only holding still, waiting, ready. A single being comes forward, moving past his darkness, or rather weaving through them, avoiding the tendrils until the last minute. It is Honey, though he does not know how he knows it. He simply does. He knows she means to hold him, and he decides to let her. Just with that simple decision, his darkness retreats.

Love in the form of light pours into him. He knows he doesn't shine as brightly as the others, and it doesn't seem to matter. The others reach out to him with the same eagerness and joy as before.

Once he is calm, Honey leads him through, and the other lights go their own way. She brings him to a place ... a field of darkness.

He has no other way of understanding it.

There are thousands of them, concentrated balls of darkness. He understands that there is a single being inside each. They are writhing in their own ... hells.

Like he once did.

A new understanding washes through him, one that shocks him. It even sends out small waves of energy, like a pebble dropped into a still pool.

This was Hell.

What he thought of as hell was this. And it was of his own making.

He wants to reject that idea. He even backs away from the field.

Honey tries to assure him, to keep him from leaving.

Safe.

You are safe.

The concept comes across to him, and he now understands he is not being put back, nor is he going to become ... stuck like this again.

Something has changed within him. Something has healed.

More light pours into his being, light that has always been there, always waiting to embrace him. He had kept it out, for fear of it consuming him.

But why?

He wants to ask, but there is no way to. Instead, the question is just understood.

And the answer returns. The others, the countless others here are also afraid. They steal energy from each other, in order to maintain this darkness, for fear of the light dissipating it. There is safety there.

He pities them.

He pities himself.

Honey moves amongst them and he follows. He does not wish to touch any of the dark orbs. She understands and agrees.

The darkness isn't dangerous. It is only the absence of light.

But those inside do not understand. So they lash out. The light holds them here and waits, peeling away at their defenses layer by layer. Hoping to get in eventually.

That which is of the light cannot be separated by the light. Only perceived to be so.

Honey comes to a stop before one of the orbs of darkness. Rafferty perceives no difference from this one than the others, but Honey touches it tenderly. It hurts her back; he can see it consuming her light. Alarmed, he surges forward to protect her, but she accepts his embrace, and her light is restored just as quickly as it is lost.

She conveys they must go inside.

He is confused. The darkness did her harm?

She indicates the orb. This time he perceives how thin the darkness seems, even though such a concept isn't right.

He struggles to understand.

He does.

The light will soon break through. Honey has waited for this orb to open. Wishes for it to open. Will continue to wait if she must, but she believes he can help. It is so close. He can reach the being inside.

He is afraid.

He recoils.

His own darkness forms around him again.

Honey reaches out more, as many times as he needs.

This darkness is too familiar. He could sink into it and never come back.

But then he remembers another light, a light so bright it cracked through this darkness once before. He let her in, and now he can and will never go back.

That realization stops him. His light returns, still dim, but there. The darkness retreats once more, also present, surrounding his light, dimming it, but not extinguishing it.

He will never go back.

He regards the other orb, floating trapped.

Honey indicates to go in once more.

Please help.

And he wants to. He feels ... not darkness. Not pity, or sadness, or anger.

Empathy.

He desires to hold the being inside, who suffers as he did. To show them, there is a way out.

And that desire is worth braving the other being's darkness.

Chapter 37

GHOSTS OF THE PAST

Rafferty's next real thought is to breathe. Reality, or what he perceived as reality, had formed around him once more. He had a body again and stood on a real floor. Pressing a hand to his chest, he felt a heartbeat and the expansion of his ribs. He was still alive.

Next, he noticed his hands, still real and a living color, instead of the dull, corpse-like gray of his demonic self. Yet, it was the sleeves that gave him pause. They were rolled up at his elbows with puffy sleeves over his upper arms. His hands hit his chest, feeling the large buttons, each stamped with the insignia of the king. Over it all was a coat of blue with red-and-white brocade, the livery of the king.

Shocked, he looked about the room and realized it was familiar. A small room that had once been above a tailor's shop, where he had lived with his mother and little sister, centuries ago.

He was home.

"This isn't real, at least not in the way you would understand it," Honey said. She stood next to him, dressed in a long gown with a sleeveless red-orange tunic, her hair gathered up under a wimple. Only a single strand escaped it, her normally honey-blonde hair having turned to a dark tendril, closer to his own coloring. "This is her dream. Remember that, so that you don't get sucked into it."

Rafferty remembered such dreams. They were always nightmares, really, memories of their lives before, and only the bad ones, the ones no one wanted to steal. It was why his memories with Helena had been so precious here. He hadn't dared trade any one of them, even though there was much he could have done with such treasures.

"Who is this?" he asked, already knowing the answer, but his voice shook asking the question all the same.

"Who's there? Who is it?" a creaking voice called out in familiar French. It was only then that Rafferty realized he had been speaking his mother tongue with Honey. "Monsieur Tomas? If it is about the rent ... I will have it next week."

"No, madame," Honey said, stepping forward into the room. "We are just here to visit with you for a while."

"Who is it? Who are you?" The form lying on a small bed at the far end of the room struggled to sit up. A ratty quilt covered her.

"No need to get up," Honey assured her, laying a hand on the frail woman's chest to encourage her to lie back down.

"I do not want visitors. Go away. Leave me to die in peace," the frail woman said, then she started coughing hard, the unknown disease in her chest shredding her lungs until she coughed blood into an already bloody handkerchief.

Automatically, Rafferty went to the bedside where a teapot sat with water in it. He picked it up and pointed the spout toward her mouth, cupping her head. The frail woman recognized what was happening and took a long drink from the spout. She swallowed and coughed again, less violently this time, patting at her lips.

Looking up at her savior, her eyes narrowed. "Who are you?"

"It's ... it's me, Maman," he said, his eyes blurring with tears.

Her narrowed eyes narrowed further. "No. No, you can't be him," she said, even as her fingers lifted up to cup his cheek.

"Maman, please," Rafferty begged, even as she pulled away. "Please, I ..." The tears escaped from his eyes as he dropped down to his knees beside the bed. "I'm so, so sorry, Maman."

Honey set her own hand on his shoulder.

"You can't be my son. My son is dead," his maman said, leaning against the wall so she could look out the small window beside her bed. There was nothing beyond it but void. She didn't seem to notice. "I failed both my children. I am a wretch of a mother. Count yourself blessed you are not my son."

Rafferty furrowed his brows as he knuckled the tears away. "I don't understand," he said to Honey. "She died before I did. Her illness took her. What is she talking about?"

"Your son is alive, madame," Honey said, raising her voice to cut through the continued murmurings of the sick woman.

"No, no, he's not. He's dead somewhere. And I'll never know what happened to him. I always feared it. That the gangs would take him away, or the army, or he'd just be killed in the streets for pocket money he doesn't have, and I would never know. They would just drop his body in some common grave, and I would never see him again."

Her words shocked him. "I never realized," he said softly.

"Realized what?" Honey encouraged.

"That my mother was so ... afraid for me." His throat thickened with regrets. "All she ever said to me was where was the money I had earned and that I needed to go out and get a job. I was the man of the house."

His maman continued to mutter her regrets, and he listened to each one, seeing and hearing her in a new way. "Oh, his toes. I loved his little toes. He was so lively and wiggled so. Oh, my baby son!" Her face melted into tears and wails again.

The world around them seemed darker, but Honey noted it without becoming alarmed. Rafferty could feel the cold despair itching at his skin. It wanted to sink into him, to feast on his energy. And he was tempted to let it, to do anything to ease his mother's suffering.

"No, you do not have to do that. Stay present or you will be pushed out, but you are not obligated to give of yourself for her. She will not disappear just yet and it is a drop compared to what she needs. It will not help her to sacrifice yourself like that," Honey said, as if she could hear his thoughts. Maybe she could.

"Then what can I do?" His question came out like a plea, filled with his self-contempt at his failure.

"Like I said, stay present with her. Hold space. We can only hope that she will hear our call and open up to us, but it must be her choice, or it means nothing."

Then she turned once more to the frail being writhing in her hell. "Madame, I have news of your son."

Rafferty's maman perked at that statement. "You know of my son? You have seen him?"

"Yes, madame. He sends you a message."

The sickly woman sat up in the bed, like she intended to leap from it. It was the most lively she had seemed yet. "What is it? Tell me!" she ordered with that sharp voice he remembered most clearly, as if she had the authority of a queen. He had found that tone grating in his youth, and he realized that it was another reason he had made the deal with Vassago. To get away from that harsh tone.

Again, Honey was not offended. She only smiled serenely and sweetly, much like her name, and curtsied to the lost soul. "He is a cook in the king's kitchen, madame."

His maman's mouth opened and closed several times, the news something too fantastical to automatically deny it. Then her eyes snapped to him, still kneeling beside her on the floor.

Rafferty laid a hand against his chest, gripping at his livery. He had been so proud to wear the king's colors. It should have been impossible for someone like him to have the honor to be one of the king's cooks. An honor only made possible, again, by his deal with Vassago.

As his mother's eyes roamed over him, she seemed to finally see him. Really see him.

Then her hand leapt to his cheek as quick as a slap, cradling it. "Mon cœur," she said, her voice cracking with warmth, sadness, and hope, all wrapped into that one term of endearment. Her other hand joined the first, holding his face, pulling him closer. "It is you?"

"Oui, Maman," he answered, holding one of her hands, so much smaller than his own. He had been barely thirteen, maybe fourteen, when he had run away from home. His hands had been the same size as hers then.

She examined his livery closer. "And it is true? You are a cook in the king's kitchen? The king's?"

"Oui, Maman. I ... I am."

"Oh, my baby. My baby!" She kissed his nose and his cheeks, making him blush even as he hungered for the familiar ritual. How had he forgotten that his mother used to do this to him even when he had gotten older.

"Are you proud, Maman?" he asked, the question a plea for approval that he had longed for. It was only now that he realized he had longed to return home and show her what he had become. He had feared what she would say about him abandoning her.

"Oh, yes. Yes. You are a man now! You are happy?"

"Yes, Maman, I was happy. I wanted you to be proud of me." His voice thickened again. "I am so sorry I abandoned you. I'm so sorry." His tears came again. He could not hold them back. His head dropped into her lap, and he wailed his pain, guilt, and grief into the worn-out bed, smelling of old hair and body odors.

It was only after there was nothing more to scream or cry that he realized that his mother's fingers threaded through his hair, brushing it back, and she hummed a wordless lullaby, a piece from some opera she had heard once and loved. Rafferty had never known what it was; the opera had been a failure and forgotten by all except his maman.

When he lifted his head, she brushed away the tears from his face, smiling warmly. "There. There now. All is well, little child of God."

He shook his head. "No, no. I am not … I am not a child of God anymore, Maman. Not after what I did to you. What I did to you and …" But he couldn't remember his sister's name, not any more than he could remember his mother's or even his own original name. He had lost those memories long, long ago. "And … my sister."

"No, no," his maman said, continuing to pet him. "That is not your fault. Not your responsibility. I am your maman. You are my child."

"But … but you said …"

"I was wrong," she answered, setting a kiss onto his forehead. "I was afraid. I did not know what to do for you. I wanted so much for you both, to be happy and safe and fed, and I failed."

He hadn't noticed the darkness retreated from them until it encroached again, eating up the world around them, stabbing through and punishing his maman. "I failed my children. I sinned, and God has abandoned me." Her words degraded into a wail.

"No, Maman! No, I am fine. I am a cook in the king's kitchen. I am fine. I am happy." He grasped her hands, pulling her back toward him.

The darkness paused as she heard him this time. "A cook in the king's kitchen?" she repeated.

"Yes, yes. I am happy," he insisted. "I live a full life."

She touched his cheek again. "You are? You are happy?"

He wanted to say yes, but it sat too heavy in his heart. He could not hide it from his maman.

"What is it, my baby?" she asked.

"There ... there is this woman."

Understanding washed over her face, mixed with joy. "You are in love?"

He couldn't lie. "Yes. But I do not deserve her," he admitted. "I have done horrible things. I have ruined her life by simply being in it. I have nothing of worth to offer her, and I have even had stray thoughts from her. She is my savior, yet I cannot bear to look at her. I am a faithless man."

"Then return to her. Beg her forgiveness and spend the rest of your life being faithful and true. Be the man I know you are," his maman said.

"It is not that simple." The words tasted wrong in his mouth.

"No, it isn't. But that is what makes it worthy," she said, tipping his chin up so his gaze met hers. "But if you do not want her, then let her go."

"But she is my savior, I owe her ..."

"Oh child, I do not want that for you," she said so gently and sweetly it silenced him. Her eyes even smiled into bright crescent moons. "I want you to find a trade, meet a nice young woman, have children, live a long, peaceful, happy life. And light a candle for your mother every once in a while. Both of you." She looked up at Honey and took her hand, squeezing tightly. "That would be enough for me to ..."

Maman stopped, words failing on her lips. Her gaze went long, looking past him.

"I see it now," she said, her voice softening and serene.

The darkness melted away and the room dissolved with it. They were returning to the beings they always had been, even as her voice continued to speak. "I understand now. I see. *Love* ..." The last wasn't a word, yet the feeling reverberated ...

... reverberates through Rafferty. She is gone. She dissolves and rejoins the light, brighter than ever. The other dark orbs move away from it, shunning the light as it pours in and consumes her. No. Takes her back, embraces her, and she returns to what she has always been. She still exists but she is home now.

Rafferty wonders why he does not do that same.

Honey is beside him, embracing him once more.

He knows it is time to return.

Chapter 38

COMING TO AN UNDERSTANDING

Rafferty felt blurry as he returned to himself. His body still felt like it floated, and time ticked by for an eternity before he was aware enough to even try to twitch.

"Take it slow," Honey's soothing voice said as she appeared in his vision. She gripped his hand and squeezed, which seemed to help him feel more real and alive.

"It's like I'm squeezing in between realities …" he muttered.

Honey laughed. "That's one way to put it. Just take it slow, waking up can be jarring."

"Waking up?" he asked, as he did not listen to her advice and tried to sit up. His head swam, and he had to yield back to gravity. Lying back, he realized he was on a couch in a normal-looking living room.

"Let me get you something cold to drink. It can help." She stood and turned, leaving his vision.

His gaze followed her, and he saw the room continue into a dining space with two exits on the other end, one leading into a kitchen and another probably turning off toward the bedrooms.

"Where am I?" he asked, too softly to really be heard, but Honey called back to him anyway.

"This is my apartment," she answered.

That didn't really make a whole lot of sense considering where he had just been, but he didn't have the will to argue about it. A few moments later, Honey returned, offering him a glass of cold water.

"Drink this; it will help. Coming back from the other side like that can be disorienting."

This time he managed to sit up properly, the world becoming more and more real and what just happened less and less. "Why ... why don't I remember?"

"What do you remember?" Honey encouraged.

He took a deep pull of the water. "It was ... it was *like* a dream. I understood ... I understood everything ... but now it's fading."

"That is alright, let it fade. What you need will remain with you and what you have forgotten will be there for you when you return, as it always has been," Honey assured.

"But what happened? I don't understand. Where is my maman? Did she ...?" His heart thundered against his ribs as that sliver of memory flashed. She had dissipated into the light, paying the price he had always feared. He pressed the palms of his hands hard against his throbbing temples. "I don't understand."

"You had a dream about your mother?" Honey asked.

He jerked, spilling some water. "Uh, yes ... no ... it wasn't a dream. It was *real*, I saw her ... You were there?"

Honey didn't answer his question, only smiled.

Then a thought occurred to him.

No.

An understanding.

She wasn't going to talk about what just happened. She would neither confirm nor deny it. It was not her way.

He had no idea how he knew that, but it was as sure a fact as the gravity holding him down to the planet.

He thought his head would explode trying to understand his understanding.

Honey sat next to him, waiting for him to keep speaking.

"How long ... have I been here?" he asked instead, looking to the window, which shone with a gray daylight. It had been night when he had arrived at this place.

"Two weeks," she said softly.

He flinched hard. "I've been here for two weeks?"

"Sleeping on my couch, yes," Honey said. "You haven't moved at all. Though that's not the worst I've ever had to deal with. Éliott stayed there a whole month once."

Rafferty furrowed his brows. He didn't understand. In his mind's eyes, he saw her again. Or perceived her? "Saw" was too small a word, but she had been brilliant and golden. It was an image that was hard to relate to the woman who squatted beside him now.

He shook his head, closing his eyes.

"It wasn't a dream," he breathed, needing to hear those words. He knew what he saw, what he felt, what had happened. It had to be real. "It has to be."

Another understanding bubbled to the surface.

No interfering.

It wasn't a voice that said it, simply ... a knowing. A rule, not given like an edict, but understood like fire burns or rain falls. Hard to define unless experienced.

"Even talking about it is interfering," Rafferty murmured.

Honey nodded sagely. A vague gesture. She could just be saying that she heard him instead of that she agreed.

"*Interfering* is what demons do," Rafferty murmured. "It's why we tell everyone about us, why everyone believes we exist, but angels ..."

But angels ...

"But angels *don't* exist," Honey said, her smile shifting a little, becoming more a knowing smirk, in the right light. "Do we?"

Rafferty laid a hand over his racing heart, pounding as the epiphany unfolded in his mind, dark and sacred as midnight rose. "Why did you do this for me?"

"I just like to help, and you looked like you needed some help. Thank you for letting me," she said.

He licked his lips. "So what happens now?"

Standing up, she gestured for his coat, hanging over a nearby armchair's back. "That's up to you. But you *could* check your phone." Then she left again, going back into the kitchen.

Any further deep introspection was interrupted by the sound of his mobile phone chirping. He found it in his indicated coat pocket. He also noted that he had no memory of taking it off.

"What in the ..." he exclaimed as he activated the screen to see the countless messages covering it and continuing down as he scrolled.

The majority of them were from Helena.

He also noted that the dates and times kept going backward.

They went back two weeks.

Before he could open the first one, another fresher one popped up, marked from Helena.

[Rafferty please. Just answer me. If this was just about you and me, I would leave it alone, but if this doesn't happen for Scarlet, I couldn't live with myself. Please, the competition is in a few hours. Just let me know if you're coming or not. Please.]

He ran a hand through his hair as he scrolled through the other messages. "Oh, Helena," he whispered, reading her struggle and desperation to reach him. Her embarrassment and apologies. For every one he read, there were three more that had been deleted.

"Are you going to go?" Honey asked, reappearing with a paper bag in one hand.

He looked from her to the bag and back to the phone.

"Of course, I'm going to go," he said with more certainty than he had ever felt in his whole existence.

"Good," Honey said, and she thrust the bag out to him.

"What is that?" he asked, even as he stood, steadier than he had been before, to take it.

"Your battle armor," she quipped.

He looked inside, but all he could make out was a bundle of dark cloth at the bottom. It took a second before it hit him what it was.

"Oh. I see," he said, setting the bag onto the couch so he could draw out the chef's coat. He held it up, but Honey took over, taking it by the shoulders to hold it against him, her eyes roving as she checked her measurements.

"Yes, I think that will fit you perfectly. The whole thing is in there, so if you want to go into the bathroom and change, that will give me enough time to find my keys. There are even shoes in the bottom," she added before whirling away toward the kitchen.

"Honey!" he called, stopping her just before she passed the threshold. "I know ..." The weight not to say what he knew pressed on his chest, but he pushed past it. "I know things now, but I still don't understand."

"Knowing something is one thing. Understanding it is something else entirely."

"I am different now," he said, pressing against his chest, which felt looser than it had in centuries. "But I'm not sure why. Something is gone."

"You paid your price. Finally," she affirmed.

He blinked at that, his mind struggling to comprehend what he knew was true. "But I'm still here."

"Yeah. Funny that," she smirked, setting her fists to her hips.

"But ... but my mother ..." He growled. "I knew all this on the other side but here ... What happened to her?"

"She returned," Honey said, her gentle smile slipping. "There are no words to describe it, so it would be best not to try."

He shook his head. "So everything that I understood when I was a demon was wrong."

"I don't know. I don't know what you understood. I am not you. You will have to figure it out. That's why we're here, after all," she said.

"It is?"

"Well, it's why I've decided I'm here," she said, her sweet smile returning. "What you're here to do is up to you, but I think you already know that."

He nodded. It was true. "But do I have the right to be here?"

"Oh, Rafferty. What does that matter? You are here," the angel sighed. "Go get changed."

Chapter 39

RENEGOTIATIONS

"Now, you go on ahead. I'm going to drop you off here," Honey said as she came to a stop in the alley behind a fairly large building. There were lights at both ends of the alleyway with another light over a familiar door.

"Of course, she booked this building," Honey said as they came to a stop.

"What about the building?" Rafferty asked, looking through the window at a structure that seemed similar to all of the other buildings in the city.

"This is the Wrightwood Ballroom," she said.

Rafferty's heart jumped in his chest.

"You didn't recognize it?" Honey asked.

He shook his head. "I never saw it from the outside. When Helena summoned me, she did it from inside the building."

Honey nodded. "Sure, that makes sense. Be careful in there."

Rafferty's legs shook as he got out of Honey's car, a very unassuming white Camry.

"Good luck," she called.

He turned around, stopping the door from closing. "You're not coming with me?" he asked.

She shook her head. "My part in this is over."

And he knew that was true. So he accepted it. Still, he hesitated. "I need to ask you one more question."

"Go ahead," she nodded.

He licked his lips. "Is what Helena told me true?" He thought he needed to say more, but before he could form it, she nodded.

"Energy freely shared compounds; it doesn't deplete," she confirmed.

It felt like the sun rose in his chest, warm and light. "Thank you, for getting me this far."

Helena nodded. "You got this, my little strudel."

He laughed as she pulled away.

The door from the picture Helena had sent him with her last plea that he come loomed before him. It was exactly the same except for the burly man standing at it with a clipboard and a bunch of cards hanging from lanyards looped over his one arm.

The guardian at the gate, he thought.

The guard lifted his head as Rafferty approached. He gave a cursory glance over Rafferty, eyes noting the chef's outfit, the red pipping visible over his chest since he hadn't bothered to zip up his coat.

"Name?" he asked without any prompting.

"Rafferty Lares."

The guard skimmed down his clipboard but didn't need to go far to find it. With his pen, he made a check, then slid a lanyard off his arm and presented it to him.

One side had an image of a stylized chef and the words "Cooking Underground" printed next to him. At the bottom of the card was a strip of purple and the word "Chef" printed in white.

"You can head on in. Keep your lanyard on at all times. You will need it on the cooking floor and to get back into the building," the guard said, then turned and opened the door for Rafferty to enter.

Immediately, warm, savory smells hit Rafferty's face. He breathed it in, savoring the ghosts of tastes dancing over his senses.

"You heading in?" the guard prompted, a little impatient at being made to wait.

Rafferty nodded and entered.

He found himself in the familiar, zigzagging back hallway of the loading dock of the Wrightwood Ballroom. It was fairly obvious which way to go. There were two tables set up to his left with catered food and drinks as well as a couple tables where other people in chef's outfits were getting something to eat themselves before they had to cook.

Still, he couldn't stop his gaze from turning around in the opposite direction. It took a second to even understand why. He wanted to feel it, to sense it. The pull of the closed summoning circle that had changed everything. It was somewhere in one of the side rooms set into the zigzags of this back area.

But he felt nothing.

"So, you did show up," Eleanor's voice said.

Whirling back, he found her standing right in front of him, her arms crossed in that stiff, irritated way that was all hers. She was dressed in her whites, but she had her hair tied back with a blue kerchief that brought out the blue fire in her eyes. His heart lightened at the sight of her, only to crash just as fast as he registered the man standing there as well.

"Nice to see you again, Lares," Vassago said, grinning as he thrust his hand out to be shook.

Rafferty didn't take it, but he stared at his own reflection in the aviator sunglasses the demon wore.

"You know you're indoors," Rafferty said.

Vassago's human eyebrows quirked over the top of the sunglasses. "I *do* know that I'm indoors. What is your point?"

Eleanor snorted. "Okay, so you two *do* know each other. He told me he knew you, but I didn't want to believe it. So, you *are* actually Lares."

The way she was eyeing him, looking him down and up, like she was seeing him for the first time, made him feel like a dried-up milk cow ready for butchering.

How does she know? Vassago couldn't have told her, Rafferty wondered.

Which meant she had to already know about Lares. And Vassago's smug grin told him there was some piece of all this that he was missing.

Still, he kept his face carefully neutral. "Yes, I told you that when I was introduced to you," he said as if it were an obvious thing. He couldn't remember if he had or not; he just needed her to doubt her own accusation that he had lied to her about it.

The quirk between her eyebrows told him it worked.

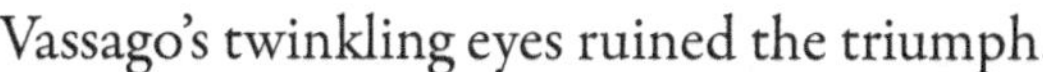

Vassago's twinkling eyes ruined the triumph.

"I'm not surprise to see you two together," Rafferty commented breezily.

Eleanor shifted her arms from crossed to fists on hips. "And why is that?"

"Oh, he's just being a bit bitter, my dear," Vassago said, grinning like a crooked salesman, which he was.

"Don't call me 'dear,'" Eleanor interjected quickly, as if it were already becoming rote. That told Rafferty this demonic relationship had been going on for a while.

Vassago continued on as if she hadn't spoken. "I previously represented Rafferty-boy here as a client, much like I'm doing for you. Unfortunately, he made a lot of personal choices that forced me to end the relationship." He sighed. "There is only so much I can do. You know. Free will and all."

"I thought we had a deal," Rafferty said, using his whole will to keep his voice level.

"Yeah, about the deal, you mind if I walk with you a minute?" Vassago slapped his hand on Rafferty's shoulder in the way he did the first time. It made Rafferty's skin crawl. Despite not being able to see his eyes, there was a smugness in the gesture that just dared Rafferty to shrug him off.

"Sure," Rafferty replied, turning to head the opposite way down the hall, using that natural motion to escape Vassago's touch.

Vassago simply took it in stride. "I will be right back with you, my dear."

"Don't call me 'dear,'" she repeated.

And he repeated it, disregarding her words.

The demon and the man walked side by side, not saying a word until they were out of sight of the others.

"You're not a judge now, so you're a ... what exactly?" Rafferty asked.

"A personal manager," Vassago stated, tugging on the lapels of his suit jacket as he scanned around them at the doors tucked into alcoves. "Though I thought of going with life coach. Ah, there it is."

He scurried over to a door, one with police caution tape hanging on only one side, still clinging to the concrete. The other side had pooled on the floor amongst some dirt and detritus.

Rafferty wasn't surprised to see this door. Of course, Vassago would bring him here, to where everything last went very, very wrong. It was the demon's natural environment.

The demon in question gave him an expectant look through the glasses, smiling a sharp smile, enjoying making his target uncomfortable. Rafferty had played all these games before, and they seemed so silly and unnecessary now.

"This is the only one that's not locked," Vassago said, answering Rafferty's unspoken question. "Trust me. I checked."

Rafferty didn't trust him, but also didn't want to dwell in this demon's company any longer than he needed to.

He had other priorities.

Turning into Vassago's chosen room, Rafferty's eyes went straight to the carved circle, etched and burned into the concrete floor. He couldn't feel a thing from it, but the sight of it still made his stomach queasy. Someone had mopped up the gore that had been left by Vassago's last victim, but Rafferty could still picture exactly how it looked. That image was burned into him. Why it should

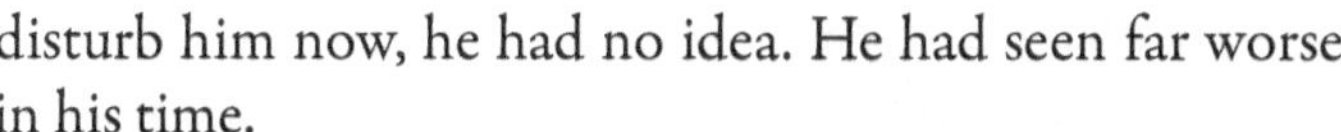

disturb him now, he had no idea. He had seen far worse in his time.

Vassago let the door drop shut before slipping his hands into his pockets, grinning under the fluorescent lights in the room. "I'll cut to the chase. I need to make a modification to our agreement, and in exchange I'll grant you one favor."

Rafferty didn't even fight to keep his forehead from wrinkling. "A favor?"

The demon nodded. "Yes, a favor, no conditions," he said. Rafferty knew from experience he was rushing things. Vassago really wanted this deal.

Looking him over, Rafferty could only come to one conclusion as to why this demon was taking a Hail Mary option. "You're running out of energy, aren't you?"

A breath huffed out of the creature who didn't need to breathe. "Don't ask stupid questions. Neither of us really have the time, do we? I believe it's thirty minutes until this show starts?"

Rafferty narrowed his eyes, an expression not lost on Vassago.

He stiffened his jaw, not willing to confirm what Rafferty already realized was true: he was still working on solidifying a deal with Eleanor.

The former demon could very well imagine it; sometimes it took an expenditure of energy, a sort of down payment or "proof of concept," to smooth the way for a more solid and lucrative deal with a target, especially if that target hadn't been the original summoner. Summoning gave the demon in question more of a toehold, already putting the target on the hook to pay the cost for the summoning.

But Eleanor was innocent of that sin. And she had always struck Rafferty as very savvy. Yet, Vassago was talented in getting the overly ambitious someones like her to fall into his traps ... as long as he delivered.

"Oh, I see," Rafferty murmured, his voice warm in its softness. "And because of your contract with me, you have been struggling to deliver the things that Eleanor would want—like a first-place win. Not if I'm there competing with her since you can't do anything to directly harm me."

"I cut very close to the line a few weeks ago, but that tarnished me in her eyes, yes," Vassago said through the teeth of his feral smile, which cut his face in half, confirmation and threat all in one. "You have been quite a thorn in my side."

"And the mortal agents are on your tail. Evading them must be costing quite a lot of energy as well," Rafferty added, poking at the wound.

"Uh, fuck you," the demon shot back.

Rafferty was completely unfazed. "I'm just saying."

"Things are different this time. I'm very close to anchoring with this powerful soul, so I just need you to—"

"Put my head on a chopping block for your convenience. Our deal is the only thing that is keeping me safe." *Keeping Helena safe*, he didn't say. "I allow you to dissolve the contract, and you could kill me now. That would solve your problem with Eleanor, wouldn't it?"

A talon burst from Vassago's otherwise human-looking hand. Pulling off his glasses, the demon's whirlpool eyes examined the talon. "You let me do what I need to do to secure myself here in reality, and I will owe you a *boon*. How about that? More than a favor, an honest-to-whomever boon. You can use it to protect yourself. Or your little old soul if you want, though it looks like you cast her aside already?"

Rafferty debated that. A boon. *That* was a powerful gift, to be able to make any wish of a demon without a cost, or rather the cost would be borne by the demon themselves. A favor didn't guarantee that. A favor was a maybe *I'll do it if it's convenient to me*. A boon had the same binding energies tied to it as a contract itself.

Still, he hesitated. What boon could he ask for that would accomplish the same thing as this current contract? "I could just command you to go back to where you belong," Rafferty pointed out.

Abruptly, Vassago slashed out with his taloned claw, which had only grown longer as they were talking and was joined by two others more. Three long gashes appeared in the concrete of the wall. The concrete bits clicked as they fell like a mini hailstorm.

The claws ended a mere breath away from Raffety's face.

He didn't back down from the clear threat.

"Absolutely not!" Vassago shouted.

The only thing holding Vassago back from ripping me to shreds is the terms of the contract, Rafferty reminded himself. He forced himself to chuckle. "You're not exactly making a convincing argument here. I think you are losing the game more than I realized."

Rafferty could see it as clear as glass as he was looking past the whirlpool eyes boring into him through to the dark being trapped in his own prison beyond. His old self would know exactly how to use such a creature, and his longest-hated rival at that, to get the most out of him.

But all he felt in that moment was pity.

"I know a way out of the game," Rafferty said, realizing that Vassago wouldn't like what he had discovered, but unable to do anything else. He felt compelled to say it, like the words were coming through him from ... somewhere else. "Just pay your price. Pay what you owe and go home."

The demon's eyes widened.

Then he bared his too-sharp teeth, grinding them with painful squeaks.

Then he laughed. "For a second there, I actually believed that you were going to give me a real answer." He dropped his threat, the claws retreating back into his fingers.

"I'm sincere," Rafferty said, amazed at his own words. But he realized that Vassago wouldn't listen, not yet. He needed to put it another way, one Vassago would understand. "Look, I've been here before. You'll keep draining yourself out until the price gets too high ... Cut your losses. Take what you have won already and go back. You will get called again. You will make it back to play the game again."

That the demon heard.

Vassago's jaw shifted, considering it. It was advice Vassago had given Rafferty at one time in a similar circumstance, though he had been more of an ass about it.

Then the jaw locked, the decision made, and Rafferty's heart sank as he realized it.

This would have been the best way forward for everyone, but it wasn't in Vassago's nature to do that. Otherwise, the demon wouldn't even be in this position now.

"Give me ... the deal," Vassago ground out between his too-sharp teeth.

Rafferty looked him straight in the eye. It would be so much easier to just relent, take the deal, and walk away.

A boon from a demon, free and clear, would be extremely beneficial.

He could just walk away.

"No. Enough is enough, Vassago. I'm done dealing with you."

He finally said it.

Despite the physical threat around him, Rafferty ducked under Vassago's too-long arm and out of the ring of his aura.

And the demon couldn't do a thing to stop him. Not with the original deal in place. The boundary would hold.

"Your new mistress is just going to have to win the old-fashioned way," Rafferty said as he moved to the door. Gripping the handle to hide the shaking of his hand, he turned back to the demon, who had rage-filled, swirling eyes. "She's going to have to beat me."

"There are other ways to destroy you!" Vassago hissed.

Rafferty nodded. "Yeah. Probably."

And he left the room, and his past, behind.

Chapter 40

RISING STAKES

His body felt like it had been slammed by a wave. As the door shut Vassago and his past behind him, there she was, walking past, talking into her phone, oblivious to his presence.

Helena had dressed in a smart scarlet suit. Her red-gold hair was twisted up and pinned in a beautiful bun, taming her waves. She wore flats that clicked as she jetted through the space.

Yet he couldn't remember how to do anything but look at her.

He was right back in that moment ... that moment when he had first laid eyes on her, standing there in the wreck of her kitchen, her eyes wide and watering from the residuals of the summoning circle. His heart ached then, and now, at the sight of her. Her eyes then had been so wide and frightened, but the entire time, she treated him with courtesy and politeness. Not something he had known much of. She had been desperate to get out of the situation. And he had let her off the hook.

Following her, like his heart was tied to a string that was attached to hers, she led him back to the staging area, which was now empty, and through another set of double doors to an enormous set.

It was in the same ballroom as before, but this time, the snowfield decorations were long gone. Up on the stage at the far end was a judge's platform with fashionably dressed people talking to each other over microphones and into cameras focused on their faces.

More cameras were set up throughout, in a dozen or so little clusters. In the center of each of those clusters were two tables set up at an angle to each other with mini-kitchen setups lined up behind. Just like every other competition, equipment was arranged, waiting to be used, on the counters, but this time there were little cards in front of them, all denoting which culinary company donated what and what website to go to find the exact ones displayed. The other chefs were setting up at their assigned places, checking equipment and ingredients, talking to each other about their game plans. The racing drivers' analogy was in full force here, with different colored chef's coats and symbols embroidered over their breast sides.

Rafferty ran his hand over where his emblem would be, his fingers finding threads. Looking down, he saw an image drawn in scarlet thread with the words "Scarlet Promotions" written beneath.

He was wearing his lady's colors.

Into that joyous chaos, Helena beelined through, encountering others from her office, all working to get this show on the road. A couple of times, her glance went to an empty station, and Rafferty knew that one was his, by, if nothing else, the deeply sad expression on her face.

Maybe he was being a coward, but he didn't want to distract her from her work. Now that he had seen her, he knew the sight of him would cause her pain. And he suddenly wasn't ready.

When she turned away, he went over to the station. He wasn't surprised at all to see it was opposite Eleanor's.

"So did you and Vassago get things squared away?" she asked, as if that were a normal thing to say.

"You call him *Vassago*?" Rafferty ran his hands over his counter, looking the equipment over.

"It's what he said his name was, so yeah," she countered.

"Fair enough," he shrugged, finding a small sheet of paper waiting for him on the end. Three rounds were typed up with lines underneath them, along with instructions and parameters for each round.

"Cookies, cupcakes, and full cakes," Eleanor said, even as his eyes discerned that from the written words. "She's practically handing me the victory." She glanced at Rafferty with a smug smile, expecting him to respond to her challenge.

"Yes, you will win," he said, setting the list down and spying the ingredients on the counter at the back end of the room closest to the ballroom kitchens. He knew his answer disappointed her, but he didn't really care. This wasn't about winning for him. It was only doing this last thing for Helena.

I've interfered in her life enough, he realized. *And after what I said, she may not want me back, but I said I would do this for her, so I will.*

Maybe what he was thinking was written on his face because Eleanor's wry, challenger smile shifted immediately. Her eyes widened as if he had slapped her, then narrowed into piercing, dark anger.

"How dare you?" she spat with righteous anger.

It was so abrupt that it jarred Rafferty out of his inner thoughts.

Confused, he met her furious gaze.

"No, don't look at me with those puppy dog eyes. You don't get to call me a cheater and then pretend you didn't just do that," Eleanor snapped.

Rafferty recognized her reaction for what it was. He had only seen it from those who knew they had used him to cheat and had deluded themselves they hadn't been.

He hadn't changed the game so they could win: *They* had won it by their skill.

He hadn't outwitted their rivals: *They* had beaten them using their cleverness and superior intellect.

He hadn't changed things so that they could reach their desired goals, shutting doors on other dreams that would have won: *They* had been more talented and worthy.

And on and on and on it went.

It was the guilt one felt when they had made a deal with a demon.

If he had needed confirmation that Eleanor was making a deal with a demon, this would have been it.

Rafferty suddenly felt exhausted. "What you decide to do is none of my business. I'm not here to win."

Eleanor crossed the space, getting too close to him. Despite the urge to, he didn't back down but instead leaned on the counter as he looked down into her fierce eyes, claiming his space.

"That is really rich coming from you," she hissed, pitching her voice down as her eyes skimmed quickly around them to see if anyone was listening or noticing.

Which, of course, they were. How could they not be? But no one came close to interfering.

It didn't deter Eleanor. "What else am I supposed to do when *you* are just like the rest of them."

That was a very loaded "you."

"What did Vassago tell you?" he asked, knowing better than to guess and accidentally tell her more than she already knew.

"Vassago didn't have to tell me anything," she said proudly, knowingly. "Neither did Helena, when she tried to make this deal with me."

Rafferty's heart skipped a beat. "Helena is not a demon," he said as if making a joke.

But Eleanor's gaze didn't waver.

She knew. He had no idea what that meant, but *she* knew about Helena already.

"Helena is not a demon," he repeated, this time very softly, not with any warning. He didn't feel the need to do that. He had a conviction that he hadn't had before. It was simply true. Helena was not a demon, and he wondered now how he could have ever doubted it.

And even if she was, she would find her way back.

Rafferty couldn't tell if that thought was his or if it came from a different source, but it flooded him with calm.

A calm Eleanor did not share, her smirk becoming more derisive, almost a sneer.

"What? You think she's an angel? Then *you* are deluding yourself. She tried to tell me the same thing; that she just wants to help me."

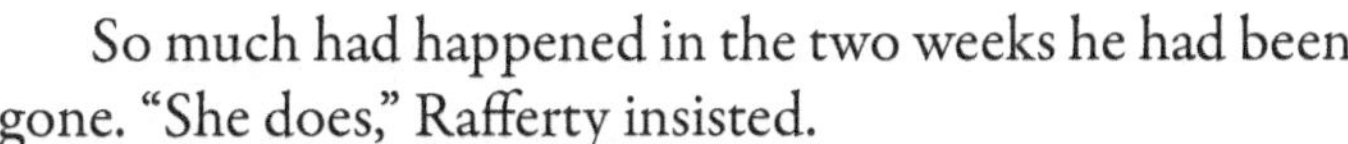

So much had happened in the two weeks he had been gone. "She does," Rafferty insisted.

Eleanor's jaw shifted. "At least Vassago is being honest about his intentions."

"And he'll drag you to hell if you go through with this," Rafferty said. "Believe me, please."

In response, just as a helper came by to drop off a package of basic ingredients, Eleanor seized the bowl of sugar from the box they carried for Rafferty's station and promptly dumped it on the ground. The helper gasped and a camera guy beelined over to record. Eleanor didn't acknowledge any of them, just simply stared down her rival, cruelty in her giggle.

"Or maybe I'm playing them both off of each other. One double-dealer to cancel the other out." She then glanced at the camera, a quick, almost-too-late calculation washing over her face. She was probably wondering if anything she had just said had been recorded and if she was in trouble. She took another step back, choosing retreat as the better part of not going to jail.

"Good luck today," she said, finally backing away now that more attention was on them. "Thanks for the head game."

Rafferty sighed, then regarded the pile of wasted sugar on the floor. He fetched the bowl she had dumped it from and angled down to try to scoop up what he could that hadn't touched the ground. Such a waste in the king's kitchen would have been unthinkable.

"Oh no, sir, you don't have to do that," the helper insisted, waving their hands at the bowl as if to shoo it away like it was a fly. "We'll get this cleaned up and get you new sugar."

"That's not necessary." But her flapping hands kept insisting, and another helper approached with a broom and dustpan, already contaminating what was left of the sugar with it before he could object again.

So, he let them, stepping back and giving himself a chance to think. It was only than that her parting words hit him. *"Or maybe I'm playing them both off of each other. One double-dealer to cancel the other out."*

His heartbeat sped up as the implications rattled him. *No, no, no. Helena made a deal?* he thought. And it wasn't really a question, it was a certainty. If she thought she could save someone by making a deal with them, putting her own freedom and soul on the line, she would do it.

Because she's trying to prove something.

Trying to prove that she's not evil.

A pair of words floated up in his mind, ones he would never use, would have never known to use. Ones given to him from ... somewhere else.

Survivor's guilt.

"Is there anything else you need, sir?" a third helper asked, interrupting his thoughts.

"Yes, I have a few special ingredients I want to use, and if I can get a moment to talk to Helena Rhodes, I would appreciate it," he answered politely, forcing himself to stay calm. Panic would do the opposite of what he wanted right then.

The helper looked like they had swallowed a bug but nodded. "Of course, do you want to report this to our HR? I can connect you up to our production manager ..."

"No, that is not necessary. It's just sugar. Eleanor and I have ... history. I just want to speak to Helena, if I could," he insisted, wishing, not for the first time, that he still had

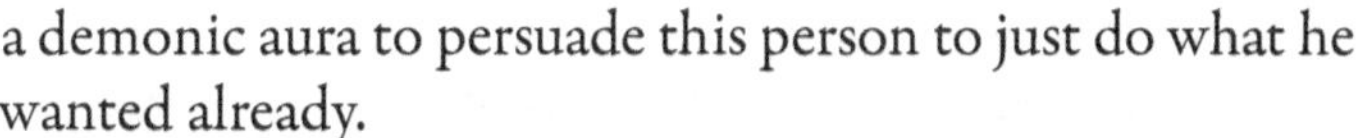

a demonic aura to persuade this person to just do what he wanted already.

"I'll see what I can do, but she is very busy," the helper said, lifting a microphone bit on a cord attached to both an earpiece and a walkie-talkie attached to their hip. They turned away to talk softly into it.

He supposed it was the most he could hope for at that moment without powers to directly snap to her location. Though he was tempted to go search for her himself.

The helper turned back after a moment. "Ms. Rhodes said to stay put, that she will come to speak with you very soon." They paused a moment, listening to their earpiece. "She also says to say, thank you for coming and representing Scarlet Promotions. It means the world to us … I mean her. And good luck winning the competition."

"So she will come talk to me?" he pressed, not liking it.

Again, another pause as they listened. "Yes. She promises. She'll be over with you soon. Just wait here and please enjoy the competition. She knows you can do it," they recited.

"Okay, thank you." His heart sank, even as it didn't slow its pace. His hands were itchy, but given no other place to put the energy, he went back over to Eleanor's station.

Before she could flinch away, he grabbed her upper arm, holding her in place. "What deal?" he demanded, the intensity in his voice too urgent to give much hush to his voice.

Eleanor glanced anxiously over at the helpers, all watching with their own worried expressions that they had a bigger problem.

Rafferty couldn't have cared less. "With Helena. What was the deal?" he demanded.

"Not here—"

"What. Deal?" He bit off the words.

Eleanor swallowed. "If I win, she'll pay my price with Vassago to get me out of his clutches."

He stopped breathing, his eyes going wide, his heart skipping a beat, then tattooing like a galloping horse.

Rafferty shook his head. "No," he said, the word falling out of his mouth, as if just saying it would change what had already happened. His mind raced. "Does … does he … does Vassago know?"

"That I've screwed him out of his deal for my soul? No, of course not. I'm not an idiot."

"Yes, yes, you are. The biggest idiot in the world," he said, and went back to his station, her retort unheard.

He needed to bake something.

Chapter 41

A Simple Entry

The rapid beating of his heart didn't abate, even as he fell into the rhythm of his work. He needed to do something while his mind worked furiously, trying to sort out what had happened while he had been ... indisposed and sorting himself out.

Vassago was bound to make sure Eleanor won the competition. By the same token, Helena must have bound herself in the same way to take Eleanor's place when she won.

How to get her out of this? How do we *get out of this?*

Those thoughts echoed in his brain as plans formed and disintegrated in his mind.

Call Agent Archon and Agent Sophia? Tell them what happened? It would not end the agreements, only delay them.

Eleanor had only to win a different competition to fulfill the terms.

Or at least he assumed so.

Yet he couldn't assume anything, he didn't know what wording was used for the agreements ...

And once a demon was bound by such things, *they* were unable to break them or change the course of the events.

He realized he understood now that the rules in regard to agreements and promises were the same whether demon or angel.

Only Eleanor could freely break them, but there was nothing Rafferty could bargain with that she had not already secured elsewhere.

Eleanor wanted this victory.

She wanted the prize money and the future it would secure.

She wanted the acclaim that winning this highly publicized event could bring her.

None of those things, he could give her. No counteroffer came to mind that he was sure would dissuade her from her chosen path.

So, he baked, and thought, and desperately looked for a new angle.

Withdrawing his shaped cookies out of his oven, the smell danced in his nose and his mouth watered.

"Those look beautiful," the cameraman recording him noted in a familiar dry voice.

"Yeah, smells good, too," noted the mic man beside him.

They were Eleanor's pair, Peter and Pedro.

Once Rafferty set the cookies on the cooling rack, however, they both turned without further comment to go back to Eleanor's station. Each pair of tables had a cameraman and a mic guy. These two were apparently his to share with Eleanor. While they had been making sure to take footage of the important steps to both their processes, evidently following a shot list required by the production company, they still focused more on Eleanor's creations.

Even without the demonic thumb weight on her scale, Eleanor's creations were definitely something to contend with. She made macarons, at least three different flavors indicated by their colors. She was in the process of setting them up on a stand shaped like a cascading waterfall.

Rafferty glanced up at the judging tables, which were taking completed creations as they came. None looked as beautiful or artistic as Eleanor's.

For himself, he didn't bother doing anything so fancy. Instead, he brushed a simple glaze over his cookies, zigzagging slashes of the white paste, while brewing some herbal tea. When it was all ready, he intended to pour the tea into a cup in the middle of the plate and set the cookies around at a slant with a sprig of holly as a garnish. The whole look was cozy and homey.

Yet, despite all this, he didn't feel cozy or homey. When he wasn't doing the next step, his eyes scanned everywhere, looking for a glimpse of Helena.

He *needed* to talk to her.

Why was she making him wait so long?

No torture he had ever endured felt as bad as this.

"Going for a cottagecore look, I see," Eleanor noted, coming back over, while the double P's moved in to take final footage of her plating.

"Come to spit on them?" he asked, the barb slipping out before he could think better of it. His worry for Helena had bled through his tongue.

Eleanor closed and opened her eyes slowly, like a cat who couldn't be bothered, then thrust out one of her macarons to him. He wasn't sure what to make of the offering and didn't get a chance to do more than take it before a helper suddenly appeared.

"Are you two ready to present your entries?" they asked, marking them off on a clipboard. The appearance was very suspect.

Probably trying to head off more issues between us, he thought.

"Yes, yes, let's hurry up," Eleanor said, swirling back to pick up her macaron design, all her focus fixed on not destroying her presentation in transit.

"Are you ready, chef?" the helper repeated, eyeing the plated cookies and the empty cups waiting for tea.

"I have been expecting to speak to Ms. Rhodes, do you know when I can see her?" he asked again, even as he reached for his steeped teapot, pouring a steaming golden-brown stream into each cup.

The helper's smile slipped. "Uh, I'm sorry. I will check while you're doing your presentation. I'm sure she just got held up," they said as they reached for the walkie at their side.

Rafferty didn't like it, but he saw little choice but to let this inefficient system work. The last thing he wanted to do was cause unnecessary trouble for Helena at her event.

Following Eleanor up to the judge's table on the stage, he waited as she presented her creation, then served each from it.

"Oh, this is fantastic," one gruff judge said with a deep voice despite his overly thin frame. He had a scarf on despite the warmth in the room and glasses that seemed more an accessory than a need. He whipped them off as he spoke. "This is sophistication and taste all in one simple dessert."

"And the presentation is delightfully whimsical," a woman said, holding her manicured fingers over her mouth as she chewed and spoke.

"I would be proud to have this served from my own kitchen," another man said, dressed in chef's whites with a very clean and jaunty kerchief tied around his neck and no toque on his head.

They heaped more praise on Eleanor's entry, which didn't surprise Rafferty in the least.

Finally, he got the signal to step up and set his own tray on the table. He then slid a plate to each of the judges and stepped back.

All three stared at his offering for a full three seconds before reacting at all.

"What in the world is this? You call this a presentation?" the glasses and scarf guy said, turning the plate this way and that.

"I almost feel insulted looking at it," the chef declared. "You do realize this is a competition of some of the best pâtisseries in the city, do you not?"

"It is my entry," Rafferty replied, tucking the tray under his arm, willing for this part to just finish quickly already.

The woman didn't say anything, simply plucked up one of the cookies and took a bite. She chewed twice, then paused, rolling the crumbs around in her mouth, then reached quickly for the tea.

The glasses and scarf man picked up his own cookie and started playing with it, crumbling off the edges. "This is terribly dry."

"It is meant to pair with the tea," Rafferty said.

"That is not an uncommon approach," the chef said chidingly at the other judge.

"I am aware," glasses judge shot back, "but a dessert that relies on the customer even liking tea is a risky move ..."

"Oh, Heavens, that's good," the woman sighed, completely oblivious to the back-and-forth banter around her. A moment later, she blinked as if coming awake and aware of all the eyes staring at her. She then refocused on Rafferty. "I have to say, this is not the most elaborate or even decadent dessert I've had today, but it is just so ... satisfying." She turned to her fellows. "It really is satisfying. The flavor is so light and clean. I feel ... almost renewed."

The other two men quickly ate their cookies and sipped their tea while she talked, trying to catch up to her impression. Both their eyebrows popped up.

The other chef nodded. "Yes, yes, I see what you did there. You used the simplicity of the flavors and the more easily digestible recipe to create a specific experience."

"But this is hardly suited for impressing a discerning audience," glasses and scarf judge said, even while plucking up a second cookie.

"No, this shows more forethought," the other chef insisted. "We have been sampling sugary, rich dishes all day, and even more to come. You knew that, didn't you?"

Rafferty blinked once, realizing the question was being directed at him. He cleared his throat. "Yes, yes, I did," he answered. "I knew that such an endeavor would be stressful on anyone's systems, so I thought to make up something that is both easy on your stomachs and cleansing for your palates."

The chef judge pointed at Rafferty rapidly. "You see, you see there, that is the sign of an accomplished chef," the other chef declared. "Considering not just the outcome of the final creation, but the audience who would be sampling it. The cohesion of the relationship between chef and diner. Well done." He slapped the table as if that were the final word, and no one could argue with it.

Rafferty could not understand what was happening here. He had not really tried to impress them, there was no point if Vassago was going to try to rig things against him, so he had just done what felt right. Glancing over at Eleanor, her face remained schooled into neutrality, with only the smallest flare of her nostril giving away what she truly felt.

"This is an impressive entry, Chef Rafferty, thank you for this pick-me-up," the lady judge declared before finishing off her tea.

The other chef nodded as well, while the glasses and scarf judge looked disgruntled by the other judges' praise. "Not to contradict or disrespect my fellow judges in any way, I'm going to need to see something more in the next round," he dismissed, popping the rest of the cookie into his mouth instead of setting it back on the plate. "Thank you."

Which implied that there would *be* a next round.

"If you will come this way," the helper said, and as they filed off the other end of the stage, Rafferty saw a flat screen where the points given by the judges were tallied behind each name. Only his and Eleanor's were blank in the two remaining entries at the bottom of the screen. It was clear that the lowest half would not make it on to the next round, indicated by the thicker black line bisecting the grid. Some of the contestants were already despairing at their loss, others congratulating one another on clearly passing, and at least three entries stared hard at the last two blank slots, waiting to see where those scores would land them.

Eleanor waited beside him with her arms crossed, not saying a word, as the blanks began to blink, their scores being uploaded. Then the entries shot up to the top of the list.

1. Rafferty Lares
2. Eleanor Rhodes

Groans and cries accompanied sighs of relief as the rest of the entrants realized what had happened.

Rafferty could only stare.

It didn't make any sense. He had taken first.

"But how?" he asked out loud.

It was only when Eleanor huffed as she whipped off her blue kerchief and spun away that he came back to himself.

"Eleanor ..." he called after, but she didn't stop, and he had no idea what he would have said next anyway.

What game is Vassago playing?

Chapter 42

ENOUGH WAS ENOUGH

"There's been a change," a helper informed him when he returned to his station. They held out a typed piece of paper. "The cupcake challenge has been altered to be a small savory challenge. And we are now pairing you up with one other competitor."

"They put us together," Eleanor said, stepping up beside him as she went over her own sheet of paper, her blue kerchief retied over her hair. "They want us to make twenty-four identical Savorys."

"Why the change?" he asked, looking over the text that basically stated that and went into a redundant explanation of what a "savory" was.

Savory Slice—A small, single-serving pastry or baked good that typically contains meat, cheese, and vegetables. It can be spicy or salty instead of sweet.

The helper sighed. "Apparently, not everyone got the same instructions and now some people have to start over.

The partnering idea was always an option, but I don't know why that was added now."

Rafferty did.

"It was an order that came down from on high, so I didn't get a vote," the helper laughed.

Neither Rafferty nor Eleanor joined them in it.

Vassago's lack of action on the first round now made sense. He let them score what they may, knowing that both would pass the first round. He then made sure they would get paired together, securing Eleanor's place to pass to the final round.

Any sabotage would come after that. Though what that would be that wouldn't violate the original agreement, Rafferty couldn't guess. Yet, a desperate demon was a clever demon. Rafferty could see the shape of what Vassago needed to do, but it didn't tell him much of the substance.

The helper then cleared their throat awkwardly. "We apologize for the mistake, a clerical error. Soooooo ... in order to make the competition fair for everyone, we've made these changes," they finished.

Rafferty looked around the room and saw there were several people talking and muttering, while others were already busy creating their second entry creations. He almost missed the helper walking away.

"Wait, I need to speak to Helena ... Ms. Rhodes," Rafferty insisted, shifting a glance over at Eleanor. Her eyes narrowed and she crossed her arms, declaring she had no intention of going anywhere now that he had said that.

The poor helper had no idea what was going on. This was a different helper from the one he had been requesting assistance from earlier, and they just blinked at him. "I'll see if I can find her."

"She said she would come talk to me after the first round," he insisted, not letting this one dodge him and heedless of what Eleanor might think about it.

"Oh, I'm so sorry. I'll go hunt this issue down for you. Don't worry. Please proceed with your savory slices. Best of luck." And then they were gone.

"Are you thinking about forfeiting? Is that part of your plan to make sure I fail?" Eleanor jabbed at him.

Staring her down, he expected to be angry at her smirking face. Such competitive spatting happened all the time before when he ...

Blinking, Rafferty's eyebrows furrowed.

I can't remember, he realized. He had the thought a second ago, but when he reached for it, it was gone. It was something to do with his past. He tried to think of other facts about his past, but everything from his first life was gone.

No, not everything.

He remembered his mother and sister, their love for him, but everything else ... Even as he tried to think of it, it slipped away, leaving an openness in his mind.

And it was a strange relief left in the wake of his realization.

This is his life now. Not then. Then was over.

What he could remember of his childhood remained, but even those were mostly impressions. Love, laughter, good moments, moments that could have happened in any age.

I trained in the king's kitchen, but he couldn't really remember what that meant anymore. The king's kitchen didn't exist anymore, but he had learned so much when he had been there.

And that's enough.

I was a demon for centuries, he thought.

But that was just a fact. He couldn't remember what it had been like to *be* one. The experience of it was a blank attached to a comfortable sadness. It was sad that it had happened, but he had made peace with it.

And I was rescued by Helena to live this life now, he thought. The memories of her flooded in. Beautiful and vivid. Her smile and laughter, her hair framing her face. The way she gasped beneath him, the weight of her in his arms. Her thoughts and fears so precisely hers as she shared them with him, making him hungry for more.

Eleanor whirled back to her station. "Ugh, I don't have time for this drama. If I have to make the whole thing myself, then I will." She then lifted out a book from her backpack and dropped it unceremoniously onto the counter.

Rafferty's heart bounced off the floor.

"Where did you get this?" he demanded, reaching for Helena's grandmother's cookbook.

"Helena," she said.

"But why would she give it to you?" he pressed, pulling it toward himself, out of her grip. She reclaimed it, forcefully dragging it back, but he didn't relinquish it, compelling her to look at him.

"She was *my* grandmother, too!" Eleanor snapped. "And seriously, this should have come to me anyway. I really don't know what my *mother* was thinking, giving it to her."

"Nana ... was your grandmother?" Rafferty's jaw couldn't be more on the floor.

Eleanor eyed him, huffing irritatedly. "Helena didn't tell you, did she? Yeah, we're cousins, fucking hell. I don't know what kind of game she is playing, being all big shot and pretending she doesn't know me or something. And it hasn't all been conflict of interest bullshit or something. but you, you were hers, right? Why wouldn't she tell you who I am?"

Because Helena doesn't remember, Rafferty realized to himself. She had lost things as well when she had paid the price for both of them. Just like him, what she needed had been returned to her, but pieces were lost. Like remembering her more distant, hostile, estranged family.

Eleanor patted the air at him, just inches from touching his chest. "I know, okay, I know it's not your fault, but I mean, when we ran into each other at the kitchen place, she didn't even try to introduce you to me. I mean, that is just fucked up. If only I had—"

Rafferty took a step back. "I have to find her," he said out loud.

"What? Wait! I don't actually want to do all of this myself. We don't have time to—"

But he didn't wait.

Turning, he rushed out of the room, grabbing the nearest helper at the door. "I need to see Helena now!" he demanded, pulling up just short of grabbing the hapless helper and shaking them.

"Uh, I don't ... I don't know ..." they said as they reached for their walkie.

Disgusted, Rafferty turned away, knowing this route hadn't produced her yet. Instead, he rushed out of the grand ballroom into the main foyer. There were almost no people here, but there were two grand staircases. They swept elegantly backward up to the second floor. It was either go that way or out the bank of doors leading out to the street.

Ignoring the obvious exit, he turned and leapt up the steps. "Helena!" he called, heedless of what anyone might say or shush.

There were a couple other helpers hanging out at the top, sitting and chatting, who both stared at him as he swept past. None moved to stop him, though. He saw up there was a hallway with a row of doors. A couple were open with papers and equipment stored within, and a couple more helpers exited out of the third room with carts filled with foodstuffs that didn't require refrigeration. They both stopped to stare at Rafferty, who moved past unheeding.

Lacking more direction, he began trying the doors themselves. Most were locked, and he almost gave up until he came to the second to the last one. It had pebbled glass set into the door, so he could see the inside was dark. He doubted she was in that one but pushed in eagerly when the doorknob yielded.

A woman stood at the far end, looking out through the window at the night city beyond.

"Helena?" he called out softly, almost fearfully. Seeing her again like this after what he had said to her last time pinged him with anxiety.

The woman turned. "Oh, it's you," Scarlet said with a sleepy drawl.

In the light from the hall, he could see her eyes were red-rimmed and wet.

"Are you ... are you alright?" He turned to look back down the hallway, but the few helpers that had watched his urgent searching were now looking away. It was a deliberate choice. They were avoiding Scarlet.

"Are you looking for Helena?" Scarlet asked instead of answering. She rubbed a finger underneath one eye, delicately brushing away the tear there and correcting her mascara in the same practiced gesture.

"I am," he said. He didn't understand the pull he felt, drawing him into the room. It wasn't that his urgency to find Helena had abated. Instead, something within him wanted him to go this way, to follow the thread of compassion he felt for this woman who was so important to Helena. He also recognized he could deny that feeling, his will wasn't being usurped. In addition, he realized he had fought feelings like this too many times, that he had always heard this call and had resisted it before.

Maybe it was time to trust it.

Closing the door behind him, he crossed the space. It was a conference room of some sort, with a long oblong table and several chairs waiting for people to sit and discuss things. There was even a whiteboard along the wall to his left with leftover writing and a rough sketch of the ballroom. Helena's plans for the evening, clearly. But it didn't interest him as much as the woman waiting for him to approach.

"I don't know where she is," Scarlet said.

"That's alright, I will find her," he answered with conviction, joining her at the window.

She looked back out it, her face lined with grim determination.

To hold herself together, to protect the world from her pain, to protect herself from the world, the understanding whispered inside him.

"Yosef should be here," she breathed, her diction the only thing that made what she said clear.

Rafferty nodded. "Yes, he should be. But he isn't."

"Yes, thank you, I'm aware," she answered bitterly.

"You know he's alright, don't you?" he said, the words falling out of him, realizing they were true only when he said them. "He loves you."

"Please stop," Scarlet said, closing her eyes against a fresh wave of pain. "It doesn't help. It doesn't help telling me that. That he's still there, somewhere." She flicked her hand at the dark window. "That love goes on. That I'll get over it! None of it helps. None of it changes how soul-crushing this feels right now." She pressed her fist to her chest. "I'm so tired. I'm so tired of thinking about it, but there is no escaping it. There is nothing that will make it stop hurting."

A long pause filled the space between them.

"You know she's doing all of this for me." Scarlet gestured another imperious hand at the hallway behind them, but he understood what was meant.

"Helena is hurting, too. She's doing what she can," Rafferty said.

"And it is all for nothing because this isn't going to make a difference. I'm already dead." Scarlet pressed her fist into her chest. "What gave me life is gone, and now I'm just a walking corpse that has been made ... to not die on its own."

"You will still die someday."

She huffed at the correction. "At least not any time soon. Not of old age and infirmity."

Which again was not necessarily true, but Rafferty held his tongue this time.

"Nor can I contemplate ending it myself." She wiped another tear, this time escaping the other eye. "You are right. It was his gift to me." A small, fragile smile graced her beautiful lips. "I have never given back one of Yosef's gifts."

More small tears bloomed from her eyes, small flickers of love over-washed again with grief.

She looked to Rafferty as she broke into a million pieces right there. He only had to lift his arm, and she tucked into it. She didn't cry, only breathed in shuddering huffs that reverberated through her entire body. "I wish she would stop," she said a moment later. "She keeps trying to save me." She sniffed in a hard, unladylike way. "To save my business."

"May I say something to you?" Rafferty asked carefully.

Despite her panged look, she gestured an acquiescence.

"None of this is about you. Helena isn't even doing this *for* you, she's doing it for herself. She's drowning and still swimming around trying to rescue everyone else around her. And none of you, not even me, have noticed."

Scarlet flinched under his arm, pulling back to her own island.

Her own orb of darkness.

For a second, Rafferty could see it clearly, hugging her pain around herself, protecting herself.

How could I never see it before? he marveled to himself.

Scarlet's gaze studied him, waiting for him to say more.

He licked his lips, letting the words pour out of him. "Everyone else's needs are too great, and she's giving everything she has to help ... well, frankly, everyone. And we're all standing around whining about how it's not enough. It's not what we wanted and it's all not good enough. So, she tries harder! Do you know that she's even risked her soul to try to save ... her cousin."

Scarlet's eyebrows pursed together. "Who?"

Rafferty ran both his hands through his hair, knocking off the black toque he wore in his frustration. "Eleanor. The other real contender down there. She's Helena's cousin. She has also, in a fucking twist of irony, made a deal ..." He couldn't say with who. His deal was still in place and the only shield he had to protect Helena.

Scarlet shook her head, her eyes going wide. "A deal? You mean ..."

He knew he was skating so close to the spirit of the agreement. He prayed he hadn't crossed it.

"Why ... why would she do that? The cousin, I mean."

"Greed," Rafferty snapped, then shook his own head. That was oversimplifying matters. "There is a lot of money at stake, and her dreams are in reach. Humans do all sorts of narrow-focused things when dreams are involved."

"Then we must tell the BDI. We have to inform them ..." But she stopped her own thought as she took in Rafferty's expression. "There is more isn't there? You've done something ..." Her eyes narrowed, as if that gave them the power to see through to his mind. "There is more to all this, isn't there?"

She would have been the savviest operator in the king's court.

"It is not my secret to tell," he landed on. "I've already said too much as it is."

"I see," Scarlet whispered, her face fixed in fury. Her jaw worked as she looked back out the black window. After a few tense breaths, where everything in Rafferty wanted to be swallowed back into hell again, she looked back at him. "There is more to you becoming human again, isn't there? It didn't just happen. She traded places with you, didn't she?"

"Helena is *not* a demon," he insisted, for what little good it would do.

"No," Scarlet said, raising her head to its full height. "She's not. Nor will we let anything happen to her."

"But I don't know what *to* do," he said, his own despair slipping into his words. "Only Eleanor has all the cards now."

"And she is not likely to play them differently," Scarlet agreed. "Even if I were to give her the money, the prestige of winning this competition is of incalculable value. My name is tainted but what Helena has done here, which has been nothing short of a miracle, Helena's enterprise has caught the attention of many. Opportunities will be rolling in to the winner." A smile of pride teased Scarlet's lips. "Helena is truly a force to be reckoned with now."

Rafferty couldn't help it. He was proud of her, too.

"So, the only option we have at this moment is to make sure Eleanor doesn't win," Scarlet concluded.

"I can't do anything to interfere. Nor can Helena," he said.

"And that is alright. It's not your duty. It is mine." Scarlet raised her head, strong and regal. "Leave this to me. I believe you have a competition to win in my name?"

Hope rising inside him again, Rafferty saluted with a fist against his chest. "Yes, my lady."

Chapter 43

I ACTED WITHOUT THINKING

Renewed fire burned through Rafferty's veins as he charged back into the ballroom. Even if Helena didn't take him back, he wasn't going to let her pay any prices that weren't hers.

But she'll be fine, a nagging voice in his head said. Even if she paid the whole price and was dragged into ... well, not hell, but the other place ...

But she loves this life, another thought whispered. *She loves this life, and she's risking giving it up.*

And for the moment, Vassago expected him to help Eleanor. Scarlet and he had agreed that being where Vassago expected bought them all some time to figure this out.

As much as he hated it, he marched straight up to Eleanor. She was in the midst of stirring up some sort of batter. She paused, her eyes going wide as he formed up beside her table, tucking his hands behind his back formally. "What do you need?" he asked.

Eleanor's gaze searched his face a moment, her mouth partially open with a hundred questions. Instead of asking them, she nodded to the cookbook beside her. Nana's cookbook. "We're making my grandmother's savory slice."

He came around her to look down at the rough sketch drawn out on one of the mostly blank pages. A printed recipe at the top only took up three lines, leaving a mostly open page. He grinned at the recipe drawn out below.

This had been one of his!

He remembered the joke of it. Nana had wanted ham sandwiches for some event, but fancy. He had given her fancy, alright.

He skimmed a finger over the lines that pointed to different layers in the sketch, listing them out. He could deduce now that Eleanor was working on the walnut sponge for the bottom of the slice. Glancing over at the stove, he spied the gammon, a pork hind leg, simmering in broth. From what he could smell, she had added flavorings like coriander seeds, peppercorn, and onions. Maybe even a little cinnamon.

But for an event like this, she shouldn't have been able to make gammon in the time allowed. "How did you acquire this?" he asked.

"What do you mean?" Eleanor asked, giving nothing away.

"This takes a day to boil, to get all the impurities out," he pressed.

"It was prepared beforehand. Don't worry. It has been prepared appropriately," she said, meeting his gaze with her own.

"But the second event was only changed a little bit ago," he said carefully.

Her gaze didn't waver.

So this move to sabotage the second round was planned all along, he thought. Either that, or she had Vassago manifest this pork for her.

As if she could hear the question, she sighed, "I prepared it entirely myself from a place I source pork from. I trust them implicitly. It is … untainted."

Rafferty took a deep, fortifying breath. "You are a good chef," he acknowledged, voicing what the feeling inside told him. It was the same as saying "I believe you."

He nodded toward the wine bottles on her counter. "I'll begin preparing the port jelly."

She nodded. There wasn't much more to say after that. Time was ticking.

They worked together seamlessly, as if they had worked in the same kitchen all their lives. He found the ingredients he needed already lined up on the counter, while she got her crust laid out and into the baking unit.

The other two teams that remained did not seem to be having the same poetry of motion. One set wasn't even in the same library, their sharp words to each other carrying their stress across the space, while he and Eleanor constructed their layers.

Before he knew it, Rafferty was slicing and plating the savories, while Eleanor dressed each with a pickled walnut, dried prosciutto, and a crisp of fried cheese arranged artfully on top.

"These are perfect," she approved. "They look exactly the same."

"Of course, they do," he said as he set the last piece on the serving tray.

Eleanor laughed. "That's your serious facade, isn't it?"

"Oui, madame," he said, the itch of a smile tugging at the corner of his lips. A familiar pride settled into his chest as he stepped back from their work, wiping his hands.

"You know," Eleanor said, grabbing up her own towel to wipe with. "I did try to summon you after Helena gave me the cookbook."

The ease Rafferty had felt immediately dissipated. Eleanor studied his reaction, smirking. "It didn't work, of course." She tucked a piece of rogue hair back behind her ear. "You know, this isn't the first time we met? Do you remember me at all?"

Slowly he shook his head. "No."

"From Nana's kitchen? Really? I would have been a child then."

He set down the towel as he tried to, but there was nothing.

"Well, I remember you. It was because of you I wanted to become a chef. You and she were preparing some food for some sick neighbor of hers, and you let me help." The way her cheeks pinked up, he got the impression that he had done more than inspire her.

And if she had intended to summon him, he understood clearly what she would have wanted from him.

It was a ... miracle ... the cookbook had ended up in Helena's hands, instead.

"Are you ready?" a helper asked, gesturing toward the stage. They were clearly the only ones who were.

"Absolutely," Eleanor said, gesturing for Rafferty to pick up the presentation tray like he was her servant.

Yes, he clearly understood what she wanted from him.

The judges' praises were over the top and fairly worthless. They had clearly won the round, even without the other entrants offering up their savories.

It would come down to points to determine who would be the third to make it through to the final round. Rafferty wasn't worried about that.

As they retreated off the stage, one of the helpers met them. "Thank you so much for your work. We're wondering if you would like to come over and do some quick interviews for us for the broadcast of this event. You know, just a real simple 'who are you' and any other color you want to share."

"Sure, that would be excellent," Eleanor said, beaming with her assured win at hand. She stepped in front of Rafferty, making it clear that she intended to go first, and he had absolutely no problem with that. He followed the both of them out of the ballroom, going through a familiar set of double doors that led into the main kitchen, where only a few months ago he had been preparing the dinner for the Winter Rose Ball.

No food was being created there today. Instead, it was being used as a sort of set with cameras set up on tripods and light stands brightening the place. Those who had already been eliminated from the competition were there giving their own interviews.

"This way," the helper said, leading them past to another set of doors that led to the back loading dock area for the ballroom. "Oh, just her," the helper added when they realized that Rafferty was still following.

"You can wait here," Eleanor said, indicating a set of stools set up along the side of the kitchen. A couple of people were already waiting there for their turns to be interviewed.

The door fell closed between him and Eleanor with no further word.

Nothing about that made him feel right, but he went and sat.

He pulled out his phone and checked it for a message from Scarlet, but there was nothing. The worries he had been suppressing leapt to the front of his mind.

Why am I just sitting here? he asked himself, then answered. *Because Eleanor told me to.*

Like she was his mistress or something. That realization jarred him up to his feet. He wasn't obligated to obey anyone anymore. Also, escorting Eleanor out made little sense. All the equipment for the interviews was here. Did they have additional setups in the docking area?

Needing to confirm, Rafferty stood up and pressed against the swinging door that led to that back area, opening a small crack.

There were only empty tables there and nothing else.

Leaning even more through the doors, he saw two figures moving away down the zigzag of the hallway. One of them was wearing a blue kerchief.

And he did not doubt where they were going.

Leaving the kitchen, he headed the direction he saw the two figures go. No one else was in the back loading dock, so he didn't worry as he moved. He reached the first bend in the hallway just as the helper let a door fall closed before they turned and walked off the opposite way. There was no sign of the second person.

Rafferty continued forward, undeterred, but to his surprise, when he got to the door festooned with caution tape, he found it empty. The circle inside sat quiet and still in the dark. If he hadn't known it was there, he would have barely made it out at all. He had been sure they would have been heading this way.

Stepping back, perplexed, he looked up and down the hallway, his mortal eyes and ears straining for any hint of where Eleanor had gone.

Lacking direction, he went to the nearest door. To his surprise, it opened into another ballroom. This one was much smaller than the main one where the event was taking place. It was also empty and dark save for a figure standing at the end of the ballroom who Eleanor was walking toward.

Immediately, Rafferty ducked back, not letting the door fall closed entirely, but keeping his fingers between it and the jamb so that he could hear what was going on.

"And there she is," the clear, boisterous voice of Vassago echoed in the smaller but still cavernous space. "How did the second round go? A success I hope?"

"Of course," Eleanor said. "And I need to get back for the third round or this whole thing is pointless. What do you want?"

"Oh, darling girl, none of this is about what *I* want, it's about getting you what *you* ultimately want. Isn't that right?"

"I don't believe that for a moment," Eleanor countered, her voice guarded.

"Ah, yes. Occupational hazard," he countered, not showing if he took any offense.

He's here to renegotiate, Rafferty realized a second before Vassago confirmed it.

"Well, then I'll get right to the point. I need to make an adjustment to the deal."

She crossed her arms. "Why? I'm clearly on the brink of winning."

"Well, it's not that simple, turns out," Vassago said. "I just learned something that is going to put that all in jeopardy."

"What?" Eleanor asked, her anger growing thick in her voice.

"Now, I just want to clarify that what has happened is not in any way my fault. But do not worry, I'm here to help you," Vassago said, then looked over his shoulders in a show of checking for eavesdroppers. Not catching the actual eavesdropper nearby, he continued. "You're going to get disqualified."

"What?! Why?" Eleanor asked, crossing her arms defensively.

"You attracted attention, little dear. The BDI is watching Ms. Kovacs and your, frankly, dramatics with Lares on the competition floor have ... well, it's simply not surprising. I thought you would have been smarter than this."

Eleanor's growl echoed in the open space.

Vassago had her right where he wanted her.

"Do something about it!" she shouted.

"I'm trying to, dear. Now, don't yell at me," he chided, opening his palms to her. "We just need to cancel this current deal and make another one."

"Eleanor! No, don't!" a beautiful, familiar voice echoed in the space. Both Vassago and Eleanor turned to another set of doors closest to their right, just out of Rafferty's view. Of course, there was another set of doors.

Helena appeared, and she glowed with her own light. She was struggling to keep her other visage from manifesting, the wings on her back and horns on her head flickering in and out of existence. Startled, Eleanor stepped back from her cousin, while Vassago slid easily between the other perceived competition for his prey.

"Oh, old soul, you aren't looking so good. Ooo, you have a tail. Did you have a tail before?" he said, drawling his words out mockingly with a Southern accent that Rafferty had never heard him use before. It was offsetting and wrong.

He's infusing his aura into his voice, Rafferty thought.

Helena ignored him, keeping her focus on Eleanor. "You have to stop, please," she begged. "You're going to lose everything if you keep going like this. Any deals with him are going to destroy you. There is no winning ..." Then Helena groaned in pain, curling around herself.

Dropping to her knees, she failed her fight to hold back her true form. The wings splayed out on either side of her as her skin paled to milky white edged with gold, casting light everywhere around her as bright as the full moon. Energy spun round and round the linking of her horns around her head until it seemed like one glowing circlet or halo.

"Helena?" Eleanor exclaimed, struggling to comprehend what she was seeing.

Vassago laughed cruelly. "You are being called home, my dear."

His laughter cut short as Rafferty skidded to a halt, dropping down beside Helena. He had crossed the space from the door faster than any conscious thought that he was doing so.

"Helena! I'm here!"

Chapter 44

SAVING AN ANGEL

"Rafferty?" Helena asked. Her voice came out small as she lifted her head. The eerie feeling he had known before washed over him, but this time, it didn't set his teeth on edge or make his skin crawl. It was warm and welcoming like the lapping waves of a summer ocean.

"You're too weak, you're giving too much of yourself," he said, reaching out to hold her, but she pulled away.

"No, don't touch me," she said sharply.

His fingers flexed just inches from her, but he respected her command.

A breath later, she looked up at him, her golden eyes asking a thousand questions. *Where have you been? How could you leave me? How can you look at me now? Do you hate me?* She didn't need her to say them for him to hear them.

"I'm so sorry," he whispered to her, heedless of Vassago's sniggering over his shoulder.

"Aww, this is so cute. You could be a Lifetime movie," the demon crowed.

Rafferty peered deep into Helena's eyes, not flinching at their intensity. How could he have ever thought her terrifying or overwhelming? "Helena, I'm so sorry—"

"Oh, for hell's sake, I'm bored now," Vassago interrupted, before turning back to Eleanor. "You want to win or not?"

"Yes ..." Eleanor answered automatically, confused and stunned by what she was witnessing.

"No matter what you do, demon, you're not going to get what you want!" Helena snapped, her eyes flashing golden fire as she struggled to her feet. She was still unsteady but didn't notice as Rafferty reacted, reaching for her waist to help her up. She braced her hands against his shoulders so that she could meet the demon eye to eye. "Any deal you make you will not get her soul."

"And what are you going to do to stop me?" Vassago laughed.

Just like that, Rafferty realized the piece of all this he had been missing, so caught up in everything that he almost hated himself, it was so obvious. At least, if he hadn't violated his agreement with Vassago.

"She's sacrificed herself to take Eleanor's place," Rafferty said, standing up to face his demon, while keeping his hands steadily on Helena.

Vassago's whirlpool eyes went impossibly large and wide as his demon understanding followed Rafferty's implication.

He then whirled on Eleanor, growing bigger as he did so, the claws sliding out of his fingers. "You made another deal with an angel!" he growled.

Eleanor whimpered as she backed away from Vassago's true self, the long teeth inside the overlarge mouth making it more difficult for him to speak.

Angel? Vassago's admission set Rafferty back on his heels. The sly old demon had known what Helena truly was. Had known this whole time that angels were real?

"Leave her alone! It was my choice to make!" Helena pleaded, pulling out of Rafferty's arms, only to drop again to the ground, her weakened legs unable to hold her and her ungainly wings up.

"Wh-what's the problem?" Eleanor stuttered out. "You're still going to get your soul food … or-or-or whatever."

"I can't touch her!" Vassago roared. "You stupid bitch! You tricked me!"

"I … I … why?! How?!" Eleanor asked, stumbling onto her back as Vassago's teeth dripped with acidic spit. She cried out as a bit plopped over her forearm.

"No! Stop!" Helena shouted.

"She didn't trick you!" Rafferty roared, his voice thundering over all of their cries.

Vassago twisted his head back nearly completely around in an uncanny spin.

"Rafferty, don't!" Helena pleaded, but he stepped around her to place himself between them. The demon's aura washed through him, but the mortal man didn't care nor heed it. He just wasn't afraid anymore.

"He can't hurt me," Rafferty said, stating it calmly.

"I could kill you in one bite. Swallow you down whole," Vassago threatened.

Rafferty leaned in, breathing in the foul odor of Vassago's teeth. "Do you feel like the deal between us has been broken?" he asked, pitching down his voice.

The stench washing over his face grew stronger as Vassago began to pant, the realization of how badly he had lost the game dawning on him. Rafferty could see it now, his own lack of control over his form. As much as he wanted those watching him to think this was a threat, Rafferty knew it wasn't. Fur had broken out over Vassago's skin, mixed in with brown, broken feathers, all pulling toward the back of the room with an invisible wind. The demon's muscles were straining, resisting a pull. His whirlpool eyes darted toward the far door, now standing open since Rafferty had pushed it in and left it there.

The circle was calling him back. The price had to be astronomical.

"They're calling you," Rafferty whispered.

Vassago flinched, then growled.

"There is nothing you can do to stop this," Rafferty pushed.

The demon's eyes flicked back. "Yes, there is," he ground out.

Without a deal, the demon couldn't take any of the desperately needed energy to pay his price, not from any of them. But he could kill Eleanor trying. Or out of spite. Rafferty's bargain didn't extend that far to protect her.

As if realizing that same thing, Eleanor bolted.

While he had the demon's attention, she had gotten to her feet and was now making a run for it. Why she chose the furthest away door, Rafferty couldn't have guessed; panicked minds didn't always make the most logical of choices.

Vassago immediately leapt after her.

"No!" Rafferty and Helena cried in unison.

Rafferty attempted to grab for the back of Vassago's coat, but the oily fur and feathers slipped through his mortal fingers.

Eleanor screamed as the teeth came after her. The demon's speed outpaced hers easily as a cheetah after a gazelle. Still, Rafferty tried to do the same, finding himself moving faster than he anticipated. Human adrenaline was no match for a demon, but it wasn't nothing either. Grasping at Vassago's fur again, he only managed to hold on a second longer, being dragged along with the great monster before slipping off.

At the same time, the overly large teeth caught the back of Eleanor's chef's jacket. The cloth ripped like tissue paper as the attack pulled her down. She *oomph*ed as the wind was knocked from her as Vassago's overly large body slammed her down. Shaking his head like a dog, the demon tore away what bit of cloth still clung to the jacket.

In the split second it took to spit the cloth out so he could clear his mouth for another attack, figures appeared at the door.

"Demon! Demon!" a woman's voice bellowed. It was Agent Sophia.

"All agents, convene at the secondary ballroom," Agent Archon ordered, though to whom Rafferty had no idea. In the same moment, she lifted a firearm and shot.

Energy arched out, striking the demon. He arched back, roaring like the monster he was as the bolt went through him.

Rafferty scrambled away, in danger of being trampled or clawed by the demon's thrashing. He encountered Helena, who had crawled after. Her wings came around him protectively, shielding him as her arms embraced his shoulders.

"I've got you," she said.

He turned in her arms and wrapped his own around her. "I've got you," he answered.

"I'm so sorry about this," she whispered, burying her face unabashedly.

"This isn't your fault," he assured, cupping the back of her head with his hand, her horns pressing along his neck. He then slid his other arm down and under her, gathering her legs. She was heavier than the last time he lifted her this way, but he remained steady on his feet. Managing to keep one wing up, Vassago was trying to protect his back as the agents battled with him. Rafferty moved the others away from the action. Helena's hands were weak, barely able to hold on to him.

"I've got you," he repeated over and over, as he marched away.

More bodies were entering the room from both doorways. Rafferty braced himself to be stopped by two agents charging toward them. He expected them to question or even demand he put down the unearthly creature in his arms. Yet, just as he approached, they went around them as if they hadn't even seen them. Maybe the demon-fighting behind them had been more urgent.

At least that had been what he thought until another agent tried to stop them leaving through the door. "You! Stop there—" and then he paused. His gaze went long and then through them, only to widen as his eyes took in the demon behind them.

"Keep walking," Éliott said, appearing beside them in the doorway. He seized Rafferty's upper arm and pulled him along. "They will walk around us and not register that they saw us. Honey is waiting outside."

With Éliott's sure guidance, Rafferty carried Helena down a short hall that drained out into the Wrightwood Ballroom's foyer. All the glass doors were standing open with other agents escorting chefs, helpers, and crew out to the street. Police vehicles and a firetruck arrived, their lights flashing brightly in various colors, blindingly bright in the dark.

Rafferty balked a moment at the sight of so much unfeeling authority, but Éliott's tug was insistent.

"Keep walking. They do not see her as she is, keep walking!" he called over the din of the emergency.

Holding to his fledgling faith, Rafferty continued to follow. And it was as the other angel had said, no one stopped them.

Rafferty's arms ached horribly as he carried her a block away.

"We're almost there," Éliott assured him, out of breath, glancing back the way they came, assuring himself no one followed them. Whatever energies the angel was expending on their escape was taking a toll.

At last, Honey emerged from a parked car and scurried around to open the doors to the back. "Come quickly."

"Honey, she's not ..." Rafferty tried to say, but he nearly dropped her. Both of Helena's wings dragged on the ground as her head lolled off his shoulder, flopping backward to hang bonelessly. "Helena!"

"Don't stop, keep going!" Éliott growled, not with anger but urgency.

"I can't get her in the back!" Rafferty snapped back, "Her wings ..."

"One moment!" Honey said, her gentle voice cutting through their fear-laden ones.

Then with an easy gesture, the car shifted into a cargo van, the side door sliding open on its own. On the floor of the van was a cushioned pad. Rafferty brought Helena to it as Honey hopped inside to help guide the broken angel into the back.

"She will be alright, sweet comfort," Honey assured him once Helena was settled on the floor.

Rafferty panted as his back hit the inner side of the van, but he didn't even wait a breath before he gathered Helena's upper body into his lap. Cradling her in his arms, he ignored everything else as Éliott joined Honey upfront and told her what happened. Rafferty couldn't care.

"Please, please, stay with me," he whispered to Helena's unconscious form. She felt so cold in his arms, but the uncanny feeling still dashed over his skin where he touched her. Brushing her beautiful red-gold hair from her face, he kissed her, willing his life to enter her and refill her.

It didn't.

Chapter 45

ACCEPTANCE OF MYSELF

"What is wrong with her?" Rafferty demanded. He crouched next to where Helena lay on a queen-sized bed, her wings hanging off to the opposite side. They had returned to Honey's apartment, carrying her inside. The whole time she still hadn't woken, nor did she feel any warmer, even as he pulled the quilt there over her.

"She has expended too much of the gift given to her," Honey said gravely. "When it is fully expended, she will return to the other side."

"No!" Rafferty cried, grabbing her hand as if that would keep her there.

"It is not something sad, corn muffin. She may return here again," Honey assured. "If she wishes to."

"She may?"

"That is not the whole of it," Éliott said. He stood on the other side of the bed, his arms crossed as he leaned against the wall. "She will not return within your lifetime.

Time is different on the other side"—then he blinked and cleared his throat—"as you probably know."

"But I can't ..." a weak voice said.

Rafferty's whole being leapt, refocusing on Helena. She remained lying on her side, her eyes closed, but her tongue licked her lips before speaking again.

"If I go ... Rafferty, I'm so sor—" Her voice failed her.

"No, no, please, don't be sorry. I'm here, I'm here," he kissed her fingers. "*I'm* sorry that I left you all alone ..."

"No, no"—her head shook weakly—"That's not ... Your life ..." She tried to open her eyes, but they fluttered shut immediately.

Honey reached out a hand, but Éliott stopped her. "What are you doing?" he hissed.

"She needs help," Honey stated.

"What is she doing?" Rafferty demanded, looking from her hand reaching for Helena to the tension between them and back to Helena.

"She's going to give a part of her energy to strengthen her, but she shouldn't do that," he said, directing the last as a warning to Honey.

"Why not? If you can help her ..."

"We are limited here," Éliott shot back. "It's not any different than you demons. The power to keep us here has a price, but we pay it from ourselves. Sharing our power lessens our time here, which is what she did." He nodded to Helena. "She spent that energy working miracles, which means she has to return sooner."

"She helped people," Rafferty snarled, standing up.

"Yes, I'm not arguing that," Éliott agreed, not at all intimidated.

"It is something we all have to learn our first time here," Honey explained, withdrawing her arm from her fellow angel's grip. "What we do with our energy is our choice."

"So it's wiser to make it count," Éliott continued. "Do what you can when it will make the most impact. Don't interfere too much, don't inhibit the mortal's choices. That's what demons do. We try to lessen the damage the demons do against people who do not make a choice to be involved with them. We all want to save everyone, but that isn't the point of all of this."

Rafferty furrowed his brow. "What is the point?"

The angels both stood quietly, unable or unwilling to answer.

Instead, the answer floated up within Rafferty.

To live.

It was as good a reason as any and better than most.

"So you won't help her because you don't want to give up a moment of your time here," Rafferty sneered. He couldn't help it, even though he understood the decision. He would have made the same one before he met Helena.

"It's worse than that," Éliott replied, keeping his patience, but his eyes narrowed a little more. "Anything we would give her would then go to you. It wouldn't help her."

"You're sure, then?" Honey asked.

Éliott nodded. "I wish I had been proven wrong, but yes, I am sure. She is giving up a portion of her energy, so that you can have this life." He gestured at the whole of Rafferty, stripping away the anger he had felt. Now he felt like water, and he yielded to gravity, crouching down once more beside Helena. With a gentle hand, he brushed his fingers through her hair through the space between her horn and her ear.

"Is this true?" he asked.

Her eyelids tensed and a tear pooled on the bridge of her nose. "I didn't realize ..."

"Helena, stop it, please."

Éliott shook his head. "It's too late. She's already spent it."

Helena whimpered. "If I go now, I don't know what will happen to you."

He leaned forward and kissed her cheek, before setting his forehead against hers. "Let go," he whispered. "I'm ready to return."

"No, you didn't ..."

He could feel it inside himself from the place of understanding.

There was a choice he could make. A gift waiting for him to accept.

He embraced it ...

Something that he held back floods over him.

He accepts the price and pays it all.

The tie to Helena releases.

Light fills him, joins the light he's already accepted.

I wasn't ready before, he thinks. *I am ready now.*

He is filled with more. He returns what was given to him and even more returns back.

He gives back to Helena what she gave to him, and she opens her eyes. She is whole again. She is more than she was before. The cycle between them passes back and forth. They are infinite.

She sees him as he truly is.

Looking down at his hands, Rafferty sees the gray skin and the black nails once more.

I am a demon again, he thought, but then he turned his hand over. The skin seemed different this time. It was gray, but as it moved in the light, shots and reflections of rainbows danced over his form. Wings brush Rafferty's shoulders. Brushed. Not scraped.

He turned his head toward them and saw instead of leathery, bat-like wings, beautiful black feathers with the same iridescence of his skin, dancing blues, greens, and purples in their sheen.

Amazed, he looked down at Helena, who had at last opened her golden eyes, and she smiled. Then she reached out and touched his face. "You're beautiful," she breathed.

Rafferty kissed her fingers, then noticed that Éliott and Honey were both standing beside them in their true forms as well. Honey's wings were the beautiful golden-brown of a hawk with equally honey skin, and Éliott's wings were the layered grays and whites of mourning doves. Like Helena, their horns crested around their heads like halos.

Reaching up to touch his own, he discovered they hadn't changed. They still pointed straight up.

A mark of who I have been, even if I am that no longer, he thought, the knowledge coming from the understanding. He liked it.

"Are you alright?" Helena asked, sitting up on the bed.

"Yes, are you?" he asked what he thought was the more important question.

She nodded, water beading in her eyes. "I think we get to stay a little longer."

"I would like to spend that time with you, if you will have me back?" he asked.

Helena laughed. "Of course!"

She was in his arms as fast as he could dive into hers. Not just their arms, but their wings, his black, hers white, wrapped around each other. His lips were met with hers, and he kissed her with every bit of his renewed self.

I will make the most of this new chance, he thought, and intended to say to Helena, when a snapping feeling cut through him.

He pulled away sharply, pressing a hand to his chest as it caught his breath.

"Rafferty? What's wrong?" Helena cried, alarmed.

He looked up, meeting Honey and Éliott's gazes, their expressions falling from sweet happiness to alarm.

"I—" was all he got out and then a circle opened up beneath him.

Light shot up, bright and blinding with a woosh of air that smelled of cold winters and forests of pine. The floor beneath him disappeared, and he fell within, torn from Helena's grasping hands.

"Raffer—" was all she could scream and then the circle closed over him. He existed in the other side, in the vastness of everything, or at least he thought he did, but he left it so fast, his senses disjointed.

The next thing he knew, he knelt on a wooden floor.

The circle there burned into the wood, creating a smelly wood and varnish cloud around him. The cold feeling vanished and the light swallowed back into the lines of the circle, leaving him once more in existence, but where was he?

"It worked. You're here," Eleanor cried, excited and amazed.

He lifted his head with dread filling his heart. She stood before him, holding Nana's cookbook.

She had summoned him.

Smiling with triumph, Eleanor snapped the book shut. "You're mine!" she crowed. "I may have lost the competition, my chance, and ... and everything else ... But you. Are. Mine!" And she laughed.

And she was right. He could feel it, the same constraining binding sensation wrapping around his chest and limbs. It had always been present before whenever he had been summoned. No matter how many times he had fought it before, tried to free himself from paying the price, these bonds were unbreakable.

Rafferty lowered his head.

"What do you wish for me to do? Mistress," he said, grinding the words out so as not to let the tears gripping his throat free for her to see.

"Nothing at this time. Just sit there," Eleanor said smugly, flipping the cookbook open more. "We're not done yet."

Epilogue

TO FORGET IS HUMAN

"Is he gone?" Agent Sophia gasped. She looked a mess, her neat little bun half undone as she leaned against the concrete wall of the small room.

Agent Archon wavered on her feet at the edge of the smoldering lines of the summoning circle that they had just sent the demon back through. She brushed a hand over her own disheveled hair. It came back with a streak of blood on it. There had been countless moments she could have acquired a wound, but that was fine. "We did our job," she said with pride.

"What?" Agent Sophia asked absentmindedly, her gaze still held by the smoldering circle.

Clapping a hand on the younger agent's shoulder snapped her out of her daze. Archon helped her back up to standing. "The answer to your question. Yes, we did it. We did our job. Our duty. That demon is gone. And everyone in this building is safe."

For a second, it didn't seem like Agent Sophia understood what she was hearing, but then, she nodded and straightened, her head held a little higher, her chest puffing a little fuller. "Yes, ma'am," she said resolutely with a nod.

The older agent patted her partner's shoulder. "Good girl, but we're not done yet. Never done yet."

"But we can count this one a win today?" Sophia asked as she followed out.

Agent Archon didn't get the chance to answer that when she spotted their informant talking to a pair of other agents on the other side of the loading dock.

"Ms. Kovacs," Agent Archon said as she approached.

The other two agents straightened up as their leader approached.

"Five with serious injuries, ma'am, they are already on their way to the hospital," one of agents reported without her asking. "A dozen minor."

"And no deaths? We got lucky," she noted, then nodded a dismissal to them so she could speak to Ms. Kovacs. "Ms. Kovacs …"

"How are you doing?" Agent Sophia interrupted on cue.

Agent Archon paused, but she just didn't have the energy to be annoyed. Her partner shot her the usual apologetic puppy eyes, but she simply chuckled a sigh and smiled. "Yes, how are you?"

"I'm fine," the young-again socialite said, pulling her shoulder wrap tighter around herself. "Though I doubt there will be any way to keep this out of the presses. It won't take anyone long to blame all this on me."

Agent Archon blinked at that statement, then furrowed her brows. "Why would anyone think that? If it wasn't for you, we would never have caught this demon."

Ms. Kovacs opened her mouth to respond, but then a pinch appeared between her perfect eyebrows as well. She blinked many times, stopping and starting. "I ... I can't remember," she said, hugging her wrap closer.

Sighing, Agent Archon reached into the inner pocket of her coat and pulled out a tin of mints. She opened it and offered one to the socialite. "It's not an uncommon effect from an encounter with a demon. Confusion and even guilt happens, but trust me, you have to realize that it is coming from outside of you."

Ms. Kovacs's face didn't change as she stared at the mints. She obviously didn't believe her.

Agent Archon sighed. "Look, if you need to talk to someone, I can recommend some people, but honestly, you probably have access to some better people than I can suggest. But please, get checked out. I can assure you that the BDI stance on the events of tonight is that you are a hero who protected all the people during your event from trouble."

She nodded at that. "Thank you. That is ... good to hear. I'm glad I could help. Now if you excuse me, I need to talk to my ..." Her eyebrows pinched again.

"I imagine you need to speak to Ms. Rhodes," Agent Archon said, supplying her the name of her protégé. It was amazing how people forgot things very quickly. Demon attacks, while sensational in the moment, were forgotten just as quickly.

Ms. Kovacs nodded. "Yes. Yes, I need to talk to Helena. She put so much work into this event, she must be devastated."

"Then I'll leave you to it," Agent Archon said, and she walked away with Agent Sophia coming up beside her.

"These wealthy socialites, thinking everything revolves around them."

"She's so young to be so successful," Agent Sophia noted.

Agent Archon pinched her eyebrows together. That didn't sound quite right. "She's older than she looks."

Agent Sophia blinked. "Well, how old is she?"

"Thirty? Thirty-five. Something like that. Do we have a suspect for who summoned this demon?"

Her partner looked at her questioningly. "Well ... Yosef ... What was his last name?"

"But ..." Then Sophia stopped, and that strange pause that Ms. Kovacs had done passed over her. "Right. Right, I'm sorry. I remember now. He was eaten and ..." Then she brightened and sighed. "Right, case solved."

"Right. Case solved. No need for further investigation," Agent Archon agreed, then rubbed her ear. It felt like someone's breath had been blowing on it, but when she looked to the side, nothing was there.

"I'm going to take a long bubble bath when I get home tonight," Agent Sophia said, stretching her back. "And maybe spend the day at my chiropractor."

"Works for me," Agent Archon agreed, and buttoned her coat to go back out into the cold. "There will be more to do tomorrow."

Neither of them saw the small, winged creature fly away and out the wide-open doors of the loading dock.

"Oh wow, that's the Wrightwood Ballroom, isn't it?" Cindy asked as she set down her cup of tea to lean forward as Charlie turned up the volume on the news program.

"It is currently reported that no lives have been lost at this time, but the incident is still under investigation," the reporter said, then paused a half second. "And I'm hearing now that we are going to bring you an exclusive interview with Scarlet Kovacs, the CEO of Scarlet Promotions who was running this event."

The screen changed, and Helena's boss appeared on the screen standing next to a reporter.

"Oh my gosh, she looks fantastic," Charlie said, but Cindy hushed him harshly.

"Thank you for speaking with me tonight, Ms. Kovacs. Now my understanding from speaking to law enforcement is that in a twist of irony, tonight's demon attack occurred during an event whose goal was to raise awareness for demonic activities?"

Scarlet nodded. "Yes. Recently, someone very dear to me was lost to a demonic attack similar to what we're experiencing right now."

"That is a cruel twist of irony indeed. Can you tell us now what the public can do to help?"

Charlie turned the sound down. "Should we call Helena? She has to have been there," he asked.

"They said no one was killed," Cindy said thoughtfully, then got up to fetch her cellphone.

"Hey, we both promised no devices," Charlie started to say, but Cindy swiped his words away with a hand as she pulled open the cabinet nearby to retrieve it.

"That was locked!" Charlie said, and he came over and ran a finger over the latch. "Okay, so that was a lot less secure that I thought it was."

Cindy ignored him as she thumbed through her contacts and found Helena's number. It rang and rang, but no one answered.

"Dammit," she huffed as she hung up. Then stared at her phone screen, trying to decide what to do next. "Quick, what was the name of her boyfriend? Maybe he knows what's going on?"

"Boyfriend? What boyfriend? Does Helena have a boyfriend?" Charlie asked.

"Yes, of course, you know ... The chef guy ... His name is ..." Then she paused.

Helena is single.

"No, she was dating him for the last few months ... Rrrr ... Raffff ... Raphael? Raffff ..." But the name wouldn't come. "Oh dammit, we met him. He was there the night Chris showed up."

"Let's not talk about Chris. That's for me and my therapist," Charlie grumbled.

"Whatever, but she has a boyfriend. I know I've met him." She stamped her foot. "Why can't I remember his name?" She stared at her phone, but it wasn't being any more helpful. Finally, she hit a different number stored there.

"Who are you calling now?" Charlie asked as he fiddled with the remote to get the closed captions on the TV.

"The ER," she said.

Charlie flinched. "Which ones?"

"All of them. Helena has to be somewhere."

A white creature chirped once and slipped away out the open back door while Charlie's little dog barked his head off.

"Zip! Shut it!" Charlie shouted, but he never went to investigate.

The little white creature hissed at the dog, then pulled the door closed with her tail before flying away.

"Helena? Are you alright?" Éliott said softly.

"I don't know, something is happening," she murmured. Then Helena seized forward, crying out. Her wings shivered, then disintegrated away, like sand being washed away by water.

Startled, Éliott's instincts urged him to reach out for her, but this time it was Honey who stopped him by seizing his arm. "No! Wait," she ordered.

Helpless, the two angels watched as her horns, wings, and tail swirled away into motes of white, sparkling energy. The sparkles gathered above her into a small, tight ball, leaving Helena's human form sitting dazed below. Once every mote had been gathered, the ball zipped away, disappearing through the wall, leaving the room darker than it had been before.

"What the ..." Éliott breathed. He had never seen anything like that before. "Is she ..."

"Revert," Honey ordered, and she did so herself, her wings fading and the sweet face she usually wore taking over.

Éliott followed suit, rubbing the top his head as his halo disappeared. "Honey, please, what is happening? I don't ... I don't sense her divine aura anymore."

"No, I don't either. She's ..."

Then Helena lifted her head, looking at both of them, but not seeing them. Then her eyes closed and opened, and she took a deep breath in.

This time she could focus on them. "Oh ... I ..." She looked around the room, pulling the quilt up over her shoulders. "Where am I? How did I get here?"

Honey beamed her award-winning smile at her and sat down on the edge of the bed. "It's alright, dear. Take it slow. You've had a nasty shock. My name is Honey."

Helena furrowed her brows. "Wait, I know you. You helped me in that clothing store. I was finding clothes for ... a boyfriend I used to have."

"Yes, that's right."

Helena pressed her fingers to her temples. "I feel terrible. I was supposed to be doing something." Then she sat sharply upright. "Oh my ... the competition ... the event ... I ... There was a demon there. I must have ... gotten hit ... or caught up in the attack." She started feeling her head for bumps or bruises but not finding any.

Setting a hand over her frantic arms, Honey extended some of her calming aura. "It's alright. You are whole, but I think you're right."

"I must have been whammied by demonic magic," Helena said, her words going monotone like something else was speaking through her.

The feeling of wrongness flashed strong, and Éliott extended his own aura into a protection circle around them.

Helena blinked again, as if waking up. "Sorry. I ... Sorry. I feel like there is someone I'm forgetting about."

"Someone named Rafferty, sugar bun?" Honey asked.

"Rafferty?" Helena wrinkled her nose. "That was ..." She chuckled incredulously. "No. No, that is the name of an old boyfriend I used to have. We didn't date very long. Wow, I haven't thought about him in a long time."

Even as she laughed and dismissed, a single tear traced down her cheek. She wiped it away. "I am so sorry, I know I'm a complete mess, but could I use a phone? I need to call people and let them know I'm okay. I should probably go to the ER or something."

"Yes, of course. Wait here," Honey said. "I'll be right back." She rose and left, giving Éliott warning eyes that he didn't need.

He knew his duty. *No interfering.* Whatever was happening to Helena, she was mortal again. And whatever happened to Rafferty …

"Sorry about this, but I feel like I know you as well. Have we met before?" Helena asked, looking up at him.

"Oui, I was the one who found you and brought you here. You were wandering around lost. Don't worry. We will take good care of you. Whatever you need."

"You are both so kind." She laughed again. "I guess guardian angels really are real."

Éliott laughed along with her, even as his heart ached. "Only if you believe they are there."

Book Club Questions

1. Were you startled by the POV changing to Rafferty? Why do you think I did that?

2. Why do you think the BDI acted so mercifully to Rafferty and Helena?

3. Do you think Helena is an Angel or a Demon?

4. If you suddenly have miraculous power, but using them would cost you life essence, would you use it? What for?

5. Where do you think Chris and Charlie's relationship is going?

6. Why do you think Helena didn't recognize or remember her cousin?

7. Did Rafferty do the right thing, breaking up with Helena? Why or why not?

8. Who do you think Honey really is?

9. Why do you think everyone forgot what had just happened? Whose at fault?

10. By the end of the story do you think Rafferty is a Demon, an Angel, or something else?

Thank you to everyone who reads and supports my books. Without your reviews, recommendations, and opening my newsletters I wouldn't still be doing this.

Thank you to Laura, Autumn, Aysha, and Oxford of being my team and delivering such a professional gold star book.

Thank you to Amy, the best personal manager and essential NPC a sister could hope for.

Thank you to my family for your love, support, and page reads. They say don't expect your family to be your fans and every one of you defies expectations!

Author Bio

Author Megan Mackie writes something for everyone—she's written cyberpunk, urban fantasy, paranormal demon romance, speculative fiction, post-post zombie apocalypse, steampunk, and mid-grade science fiction. She's also a contributing writer for RPGs Legendlore and Legendlore: Legacies by Onyx Path.

She's a popular figure at comic cons across the country, so if you come across her, ask about the Lucky Devil series and prepare to get your mind blown.

Whats the news, Barman?

Sign Up for Megan's Newsletter!

https://www.meganmackieauthor.com/newsletter

Also check out her free Wattpad novel!

https://www.wattpad.com/1423396171-i-can%27t-get-the-vampire-rogue-to-romance-me

**It was all fun, until she got
sucked into the game.**

OTHER BOOKS BY MEGAN MACKIE

URBAN FANTASY/CYBERPUNK

THE LUCKY DEVIL SERIES
The Finder of the Lucky Devil
The Saint of Liars
The Devil's Day
The Digital Mage
Demonic Inc. – Coming Soon

THE SAINT CODE SERIES
The Lost
Constable – Coming Soon

MID-GRADE SCIENCE FICTION

THE ADVENTURES OF PAVLOV'S DOG AND SCHRODINGER'S CAT
Maxwell's Demon
The Ship of Theseus - Coming Soon
Sniffy the Virtual Rat – Coming Soon

POST POST-ZOMBIE APOCALYPSE

DEAD WORLD
The Prisoner of the Dead
The Journey to Naraka – Coming Soon
The Damned Road – Coming Soon

SUPERHERO

WORKING MASKS
The Vilification of Aqua Marine
The Indemnification of Black Heart - Coming Soon

EPIC FANTASY

SILVERBLOOD SERIES
Silverblood Scion